The Girl Who Came Back

£1-25 9

KT-557-619

Susan Lewis is the bestselling author of thirty-four novels. She is also the author of *Just One More Day* and *One Day at a Time*, the moving memoirs of her childhood in Bristol. She lives in Gloucestershire. Her website address is www.susanlewis.com

Susan is a supporter of the breast cancer charity, Breast Cancer Care: www.breastcancercare.org.uk and of the childhood bereavement charity, Winton's Wish: www.winstonswish.org.uk

Praise for Susan Lewis

'A gripping story of love, uncertainty and betrayal . . . a guaranteed tear-jerker that will keep you at the edge of your seat.' *OK!*

'A master storyteller.' Diane Chamberlain

'Spellbinding! You just keep turning the pages, with the atmosphere growing more and more intense as the story leads to its dramatic climax.' *Daily Mail*

'Utterly compelling.' *Sun*

'Expertly written to brew an atmosphere of foreboding, this story is an irresistible blend of intrigue and passion, and the consequences of secrets and betrayal.' *Woman*

'Sad, happy, sensual and intriguing.' *Woman's Own*

Also by Susan Lewis

Fiction

Susan Lewis

The Girl Who Came Back

arrow books

1 3 5 7 9 10 8 6 4 2

Arrow Books
20 Vauxhall Bridge Road
London SW1V 2SA

Arrow Books is part of the Penguin Random House group of companies
whose addresses can be found at global.penguinrandomhouse.com.

Penguin
Random House
UK

First published in Great Britain by Century in 2016
First published by Arrow Books in 2016

www.randomhouse.co.uk

A CIP catalogue record for this book is available from the British Library

ISBN 9780099586548
ISBN 9780099586531 (export)

Typeset in Palation (11.83/14.56pt) by Palimpsest Book Production Limited,
Falkirk, Stirlingshire
Printed and bound in Great Britain by Clays Ltd, St Ives Plc

To James, again and forever

It wasn't right to feel this way.

Not about her own daughter.

The child was only nine, for God's sake. She was an innocent, a tender young soul still trying to find her way in the world. Except that wasn't how she seemed, innocent and tender, or how she behaved.

She wasn't like other children. She didn't run or skip or play childish games. She didn't sing or tease or sleep like an angel.

She didn't look at people, she stared; she didn't laugh, or when she did the sound was false, jarring, sadly humourless. Olivia had never heard girlish giggles erupting from bubbles of happiness or excitement inside Amelia. Little seemed to amuse her, or even please her, although she was often fascinated by things: insects, small animals, dolls; tools, gadgets, other children's toys. She always wanted what wasn't hers, which perhaps didn't make her so very different from other children; Olivia had come across plenty of kids like that.

Amelia didn't speak very much either, at least not to her mother.

She chatted away with her father when he made time for her.

She was the apple of his eye, when he remembered she was there.

As far as he was concerned, nothing was too much for his girl, provided it didn't get in the way of his other commitments.

Olivia felt sure that Amelia was the only human being her husband had ever come close to loving, although she'd thought he loved her once.

That seemed a very long time ago.

She wondered how she'd ended up in this marriage, how she'd allowed herself to become the victim of such an egotistical man with such a dismissive air towards those he considered of little use.

Olivia was never entirely sure how useful she was to him.

In a material sense she wanted for nothing. They lived in a large, imposing house a stone's throw from Chelsea Bridge. She had her own suite of rooms, a fancy car, a generous allowance and all the freedoms she could wish for.

She also had a daughter who was healthy and intelligent, meticulously clean and tidy, but never seemed joyful or carefree. Amelia was sullen and sly.

Yes, really – sullen and sly.

Olivia had never voiced her feelings about Amelia to anyone, least of all to her husband, Anton. Of course he would say the problem, if there was one and he probably wouldn't admit that there was, lay entirely with her. She was Amelia's mother, therefore she was the person Amelia spent the most time with (when she wasn't away at school), so it stood to reason that she was the biggest influence on Amelia's life.

Amelia was on her third school now, fifth if Olivia counted the two kindergartens she'd attended.

Amelia couldn't settle. Other children didn't warm to her, or were afraid of her, or ruthlessly tormented her. Olivia felt sorry for her when she was bullied and tried to soothe her, but Amelia hated being babied.

What was to become of her?

Would she change as she got older, and start to understand that she needed to be more like others if she wanted to be accepted by them? It was pointless trying to have the conversation with her; she simply got up and walked away. Or she'd tell her mother to shut up, or to leave her alone, she was busy.

Anton's parents were bewildered by the girl, although most things bewildered them these days.

As for Olivia's parents, they'd separated many years ago and she hadn't seen either of them in a very long while. She didn't even know where they were living now, though she guessed she could find out easily enough if she tried.

She'd felt so painfully alone since marrying Anton, which wasn't how she'd felt when she was still single. She'd had lots of friends then, a career as a legal secretary, a great social life and she'd always been up for something new. Anton had been like that too, dashing and daring, successful, romantic and always attentive.

So what had changed him?

Maybe his irresistible charm had been an act that

he'd simply dropped once he'd made her his wife, seeing no need to go on pleasing her as he had when they first met.

She had no idea if he ever had affairs, but she hoped he did, they would provide her with a solid excuse to leave when the time was right.

Wasn't the time right now?

Not while Amelia was still so young.

So you see, I'm not such a bad person. I really do care about my daughter, I want what's best for her, I'll never turn my back on her, I'm determined to find a way through to her heart.

In the meantime Anton could ridicule and humiliate, neglect and even beat her, but only until Amelia was able to make her own way in the world. That was when Olivia would go and never come back.

Looking around for Amelia now, she found her staring at her from an upper deck of their cruiser. The breeze was ruffling her mousy hair; the sun was burning her freckled cheeks.

'Have you used sunblock?' she called out.

Amelia held up a tube, presumably to show that she had.

'Are you going to swim?' Olivia asked.

'Only if you do.'

Olivia's heart twisted around her conscience. 'You know I can't.'

'Why not?'

'Because I've never learned.'

'That's just stupid.'

'Yes, it is.' Olivia didn't admit that she was afraid of the water; if she did Amelia would ask why and

4

Olivia could never find a good enough answer to that. Or not one that would satisfy Amelia.

'Where's Daddy?' Amelia demanded.

'Inside, sleeping. Or working.'

Amelia turned away and a few minutes later she was on the deck beside her mother. 'I want you to swim,' she told her bluntly.

'One of these days I'll learn,' Olivia promised.

'I want you to do it now.'

'It doesn't happen just like that. I need someone to teach me.'

'I can teach you.'

'OK, but not here. We're too far from the shore and I'll need to be able to touch the bottom in case I panic.' She smiled, hoping that Amelia might too, but she didn't.

'Are you afraid of drowning?' Amelia asked.

'Of course. It would be a horrible way to die.'

Amelia seemed to think about that, then suddenly pulling back her arms she gave her mother an almighty shove, sending her over the rail into the sea.

Olivia was too startled to scream. Her hands and legs flailed desperately in the water. 'Amelia,' she tried to gulp. 'Throw . . . throw me . . . the lifebelt.'

Amelia only watched her.

'Amelia! Please!'

Amelia turned away and went to sit at the table where she'd left the book she was reading.

Fifteen or so minutes later her father appeared from below.

'Hello sweetie,' he yawned, ruffling her hair. 'Are you OK?'

Amelia nodded.

He looked around, taking in the fresh sea air, calm waters and distant shore. 'Where's your mother?' he asked.

Amelia shrugged and carried on reading.

Sixteen Years Later

Chapter One

'Hello Jules? How are you?'

Jules Bright didn't answer. These days she wasn't used to unexpected visitors ringing the doorbell; if they did it was usually someone to read one of the meters, or young hopefuls collecting for a worthy cause. She was always polite to the former and gave generously to the latter, but friendly though she was, she never invited anyone in if she could help it. In truth, she didn't think anyone wanted to come, not because they were scared of her, or any nonsense like that, she was sure they just didn't want to get caught in conversation with her. No one ever knew what to say. She had to admit that she didn't either.

There had been a time when every day was filled with people seeking her out for one reason or another. Sometimes simply for a good laugh, or maybe sympathy for some troubles, the sharing of secrets, breaking of confidences, gleeful horror over the latest scandal . . . Her door had always been open, not this one, she'd lived somewhere else back then where her world had been full of people, music, rowdy applause, the clinking of glasses and cheers for whichever team they were supporting that day.

So who was this woman at the door of the home she had now, tall, dark-haired with aqua-green eyes that tilted at the corners towards a subtle, but quite arresting, beauty? Her smile was making Jules want to smile, although there was something hesitant about it, as though she was worried about intruding, or perhaps she didn't really have anything to smile about.

Jules knew she should recognise her, the certainty of it was climbing all over her memory trying to find the right images to rouse from the shadows, but so far unsuccessfully.

Then out of nowhere it came to her that this woman used to wear black-rimmed glasses and her hair was usually severely scraped back, as though she'd been trying to hide her beauty, or at least downplay it. No glasses today, and a glossy abundance of curls tumbled around her collar and slender face.

Suddenly the mental Googling hit the right link and Jules's heartbeat slowed as her smile both formed and drained.

She liked this woman a lot; there was a time when she'd felt she was the only person she could trust. She just hadn't imagined, once it was all over, that she'd ever see her again. Or not here, knocking on this door.

'It's Andee,' the woman told her. 'Andee Lawrence.'

Jules nodded. The name had come back in the instant it was being said. Detective Constable Andrea Lawrence, but please call me Andee. Hadn't she been promoted since Jules had known her? Jules was sure she had, and was now stationed locally, in Kesterly.

Why was she here?

'How are you?' Jules asked quietly.

'I'm fine. And you?'

Jules shrugged. No one expected her to be fine, so she often didn't bother to pretend.

'May I come in?' Andee asked gently.

Jules stood aside to let her pass, not quite able to summon a stronger voice yet, if she was even looking for one. She was too stunned – and anxious, and curious; she might even be slightly afraid.

There was nothing to be afraid of, she reminded herself as she led the way into a spacious open-plan kitchen area at the back of the house she now called home. It was a modern three-bed detached, on a street named the Risings, which was shaped like a banjo with two rows of semis lining the neck and fingerboard of the road in, and five individual properties forming the head around a central green. Her house was at twelve o'clock on the green. To continue with the banjo simile, overhead BT and power cables formed some random strings, though there was nothing musical about them. Where the instrument's tailpiece would have been, however, was a quaint iron footbridge nestling amongst trees and crossing the stream that ran its tuneful way through Jules's back garden.

She caught Andee Lawrence casting a subtle look around the room and wondered what she might be making of this modest new abode with its shiny black and white kitchen, natural pine dining table for six, and faux-marble fireplace with gas fire and lava logs. It was a fraction of the size of Jules's previous home, had none of the period features, and could boast nothing more than a postage stamp of a garden.

11

However, Jules was comfortable here; it was an easy home to take care of, bits didn't randomly fall off the ceiling the way they had in the previous place, pipes didn't burst, jackdaw nests didn't clog up the chimneys and there was no whimsical ghost floating about in the wee small hours.

How she missed that ghost, and sometimes wondered if the ghost missed her too, mischievous little minx that she'd been. She had other people to tease now, although Jules didn't think she bothered.

Had she ever told Andee about the ghost?

She doubted it; they'd had other things to talk about at the time.

'Can I get you some tea?' she offered, going to the kettle. 'I have all sorts.'

'How about peppermint?' Andee suggested, unfastening the smart cream leather jacket that had clearly cost her quite a bit, and draping it over the back of a dining chair.

Jules owned classy, expensive clothes too, but she hardly ever wore them now. She had no place to go that called for them. Not that she'd let herself go, she really didn't want to do that, though there were times when she felt so drained, so lacking in purpose, even life, that it surely could only have been habit that drove her to make herself up in the morning, and do the necessary to keep the grey from her hair. Despite what she felt, others would describe her as an attractive woman, tall, a little too slim, with the kind of boyish frame that meant clothes usually looked good on her. Her fine, straight hair was raven dark, and sometimes fell loosely around her shoulders, or was

12

scrunched up in a knot at the back of her head. Not so long ago she'd had the liveliest brown eyes, with spiky dark lashes and such a readiness for compassion or humour that she almost always seemed to be empathising or laughing or simply taking an interest in whatever was happening in that moment. Her eyes were different now – the same colour, just a sadder, more cautious version of what they used to be. As for her age, since she'd been blessed with the kind of complexion that made her seem much younger than her years, she still looked under forty in spite of all she'd been through.

Once, her spirit, her *joie de vivre* had seemed as inextinguishable as a joke candle, an inner flame that just wouldn't stop burning . . .

Until one day it did.

'You're looking well,' Andee commented, perching on a barstool.

'Thank you,' Jules replied, in her faint but unmistakable West Country burr. 'Out of interest, how did you find me?'

'I went to the pub.'

Of course, it would have been the easiest way. 'Are you still with the police? You didn't use your rank just now.'

'I quit, about a year ago.'

The answer surprised Jules, although she wasn't quite sure why.

'I never really felt cut out for it,' Andee admitted. 'I mean, I always took it seriously, and gave it my best, but I . . . Let's just say I reached a point where I felt I needed a change.'

'You mean you needed to get away from the ugly side of life?'

Andee didn't deny it. Why would she when, in Jules's opinion, no one in their right minds would want to spend their days confronting the hatred, violence and evil which seemed so large a part of today's world. Not that this town had an especially high crime rate, in fact it was one of the reasons people moved here, to get away from unwholesome inner cities. Although it had to be said that Kesterly-on-Sea could boast some terrible stories of its own. Now Jules came to think of it, the last time she'd heard news of Andee was about a year ago when a teenage girl had gone missing from a caravan park over at Paradise Cove. Detective *Sergeant* Andee Lawrence had led the search, so she *had* been promoted since the time Jules had known her, and apparently she had moved to Kesterly.

Though the missing girl had been found, the circumstances would have been hard for Andee, Jules realised, for Andee's sister had vanished when she was in her teens and had never been traced.

Imagine that, never knowing what had happened to someone you loved.

Could it be worse than knowing? That clearly depended on what there was to know.

So it was over two years since Jules and Andee had last met, though Jules couldn't quite remember where they'd been on that occasion, how they'd ended up saying goodbye. However, she had a clear recollection of their first meeting, at the Crown Court in the centre of Kesterly.

'Are you working these days?' Andee asked as Jules passed her a mug of peppermint tea.

Yes, Jules was working, but at a very different kind of job to the one she'd had before. 'I'm an administrator for the Greensleeves Care Home, down near the seafront,' she replied.

Andee's eyebrows rose in surprise.

Managing one of her old ironic twinkles, Jules said, 'My mother's there, and it's only part-time. I usually end up doing most of the work from here. How about you? What are you up to now you've left the force?'

Andee looked faintly sheepish as she took a sip of her tea. 'Well, I tried being a full-time mum for a while, but my kids soon got fed up with that. They're eighteen and sixteen now, so you can probably imagine, I was just in the way. Actually, their father and I finally got married a few months ago, they seemed to enjoy that, and of course they had to come on honeymoon with us, as did both our mothers, although we did manage a few days in Paris on our own.'

Jules felt dizzied by the image of three generations enjoying one another so much that they'd willingly travel together even for a honeymoon. Her own family had been just like that, doing everything and going everywhere together.

'. . . so I'm now toying with the idea of studying for the Bar,' Andee was saying.

Though Jules immediately saw beer taps and optics, she quickly realised Andee was talking about the law. Actually, she could see her as a barrister. She'd be good. Scrupulous, thorough, ruthless where necessary, sensitive, sharp, effective, but above all honest and incorruptible.

There were lawyers like that, Jules was in no doubt of it, it was just that she and her family hadn't come across them.

'What about the women's refuge?' Andee asked. 'Are you still involved with that?'

Jules both nodded and shook her head.

It seemed such a long time ago that she'd set up the refuge for battered women, probably because it was. It had happened in another lifetime, when she'd been as fearless of consequences as she had of raising money; she'd thought nothing of taking on the council for permissions, getting the social care they'd needed, financial support and even protection for the women and children to keep them safe from their tormentors. Memories of the fund-raisers they'd staged for the place and shows they'd put on for the children began flickering as though trying to find a focus, but she quickly shut them down again. 'They still have lots of volunteers doing their bit,' she told Andee. 'It's lovely how supportive some people can be, especially when there's nothing in it for them.'

'Apart from the satisfaction of knowing you've done something good for someone else. That's always rewarding.'

Jules didn't disagree, although she couldn't remember ever thinking much about how she felt when helping others. It was just something she'd done, because she could, and what sort of person turned their backs on someone when it was in their power to make a positive, even life-changing difference to a wretchedly unfortunate soul?

She wondered if they were now getting round to what this visit was actually about. Perhaps Andee had come to solicit her help in setting up some new kind of social project? She'd happily work with Andee on anything, since she had no doubt it would be a worthy cause. In fact she felt a stir of excitement, as much at the thought of getting involved in something new, as at the idea of becoming friends with Andee. It seemed such an age since she'd had someone to chat to, confide in, share a goal with, apart from Em, but with Em being so far away now she couldn't count on her in the same way as if she were still in Kesterly.

Andee was here, and they'd got along very well the last time they'd known one another, in spite of her not really being Andee's type. Actually, they probably were quite similar in some ways; it was just that they were from very different backgrounds. She, Jules, had started out life on the notorious Temple Fields estate, across the other side of town, whereas Andee was from the right side of London, where her father had been high up in the police force before his retirement. Not that she could imagine anything like disparity in social backgrounds being a problem for Andee; during the time Jules had known her she'd never shown any signs of considering herself superior to anyone, which made her pretty unique for someone doing her job. No, as connected and cultured as Andee might be, she'd been every bit as appalled as Jules had when the wheels of justice had turned the way they had almost three years ago.

It was time, the therapist had told Jules only last week, to start making efforts to move on. Though Jules had known it, hearing it had made her want to bury herself even deeper in her grief and anger, to tell the wretched woman that she had no idea what she was talking about, that if she were in her shoes she'd know what a ridiculous, insensitive and impossible suggestion that was. However, when she'd got home she'd found herself collecting up photographs and other treasured mementos and putting them away. That was all she'd done. It had felt huge at the time, exhausting, debilitating, but now, like some guardian angel, Andee had arrived, maybe to help her on the next stage of the journey?

She could do it. Whatever Andee was about to ask of her, she was going to say yes.

'I have some news,' Andee said, and her lovely blue-green eyes seemed to search Jules's in a way that made Jules start to tense.

She'd read this wrong. Andee wasn't here for a worthy cause, or to make friends, she was here for only one reason, and now Jules wanted her to leave before she confirmed her worst fears.

'I had a call from an old colleague,' Andee continued. 'He thought I should . . . He asked me if I would break it to you.'

Though Jules's heart was starting to thud, the beats were all wrong, fast, slow, harsh, so faint it might have stopped with dread. She knew what was coming, and yet she couldn't allow herself to think it, much less believe it.

'Amelia Quentin is being released,' Andee said quietly.

Jules's insides turned so hard they might crack. The hand she pressed to her head, to her cheek was stiff like a claw, yet shaking. She knew she shouldn't feel shocked, if anything she should have been expecting it, but so soon . . . It was as though no time had passed; considering what the girl had done, no time had.

'Come and sit down,' Andee said gently, pulling out a chair at the table.

Doing as she was told, Jules said, 'When?'

'I don't have an actual date,' Andee replied, 'but it's imminent.'

'And where will she go?'

Andee swallowed and her eyes moved briefly away before she said, 'I believe she's returning to Crofton Park.'

The reply was like a slap. Crofton Park, one of the Quentins' several country homes, was less than four miles from this part of Kesterly, out on the moors, close to the medieval village of Dunster. The old folks, Amelia's grandparents, the judge and his wife, had spent their final years at Crofton Park and no one locally had liked them. Good riddance, they'd all said when the ill-tempered, tight-fisted old beak had followed his snobbish, petty-minded, unpleasantly outspoken wife to the grave. Since their passing the place had become little more than a weekend retreat for their only son, Anton Quentin QC, and his despicable toff friends from London. They hardly ever mixed with the locals, unless it suited them for some trifling reason, otherwise they were far too exclusive to entertain even the idea of becoming involved in the local community. Theirs was an overprivileged, overmoneyed, overtitled, rarefied existence that the rest of the world – the every day pleb world – only read about in expensive glossy magazines and society columns. They were also, Jules had come to learn the hard way, a section of the upper-class British Establishment that stuck together no matter what, and even believed they were entitled to play by rules of their own.

'Doesn't she have to go to a halfway house first?' Jules murmured, still trying to take it in. 'That's what usually happens when someone's released, isn't it?'

'Often, yes,' Andee confirmed.

Jules looked at her briefly. Of course the rules were different for the likes of Amelia. How stupid of her to have forgotten that.

Amelia Quentin was to be released; she was returning to Crofton Park . . . How could the girl even think about setting foot in that place again, never mind actually want to? 'It shouldn't be happening,' she said hoarsely. 'It's just not right.'

'I know,' Andee responded.

'Her sentence was a farce! An outrage!'

Andee didn't disagree.

'There are other places she could go,' Jules cried angrily. 'Why does it have to be there?'

Andee had no answer to that.

'She should *never* be allowed out,' Jules declared fiercely. 'If we hadn't been cheated of a proper trial . . . What about Dean Foggarty? Is he being released too?'

'I haven't had any news about him.'

Thinking of Dean caused Jules to see red again. 'It was one massive injustice from start to finish,' she growled. 'We were treated like the little people, cretins who don't matter . . . Dean shouldn't be where he is, everyone knows that. *She's* the one who should be paying.'

Andee's eyes showed her sympathy; the words she'd spoken at the time of the trial had expressed how disgusted she too had felt at the way things had turned out.

'If I see her, if she comes anywhere near me . . .' Jules raged. What would she do? She knew what she'd like to do.

'She won't, I'm sure.'

Jules's breathing was still ragged as she struggled with a tangle of fury, frustration, helplessness and the deepest, bitterest resentment. Just as she was finding the heart to start moving forward . . .

She couldn't cope with this . . .

'Where's Kian?' Andee asked softly.

Jules looked at her, her eyes feeling as wide as the jagged holes in her heart. From the kindliness and concern of Andee's expression it was clear that she had no idea about Kian.

Andee Lawrence had gone now, leaving Jules alone with the stark reality of a nightmare with no end. She knew that if Andee had been able in any way to soften her news, or to change it to what everyone wanted to hear – that Amelia Quentin was never coming out of prison – she would have done so. But it hadn't been in her power. All she'd been able to do was come here in an act of selfless consideration that went above and beyond what was called for, given that she was no longer with the police. She had her own life to lead now, there was no need to concern herself with anything that had happened during the time she was a detective. And it wasn't even as if she'd been assigned to the Bright family case back then; what she'd done had been out of genuine kindness, something Jules would never forget.

Jules suspected Andee was driving home now worrying about leaving when she had. In a way it was reassuring for Jules to know that she had someone on her side. On the other hand, maybe she didn't want to connect too strongly with Andee when the thoughts in her mind were so chaotic and dark.

Glancing at the clock, she calculated the time in Chicago where her best friend Em was a first-grade teacher, and Em's American husband, Don, was the Director of Alumni Relations at one of the city's exclusive private schools. They'd met, by chance, in London, over two decades ago, at which point in time Em would have been the last person to envisage herself leaving Kesterly, never mind Britain, and going to live in the States. However, that was what had happened, she'd even married in the States at Don's family's lakeside villa in Indiana, where Jules and Kian had spent just about every summer vacation since.

'You're kidding me,' Em cried when Jules broke the news about Amelia Quentin, sounding every bit as sickened as Jules had expected. 'How the hell can that happen?'

'It's called parole. Apparently she's eligible – or someone's seen to it that she is. I'll need to look it up, because I don't know how these things work, but she hasn't even served three years.'

'What about Dean? Are they releasing him too?'

Jules winced, as she often did when Dean's name was mentioned. There were so many emotions attached to him, guilt, confusion, anger, love, despair . . . One day, when she could think straight again, she might work it all out. 'She didn't know about him,' she replied, 'only about Amelia.'

With a sigh Em said, 'Oh hell, Jules. What are you going to do? Is it absolutely certain she's coming back to Kesterly?'

'To Crofton Park, is what Andee said. So close enough.'

'Then why don't you just pack up and come here? I could help you . . .'

'You know why,' Jules interrupted. 'Apart from everything else, I can't just abandon my mother, even though she hardly knows who I am. I like to think we're still connecting on some level. I have to tell myself we are, or there wouldn't be a point to anything.'

'Poor Marsha. No better, huh?'

'That's never going to happen, and I have to be honest, I sometimes feel glad of it. At least she didn't have to go through what the rest of us did. It would probably have killed her if she had.'

'I get what you're saying,' Em assured her, 'but listen, I've just noticed the time and I have to be in class in half an hour. I'll call again at noon, OK? Just tell me, do you think you're going to be safe with that girl on the loose?'

Jules's insides clenched with a sour blend of hatred and unease. 'She's got more to fear from me than I have from her,' she declared tightly.

'Mm, you, and the rest of Kian's family. When's it supposed to happen?'

'I don't have an exact date, but apparently it's imminent.'

'Is Stephie around?'

'No, she's in Thailand.'

'How about Joe? Are you going to be in touch with him?'

'I had an email from him a couple of weeks ago. He's coming here at the end of next month to kick off a tour of Europe.'

'That's cool. It's great that he's kept in touch. And it was real kind of Andee to come and tell you about the release. I always liked her.'

'Me too. She didn't know about Kian.'

'That surprises me. Did you tell her?'

'Yes. I think it came as quite a shock. Anyway, I should let you go. Call me back as soon as you can.'

After ringing off Jules sat down in front of her laptop not quite sure what to do next, apart from check her emails and maybe catch up on some work. She knew she should email Stephie and Joe, and call Kian's family, but all she did was walk to the window and stare out at the rain. Lucky she hadn't put any washing out; she'd been about to when Andee had arrived. Now all she could think about was what she was going to do if, when, she ran into Amelia Quentin. She could see, almost feel the girl creeping up on her as she draped sheets on the line, or walked out to her car, grabbing her, forcing her to the ground and stabbing her, over and over . . .

Her vision blurred as the past loomed up in all its frantic and bloody glory.

She was aware of her hand tightening around the handle of a knife; there were spasms in her arm as if it were trying to make a frenzied attack; there was sickness and murder in her heart that was blackening all the natural goodness and love . . .

Wrenching herself free of the chaos, she ran upstairs to the spare room and dragged out the box she'd stored there so recently. With trembling hands she took out the photo of Kian that she used to keep next to her bed. Why had she removed it? There had been no need to. He was her husband, it was only right that she should look at him every day.

Hello my love, she whispered, her slender fingers tracing the easy line of his jaw and the fair, tousled curls that made him look so fun-loving and rakish. He was laughing straight into the lens, carefree, happy, as though nothing could touch him, no one could be as lucky as him.

It was what he used to say, 'Being married to you makes me the luckiest man alive.'

Jules could hear the words so clearly he might be saying them now. They were falling around her as softly as petals, and felt as refreshing as spring rain. He was pouring his love into her heart, driving out the darkness, filling it with light and laughter, the way he always had when she was afraid, or sad, or angry, or starting to lose hope. She'd never doubted him or his love, the way she knew he'd sometimes doubted hers.

'I didn't mean to shut you out,' she whispered, tears shining in her eyes. 'Is that what I did?'

He'd never accused her of it, but she'd sensed a loneliness in him at times that she knew she could have done something about, but she hadn't. It broke her heart all over again to think of it now.

'I should have made the time,' she said hoarsely. 'If only I'd made the time. Maybe none of it would have happened if I had.'

She didn't really think that was the truth, or not all of it, anyway, but sometimes there was comfort to be found in punishing herself with guilt. If she was responsible then it meant she was in control, and if she was in control she could have stopped it . . .

Her therapist was having none of that. 'You know that doesn't make any sense,' she'd tell her, and Jules never argued. She understood why the therapist always steered her away from the self-destructive thoughts. It was her job, what she was trained to do – in her shoes Jules would do exactly the same.

'Hey, you,' she said tenderly as she stroked Kian's face again.

He was still smiling at her, so she smiled too and did nothing to stop her mind drifting back over the years to a time when just about everyone they knew had smiled with them . . .

Chapter Two

The pub door crashed open loudly and in stepped a man in black.

On the man's head was a *montera* – a flat-topped hat with round fluffy bulbs above each ear. Swinging from his shoulders was a heavy cape, flashing flirty glimpses of a blood-red lining as it swayed. His silken shirt was slicked tight to his manly body, opened down the front to reveal his even more manly chest. Around his waist was a crimson sash; his trousers hugged his hips like a lover's hands and flared like sails around his ankles.

He stamped his feet, threw out his long arms and shouted, *'Olé!'*

Jules's eyes were alight with laughter.

Tap-dancing across the bar, the matador (or was he a flamenco dancer?) clicked his fingers, flourished his cape and declared, 'I am come to see the beautiful lady. You must follow me outside, oh lovely señorita, I have special surprise to make your heart happy and your husband very jealous.'

Glancing at the laughing decorators, watching from atop their ladders, Jules was about to ask if they were in on this when Ruthie Bright bustled in from the next bar with a bucket and mop in one hand, and something indefinable in the other.

'Mary, Mother of God!' Ruthie muttered as she spotted the man in black. 'What the devil has he come as this time?'

'I'm still trying to work it out,' Jules twinkled, as the flamboyant Don Juan planted a trail of noisy kisses up her arm, and whisked her from behind the bar to dance her out through the door into the morning sunshine.

The pub garden was cluttered with boxes, pallets, skips, all manner of builders' paraphernalia and a freshly painted sign waiting to go up. The Mermaid of Hope Cove, it declared. The garden's grass was long and ragged, coated in cement dust, and appeared on a steady slide into a glistening bank of pebbles that dipped abruptly on to the shale beach beyond. Beside the garden was a slender stone footbridge over an inlet that led into a small harbour, where a mere handful of boats bobbed and jangled in the watery undulation.

Rising up alongside the cove, as though protecting it, or maybe even threatening it, were dark and jagged cliffs, dropping straight from the vast and mystical wilderness of Exmoor National Park. Nestled at the heart of the cove, with a gentle flow of fields and forest to the back and the tempestuous estuary to the front, was the legendary Mermaid Inn, one of Kesterly's oldest and quaintest public houses.

It was said somewhat intriguingly, or even absurdly, that the pub was responsible for choosing its owners. It was also said that its walls had ears and no secret was safe if spoken within, but no one had any proof of that. Everyone knew it had a ghost though no one could actually lay claim to having seen it. The records showed that the oldest part of the inn dated as far back as 1462, with various rooms, stables and outhouses being added over the years to form the characterful, although rundown establishment it was today. Until a dozen years ago it had belonged to an investment banker from London who'd visited often, but had left the running of the place to those more qualified than he. Since his untimely death in a skiing accident the Mermaid had stood empty, the subject of a bitter inheritance dispute. Those who knew Dickens's work had referred to it as a Jarndyce v Jarndyce situation, though mercifully the case hadn't dragged on anywhere near as long as its fictional counterpart, and there was certainly nothing bleak about this house.

Its outer walls were silvery white and glistened like mother-of-pearl in the after-rain sunshine; its windows were black-framed and randomly placed, and seemed to gaze out at the channel like a wise old soul seeing all, judging nothing, simply waiting for storms to pass and seasons to change. Its roof was slate, its beams gnarled and black and its history as colourful as the sunsets that cast their fiery glow across the waves to turn the entire setting into a dreamland.

Fortune had bestowed a dazzling smile on Jules and Kian the day it had decided to make the place theirs. It had been a dream, albeit an idle one, almost since they'd first known each other, and now, amazingly, unbelievably, ten years on and still only in their twenties, here they were, the owners of this historic, heart-stirring jewel of a freehouse.

It would also seem, Jules realised, as the crazy Spaniard began flamenco dancing around a vintage Austin Healey Sprite with a convertible roof and maybe even a starter handle it was so old, that they might just be the owners of this little charmer too.

'Ees-a for you,' he announced, 'with all-a my love-a.'

Laughing, Jules took the keys and slipped into the driver's seat. 'You're seriously going to let me loose in this?' she challenged the ludicrous figure in its nylon moustache and flame-retardant wig. Her husband's sparkling violet eyes narrowed playfully. 'I let you loose-a with everything. This is how we make-a loose-a woman out of you,' and with a swirl of his cape to shield them from watchful eyes he stooped to kiss her.

'What are you like?' she chuckled, as he raised his head to gaze into her teary eyes. 'And the car's not even Spanish.'

He grimaced an apology. 'Is only costume Nola have left in shop that fit me.'

Loving him, and wanting to hug him almost as much as she wanted the reason for this gift to go away, she put a hand to his face as she whispered, 'You didn't have to do this. It's fine, honestly.'

Removing his hat and wig to reveal a flattened riot of ash-blond curls, he said, gravely, 'It's not fine, but it will be, I promise.'

Turning at the sound of an admiring whistle, he immediately flourished his cape again, clicked his heels and thrust out his macho chest. 'Come meet my wife's new car,' he told Ruthie and the decorators. 'She will be the envy of all Kesterly for this cheeky little minx, just as she is for her dashingly handsome Romeo of a husband.'

'Will you just listen to him?' Ruthie was trying not to laugh as she came to join them, her wide brown eyes and cheery moon face showing as much fondness as humour as she tweaked Kian's rugby player's nose. 'If only I'd been lucky enough to catch myself one like you,' she sighed. 'I got the wrong cousin, so I did.'

'Now you won't want our Connor to be hearing you say that,' Kian chided, 'when we all know you worship the ground the dear bloke walks on.'

'Yeah, like I worship his betting and boozing and big-talking buddies.' Ruthie had always had a knack with alliterations. 'Now, what's this dear little car all about?' she wanted to know. 'Don't tell me I forgot your birthday, Jules. If I have I'll rush off somewhere right now to put things right, though heaven only knows what I'd get you when the mad Manuel here spoils you half to death already.'

'It's not my birthday,' Jules promised, 'and actually it's not my car.'

'What are you saying?' Kian protested in a Spanish fluster. 'The lovely lady no want the lovely car?'

'I know *you* do,' she countered. 'You've had your eye on it ever since your Danny told you it was in Damian Boyle's showroom.'

'But my eye is looking out only for you, to present this gift to make you smile.' She knew at least a part of that was true. He always hated it when she cried. The last time it had happened he'd come home with his face painted like a clown and had injured his back trying to somersault down to the beach. 'Of course,' he ran on nobly, 'if you would like me to be your chauffeur, it would be my honour to do this favour for you.'

'Take the car,' Ruthie told her. 'I know I would. Imagine yourself driving around town in that, up and down the coast road, on to the Temple Fields estate. Take it there for half an hour and you won't have any wheels left to get out again.'

'Sad, but true,' Kian conceded. Coming from the wrong side of the estate himself, there wasn't much anyone could tell him, good or bad, about what went on there.

Jules herself was from the right side of the estate, which meant south of the high street, where many of the cul-de-sacs and avenues were quite leafy and smart, with dustbins taken in after collections, front lawns regularly mowed and net curtains washed with bleach and ironed with starch.

The Mermaid was about as far along the coast from the estate as it was possible to get while remaining in Kesterly. However, there was no doubt in either of their minds that Kian's enormous Irish family and their numerous friends from all over town, including the estate, would make regular trips to see them.

The grand opening wasn't too far off now, since the major repairs were all but complete, the new kitchen was due to be installed tomorrow and joy of all joys, their licences from the local authority had come through in plenty of time. They'd been on several training courses by now, and the experience they'd had of working at the Red Lion, Kian's Uncle Pete's drinking man's pub, over on the estate, hadn't done them any harm at all. However, running their own establishment was going to be a whole other sort of challenge, which was why they'd taken professional advice every step of the way – and were still doing so now. They understood how important it was to go above and beyond their training to know the rules and regulations of the licensing trade, to comply with the health and safety requirements imposed by the government, they'd even gained something close to medical training on how alcohol affects different people, and what to do in all kinds of emergencies.

Their most vital needs right now were for a cook – Fliss at the Seafront Café in town had told Aileen, Kian's mother, only yesterday that she knew of someone good who was looking for a job, so that might be sorted – and an experienced bar manager to run the front of house while Jules and Kian took their turns at shifts, but mostly concentrated on everything behind the scenes.

Since they were fully confident of finding the right person for each role by the deadline they'd set, the recruitment wasn't an issue that vexed them unduly. In fact, being the type of people they were, very little worked them into a frenzy of sleepless nights and fraught, overstretched days. There was always an answer to a problem, they'd remind one another, it was just a question of finding it, and stressing out wouldn't make things happen any quicker; more likely it would steer them off in a wrong direction and end them up flat on their faces.

Watching Kian now in his hilarious costume, showing off to the boys, Liam and Greg (his second cousins who'd been tasked by their builder father, Davin, to paint the pub without making arses of themselves), Jules felt so much love and sadness engulfing her that she had to turn away.

'What is it, pet?' Ruthie asked softly, all concern.

Jules instantly brightened. 'Nothing,' she assured her. 'Just something in my eye. Is that the phone? My God, they've connected it at last!'

Ruthie cocked an ear to listen. 'Miracles will never cease,' she cried gladly, and off she bundled back inside leaving Jules to slip out of the car, close the door and lean against it as she stared off towards the milky horizon.

The sea was like shattered glass today, sparkling with sunlight, barely seeming to move apart from the waves sighing quietly on to the shore. They might still be young and foolishly naïve, but they were going to love it here; there wasn't a shred of doubt in her mind about that. It was such an idyllic spot people *wanted* to come here; some said they wouldn't even have to bother with any publicity, because word of mouth would do it all. That could be true given how fast news travelled in Kesterly, and how well known Kian's family was. However, they'd already hired an agency to work on a marketing strategy, which was the kind of thing most new businesses were doing these days. They didn't want to try and make out they were anything more than they were, they simply wanted it to be known that they were going to serve some fine ales from local breweries, a good selection of French and New World wines that a local merchant was advising them on; and as wide a range of spirits as any self-respecting bar could boast. As for food, they were going to start out fairly modestly by offering all the traditional fare of scampi or chicken in a basket with chips, jacket potatoes with four different fillings, an assortment of sandwiches, a full-blown roast on Sundays and of course the usual packets of crisps, peanuts and pork scratchings.

Later, if things went well, they intended to make the catering a bit posher, and might even turn a section of the pub into a restaurant. But that was for the future. For now, since under-fourteens weren't allowed in the main bar a family room was already being set up at the back complete with pool table, dartboard and the game of devil among the tailors, aka table skittles, that they'd found in the cellar during the renovations. Of course there was also the garden and the beach for when the weather was fine, and what had once been the old off-licence was now a spacious boot room for hikers and dog-walkers as they came down from the moor.

The upstairs rooms had already been transformed into a luxurious three-bedroom, two-bathroom apart-ment, and now all the work was complete it would be hard to love it more. An interior designer from London had taken on the project, since Jules had hardly known where to begin, especially when so much of the building was listed. So, working together with Kian's Uncle Davin, the designer had managed to retain most of the original features, while knocking down partition walls, opening up fireplaces, repairing decaying oak beams, sanding and resetting Victorian pine floors, and recrafting ornately corniced ceilings.

Afternoon and evening light now flooded across the sea and beach in through the casement windows of the romantically cosy master bedroom, also into the sitting room and kitchen, while the two bedrooms and bathroom at the back could boast their own mesmerising, even haunting views of the moor.

It seemed that the whole place now felt as full of happiness to be alive again, as Kian and Jules did to be there. Jules even swore she could see it smiling at them, especially last night, after all the workers had gone, and they'd laid out a picnic blanket on the beach and toasted a week of being in actual residence. They'd looked at the Mermaid, raised their glasses and at that very moment the sun had caught a window, making it seem as though it was winking at them. They'd laughed, hugged each other and toasted the place again. Kian had chosen a new beer they were trying out from Exmoor Ales, while Jules had gone for an unexciting lime soda. This morning she'd discovered that she too could have had beer, or even champagne, because the evidence had been right there to show her that in spite of all their efforts she still wasn't pregnant.

She'd felt so crushed, so angry and helpless that she'd hurled a box of tampons at the wall with such force that it had split and scattered the contents all over the place. As if being violent was going to change things. What difference did a temper make when the body clearly wasn't listening?

Because they were still only twenty-six and twenty-seven everyone kept telling them they had plenty of time, but they'd been trying for over four years now, and still nothing had happened. Their lovely doctor over on the estate had sent them for one test after another, after another; they'd attended all sorts of counselling sessions, had spent hours with their legs in the air (Kian always joined in) to encourage a happy bonding, had even gorged on leafy greens, lentils, oysters, everything that was recommended to help the little miracle occur.

It shouldn't matter so much. Jules told herself that repeatedly, angrily, fiercely, sadly, reasonably, because she knew very well how lucky she was in every other way. She had a wonderful husband, more friends than she could begin to count, this dream-come-true of a pub, they even had enough money for it not to matter too much if things didn't work out the way they'd planned. So how dare she be so desperate about failing to conceive? It didn't diminish her as a person; it wasn't destroying her health; it made no difference to their plans for the pub; and it wasn't affecting their marriage.

At least not yet.

Kian swore that it never would. She was all that mattered, he always insisted, but she knew that his longing for children ran just as deep as her own. They'd talked about it so often, even as far back as when they hadn't been much more than children themselves, laughing and thrilling at the prospect of becoming parents to four, five, six, even seven kids all with personalities, dreams, looks, quirks and passions of their own. Perhaps it was being only children themselves that made their desire for a large family so overwhelming. Or maybe, these days, it was because so many of their friends were managing it with no trouble at all. It made their own failure seem so pathetic and cruel. Whatever the reason, biological, psychological, or nothing logical at all, it was beginning to turn their irrepressible urge to become parents into an out and out obsession.

This last failure had been the bitterest blow of all, since it had followed their first attempt at IVF. Clearly even that wasn't going to work, which could only mean they weren't meant to have children, and if that was the truth then Jules just wanted to walk into the sea right now and never come back. She felt so miserable, unworthy, useless, and . . . *cheated.* Yes, cheated. Which just went to show how selfish and shallow she was to think she had the right to be a mother when no one actually had that *right*, and anyway, she already had so much.

Round and round; round and round.

Kian's laugh suddenly broke into her thoughts, and she turned to watch him sending his cousins back to work. 'That's enough now,' he told them with a wink at Jules. 'I'm not paying you to stand about all day admiring Jules's car, or her ass, *Liam* . . . That's right, you little tosser. She's family, for God's sake . . .'

'Stop,' Jules cried, as the sixteen-year-old lad blushed to the roots of his fiery red spots.

'I was not looking . . .'

'Get out of here,' Kian told him fondly. 'And you, Greg. You're supposed to be done in the main bar by the end of today. How likely is that looking?'

'Hundred per cent if you'll let me take a spin in that car,' Greg promised.

'Yeah, like that's going to happen. Anyway, it belongs to Jules so you have to ask her.'

Greg immediately turned to Jules.

'The answer's no,' Kian informed him. 'Ruthie, my darling, do you think we can rustle up a cup of tea for us all?'

'Who was that on the phone?' Jules called out.

'An engineer testing the line,' Ruthie replied, coming to the door. 'Very polite he was, and he told me if we have any problems . . .'

'Tea?' Kian interrupted.

'Just what I was thinking,' Ruthie told him, 'you know where the kettle is. Two sugars for me,' and allowing the boys to pass she grinned at Jules before following them back inside.

Sighing, Jules rested her head on Kian's shoulder as he slipped an arm around her.

'I know the car doesn't make up for anything,' he said softly, 'but it did make you smile.'

'Not as much as the outfit,' she assured him. 'You look a complete dick, and I suppose you went parading through the town dressed like that making sure everyone saw you.'

'Well, I wouldn't be wanting them to miss out on a good laugh, now, would I?' he admitted. 'Which reminds me, I was thinking we could make our grand opening a fancy dress affair. Can't you just see it? We could go for a nautical theme, you know, pirates, smugglers, jolly matelots, *mermaids* . . .'

Jules looked at him askance.

'OK, maybe not mermaids, they wouldn't be able to walk, but the topless bit would go down well.'

'I wonder what you're going to think of next?' she laughed. '*You're* the one who loves dressing up, not everyone else. Well, maybe everyone in your family . . .'

'Who's that?' he broke in as a large white van came trundling along the cove's only access route from the main road. 'Oh, great, it's Bob. I bet he's brought our new computers.'

'That fell off the back of a lorry?'

Kian's hands went up. 'He knows we don't take any of his dodgy stuff,' he assured her. 'Apparently these are totally on the level, still in their boxes. I thought you wanted one.'

'I do. Definitely. Who's going to teach us how to use them?'

'We'll find someone. You know they're saying that within ten years everyone's going to have one . . . I'll go give him a hand to unload. Christ! He nearly hit my new car, stupid b . . .' He turned sheepishly to Jules. '*Your* new car,' he corrected.

Her eyes were shining as she watched him taunting Bob with his cape, zigzagging over to the van where Bob was clearly enjoying the performance as he jumped down on to the gravel. They'd been friends all through school, had lived on the same street, played on the same football and hurling teams, were best men at each other's weddings, and had promised to be godfathers to each other's kids when the little rascals finally came along. (Bob's wife, Izzie, was expecting their first at the end of next month.) There probably wasn't anything the two men wouldn't do for one another, although Jules had to admit there wasn't much Kian wouldn't do for anyone.

He was just that sort of bloke. He absolutely loved to help others, to the point that he found it almost impossible to say no, and it didn't even seem to bother him if he was taken advantage of, which happened more often than he probably knew. Not that anyone ever did him wrong, it wouldn't have been wise given the family he came from, and besides everyone was far too fond of him to want to hurt him in any way, or to cause any deliberate offence. It was simply that he was a lot of people's first port of call when something needed doing, since he had a knack of sorting out problems and making things happen. He filled in complicated forms for the elderly and infirm, organised transport for their hospital visits, found plumbers for their leaks, made sure cars were properly fixed before bills were paid, dealt with snooty power companies, called in the Brightest Spark (his cousin Finn, the local electrician), or another cousin who was a nurse, or Carrie who worked for social services. He had a bigger network in and around Kesterly than British Telecom, his mother would often tease, and Jules was convinced that Aileen was right.

Like Jules's mother, Marsha, Aileen had lost her husband at a young age, and had had to bring up her child alone. However, with so many brothers and sisters all over the Temple Fields estate, as well as back home in Ireland, and all the nieces and nephews that entailed, plus further extended family and of course friends of family, it could hardly be said that Aileen had lacked support. In Marsha's case the circumstances had been entirely different. Apart from her lovely next-door neighbours Trisha and Steve, parents to Jules's lifelong best friend Em, she'd had no one to help with the burden – or share the joys – of being a single parent. Unless she counted her mother-in-law, Florence, but it was hard to do that when Florence had always seemed to resent every single finger she was forced to lift in assistance of others.

'It's a miracle your father turned out to be as kind and lovely as he was, having a mother like that,' Marsha would often sigh when she and Jules were talking about Florence, 'so let's just be thankful he didn't take after her.'

Jules's father had died when she was five years old. It was an accident that should never have happened, and wouldn't have if he'd left work a minute earlier or later. In the event he was driving home when a tree fell on his car, crushing it.

Whether it was the shock of fate changing her world so abruptly that had made Marsha so nervous of life, or whether she'd been like it before her husband was killed, Jules couldn't be sure. She only knew that her mother, as sweet and funny and wise and supportive as she could often be, would leap out of her skin at the merest unexpected noise, constantly shy away from confrontations in case she ended up being punished in some ghastly cosmic way, and worried herself ragged from the minute Jules left the house until she came home again. It was a part of her mother's character that Jules had always found wearing – and intensely annoying when she was in her teens – although it had made her extremely protective of her.

Since Grandmother Florence had departed the world when Jules was eleven, it had been just Marsha and Jules, with Trish, Steve and Em providing all the family they needed. And when it became evident, a few years later, that Jules's relationship with the dashingly lovely

Kian Bright was turning serious, they were all more than happy to be a part of Kian's chaotic family, in spite of them living on the wrong side of the estate. (This was something that had only ever mattered to Marsha and Trish, until they met Kian and Aileen whom it was impossible not to adore.)

It hadn't even seemed to bother Marsha too much that Kian had no plans to go to uni. He'd seemed quite chilled about continuing to divide his working hours between his cousin Danny's boxing club on the edge of town, and the Red Lion, for as long as it floated his boat – a phrase that had tickled Marsha to bits when she'd first heard it. (She'd known in her heart that Kian was going to amount to something, everyone did, it was just going to take time to find out what.) Jules had also worked at the pub back then, but being only sixteen her duties had been restricted to washing glasses, wiping tables and sweeping the floor. By the time she was seventeen, and halfway through sixth-form college, she was a part-time server behind the bar (Kian's Uncle Pete with his flamboyant moustache and twinkly eyes had always considered the law something to be stretched and moulded to suit a person's needs), and she and Kian had already decided that one day they were going to run their own pub.

'Wouldn't you just love it to be the Mermaid?' he'd sighed one warm Sunday afternoon as they'd strolled on the deserted beach in front of the forlorn-looking inn. 'Just think what we could do with it if we had a bit of cash.'

'A lot of cash,' she'd corrected, 'and then we could

make it the best pub in Kesterly by a mile, the way everyone says it used to be.'

And now, miraculously, here they were happily married with their extravagant plans built up over the past several years coming to fruition, and enough in the bank to create even more.

When the money had come to them, back last year, Kian had been working in Damian Boyle's car show-room on the outskirts of Paradise Cove. One of his many tasks, besides selling the second-hand rides at which he was extremely good, was to run the staff lottery scheme. This meant collecting the money, popping out to the newsagents to buy the tickets, and checking the results when they came in.

However, it wasn't the syndicate that owned the only winning ticket one momentous Saturday evening, it was Kian who'd tossed over a pound coin before leaving the shop, saying, 'Give us one for luck, mate.'

So the newsagent had, and by the end of the day Kian was in such a profound state of shock that he hadn't been able to speak to tell anyone what he was sure couldn't be true. It was only when he made the call and found out it was true that he finally owned up to Jules, who'd as good as fainted when she'd heard how much he'd won.

Being Kian, he couldn't face telling his colleagues in the syndicate that by some mind-boggling fluke he was rich and they weren't, so when the winnings came through he'd ended up giving them all twenty grand each, no strings attached. There were handouts for his family too, naturally, and the biggest of all for his mother. Weirdly – or perhaps not, since his family wasn't like most others – no one had used their windfall to leave the estate. A few spent it on home improvements, others lost it all on the horses or dogs, a couple made good investments in a new waterside development next to Paradise Cove, and just about every one of them, including his mother, had bought themselves a brand-new car and taken a fancy holiday. Aileen's choice of car had been a funky blue Fiat Panda, which she'd picked up a day before taking off on a luxury cruise around the Med with her best friend Marsha. In return Marsha had used some of her own little windfall from Kian to take Aileen, Trish and Steve on, of all things, an African safari. Such courage from her mother! Jules could hardly believe it when Marsha, who worked at the dog-rescue centre, had owned up to this secret, lifelong desire to see wild animals in their natural habitat.

Now, Jules was about to start back inside when Aileen's funky Fiat, as everyone called it, swerved in from the main road and skidded to a halt inches from Bob's white van.

Realising Em was at the wheel – Aileen had given Em the keys the day Em had arrived from the States, telling her to think of the car as her own for the duration – Jules ran over to greet her.

'Did you get through?' she asked, as Em climbed out of the driver's seat, beaming all over her dear sweet face.

'I did,' Em confirmed, her spiky blonde hair and riot of gingery freckles making her look as airy and frivolous as a teenager, when she was actually twenty-six and already a mother. 'Kian! *What* have you come as?' she shrieked.

'Julio Rivero at your service,' he responded, with an extravagant flourish of his cape and clatter of heels. 'So, tell us, *chiquita*, are you staying a bit longer?'

'Two days,' she told them excitedly. 'The travel agent was such a sweetheart. He actually let me use his phone to call Don while he checked out the flights. Don's totally cool about me extending, he's just really sorry that he can't be here too, but you're all to come visit us just as soon as you're able.'

'You can count on it,' Kian assured her.

'How's Matilda?' Jules wanted to know, referring to Em's almost two-year-old bundle of joy.

'Oh, she's doing just great,' Em replied, seeming to melt. 'Apparently she's being really good for Grandma, Grandpa and Daddy and when Don put her on the phone she actually said, "Hello Mommy, miss you." I swear I nearly sobbed. I wanted to get on a plane that very instant, but you and I get so little time together these days, and I'll see her again by the end of the week. Bob Stafford, as I live and breathe! How are you? I haven't seen you in so long.'

Appearing slightly perplexed by this new Em, who was actually the same as the old Em, full of warmth and exuberance, except she had a kind of mid-Atlantic accent now with little West Country waves washing all over it, Bob allowed himself to be hugged.

'Looking good, Em,' he told her gruffly. 'Suiting you over there, is it?'

'I love it,' she assured him, 'but I love coming home to visit. Nothing changes, which is the most wonderful part of it, and yet it does, because look at these guys getting this fabulous old pub up together . . . I only wish I could be here for the opening, but the Fall semester starts on August 18th and I have to be back for that.'

Flooding with pride at her friend's achievements, Jules was about to slip an arm around Em's shoulders when another car pulled in from the main road. This time it was a silver Mercedes with blacked-out windows that neither Jules nor Kian recognised, but as it came to a stop and two men dressed entirely in black stepped out Jules felt a chill run through her.

'Who is it?' she murmured to Kian.

'Go inside,' he told her.

'I want to know who it is.'

'Go and call our Danny,' he growled. 'Tell him to get himself over here *pronto*.'

Even before she'd made the call to Danny, Jules had realised who the unwelcome visitors were.

'It's the Romanians,' she said softly as she, Em and Ruthie watched from the window. 'Or Albanians. I'm not sure about their nationality, but you can guess why they're here.'

'They're messing with the wrong family if they think they're going to get anything out of us,' Ruthie muttered fiercely.

'Are you saying it's protection they're after?' Em asked, appalled.

Jules nodded. 'They turned up in Kesterly back in April or May and they've been harassing businesses all along the coast ever since, especially in Paradise Cove.'

'Is anyone paying up?'

'I've no idea, but I'm guessing some are or they'd surely have cleared off by now.'

'Or someone would have been hurt,' Ruthie added ominously.

To Jules Em said, 'Will Kian pay?'

Jules was indignant. 'No way!' she declared hotly. 'I'd rather close the place down than start bowing to the likes of them.' In a sudden blaze of fury, she started for the door. 'I'm going out there.'

'No, Jules, you can't!' Ruthie and Em cried, grabbing her back.

'You don't know what they're capable of,' Ruthie cautioned wisely. 'If you go upsetting them they might take it out on Kian.'

Jules returned to the window, still steaming and frustrated. When she saw what was happening now her jaw dropped in shock. 'Oh my God! He's only treating them to a bloody flamenco,' she exclaimed, starting to laugh. 'He's out of his mind.'

The others started to laugh too. Kian was nothing if not unpredictable.

Suddenly Jules froze. '*Christ!* Is that a gun?' she gasped, fear coursing through her so fast she started to shake.

Bob was backing off, white-faced, hands in the air.

Kian carried on dancing, clicking his heels, waving his hands and throwing out his cloak.

'This is like the scene from *Indiana Jones* when he pulls the gun and shoots the baddie,' Liam declared over their shoulders.

'Except in this case the baddie's got the gun,' Ruthie pointed out.

Jules couldn't watch for another minute. She had to get out there and put a stop to it all.

'Come back,' Ruthie seethed, grabbing her again. 'I'll tell you what he's up to. He's making out he's a nutjob, or drunk, someone who isn't the owner of the business, so they're wasting their time trying to get anything out of him.'

'If you go out there,' Em told her gravely, 'there's every chance you'll get hurt, and that definitely wouldn't be Kian's plan.'

Unable to argue with that, Jules turned to Liam as he said, 'Looks like they're going.'

Returning to the window she watched the thugs getting into their car while Kian, unbelievably, just carried on dancing and Bob, by the look of him, was bending double trying not to laugh.

As the Mercedes reversed back to the road and disappeared, Jules threw open the door and shouted across the garden, 'My husband and his best friend have to be the only idiots in the world who treat a visit from the mafia as a joke.'

Kian spluttered, 'Did you see their faces? They didn't know what the hell to do.'

'So they pulled a gun. These guys are dangerous, Kian. People who mess around with them end up dead.'

'Did you call Danny?' Kian wanted to know.

'He's on his way, with backup.'

'OK, we'll deal with it from here, so you just go on about your day and don't worry yourself any more about nasty little men who make nasty little threats that they can't carry out. Especially not with Julio Rivero!'

Unable not to laugh, Jules turned back inside, still worried, although loyally confident that Kian and his cousins would find a way to see the Romanians, and any other chancers with similar aims, off for good. If they didn't then their dreams really might be over before they'd begun, since she was serious about not working for some lowlife hoodlums of any nationality who had the audacity to try and set up their vile racketeering in her home town.

'Have you had many visits like that?' Em asked as Jules led the way past the bar to the stairs.

'No, that was the first, and let's hope it's the last or things could really turn ugly. Actually, I heard the other day that the police are calling a meeting with local business-owners to come up with a solidarity type of plan to try and sort this out. Kian will be sure to go, especially now, probably along with half the Temple Fields estate. You know how they're always spoiling for some sort of fight.'

'It'll make a change for them to be on the same side as the police,' Em remarked drily as they climbed the stairs. 'So, are you missing being over there? It must seem very quiet on the posh side of town by comparison.'

Jules paused as she reached the top of the stairs where boxes were piled on the landing, and a warm breeze was stealing through an open sash window.

'What is it?' Em asked, trying to peer around her.

Jules shook her head. 'Nothing,' she said. 'I just thought . . .' She picked up an old-fashioned cream leather shoe with a fraying lace and broken stitching around the pointed toe. There was no heel as such, and the sole was worn thin, though not through. 'The builders found this lodged in one of the window frames while they were carrying out the renovations,' she said, showing it to Em. 'I keep wondering about who might have owned it.'

'It looks very old,' Em commented, treating it carefully as she turned it over in her hands.

'It is. Mum took it to one of the antique dealers in town, who reckons it dates from the mid-nineteenth century and probably belonged to a young girl or small woman. Because it's leather and is clearly for the right foot he says she was unlikely to have been a peasant.'

'What does the right foot have to do with it?'

'Apparently only the better off were having shoes shaped for each foot around that time. I've been trying to decide where to put it, and I was sure I took it down to the bar this morning . . .' Shrugging, she put it on the top of a box and carried on along the landing.

As she pushed open the sitting-room door she felt her heart swell to see how elegant and welcoming it was with its up-to-the-minute fawn suedette sofas, thick-pile champagne-coloured rugs, whitewashed stone walls and perfectly restored Georgian sash windows, all open and allowing the sun to cast the room in an almost dreamlike glow.

'I'm still having to pinch myself,' she confessed, as Em followed her in. 'I mean, imagine me and Kian having a home like this. It's straight out of a magazine.'

'And it's no less than you deserve,' Em told her fondly. 'If that money had gone to someone else I bet they'd never have given as much away, or done as much for the community as you two are doing.'

'Who knows,' Jules shrugged, 'I'm just glad we're bringing this place back to life, because right from the minute we stepped through the door, when it was still practically a ruin, it's felt like we belong here. Mum's been digging out stuff from the library so we can read about its history. I mean, we know from all the searches and everything that it's always been an inn, but it would be fascinating to know something about the people who've lived here.'

'Wouldn't it just,' Em agreed, rapt by the romance of it.

Heading for the windows, Jules said, 'We've already had a few locals dropping in to tell us stories, and even give us photographs of when their great-grandparents used to come here, back at the beginning of the last century. Apparently it was called the Smuggler for a while during the twenties, but it became the Mermaid again in 1930. We're going to hang the photos in the main bar, and Mum's been rummaging around local charity and antique shops to see what else she can find that might be fitting.' She was watching Danny and his entourage of hard men with shaven heads and tattoos piling out of Danny's battered old Land Rover, apparently torn between bristling for a fight and laughing at Kian's crazy costume.

'To think,' she murmured teasingly as Em joined her, 'Danny Bright could have been all yours if you hadn't met Don and skedaddled off to the States.'

Sighing nostalgically, Em said, 'I was so in love with him when I was twelve.'

'Sixteen,' Jules corrected.

Em twinkled. 'You've got to admit he was a real

looker back then, and he still would be if it weren't for the broken nose and scary scars.'

'He's been in a few scrapes,' Jules admitted. 'And when you consider the kind of club he owns . . . Shall we go and say hello?'

As she made to turn away Em caught her hand and gently pulled her back. 'In a minute,' she said, her grey eyes full of concern. 'I want to make sure you're OK first.'

Jules made herself smile. 'I'm fine,' she promised. 'It's just one of those things. If it's not meant to be, then it's not meant to be.'

Hearing the emotional tear in her voice, Em drew her into an embrace. 'You've got so much going on at the moment,' she soothed gently, 'so maybe now isn't the best time for a baby.'

Pulling away, Jules said, 'How would you have felt if someone had said that to you when you were trying for Matilda? Oh that's right, you didn't try, it just happened, the way these things do for most people.'

Em regarded her helplessly.

'I'm sorry,' Jules sighed. 'I'm not bitter really, or maybe I am. I mean I don't begrudge you Matilda, please don't think that for a moment, I just can't understand why it should be so difficult for me when no one can find anything wrong with me.'

Clearly desperate to keep hope alive, Em said, 'I'm a firm believer in everything happening when it's supposed to. So there'll be some divine reason why you're not getting pregnant now, and in time you'll look back and think, thank God it didn't happen then, because it's much better that it's happened now.'

Though Jules smiled gratefully, in her heart she was wishing her best friend had been able to come up with something a little more original, or at least some form of comfort that both their mothers and Aileen didn't regularly trot out. 'Remind me,' she said, needing to change the subject, 'why did we come up here?'

Em shrugged. 'I just followed you.'

Jules gave a laugh as she looked around. 'I guess I love it so much up here that I can't stay away. Actually, I feel like that about the whole place, and it's fantastic that you're going to stay with us for your last couple of days. Did you bring your stuff?'

'Mum and Dad are driving it over later so they can see for themselves how things are going here. I just love the way the whole town is talking about it. There's such a buzz going on. I can't believe I'm going to miss out on the grand opening.'

'But you'll come for Christmas,' Jules reminded her. 'All of you.'

'You bet. Don's folks are even talking about coming too, but don't worry, no one will have to put them up,' Em hastily added. 'They can afford one of the smart hotels on the front, and would probably prefer it anyway.'

Relieved to hear that, since she, Kian and her mother had found Don's wealthy parents a little daunting when they'd been in the States for the wedding, Jules said, 'Obviously they'll be very welcome, but I hope they're prepared for the Brights en masse.'

Em laughed. 'Rosemary and Gray are much easier-going than you think, and I'm sure they'll love all you Brights every bit as much as I do.'

Feeling suddenly downcast at the thought of Em being part of a family that was so far away, and so very different to her own, Jules turned to the door. 'I'll just pop to the bathroom,' she said awkwardly. 'Meet you downstairs?'

As Em started along the landing Jules watched her go, wondering what she was thinking now, if her thoughts had already flitted off across the Atlantic to Matilda and Don. Jules couldn't imagine thinking of anything but her child if she had one, no matter where she was; there again, she was thinking about it anyway and it didn't even exist.

Turning into the bedroom, she gave a sigh of exasperation to discover that she'd left most of the dresser drawers and the wardrobe doors wide open. As if she needed any evidence of the state of mind she'd been in when she'd dressed earlier.

Annoyed with herself, she closed everything up and went into the bathroom to sort out the mess she knew she'd left there. However, to her surprise everything was as it should be. The tampons were back in their box and inside the cabinet, and the towels were hanging neatly on a heated rail when she was sure she'd left them heaped on the floor.

Realising Kian must have found a moment to tidy it all up, she sank down on the edge of the bath and dropped her head in her hands. Though she loved him for doing it, it was making her sadder than ever to think of how he must have felt when he'd walked into the evidence of her frustration and grief. Everybody made this all about her, including him, but she knew that he was suffering too, yet instead of sitting around feeling sorry for himself, or throwing things about the place, he'd gone out and bought her a car. Not only that, he'd got himself all kitted out as a dancing Spaniard simply to make her smile. Only she knew that it had provided a crazy persona for him to hide behind, which, as it turned out, had served him well when the Romanians had come calling.

She wondered if they'd come back, and in that moment she wasn't sure that she cared. All that mattered was the baby that she and Kian couldn't produce. Her heart was already swollen with love for it; her arms were so ready to hold it she found it hard to keep them at her sides. There were times when she was sure she could feel it, even hear it, and whenever she went shopping she had to force herself not to buy things ready to welcome it into the world.

'It doesn't do any good to remind you of how young you are,' her lovely doctor had said the last time she was there. 'When the instinct is upon you the way it is now, it's one of the fiercest things in the world, which is why I'm going to do everything I can to help you.'

Jules wondered if Dr Moore would still feel the same when she let her know that the IVF hadn't worked. It was extremely expensive, and not everyone was lucky enough to get it, so maybe they'd decide that Jules was too young to be given a second chance; she would either have to wait for conception to happen naturally, or go to a private clinic. She and Kian had already discussed that, and were perfectly prepared to pay. In fact, they should probably have done so anyway, given how well off they were. Now she came to think of it, it could very well be the unfairness of that that was at the root of the problem. It wasn't her turn. Whoever handed out babies up there had decided she'd elbowed her way into the wrong queue, and until she got into the right one nothing was coming her way.

Hearing a noise in the bedroom she lifted her head, expecting someone to call out her name. When no one did she concluded that the wind must have blown something over, and getting to her feet she went to check her face in the mirror.

As she gazed at her reflection she found herself blinking several times, trying to work out why there seemed to be two of her, one in front of the other.

'Jules! Where are you?' Kian shouted along the landing. 'You've got to come and see these computers. Bob's brought the lot, monitors, towers, keyboards, there's even a printer. We are so bang up to the minute, or we will be when we know how to use them.'

Chapter Three

Something was tapping the window, and had been for some time. A gentle, lacklustre rhythm that took a while to make Jules lift her head. For several moments she watched the guilty branch drifting back and forth like a useless limb in the wind.

She couldn't think where she was, though she knew it wasn't the pub, as real as it had seemed a moment ago with crazy matadors, mafia thugs and dear Em . . .

Her heart emptied as the present pushed aside the past to bring her into the spare room of her new home at number fourteen, the Risings. Andee Lawrence had left a while ago, though Jules couldn't be sure how long it had been since she wasn't wearing a watch and there was no clock in the room.

It didn't matter. She had no pressing engagements today.

The branch continued to tap, making her think of Ruby, the ghost at the Mermaid. She willed the girl's face to materialise in the sky beyond the tree, but the clouds simply carried on sailing by like purposeful boats on a steady sea.

Taking one last lingering look at the picture of Kian,

she put aside the box of photo albums and other precious mementos and went downstairs.

Andee Lawrence's card was still on the table where she'd left it. 'Call any time,' she'd said as she'd handed it over, and Jules had felt sure she'd meant it.

Slipping the card into a drawer, she checked the time on her mobile phone and wondered how long it might be before Em rang back. She was so busy with all her teaching and committees and after-school coaching that she often said she'd call and ended up being unable to.

Jules jumped and almost dropped her mobile as it suddenly started to ring.

She looked at the caller ID, half expecting it to be someone from Greensleeves needing to talk about her mother, but it wasn't a number she recognised.

Perhaps it was Andee, checking to make sure she was OK.

She clicked on, wondering how she'd answer the question if she turned out to be right.

It was a reporter from the *Kesterly Gazette*.

Jules ended the call and turned off the phone.

A moment later she turned it on again. If the press had been tipped off about Amelia Quentin's release there were people she needed to warn before reporters started harassing them too.

Her first call was to Aileen, in Ireland. Aileen's sister answered, explaining that Aileen had just popped out, but would be sure to want to speak to Jules when she got back. Jules left a message, knowing there was no doubt about it being passed on.

Realising she didn't want to speak to anyone else

yet, she composed a text to a dozen or more family members that read, *She is being allowed out. No date yet. Will let you know as soon as I hear.*

Knowing she'd be inundated with calls as soon as the message was received, she turned her phone off again and opened her laptop.

> *Dear Joe,*
>
> *I know I've already told you how happy I am that you and your friend have decided to start your European trip here in Kesterly, it will be lovely to see you again and catch up with all your news. That hasn't changed, but I'm afraid I have some news of my own that I think I should tell you before you come in case it changes things for you. Amelia Quentin is being released from prison, and will very probably be back at Crofton Park by the time you get here . . .*

The mere thought of that caused her breathing to stop and her heart to beat viciously.

She envisaged the girl in the big house on the moor, moving about it like an evil force, spinning her lies and treachery, maybe even reliving what she'd done and enjoying it . . .

She looked at the email.

There was more she wanted to say, much more, but for the moment she couldn't think how to phrase it. Her thoughts were tangled in the traps they were laying for revenge and memories, mixing them up, colouring them with prejudice and grief, drawing her into a terrible confusion.

Getting to her feet she put her hands to her head

and closed her eyes as she focused on sweeter memories, forcing herself to let go of all thoughts of revenge, at least for now.

Though the shallow depths of the past were torturous, the deeper in she went the softer her heart became and the wetter her eyes. She could smile, even laugh at those early days at the Mermaid, the exhilarating success of the grand opening; their first glowing reviews in local papers and even the local news. It might have been before the days of the Internet, but word had still spread like wildfire, so that party bookings had come flooding in and the takings had surpassed all expectations.

They'd received no more visits from chancing thugs trying their hands at extortion. The Rafia, as Kian liked to call them, had been seen off by a hard-core group of local businessmen and traders working with the Dean Valley police, and a handful of undercover officers from the Met. What a thrilling time that had been for the blokes of Kesterly, getting involved in such a dangerous operation, and of course the Bright family men were amongst the first to volunteer.

After a crash course in computer studies Jules and Kian had soon begun to wonder how on earth they'd ever managed without their new machines (this was when they weren't threatening to chuck the bloody things out of the window). Jules then followed up with a six-week course in bookkeeping, while the new bar manager, Misty Walsh, whom they'd enticed from a very la-di-da hostelry in Berkshire, had set about teaching Kian everything she knew about running pubs, which was a lot.

Em and her entire family had come for the first Christmas at the Mermaid, and though Em's upright and slightly stuffy parents-in-law had seemed awkward, even perplexed by the unruly Brights for the first few days, by the time they'd left they were inviting everyone to Chicago any time they wanted, they'd always be welcome to stay.

Jules and Kian had crossed the Atlantic the following Easter, leaving the eminently capable Misty in charge of the Mermaid and its loyal workforce: two cooks, four full-time bar staff and four part-timers. While they were in Chicago Em had gently broken the news to Jules that she was expecting her second child. Jules had felt terrible on every level, not least for the way Em had seemed so apologetic, when she should have been rejoicing. Of course, Jules couldn't deny she was jealous, she was insanely so, but it didn't mean she wished Em anything but happiness and as many beautifully healthy children as she desired.

She just wished she was capable of producing the same, but by then she and Kian had experienced two more failures with IVF, and were being told, mainly because of the emotional stress, that they should maybe start considering adoption.

'I'm sure you've heard about couples who've adopted and then suddenly found themselves pregnant,' lovely Dr Moore had pointed out. 'That's not to say I can guarantee it happening for you, but it's amazing what can happen when you take off some of the pressure.'

Jules hadn't doubted it; it was just that she hadn't felt right about using an innocent child that way.

Em and her family didn't come for the second

Christmas at the Mermaid, not because their adorable new baby son, Oscar, was too young to travel. It was because a week before they were due to leave Em's mother-in-law died quite suddenly from a heart attack.

Em's parents flew straight to Chicago; Jules and Kian would have followed were it not for the fact that they had an appointment they simply had to keep, and Em had refused to let them change it.

'Jules! Jules!' Kian shouted. 'Will you hurry up or we're going to be late.'

Jules ran out of the pub, tugging a white bobble hat on to her head, and trying to wrest the toggles of her duffle coat from a tearing wind so she could fasten them. The estuary was kicking up a right royal storm this morning; what a mood the heavens must be in to be bearing down on the world with such a thuggish display.

Kian was already behind the wheel of their Range Rover – it was no weather for the plucky little Sprite – and as Jules jumped in he began pulling away.

'Will you wait for me to close the door?' she cried, struggling to grab it from the wind.

He hit the brakes. 'Sorry, I'm getting myself in a bit of a state. Are you OK?'

'I'm fine. Just don't go too fast, we need to get there in one piece.'

Fifteen minutes later they turned on to Kesterly seafront to find awnings being ripped from their frames and an upturned carriage from the white tourist train blocking the road. Police were redirecting traffic into North Road, but Kian took a quicker route through the old town, not officially open to non-residents, and brought them out on the ring road just as it was being closed due to an accident.

'What the hell!' Kian cried, thumping the steering wheel.

Blinking back tears of frustration, Jules looked away as he reached for her hand. She felt angry with him, even though it wasn't his fault.

'We might still make it,' he said lamely.

After months of indecision and then waiting for an appointment . . . These hold-ups were already making their next attempt at IVF feel doomed, as though someone up there was trying to stop her putting herself through it again.

Taking out his new mobile phone, Kian called the clinic to warn them they'd be late. As he listened to the reply he turned to Jules. 'That's great,' he responded, raising his eyebrows. 'Yep, we can do that. Thanks very much. We'll definitely be there.' Ringing off he said, 'They've had a cancellation next Monday, so they're going to slot us in at eleven.'

Jules's head fell back against the seat. It wasn't only relief pushing tears to her eyes, but the fear of her own hope as the terrible waiting continued.

Half an hour later, having collected their mothers from a yoga class, Kian dropped his girls outside the Mermaid while he went to park the car.

'Oh, look, a lovely log fire,' Aileen cried, going to warm her hands in front of the lively flames. 'Marsha, come and sit yourself here in the armchair and get yourself warm.'

'I'm all right,' Marsha insisted. 'It's you we want to

be taking care of. You're not properly over your cold yet.'

'Ach, me, I'm as fit as a fiddle and never better. Me oh my, is that you over there, our Danny? What are you doing here at this hour? It's not even the middle of the day yet. Shouldn't you be running that club of yours?'

'It doesn't open until five on Tuesdays,' Danny grinned, strolling over from the bar with a pint of best in one hand and a half-smoked cigarette in the other. 'It's good to see you, Auntie Aileen, so it is. And Marsha. Out doing the ladies-who-lunch thing, are we? Got some shopping lined up for after?'

'Now there's a good idea, Marsha,' Aileen declared. 'We should go and spoil ourselves this afternoon, why not? Now don't be blowing that smoke in me face, Danny. And it's time you gave up those filthy things.'

'It's what keeps me going,' he informed her, stifling a cough. 'So now, can I get you two gorgeous girls a drink? Pint of Guinness, Auntie Aileen? Put some hairs on your chest?'

'Oh, you're funny you are,' she retorted. 'I'll have me usual lager shandy, and I expect Marsha'll have the same.'

'I will,' Marsha confirmed. 'And how's your lovely wife, Danny? I don't think I've seen her since Christmas.'

'Cheryl? She's all right, but with the baby due in a couple of weeks, she's feeling too heavy to go out much. Kian, my man!' he cried as his cousin came through the door. 'Just the person. I've got myself some tickets you're going to want, and they won't cost you a penny more than I paid for them myself.'

'Which means they'll be double,' Jules muttered to Misty, making her laugh.

'That couple's in the family room again,' Misty told her, moving towards the pumps to start serving some newcomers.

Jules frowned.

'You know, the posh ones I told you about last week, with the spoiled brat of a little girl. Apparently she wanted to play with the devil among the tailors again. The way she's going at it it'll be in pieces before she's finished.'

Since Jules considered the game one of the pub's prized possessions, she wandered through to the family room to find the couple sitting incongruously at a table close to the unlit fire, and the child standing at a table flinging the ball on a string at the tiny wooden skittles. Being so young, probably no more than three, it was unlikely she could cause much damage, although she seemed fairly intent on it considering the oomph she was putting behind her throws.

'Hi,' Jules said chattily. 'If you like, I'll get someone to come in and light the fire.'

'Oh, no, no,' the woman hastily answered, 'we don't want . . .'

'That would be welcome,' the man interrupted, turning in his chair to look at Jules in a way that immediately irked her. There was such a condescending air about him that she'd have liked nothing more than to turn on her heel and leave him in the cold.

'We'll stay for lunch if we may,' he told her. 'My daughter enjoyed the jacket potato she had before. It's partly why we came back. She's also taken rather a shine to your little table game, as you can see.'

Jules watched the child hurling the tiny ball with all her might, as though some deep-seated anger was making her want to destroy the harmless, deftly carved little skittles.

Apparently unaware she was being spoken about, or simply not caring, the girl carried on flinging the ball.

'Hello,' Jules said gently. 'And what's your name?'

The child simply ignored her.

'Amelia,' her mother admonished.

The father put up a hand to silence his wife. 'Amelia, the lady's talking to you.'

The child turned to look up at Jules and her eyes, round, direct and coldly assessing, almost caused Jules to blink. She'd never seen someone so young with such an adult expression, or with such translucent skin that she might never have seen the sun.

Jules made herself smile.

The girl didn't smile back.

'Do you like the game?' Jules asked, going towards her. When was the last time someone had brushed this child's hair? It was so tangled it must have been a while, though she could easily imagine the kind of tantrum the girl might throw if someone tried.

The girl's fist was tightening around the ball, as though she was afraid Jules might be about to take it away.

It didn't matter that the pull on the string was making the narrow pole bend; being metal it was unlikely to break.

'We've tried to find something similar,' the father announced, 'but I'm afraid this is the one she's set her heart on.'

Jules looked at him.

'I'd like to buy it,' he explained, as if Jules was becoming tiresome.

'Well,' Jules began, 'I'm afraid it's not for sale.'

'Oh, but I'm sure it must be,' he protested. 'A little old thing like that. I can't imagine anyone else plays with it.'

Sensing that he wasn't used to taking no for an answer, Jules said, 'It's been at the pub for a very long time, possibly over a hundred years, so we feel that it belongs here.'

His laugh was more of a scoff, but before he could speak his wife said something that Jules didn't catch. Whatever he muttered through his teeth in reply Jules couldn't make out either, but there was no mistaking the way the woman seemed to shrink back inside herself.

The man was clearly a bully who had little regard for women, including his own wife. However, he wasn't going to get away with anything here, especially not the game. 'I'll have someone come and take your order,' Jules informed him shortly, and turned on her heel.

'Excuse me,' he barked, 'we haven't finished here. I said I want to buy the game . . .'

Jules turned around. 'And I said it wasn't for sale.'

'For heaven's sake, look at her. You can see how much she loves it, would you really begrudge a small child something so . . . so . . . worthless?'

'I'm sure you'll be able to find another . . .'

'I want this one,' the girl informed her. 'It's mine.'

'No it isn't,' Jules replied gently.

The girl flung the ball with all her might. It spun round the table, missing the skittles, and ended up with the string wrapped tightly around the pole.

'I really don't see what the problem is,' the man declared, getting to his feet. He was far taller than Jules had expected, certainly over six feet, and there was a menace to his manner that made her wonder if he was actually going to try and take the game by force.

'Anton, please,' the woman begged.

Ignoring her, he continued forward.

The child suddenly screamed and they all turned round.

'It hit me, it hit me!' she wailed, clutching her head.

Her father scooped her up as Jules looked at the game. The child must have spun the ball again, although how she'd managed it when the string was still wrapped around the pole was impossible to say.

'It's all right,' the father told her, making it sound more of a fact than an attempt at comfort.

'I hate it! It hurt me,' the girl sobbed. 'Naughty game.'

The mother was on her feet too, trying to take the child.

'No!' the child growled, and turning her face into her father's shoulder she clung to him and wailed loudly.

'I'm sorry,' the woman mumbled, not quite meeting Jules's eyes. 'I . . .'

'What the hell are you apologising for?' her husband

snapped. 'We haven't done anything wrong,' and as though neither Jules, nor his wife, nor even the game existed, he stalked out of the room, taking his sobbing daughter with him.

'I'm sorry,' the woman whispered again, and before Jules could respond she went scurrying after her husband.

Realising Misty was standing behind her, Jules said, 'Did you see any of that?'

'Enough,' Misty answered. 'A total dickhead if ever I saw one.'

'And the game fought back,' Jules smiled. 'It wants to stay here, so it saw the child off.'

'Yeah, like it's got a life of its own.' Misty's cynicism was as playful as the light in her eyes.

Jules simply shrugged. She wasn't going to comment one way or another, for she was feeling far too tired and anxious to get into any banter right now about whether or not there was something, or someone, living alongside them at the pub, but she rather thought there was.

Chapter Four

Dear Ruby, where was she now, Jules was wondering as she drove past the shady spur road leading to Hope Cove and the Mermaid, and continued along the coast towards town.

Misty, who was still running the pub with her Italian husband, Marco, had told her they'd never sensed any sort of other-worldly presence since Jules and Kian had left, and the cream leather boot that Jules had placed on a mantlepiece in the library the day of their departure – yes, they'd had a library by then – had never been moved other than by human hand.

It was funny, that, because it used to move about all over the place when Kian and Jules were there, turning up between her and Kian's pillows at night; alongside Jules's shoes inside a cupboard as though trying to blend in; it even showed up in the car once, as though it was ready for a day out. For a long time Jules had been convinced Kian was doing it as a tease, despite his denials, but after her mother had found the story of Ruby Gideon in an old newspaper cutting at the Kesterly library she'd actually started to believe that they weren't alone at the Mermaid.

Girl loses life in fire, the small headline in a late-nineteenth-century edition of the *Kesterly Chronicle* (now the *Gazette*) had read. There were only a few lines below, providing scant detail of how Rose and Robert Gideon, innkeepers of the Mermaid public house, had lost their twelve-year-old daughter, Ruby, in a fire that had broken out in a bedroom, due to an overturned oil lamp. Of course, there was no way of knowing for certain that the owner of the cream leather boot really had been the Gideons' daughter, but given its age (according to the antique dealer) and its size, Jules had decided that the little rascal living alongside them just had to be Ruby.

She could feel herself warming to Ruby even now as she approached the outskirts of town, remembering the way she used to talk to her at times as though she was actually there.

'Are you hungry, Ruby? Shall we make ourselves a sandwich?'

'Was it you who set the alarm off at one o'clock this morning, Ruby?'

'Ruby, what is your boot doing on top of the cigarette machine? You know you're too young to smoke.'

And there had been the sadder times when Ruby's presence had felt as real as anything she could touch, and in a way had seemed as comforting as if the ghost somehow understood what she was feeling.

It was crazy, but true, that she'd hardly been able to wait to tell Ruby when she and Kian had found out they were pregnant. People were saying that by then, 'we are pregnant,' as if the man was going to blow up like a balloon and give birth at the end of it all. They'd received the news when they'd gone to their rescheduled appointment at the clinic to find out if they were clear to start a new round of fertility treatment.

'It would appear from these test results, Mr and Mrs Bright,' the doctor had announced, eyes still on the file in front of him, 'that you've beaten medical science to it and achieved a conception all on your own.'

Jules's heart caught on the memory. She could see herself, as clear as day, staring at the doctor in disbelief . . .

. . . She was dreaming, she had to be. She hadn't heard him right . . . Yet he was smiling, and Kian was standing up to shake his hand, as though the doctor had played an actual part when he'd just said he hadn't . . .

Jules was suddenly sobbing so hard that she could barely catch her breath. Relief, elation, shock, so many emotions were coursing through her that she had no clear idea of what any of them were.

She was carrying a baby.

Right now, this minute, a tiny little speck of life was starting to grow inside her, a speck of life that she and Kian had created, and that would be loved and wanted so much it would surely come right now if only it knew.

'Oh God,' she gasped, over and over. She'd prayed so hard, had tried everything it was possible to try and now, without them even realising, it had happened. Their beautiful little son or daughter was coming to them at last.

'How – how far along?' she heard Kian asking.

'About eight to nine weeks,' the doctor replied.

Out of nowhere Jules was suddenly struck by fear.

'Do you think it'll be all right?' she cried. 'I mean, after everything we've been through . . . Is there a chance . . .'

She was thinking of miscarriages, deformities, complicated births that might leave one or both of them dead . . .

'There's no reason why everything shouldn't be just fine,' the doctor smiled. 'You're young and in good health.'

'But even healthy women . . .'

'Jules, stop,' Kian came in gently, taking her shaking hands in his own. 'You can't start looking on the black side now. We've got what we've always wanted, our very own little miracle, and the doctor just said, there's no reason why everything shouldn't be just fine.'

It had turned out to be more than fine; no problems at all with the pregnancy, only excitement and trepidation, the like of which neither Jules nor Kian had ever experienced before. It was as though both their families, all their friends and even the pub's clientele were pregnant with them, for it was hard to imagine a baby stirring so much interest or relief or belief that everything happened in its own time, especially the birth of babies.

In the end it was on a humid, lazy afternoon in late August that Jules went into labour. Kian instantly leapt into action, and by the time he'd rushed her to the hospital, fraught with nerves and exhilaration, the highly active Kesterly grapevine was already buzzing with the news.

Jules would never forget the look on Kian's face when the nurse handed him his tiny scrap of a daughter to hold for the first time. It was a comical blend of alarm, confusion, adoration and pride. Exhausted though Jules was, the sheer joy of those moments gave her the strength to hold their baby girl too, and even feed her, and the surge of love that rushed in as though to bind the three of them together had felt so powerful and real that she knew right then that nothing could ever break it.

'Hello Daisy,' she whispered, gazing down at the flushed, sleepy little face. 'You're a very beautiful little girl.'

'Daisy,' Kian echoed, staring at her as though still unable to believe she was there. 'Do you like the name? If you'd rather have another, I promise I won't mind.'

The baby's eyes opened briefly, but whether she could see them it was impossible to tell.

'I think she likes it,' Jules murmured. 'Daisy Bright is a lovely name, so why wouldn't she?'

'She's all things Bright and beautiful,' Kian whispered with a sob in his voice. 'Oh Jules, she's wonderful. Thank you, my darling, thank you so much.'

'I didn't do it alone.' Jules smiled at him. 'And I think we should have that hymn at her christening.'

They took Daisy home the following day to a rousing welcome, with balloons and bunting decorating the entire cove right down to the beach. It was hard to imagine what they were going to do with all the gifts, much less how they were going to work out who each one was from.

Knowing the party was likely to go on all day, probably through to the wee hours, Jules soon made her excuses and took Daisy upstairs to her and Kian's bedroom where they'd set up the crib.

She didn't lie her down, she simply went on holding her, feeling her weight, smelling her wonderful baby smell, watching her eyes open and close and her tiny lips pursing and popping. As real and precious as she was, it was still taking time for Jules to believe that this wasn't all a dream. She and Kian had their very own baby at last. Their lives were going to change in ways they probably couldn't even imagine, but they were ready for it. Whatever being a parent meant, they were going to do the very best they could and make sure their little girl never wanted for anything.

Lifting Daisy's silky cheek to hers, she looked around the room. Of course there was no sign of Ruby, because there never was, it was all about feelings and sensing and somehow knowing she was there. And she was, Jules felt certain of it. It was as though Ruby had been waiting too, and was watching in her own way as the baby came into their home.

What if she was jealous and worried, and afraid that the baby would become more important than her? It was crazy to think that way, but maybe believing in Ruby's goodness meant she had to accept that there could be another side to her as well.

She didn't speak out loud; she said the words silently in her mind, certain that on some level Ruby could hear. 'Ruby, this is Daisy. I hope you're going to love her, because it would mean the world to me if you do.'

Naturally there was no reply, but she sensed no change in the atmosphere, no withdrawal or coming forward, so maybe Ruby was just watching, as fascinated by a newborn as any twelve-year-old girl might naturally be.

Responding to a knock on the door, Jules called out for the proud grandmothers to come in. She'd known they would follow and she was glad that they had. Daisy was as special to them as she was to her parents. She was the baby they'd longed for too, and was, for them, living proof that God really did answer prayers.

No sooner were they in the room than the phone started to ring.

'It could be Em,' her mother declared as Aileen took the baby. 'I called before Aileen and I left to let her know you were on your way home.'

'Oh, she's a little darling, so she is,' Aileen crooned as Jules reached for the phone.

'Jules! Oh my God! It's so wonderful,' Em gushed down the line. 'Your mum rang yesterday to tell me you were in labour, and now you have a beautiful baby girl. Daisy. I just love her name. I can't wait to meet her. I promise, if school hadn't already started I'd be on the first plane out, but I'll definitely be there for half-term. How are you? Was it gruelling? How many stitches?'

Laughing, Jules lay gingerly down on the bed, loving the way Aileen passed Daisy to Marsha so she could hold her too. She had never felt so much elation and tiredness in her life, or such a powerful sense of belonging to another human being, tiny as Daisy might be.

An hour or more passed as she and the grandmothers gossiped and laughed with Em on the phone, passing the baby between them to be fed or winded or simply admired. Daisy took it all without complaint, sometimes gazing at them curiously, or yawning, or waving a little fist in the air.

When Kian escaped the celebrations to come and join them the baby settled comfortably into her daddy's arms, and within minutes they were both fast asleep.

'We'll leave you to get some rest too,' her mother whispered, running a hand over Jules's hair. 'Don't worry about anything, we've got it all under control.'

With her eyes already half closed Jules said, 'Why would I worry when I have you to do it for me?'

Marsha smiled and turned to Aileen, who was gazing at her son and granddaughter in something close to awe. It was a truly special moment for them all. Their son and daughter had finally been blessed by the Almighty with the beautiful baby they so desired and deserved.

As the door closed behind the grandmothers Jules forced herself up to close a window, hoping to block out some of the noise downstairs. It helped, a little, but since she wanted to fall asleep to the sound of the celebrations, she left the others open and turned back to the bed.

On the way she stopped at the exquisite, hand-carved crib that Kian's second cousin's wife, Terry, had found in an antique shop somewhere in Devon, and had spent the last few months lovingly restoring. When she'd brought it to the pub, just over a week ago, Jules had immediately fallen in love with it. It was impossible not to.

Going to the crib she ran a hand along the smooth sandy oak, and lace bows that Terry had tied on to the rails. Ruthie and Connor had given Terry the cream silk coverlet to put inside the crib, along with a mobile of small white fluffy animals that was currently curled up in one corner waiting to take its rightful place. As Jules went to reach for it her hand came to a stop. Ruby's dainty little boot was nestled in amongst it, looking for all it was worth as though it belonged there.

Jules smiled and frowned curiously. She hadn't noticed it when she'd come into the room, but there again she hadn't looked very closely. And anyway it must have already been there, because it couldn't possibly have turned up since, and now what she was wondering was *why* it was there. Could this be Ruby's way of offering Daisy a gift, since it was all she had to give?

It seemed the most likely answer, and because it felt so typical of Ruby to do something a little whimsical, yet kind, even funny in its way, she decided that she had read the gesture correctly.

Returning to the present, Jules stopped the car and looked around. She was in a street she knew well, but hadn't visited in several years, and she couldn't think what had brought her here now. Hadn't she been on her way to the care home to visit her mother and drop off some of the paperwork she'd promised to have ready by today?

She glanced at her watch and seeing the time she sent a quick text to Maurice Rich, the care home's manager, assuring him she'd be there before five.

As she put her phone away her gaze wandered to the house where Kian had grown up, a compact two-up, two-down in the middle of a pebble-dash terrace. Aileen had always kept it shiny and clean: a

Bright jewel in a necklace of worn stones was the way Em had once described it. It was as dreary and neglected as the other houses now with dull, skewed nets, a boarded-up pane in the front door and peeling paint on the window frames. Aileen's sister-in-law, Bridget, still lived in one of the semis opposite, but there was no sign of her today. Nor of her eldest son, Danny.

He'd done time, had Danny; an eighteen-month-stretch for assault and two years for actual bodily harm. He wasn't the only member of the family who'd been inside, several had, and there was a good chance one or two more distant cousins were still there. They had a reputation for fighting hard; no one wanted to be on the wrong side of them. However, if you were one of them, family or not, they'd do anything for you, and top of their list was Kian. They'd walk through fire for him, cut off their right arms, sell their grannies into white slavery, basically anything anyone asked of them just as long as it was for Kian.

To most of the Bright clan Kian was a god, and made even more so for never becoming involved in his cousins' shadier schemes. Jules didn't doubt that he often knew about them, might even have helped connect them with a fence or a bent cop who could further them, but he was always careful to remain on the right side of the law himself. He was a good man, everyone knew that, and no one ever tried to change him. It was as though they all needed him to be as straight and loyal as he was, a kind of priest without actually being one, as well as a madcap, fun-loving bloke about town who could stop fights before they began, and get behind a worthy project in a way that often made all the difference.

Daisy coming along didn't change him; he just seemed to become even more of what he already was. He was devoted to her in a way that made everyone smile, while Jules would roll her eyes and wonder what their little minx of a toddler would get her beloved daddy to do next. She was like him in so many ways, not only to look at with her bouncy blonde curls and captivating violet-blue eyes, but in how sweet-natured and patient she was, how she loved to meet new people, and how outraged she became if she sensed an injustice, or a lie, or someone being mean just for the sake of it.

'Daddy? Have you been naughty again?' she'd whisper to Kian if Jules raised her voice to him.

'I think so,' he'd whisper back.

Daisy's big eyes would come to Jules. 'Daddy doesn't mean to be naughty,' she'd explain, 'he was just born that way.'

How could you not love her and laugh?

'Mummy? Can I make my bedroom like somewhere mermaids live, because I think I'm a mermaid.'

Holding back her smile, Jules said, 'Why do you think you're a mermaid?'

'Because that's what our house is called, and Uncle Danny said I swim like a mermaid. Is Uncle Danny coming to my birthday next week?'

'I think everyone's coming, sweetheart.'

'I'll be three and the week after that Granny Aileen will be twenty-three.'

Laughing, Jules said, 'Is that what she told you?'

Daisy giggled and twirled and crashed into a chair where she found her Polaroid camera, so ran off downstairs to take yet more photos of Misty and the staff. Even at such a tender age Daisy loved nothing more than to take photos or videos of her friends and family to show to the grannies every time they came over.

It was funny the little scenarios that drifted randomly in from the past for no particular reason, apart from to remind and cause smiles and heartache.

When Daisy had started playgroup it had amused Kian and Jules no end to hear of how little time it had taken her to set about tackling the bullies. 'She kills them with kindness,' the group leader told them, 'and they just don't know what to do with it, apart from make her a friend.' Apparently she was afraid of no one, would always speak up for someone too shy to do it for themselves, was quick to take new children under her wing, and wasn't backward in clocking someone round the ear if she felt they deserved it. She was generous to a fault, giving away her toys, her sweets, even the favourite teddy she'd had since birth. She'd cried over that, confiding to Jules that she wished she could have him back, but she didn't think it was fair to ask when Dean Foggarty didn't have a teddy at all.

'You don't have a teddy?' Jules said to Dean, adoring the sweet little face that was tilted worriedly up to hers.

He shook his head and turned his big grey eyes to Daisy as she said, 'His mum and dad don't allow toys or anything like that, and he can't have sleepovers either, but they will allow him to come here, so I said he could. Do you think he could live with us, Mum?'

Smiling, Jules dropped to their height as she said, 'I'm sure he'd rather live with his mummy and daddy, but you're always welcome here, Dean. All Daisy's friends are.'

'She's got lots of friends,' Dean told her earnestly. 'Stephie's her best friend, and I'm the next.'

'That's right,' Daisy confirmed, nodding her blonde head up and down.

'Yes, I'm definitely the first,' impish Stephie piped up, all bright red hair and chaotic freckles.

'So what are you three up to this afternoon?' Jules asked, going to pour them all a juice.

'We're going to do a play on the beach,' Daisy shouted triumphantly, 'and Millie, Georgie, Mary-Jane and Max are coming too. Can they all stay for tea, please? We'd like fish fingers and chips, or beans on toast.'

'Would you now? And should it be served here at the table, or down on the beach?'

Daisy burst out laughing, and Jules didn't ask why. It was simply Daisy's way to laugh when she was happy, and generally everyone laughed along with her.

It turned out to be true that Dean hadn't had a teddy before Daisy gave him hers, and he didn't have much of a life either, as far as Jules and Kian could make out. His parents were members of a devout religious sect, some kind of brethren who'd moved into the Southwell area of Kesterly, and who didn't want much, if anything, to do with anyone outside their exclusive

83

enclave. However, for reasons known only to them (Jules thought Dean's mother was behind it), they seemed to approve of Daisy and never tried to get in the way of their delightful little son's eagerness to spend time at Hope Cove. Indeed, once he started coming on a regular basis he all but burst from his shell on arrival, making everyone laugh with his terrible jokes and useless magic tricks, and enchanting them with his gift for inventing stories, mostly featuring three children called Daisy, Stephie and Dean. It could make Jules feel desperately sad to think of the way he had to shut himself down each time he went home; she could see it happening when she drove him, as though he was carefully detaching himself from Hope Cove to slip quietly and unobtrusively into the darkly religious world at Southwell, where Jules didn't imagine there was much laughter or fun.

However, as time went on his parents, to everyone's surprise and Dean's delight, began coming to the shows that he, Daisy and Stephie had started putting on at least once a month in the function room at the Mermaid, or, weather permitting, on the beach. Though Gavin, Dean's dad, usually looked disapproving throughout, he never uttered a negative word about anything, or disagreed when it was claimed that his son must have it in his genes to entertain.

'His great-great-grandfather on Gavin's side was one half of a vaudeville act,' Dean's mother confided to Jules.

So there was no doubt this was who Dean, with his love of slapstick and great comic timing, took after, while Stephie's talents for writing plays and acting were all her own, her modest parents insisted, and Daisy's remarkable ability to organise, photograph, direct video, and get the very best out of her little troupe of players was just another way, claimed her father, of proving that she was all things Bright and beautiful.

'What you could say about her,' Kian would proudly comment, 'is that she's extremely good at bossing people around, especially me.'

He had indeed been a devoted slave to the Hope Cove Performing Arts Society, as they'd later very grandly called themselves. They'd been twelve or thirteen by then, with hundreds of shows behind them and a reputation that had long ago broken out of Kesterly to work its way all over the West Country and even beyond. However, for most of their younger years they hadn't had a name at all, just an unstoppable enthusiasm for putting on singing competitions, Christmas pantomimes, stand-up comedy routines, dance-a-thons, all kinds of sporting events, specially choreographed ballets (with the help of Daisy's ballet teacher), even poetry readings by Melissa Harding, who wrote rhyming couplets that were more hilarious for not being funny, or even particularly comprehensible, than they were for any natural gift in that field.

Everyone wanted to be a part of their group, so just about everyone was, since Daisy didn't have it in her to exclude anyone, even those who meant mischief or had no real talent for anything apart from turning up.

'My mum says that Daisy is a very special girl,' Dean told Jules one day when she was driving him home, 'and I'm lucky to have her as a friend.'

Jules's heart contracted as she smiled. 'She's lucky to have you too,' she said, ruffling his thick dark hair and wondering what his life was really like inside the Foggartys' Victorian-Gothic manse. He never talked about it, either to complain, or show off, or simply to state something ordinary like 'my mum cooks that too,' or 'my dad likes digging the garden.' All that Jules and Kian really knew about the Foggartys' private existence was that their son must be at home on Tuesday and Thursday evenings and all day on Sundays for worship and Bible study.

Dear, sweet, complicated, kind and inwardly tormented Dean.

Jules's eyes closed as a deep and heavy pain lodged in her heart. She'd loved that boy – and Stephie – as if they were her own.

Realising her phone was vibrating she pulled it from her bag to check who was calling. Since it was a number she didn't recognise she let it go to messages and called up her emails.

Finding one from Joe she clicked it open.

I can't believe they're letting that evil bitch loose on society again. I feel so mad, so enraged by it that I can't think about anything else. It's definitely not going to stop me from coming. I say bring on the opportunity to meet her face to face. She's going to regret everything she did, there are plenty of us who'll make sure of that. Do you know a date yet?

Closing down the email, Jules let her head fall back against the headrest. It was both easy and hard to imagine Joe at his college in North Carolina, easy because she knew his strong, handsome face so well, hard because she'd never been to North Carolina so had no idea what his surroundings were like. Perhaps he wasn't there now. Perhaps he'd already returned to his family in Chicago. Indeed, when she considered the date, he must have done, so the chances were he'd go to see Em before coming to Europe, and they'd talk about Amelia Quentin and how she was about to disrupt and poison their lives all over again.

She wondered where Amelia Quentin was right now, this minute. In the prison, of course, unless she'd already been released, but that couldn't be the case, Andee would have let her know, and besides it was likely to make the news. So for the time being she was still being kept away from decent, law-abiding people, was only being allowed to mix with her own type, although Jules was reluctant to tar junkies and shoplifters, delinquents, fraudsters and forgers with the same brush as someone as inherently evil as Amelia Quentin.

Realising the last caller had left a message, she clicked through to voicemail and felt a tight band close around her head as Andee Lawrence said, 'Hi Jules, it's Andee here. I've been thinking a lot about you since I came to the house last week, wondering how you are, hoping you might get in touch. You know where I am if you'd like to talk. No pressure, I just don't want you to think you have to handle this alone.'

Andee, who had been her rock throughout everything, and would be again if Jules allowed it.

Clicking off the line she started the engine and drove on to the end of the street where she turned to head back the way she'd come. It was good of Andee to offer her friendship, but she had the support of just about every member of Kian's family, each of them willing to be there in any way she chose.

'If you don't want the bitch around these parts, Jules,' Danny had snarled as soon as he'd learned of the imminent release, 'just say the word and I promise it won't happen.'

Jules hadn't asked how Danny could prevent it, he'd have his methods and as Kian had always said, it was best not to know too much about them.

By the time she pulled into the Greensleeves Care Home her phone was ringing again. This time it was Kian's cousin, Terry. She could rarely think about Terry without remembering the beautiful crib they'd eventually auctioned off for charity. Daisy had always kept a photograph of it on a shelf in her room.

Jules didn't know where the photograph was any more.

'Jules, was that you I saw driving through town about twenty minutes ago?' Terry wanted to know.

'Probably,' Jules replied. 'Where were you?'

'Coming out of the butcher's on Market Street. I waved, but I could tell you didn't see me. So how are you? I've tried calling a few times. Did you get my messages?'

'Yes, I did,' Jules admitted. Everyone had been in touch, Ruthie, Bridget, Cheryl, Brad, Uncle Pete, Finn . . . Just everyone. 'I'm sorry I haven't rung back,' she said, 'but things have been pretty hectic. How about you? Is everything OK at the women's refuge?'

'Sad to say, we're as busy as ever. Penny was remarking the other day that you haven't called in to see us for a while. Of course, you've got a lot on your plate right now. Have you had any news about a date yet?'

'No, not yet.'

'Will you let me know when you do?'

'Of course. I'm sorry, I should go now . . .'

'Before you do, I was wondering if you're thinking of going to Ireland?'

'I don't expect I will this year.'

'OK, but if you do, I'm happy to come with you. I'd like to see Aileen, and if . . .'

'I know she'd love to see you too, so if I do go, I'll be sure to let you know.'

As she rang off Jules found she was gritting her teeth, not in anger so much as resistance to all the kindness and concern, as she could find no proper way to respond to it. She knew everyone was making excuses for her, that they'd never bear her any ill will for wanting to keep herself to herself. They would probably even understand if she told them that she simply couldn't take their pity and constant need to make things better, when that was totally impossible.

'Sure we can make things better,' she suddenly heard Kian crying cheerily from another dimension, 'and that's exactly what we're going to do, and do you know why?'

'Tell me,' Jules prompted.

'Because we can,' he laughed, and throwing his arms around her he danced her across the bar towards the stairs, leaving an appreciative crowd of late lunchers finishing their coffees and wondering what on earth the Brights were going to get up to next.

Chapter Five

Jules and Kian were halfway up the stairs, heading for the office they shared on the first landing, when some sort of ruckus began kicking off in the main bar.

Groaning, Kian threw out his hands. 'You leave them alone for thirty seconds . . .'

Laughing, Jules started back down to investigate. 'I'll handle it, while you go and look at my proposals.'

'Your proposals? Now there's an offer,' he teased, and treating her to a bawdy wink he disappeared into the office just as his mobile started to ring.

'What the hell is this?' a smartly suited man was demanding as Jules returned to the bar. 'It's disgusting.'

'It's what you ordered,' Misty informed him, barely concealing her annoyance.

'The ice cream, yes,' he snarled, 'but not this revolting gloop you've spread all over it.'

Clocking the way everyone was staring, evidently sympathising with Misty, Jules moved in to take over the dispute. 'It's called coulis,' she told the man, recognising him right away. She hadn't seen him in a long while, and had hoped never to again, but here he was in all his grandiose glory, making himself no more agreeable now than he had the first time they'd met. 'It says on the menu that chocolate ice cream comes with a raspberry coulis, but if you . . .'

'Show me,' he demanded pompously.

Jules nodded for a barman to bring a menu. To Misty she said, 'Perhaps you can take this one away.'

'Did I ask you to do that?' he challenged. 'I just wanted to know what it was and why it's all over the ice cream when I *didn't order it.*'

Jules glanced at the woman beside him, recognising her too, and felt a stirring of pity for how embarrassed she looked. 'We'll bring you another ice cream without coulis,' she informed him affably. 'Would you prefer one without coulis?' she asked his wife.

'No, no this is fine,' she stammered.

'Yes, she would,' he corrected. Misty picked up the ice creams. 'You should have it there as an addition, so it can be ordered if you want it, not forced on you. What the . . . !' he cried, as he knocked Misty's arm and one of the ice creams landed smack in his lap.

To his outrage and Jules's hidden amusement a cheer went up.

'Hey!' one of the regulars shouted over, 'a little less of the attitude, mate.'

'I don't recall asking for your opinion.'

'Well you're getting it. You're bang out of order the way you're speaking to these ladies. Hey, I'm talking to you . . .'

Ignoring him, Anton Quentin strode off in the direction of the Gents, presumably to clean himself up.

'Are you OK?' Jules asked his wife.

'Yes, I'm . . . I'm sorry about that,' she mumbled,

blushing deeply. 'He's – he's very stressed at the moment. We're here to get away for the weekend, but his parents . . .' She glanced briefly at Jules and fell silent.

'I've seen you in here before, haven't I?' Jules said chattily. 'With your little girl. Amelia, is it?'

The woman nodded, but the weakness of her smile showed that she hadn't forgotten the last uncomfortable episode either.

'How is she?' Jules asked. She wasn't sure why she wanted to be kind to this woman, apart from feeling that someone ought to be. 'I imagine she's started school by now.'

'Yes, she has. She's doing . . . Well, I'm afraid she doesn't always find it easy to make friends. She's very . . . shy.'

'Does she go locally?'

'She did for a while, but it didn't work out too well . . . With Anton's work being in London, it made more sense for her to go to school there. I heard . . . You have a little girl too, don't you?'

Jules couldn't help but smile, since it was the effect any mention of Daisy always had on her. 'Yes, she's almost four,' she replied. 'A proper little whirlwind who takes after her daddy with all her mischief and madcap schemes. She's at playgroup today.'

'That's nice. Which one does she go to?'

'The Pumpkin, near the station?'

'Yes, I know it. Amelia went there for a while a few summers ago. I guess before your little girl's time.'

'Daisy,' Jules told her. 'My daughter's name is Daisy.'

The woman nodded. 'I've seen her,' she said, 'she's very pretty.'

'Thank you. You should bring Amelia in again, the next time she's here. I'm sure Daisy would love to meet her.' *Provided she's a bit more agreeable than the sour-faced little madam she'd been four years ago.*

'Oh, she's here,' the woman replied. 'She just went . . .' She was looking worriedly in the direction of the Ladies. 'She can be very independent . . . I should have gone with her.'

'I'm sure she's fine. There's nowhere to get lost around here. So did you ever get her a game of devil among the tailors?'

The woman frowned. 'Oh, you mean the table skittles. No, she went off the idea. Children are like that, aren't they? Screaming for something one minute, forgotten about it the next.'

Although she couldn't accuse Daisy of ever screaming for anything, Jules rolled her eyes anyway. 'Such handfuls,' she sighed, 'they drive you nuts at times, but you have to love them.'

The woman nodded distractedly. 'Yes, yes you do,' she mumbled.

After a few awkward moments Jules accepted that the conversation had gone as far as it could and stepped back, almost treading on one of the kitchen staff. 'Ah, here are the fresh ice creams,' she declared, moving out of his way. 'Of course there won't be any charge . . .'

'I should hope not,' Anton Quentin cut in, coming towards them. 'And I've a good mind to send you the bill for cleaning my suit.'

Jules's eyebrows rose. Apparently he went out of his way to make himself as obnoxious as possible. 'You know where we are,' she responded mildly, and with a quick glance at the girl coming out of the Ladies she left them to it.

'It was an accident,' Misty hissed crossly as Jules joined her behind the bar. 'He knocked the dish out of my hand . . .'

'I know, I saw. Just put it out of your mind, it's not worth getting worked up over.'

'He's just like his father,' Rustie Belham, a local fisherman, grunted, 'old Judge Quentin. So far bloody up themselves, that lot, they got nothing but shit coming out their cakeholes.'

'Lovely image, Rust,' Misty muttered, 'thanks for that.'

'You're welcome. They say the old boy's gone a bit barmy now, and the wife's not much better. Old fancy pants over there will inherit when the time comes, being the only son.'

Glancing at the unpleasant barrister, Misty said, 'I don't know why he bothers coming in here, he always finds something to complain about, and I can't imagine we're up to his *usual standard*.'

Amused by the sarcasm, Jules asked, 'Is he in here often, then? I've only seen him once before.'

'I wouldn't say often,' Misty replied, 'but he's been in a couple of times lately, the last was about a week ago when he was with the mayor and your Kian. Nice as pie he was then. Polite to everyone, giving out tips like he was made of money. Apparently he's involved in the project to get the old cinema up and running again.'

Blinking, Jules said, 'He's in on that? Wow, I'd never

94

have put him down for philanthropy, much less community spirit.'

'In his case it'll be a tax dodge,' Misty muttered, starting to pull a lager for Bob Stafford who'd just come in. 'And you have to wonder what it's like being married to the tosser. He might be rich, but that's about all he's got going for him. And as for that child, you should have heard the way she spoke to her mother just now. She needs her mouth washing out if you ask me.'

Deciding not to ask what was said, Jules watched the child slap the ice cream spoon from her mother's hand and turn to her father. 'He spoils that girl,' she said softly, 'and his wife's too scared of him to do anything about it.'

'I heard he knocks her about,' Rustie grunted.

'Who's that?' Bob Stafford wanted to know.

'Bloke over there, what's-his-name Quentin.'

'Oh him, yes I heard that too. Makes me sick to my stomach that, blokes hitting their women about. Bloody cowards, the lot of them.'

'Couldn't agree more,' Kian retorted when Jules repeated the conversation to him later. 'Maybe we should let her know about the women's refuge we're starting, just in case she needs it.'

Jules's eyes lit up. 'So you're going to back the plan?' she cried ecstatically.

Kian regarded her carefully. 'Let's make sure I've got this straight,' he said. 'You want us to buy and convert the old convalescent home over on Hanfield Common into a kind of safe haven for abused women and their kids?'

'Exactly,' Jules confirmed.

He nodded thoughtfully. 'So you girls get to take care of them, and we blokes get to beat the living shite out of the bastards who are hurting them?'

'Yay! What a great idea,' Jules exclaimed, clapping her hands. 'Let's all get sent to prison for trying to do a good deed.'

Laughing, Kian said, 'I reckon it's something the mayor and his wife would get behind. We should set up a meeting, talk it through with them, and see who else they can bring on board, such as the head of social services and the like, because even if we manage to get private financing, we're going to need their support when it comes to everything else, not least of all planning.'

'You've really been thinking about this,' she told him delightedly.

'You knew I would be,' he laughed as she threw her arms around him.

It was true, she had known, because he never shied away from supporting a good cause, especially those cooked up by the women of his family. 'Our mothers are going to be over the moon,' she informed him, her eyes softening as she gazed into his. 'Did I ever tell you how much I love you, Kian Bright?'

He frowned as he thought. 'I'm not sure,' he replied, 'but I do happen to know of a way you can show me.'

Always ready to do that, she melted against him and began a game they often played during private moments, of talking business while making love. 'Did you look at my proposals?' she murmured as he pushed his hands into her hair.

'I'm with them all the way,' he assured her, pulling her more tightly to him. 'The smoking ban's bound to come and we need to be prepared for it. Have you discussed anything with Misty yet?'

'Not in any detail, but she agrees we have to up our game where food's concerned so we're as much a restaurant as a bar, and that's going to mean finding ourselves a really good chef. I've listed all the best catering colleges in my proposals, but I think for the head guy we should look at poaching someone who already has a reputation.'

Kian's eyes widened. 'Oh, I love it when you're ruthless,' he growled, pretending to bite her neck.

'And then we need to start turning ourselves into a B & B,' she informed him as he began unbuttoning her blouse, 'or even a full-on hotel, you know, serving dinner as well as breakfast. Quite a few pubs are doing it already, so I think we, you me and Daisy – probably Stephie and Dean too, if his parents will allow it – should go on a road trip round the country checking everyone out and picking up ideas.'

'Just tell me when to be ready,' he murmured against her lips.

'I've no idea how many of these pubs can be found on the Internet,' she ran on, 'but they're saying everyone will be on it soon, so that's another thing we have to get sorted, a website. Kian, my darling, I think we'll have to take a rain check on what you have in mind, because if you can't hear your adorable daughter outside I certainly can.'

Sighing, he drew back and looked at her, both merriment and regret in his eyes. 'We need to talk to her about timing,' he decided, 'and the part she can play in helping us to get her a brother or sister.'

'You're the one who encourages her into our room every morning,' Jules reminded him.

'And we're both too tired by the time we go to bed at night. Ah, here she comes.'

'Mummy! Daddy!' Daisy shouted, charging up the stairs. 'I'm home and I've got a surprise that I made. Mrs Janet said it was really good. Mummy! Where are you?'

'We're in here,' Kian called out.

A moment later the door burst open and in bounced Daisy, breathless, bright-eyed, ribbon tumbling from her mussed-up hair and paint smudged all over her cheeks.

'Look at you,' Jules laughed, scooping her up for a bruising embrace. Just the feel of her skinny limbs in her arms could turn Jules's heart inside out, and she knew it was the same for Kian.

'You have to come and see what I made,' Daisy was informing them earnestly. 'I really think you're going to like it.'

'I'm sure we'll love it,' Kian laughed as she threw herself his way for another cuddle. 'What have you done with your grannies?'

'They're down in the bar talking to some people. We saw a lady in town that looked just like the one on *Sesame Street*. It was really funny, but it couldn't be her, because that's in America where Auntie Em lives. Mum, Stephie and Dean are coming over in a minute for tea. It's not raining so we could have a picnic on the beach and play some games after. Can we, Dad?

Please, please, please. I promise I'll be good, and I won't push you over in the waves.'

Before he could answer she was wriggling to get down, and whizzing off in her blue dungarees and purple jellies, getting almost to the stairs before shouting, 'You haven't seen what I made yet. Come on, or Ruby might get it.'

'*Ruby* might get it?' Kian echoed in a whisper.

Jules could only shrug and wonder, as she had many times before, if Daisy had ever actually seen the ghost. Certainly when she was a baby there had been times when she'd seemed to look right past whoever was standing over her, giggling away at what appeared to be nothing at all. Or she'd tilt her head to one side as though listening when the room was silent. Or her eyes would seem to follow someone across the room when no one was there. Whatever, it was good to know that Ruby didn't frighten Daisy. To the contrary, Daisy seemed to accept their invisible friend as a living, breathing member of the family.

'Let's hope your new friend and his family have gone by now,' Jules commented to Kian as they started down the stairs.

'What new friend?' he asked curiously.

'Anton Quentin. The wife-beater.'

'Keep your voice down.'

'No one can hear me.'

'And you don't know if he's a wife-beater.'

'I know he's a misogynist.'

'How come we didn't see them when we came in earlier?'

'They're in the alcove, next to the fireplace,' she

99

replied, and to her dismay, as Daisy urged them across the bar towards the grannies, she saw that the Quentins were still where she'd left them.

'Look! Look!' Daisy demanded, holding up her latest creation in Play-Doh.

Realising right away what it was, Jules started to laugh.

'It's to go with Ruby's other shoe so she has two,' Daisy proudly informed them. 'I know this one's smaller and it doesn't have a proper lace, but I think she'll like it, don't you?'

'I'm sure she'll love it,' Kian responded, sweeping her into his arms. 'And it's very kind of you to think of it, because she's only had one shoe for a very long time, so I expect her other foot has got very cold by now.'

'That's what I thought,' Daisy told him seriously, 'and it's not good to have only one shoe because you have to hop all the time.'

'Out of interest,' Jules said, 'did you tell Mrs Janet and the others who you were making the shoe for?'

Aileen chuckled. 'Oh, she did that all right,' she responded, pinching Daisy's cheek. 'Go on, you little minx, you'd better own up.'

Clasping her hands round Kian's face, Daisy said, 'I told them it was for Ruby the ghost and now everyone wants to come and see her.'

His eyes started to dance. 'And you said they could?' he prompted.

She nodded eagerly.

'They understand that she's invisible?' he asked carefully.

'Yes, I told them that, but they still want to come.'

'And how many are there in your playgroup?'

Daisy started counting on her fingers, giving up around five. 'About a hundred,' she declared.

As everyone laughed, Marsha said, 'Provided it's all right with Mummy and Daddy, Mrs Janet is going to organise a little trip to the pub so everyone can hear about Ruby, and then, if the weather's good, she'll organise some games on the beach.'

Daisy's eyes were shining with excitement at the mere prospect. 'We have to invite everyone,' she hurriedly told her father, 'because it wouldn't be fair to leave anyone out, would it?'

'Absolutely not,' he agreed. 'And if you speak nicely to Misty, I'm sure she'll get the kitchens to rustle up a little feast for you and your hundred-odd friends.'

Daisy punched her hands in the air. 'Yes,' she cheered, straightening her legs to slide to the floor, but just as she was about to hare off to the kitchen she spotted Amelia Quentin standing to one side, watching her.

Unusually for Daisy she didn't immediately introduce herself, but simply watched the older girl, seeming unsure what to say, while Jules wondered why so many well-off people dressed their children like paupers. Amelia was wearing dark socks, a long plain dress, scuffed shoes and an ill-fitting cardigan.

'Not all ghosts are invisible,' Amelia informed Daisy.

Daisy glanced at her mother. 'Ours is,' she said softly.

Amelia shrugged. 'So how's she going to wear the shoe?'

Apparently lost for an answer Daisy said, 'Her

101

name's Ruby and she's lived here for more than a hundred years.'

'That shoe's stupid,' Amelia snorted. 'No one can wear that.'

'Amelia, that's not kind,' Jules chided as Daisy's eyes rounded with surprise.

Amelia apparently didn't care whether it was kind or not.

'Amelia, come away,' her father called out.

'She's OK,' Kian told him. 'We're just getting to know one another, aren't we, Amelia?'

Amelia's intense eyes went to his, narrowing with what appeared to be something like annoyance, or maybe suspicion.

'I'm Kian, Daisy's dad,' he smiled, holding out a hand to shake.

Taking the hand, Amelia said, 'Do you own this pub?'

Apparently surprised by the question, Kian glanced at Jules. 'As a matter of fact, I do,' he replied.

'So you live here?' Amelia said to Daisy.

Daisy nodded. She was still, Jules noted, being unusually reticent for her. It was as though she was sensing something about the girl beyond her understanding. It was beyond Jules's, too.

Amelia was regarding Daisy carefully, her dark, unsettling eyes giving nothing away.

She really was the most unusual child, Jules was thinking to herself. She seemed so much older than her years, so self-assured and unnervingly intense, as though she was seeing things that no one else could.

In the end, the girl said, 'The shoe's still stupid,' and

turning on her heel she marched back to her parents.

Aileen's eyebrows arched. 'Charming,' she muttered, as a baffled Daisy reached for Kian's hand.

Looking up at her father, Daisy said, 'I was going to ask her if she wanted to play with us when Stephie and Dean come, but I don't think she does.'

Going down to her height, Kian replied, 'I expect she's going home now, but it was very nice of you to think of it.'

Daisy looked over to where Amelia was standing beside her father, watching the girl who lived at the pub. 'She's funny,' Daisy whispered in Kian's ear.

'I think she wishes she was you,' Kian whispered back, 'because you're going to be playing on the beach in a minute and having a lovely picnic that . . .'

Suddenly remembering what they'd been talking about before Amelia had joined them, Daisy gasped with excitement and ran to the kitchens shouting, 'Misty! Misty! Please can we have a great big feast? Daddy said it was all right.'

Hooking an arm round Jules's shoulders, Kian glanced at his watch and pressed a kiss to her forehead as he said, 'Gotta run. Seeing a man about a sailing school.'

'Seriously? Here, in the cove?' They'd been talking about it for a while, so apparently he was setting things in motion.

'You got it, here in the cove, but we're meeting in town.'

'Could I catch a lift back with you?' Marsha quickly asked. 'I'm helping out at the community centre this evening. Unless you're ready to leave,' she said to Aileen.

'You're due at the animal shelter this evening,' Aileen reminded her, dropping into an armchair next to the hearth, 'and I'll wait here. With any luck, if I hang around long enough, someone might offer me a nice cup of tea.'

Moments after Kian and Marsha had left, Misty appeared with a tray of Tetley's best and a scrumptious pile of scones. 'Thought this might go down a treat,' she declared, setting it out in front of Aileen, while watching the door close behind the departing Quentins. 'I thought they were never going to leave,' she muttered under her breath.

'That dreadful child was so rude to our Daisy,' Aileen snorted indignantly. 'I'd be surprised if she had any friends, carrying on like that.'

'Her mother mentioned that she was finding it difficult to make any,' Jules told them. 'Personally, I think the problem in that family is the father.'

'Well, anyone can see he spoils the girl rotten,' Misty commented.

Jules didn't disagree. 'But it's not in a normal, loving sort of way,' she said pensively. 'Or not that I'm detecting, anyway. He definitely doesn't come across as the affectionate type. I didn't see him touch her once . . . In fact, I wouldn't be a bit surprised if the poor girl is horribly neglected on an emotional level, and horribly lonely into the bargain.'

Aileen waved a hand. 'If she is, it's not our concern,' she declared dismissively. 'We've got more than enough to worry about without adding them to our list. Has our Kian agreed to get behind our refuge project yet?'

'He has,' Jules confirmed. 'So we can start negotiations

for the old convalescent home on Hanfield Common just as soon as we like.'

'Count me in, anything I can do,' Misty told them, starting back to the kitchen.

Waiting until the door had closed behind Misty and Jules had finished pouring the tea, Aileen glanced around to make sure they were alone, and said, 'I'm glad to have this opportunity for a little chat.'

Startled, since this sounded quite serious, Jules asked, 'Is everything all right?'

Aileen frowned as she lifted her cup. After taking a sip of tea she said, 'The honest answer is I don't know, but I'm worried.'

Tensing as her imagination leapt into action, Jules said, 'Are you unwell?'

'No, no, I'm fine, fit as a fiddle,' Aileen assured her. 'No, it's not me I'm worried about, it's your mother.'

Jules's heartbeat slowed.

'There's this bloke who goes to our yoga class,' Aileen continued, staring off at nothing. 'Lovely person, always polite, has a little laugh and joke with us . . . To tell the truth I think he fancies Marsha, and no one could blame him for that, she's an attractive woman. Anyway, I was talking about him yesterday, you know, teasing her a bit, the way you do, and it was the strangest thing, because she didn't seem to know who I was on about.'

Jules frowned.

'It came to her in the end, or she said it did, and I probably wouldn't have thought any more of it if there hadn't been other instances lately when she's seemed a bit . . . well, I suppose you'd call it forgetful.'

Jules's insides were starting to knot.

'I'm not the only one who's noticed,' Aileen went on. 'Em's parents rang me a couple of weeks ago to say she'd run back into the house when Trish called over the fence from her garden. Of course she went round to find out what the problem was, but Marsha wouldn't let her in.'

Dumbfounded, and feeling for the shock of Em's mother, Jules asked, 'What happened then?'

'I got in my car and drove over there. By the time I turned up they were all having a nice cup of tea on Marsha's patio, laughing and chatting away as if there was never a cloud in the sky.'

'So did Mum explain why she'd behaved that way?'

'Not really, but that could be because no one asked her. We didn't want to upset her, or make a big thing of it, so we just carried on as if everything in the garden was rosy, and it was by then. Trish told me on the phone later that Marsha had eventually opened the door with the chain on, and when she saw it was them she'd immediately let them in. It was like, Trish said, she was scared of something, or hadn't recognised their voices, but then suddenly she did.' She regarded Jules carefully. 'Have you noticed anything yourself?' she asked.

Jules didn't want to admit that she had, in fact she was on the point of denying it, but burying her head in the sand was going to help no one, least of all her mother. 'She's always been the nervy type,' she said, as though this well-known truth might explain the oddness of how her mother had seemed unwilling to answer the phone lately, or the way she repeated herself, or constantly lost things. 'I know she's forgetful at times, but we're all guilty of that . . .'

'Tell me about it,' Aileen sighed, rolling her eyes, but her tone remained serious as she said, 'I just think it might be worth her having a little check-up with Dr Moore. I mean, we're none of us getting any younger . . .'

'But she's only fifty-eight,' Jules protested, as though her mother's age were some kind of protection against the awful possibilities her imagination was dragging up.

Aileen took another sip of tea.

Finally realising that Aileen was asking her to take a lead on this, Jules braced herself and said, firmly, 'OK, if you're saying she should see a doctor then I agree, but how am I going to persuade her if she doesn't think there's anything wrong with her?'

Aileen regarded her gravely, as though she'd expected the question. 'I've been thinking,' she replied, 'that it might be a good idea for you to start by having a little chat with Dr Moore yourself. You can tell her what's bothering us, and ask her advice on how to proceed from there.'

Accepting that was probably the best way forward, Jules swallowed hard as she looked into Aileen's eyes. In her heart she knew what Aileen was thinking, it was what she was thinking too, but neither of them was prepared to speak the words aloud in case fate overheard and turned them into an unthinkable reality.

Now, all these years later, Jules was signing herself into the Greensleeves Care Home where her mother was a permanent resident. Since there was no one in reception she went on through to the manager's office, where she dropped her workload on his desk and decided to wait a few minutes in case he came back.

Her mind was filling again with that first time Daisy and Amelia had met, reliving the strangeness of it, while realising that she hadn't remembered it all, because she was recalling now how at some point Daisy's eyes had sparkled as she'd said, 'Is your name really Amelia? Like naughty Amelia Jane?' and Amelia had smiled in a sly sort of way as she'd replied, 'Yes, exactly like that.'

Something else that was coming back to her was the memory of Stephie and Dean hurtling into the bar in their usual overexcited way and coming to a dead stop when they'd spotted Amelia. It was as though they too had realised, in the instinctive way children have, that there was something different about this girl.

She couldn't remember how Amelia had reacted to their arrival, or if they'd spoken to one another, but she was sure now that when Daisy had gone racing off to the kitchen calling out to Misty, Stephie and Dean had followed.

Did any of it matter now?

She guessed not, and yet the memories were there, staging themselves sketchily, unreliably in her mind – feeling like an early warning that she'd failed to see. Even if she had seen it, she'd have had no idea what the warning was about.

Deciding to leave the manager a note to let him know she'd arrived, she went upstairs to the dementia wing, using the security code to release the door. The communal lounge was sunny and crowded with wing-back chairs, though not so many people. The TV was showing an old Gregory Peck film and half a dozen or so grey- and white-haired women along with Alan, one of only four men in the unit, were being served afternoon tea.

'Jules!' Chona the senior nurse declared cheerily as she came out of her office. 'How are you?'

'I'm fine,' Jules assured her, trying not to wince as one of the old ladies let out a piercing scream.

'Your mother was asleep when I went in just now,' Chona was telling her. 'There were a few episodes of wakefulness during the early hours, which will account for her tiredness today.'

'Is she eating?'

'She managed most of her lunch, and if you want us to we'll try waking her up for tea.' Chona's watchful eyes came inquisitively to hers. 'How about you, Jules?' she asked softly. 'Are you managing to eat and sleep?'

Jules forced a smile. Obviously news of Amelia Quentin's release was spreading. 'I'm fine,' she assured the nurse. As well meaning as Chona was, and as much as she liked her, the last thing Jules wanted right now was to get into a discussion about her own state of mind. It was why she hadn't returned her therapist's calls this past week, and probably wouldn't in the foreseeable future. 'I should go and see if Mum's awake,' she said.

Her mother's room was at the end of a wide, pale green corridor with stuffed animals perched on the handrails that lined the walls, and all sorts of memorabilia pinned to various boards. The photograph on her mother's door was of a seventy-year-old Marsha looking smart and alert (though she hadn't been) in a navy pinstriped blouse and knee-length pleated skirt.

Marsha Symonds, her name tag read, and underneath,

Marsha is from Kesterly-on-Sea. She likes animals, music, bedtime stories, Strictly Come Dancing, *having her hair brushed and daisies.*

Seeing the last always made Jules's heart ache to a point that could bring tears to her eyes.

Though Marsha had been at the home for over three years now, Jules still wasn't finding it any easier to see her here, had probably never quite accepted that the stranger who looked like her mother but wasn't was the woman who'd brought her up single-handedly, had loved her unconditionally and would have far rather died early than end up like this.

She found her fast asleep with her mouth half open and her tiny, claw-like hands bunched together on her meagre chest. The skin on her cheeks sagged in papery thinness, the healthy gloss of her silvery hair seemed an impossible accomplishment for such a fragile skull.

Going to sit on the bed beside her, Jules gently lifted one of her hands into her own and held it to her cheek.

Marsha didn't stir, and in truth it was such a relief not to have to try and engage with her today that Jules's eyes burned with a painful mix of sadness and guilt. All too often when she came in her mother would cower away in fear, saying sorry over and over as if she'd committed some sort of offence, or she'd shout at someone only she could see to go away and leave her alone.

'Please, Nurse, please, please, make him stop,' she'd cry, and Jules could only look on helplessly, having no way to comfort her, or to convince her that what she was seeing wasn't real.

Deciding to sit with her for a while, Jules moved to the armchair next to the bed and used the remote control to find a classical-radio station on the TV, something soothingly spiritual that might help to untangle at least some of the chaos in her own mind.

As her eyes closed she almost smiled at the memory that drifted into focus. 'What are you doing with that?' she'd asked her mother once when she'd found her prodding at the buttons on one of the remote controls.

'I'm voting on *Strictly*,' her mother had breathlessly replied. 'I want her to win.'

The news had been on at the time, and the remote had actually been to operate the electric bed, but at least her mother had been able to utter sentences that made some sort of sense back then. It was rare for her to manage any now.

The diagnosis of early onset hadn't happened overnight. The tests, appraisals and endless consultations had seemed to go on for ever before a psychiatrist had finally confirmed that Marsha had Alzheimer's disease. Jules would never forget the look of horror that had come over her mother's face, as though she hadn't expected it, when she'd been living in dread of it since the tests had begun.

Yet, in spite of the tragedy of what was happening to her, over time she'd begun showing a courage and stoicism that Jules would never have believed her capable of, had she not seen it with her own eyes.

'You know my biggest fear?' she'd once confided to

111

Jules. 'It's that I might reach a point where I won't know you and Daisy any more.'

Unable to bear the thought of it herself, Jules had embraced her hard. 'That won't happen,' she'd promised her, never dreaming that one day Marsha's tormented oblivion would be a blessing.

Her memories of Daisy were intact.

'How's Amelia?' Daisy asked Anton Quentin, surprising Jules that she remembered the name and the father, when more than a year had passed since she'd first met them.

'She's very well, thank you,' Quentin had replied stiffly. After a moment he looked down at her. 'Daisy, isn't it?' he asked.

Daisy nodded. 'Is she really like naughty Amelia Jane?' she whispered with a giggle.

The barrister's hawkish eyes glinted.

'Daisy, that's enough,' Jules said, going to take her hand.

Looking up at her, Daisy said, 'She said she was, but I don't expect she is really, do you?'

'Probably not,' Jules smiled, while thinking she probably was.

Chapter Six

'Mummy! Mummy!' Daisy shouted as she came bursting into the kitchen with Stephie, Dean, Millie, Max and three other children Jules hadn't seen before hot on her heels. 'Guess what, I think Ruby's a mermaid and she . . .' She stopped suddenly, lighting up as she spotted her second cousins, Robbie and Tilde, at the table with cookies and squash. 'I didn't know you were going to be here,' she cried, going to throw her arms around them.

Everyone was always made to feel welcome in Daisy's world.

'Auntie Aileen brought us,' five-year-old Tilde told her. 'Mummy and Daddy have got some things to sort out.'

'Why weren't you in school today?' Stephie asked Robbie. 'You were supposed to be my partner in the three-legged race.'

'It was OK, I did it twice,' Dean piped up, 'once with Daisy, which we won, and then with Stephie. We came second in that race. Did you bring your football cards?'

'Yes, I got them all.' Robbie dived into his holdall.

'I've got two Michael Owens so I'll swap one if you've still got two Thierry Henry.'

'Where's Dad?' Jules asked Daisy.

'Downstairs talking to Granny Aileen. Are you going to stay here?' she asked Robbie and Tilde. 'Mummy, can they sleep in my room?'

'If they want to,' Jules assured them.

Thrilled, Daisy turned back to them. 'You can have the bunks, or the lilo or the hammock, I don't mind,' she announced generously. 'I can sleep anywhere.'

'Will Ruby be there?' Tilde asked worriedly. She was no doubt still remembering the playgroup outing to the Mermaid, when they'd come to learn all about Ruby the ghost and Kian had gone overboard with the sound effects. While half the group had screamed in delight, the other half had ended up having night- mares. Kian had felt so terrible about it that he'd arranged another trip to show them exactly how he'd made the noises, and as an added bonus he'd produced an enormous box of dressing-up clothes from Nora's costume shop. That day had been a far greater success than the first, with impromptu little plays being staged all over the place, a rowdy picnic in the family room and to top it all Kian's cousin Finn, the Brightest Spark, had turned up to show off some of his magic tricks.

Now Daisy was saying to Tilde, 'Honestly, you don't have to be scared of Ruby. She just sits around watching us . . .' She suddenly gasped, remembering what she had started to tell Jules earlier. 'Mum! I think Ruby was a mermaid, you know like in the story, and because she couldn't kill the prince she's turned into a daughter of the air, you know like a ghost. Have you seen the film?' she asked Tilde.

Tilde shook her head.

'It's brilliant,' Stephie told her. 'We've seen it about a thousand times, haven't we, Daise?'

'Can we watch it now, to show Tilde?' Daisy asked her mother. 'We've got it on video,' she added grandly to Tilde.

'Do the boys want to watch it too?' Jules asked, as the girls began hurrying off to the TV room.

'No way, not again!' Dean protested. 'We'll go down on the beach and play with our cards and collect crabs and sea worms and shells and stuff.'

'Are you staying for tea, Dean?' Jules called after him.

'Yes please,' he called back. 'I'll have three of everything.'

Thinking how adorable he was, Jules went to start preparing Daisy's mermaid emporium for its new 'underwater' guests. With its walls painted to resemble waves, its sand-coloured carpet with shell-like rugs, lacy fishing-net curtains, foaming ceiling and moody lighting to create bubbles and shadows, it could have been a set straight out of the movie. Although Daisy had been given many posters from the Disney film by friends and family she hadn't wanted them to spoil her mermaid cave, so Kian had helped to place them in a large artist's portfolio which she could pull out any time she wanted to look at them or to show her friends. The rest of her amazing mermaid collection, most of which had come as Christmas or birthday presents, was laid out carefully on the rugged-rock shelves Kian had commissioned a set designer to fashion for her. It ranged from snow globes to musical figurines, bracelets, headbands, caps, jigsaw puzzles and a set of dolls representing the rest of the cast from the movie, including Eric, the prince, with whom Daisy was currently passionately in love. She even had a *Little Mermaid* swimsuit and swim bag, and the cutest imaginable mermaid jellies that Em had sent over from the States.

In the midst of this treasured hoard, holding pride of place, was Ruby's cream leather shoe, which didn't seem to wander about the place half as much as it used to.

'There you are,' Kian sighed, finding Jules on her knees inflating a lilo just in case one of the children might prefer it to a bed. 'So Robbie and Tilde are staying with us while their father moves out of the house to go and shack up with his girlfriend?'

Knowing only too well how furious Kian was about the situation, Jules said, 'It's better than them having to watch him go.'

'You're right about that. So who's there for our Terry? I hope she's not having to cope with this on her own.'

'Everyone's rallying, you know that, and let's be honest, Kian, she's well shot of him. It'll be a relief not to have to put up with his moods any more. She's said so herself. In fact, she's admitted she can't stand him, so all I can say is good luck to the other girl.'

His eyes remained dark and troubled. 'Our Danny's been told what's happening,' he said distractedly. 'I've been trying to call him, make sure he doesn't do anything stupid, but he's not picking up. Bob and Finn are on their way over there, I reckon I should go too, because the last thing we need is a bloody murder on our hands.' Taking out his mobile as it rang, he groaned. 'It's the bloke who's trying to get me interested in setting up safaris on the moor. I'll have to rearrange,' and turning back along the hall he clicked on to take the call.

By the time Aileen had collected Terry, two days later, and brought her over to see the children, Danny had been arrested and charged with grievous bodily harm. Though the injuries Keevan had inflicted on his wife before leaving were far worse than those he'd received from Danny, he ended up being charged with the lesser offence of actual bodily harm, which was later reduced to common assault. Apparently this was to allow the magistrates to impose a quick, custodial sentence that would keep him away from his wife and children for the next six months.

Danny, on the other hand, stood trial at the Crown Court and to everyone's dismay was sent down for three years.

As far as Terry's family, friends and the media were concerned, the judiciary had made its position clear: hurting a man was a far more serious offence than hurting a woman.

There was an outcry amongst women's groups from as far afield as Edinburgh, Manchester and Dublin, who all tried to get in touch with Terry to turn her into some sort of poster girl for their cause. Though Terry was too shy to accept so much exposure, she wasn't so faint-hearted that she'd back away from trying to help others in her situation. In fact when

Reynolds House women's refuge finally opened its doors just over a year later with Penny Grace, an ex-social worker and committed women's rights campaigner, at the helm, Terry was her number two. Jules and Misty, along with the mayor's wife and several well-connected women from the area, took charge of fund-raising, while Marsha and Aileen and most of the women in Aileen's extensive family helped out in any way they could.

'I don't believe it,' Jules exclaimed when Kian told her that Anton Quentin had been amongst those who'd put money into the project. 'Someone who bullies his wife the way he does . . .'

'You don't know that for certain.'

'I know what I saw.'

'Jules, it was a long time ago. You've got no idea what's going on with them these days . . .'

'Because he never brings her here.'

'She's in London, it's where they live, and ask yourself, why would he put money our way for Reynolds House if he was an abuser himself? It doesn't make any sense.'

'Of course it does. It's the perfect cover. Surely you can see that.'

Sighing, he said, 'I can also see that you have a blind spot where he's concerned . . . No, no listen, I don't like the bloke any more than you do, but slagging him off isn't getting us anywhere so let's just drop the subject, shall we?'

They did, and Jules also resisted the urge to write to Olivia Quentin to tell her about Reynolds House. Apart from not being very subtle, she didn't know the

messages on her mobile too. She'd get round to them eventually; for the time being she needed to recover after the hour or so she'd just spent with her mother. Not that Marsha had woken up, or even as much as stirred while Jules was there, it was just that seeing someone she loved in such an undignified and desperate state was so distressing that she always needed time to adjust when she'd left the home.

I should kill her.

It wasn't the first time the thought had entered her head, it was probably always there, if not in the foreground, then lingering close by every time she saw her mother. However, today she wasn't only thinking about Marsha. In fact she might not have been thinking about Marsha at all.

Sometime soon, possibly only days from now, the Quentin girl would taste freedom again. She would breathe the cleansing air of the coast, shield her eyes against the dazzling sun; fill her mind with all she was going to do with the rest of her life.

Jules wondered if she already had plans. How easy was it going to be for her to find a job, make friends, settle back into the society she'd never really been a part of, even before? Everyone knew what she'd done, so who'd want to befriend her? Who'd have the courage, apart from social outcasts or the deeply religious? No one from Dean's family's sect would go near her; surely almost everyone else would give her as wide a berth as she deserved. Maybe some would tell themselves, 'She's served her sentence, it's time to put it behind us and move on.' Some might even say, 'Poor thing, I'm sure she bitterly regrets it all now, and we should find it in our hearts to forgive her.' There would be others, such as the Bright family and their closest friends, who would declare, 'Someone should make her pay, because the law sure as hell didn't bother.'

'Just say the word,' Bridget, Danny's mother, had urged when Jules had last spoken to her, 'and it can all be made to go away.'

Jules had said nothing as she'd tried to make up her mind what she wanted. So many images and voices were crowding her mind that there seemed no room for words to form, much less to be spoken.

Bridget said softly, 'You don't have to know anything about it. There are ways we can make it happen . . .'

Danny-type ways? What good would that do?

'Remember, we're all here for you,' Bridget soothed.

Still Jules had said nothing. There was no point reminding Bridget that those closest to her had all gone. Daisy, Kian, Aileen, her mother . . .

Starting as the telephone brought her back to the present, she checked who it was and felt relieved by the timely reminder; Em was always there, even if she was four thousand miles away. 'Hi,' she said into the receiver, 'I wasn't expecting you yet. It's still early with you.'

'Don's out, so I have the place – and the phone – to myself for a while. How are you?'

'OK. Before you ask, no I haven't heard from Andee about a release date, but she left a message earlier asking how I was and reminding me to be in touch if I needed to talk.'

'That was nice of her. Maybe you should take her up on it.'

'Maybe. To be honest, I'm not sure what I want, apart from to be somebody else.'

With a gentle sigh, Em said, 'I wish you'd come here, to us. We've got plenty of space now the kids have gone . . .'

Gently changing the subject, Jules said, 'How are your parents? I had a postcard from them a couple of weeks ago, it sounds as though they're still enjoying Spain.'

'And the old-fashioned methods of communication. They still won't email, and I have to admit in some ways I envy them the freedom of not being tied to a computer or a phone all the time.'

With a smile Jules said, 'I know what you mean.' And after a beat, 'I had an email from Joe. He's still intending to come here. Do you know if he's in Chicago at the moment?'

'I believe so, but I haven't seen him. I ran into his father the other day.'

Jules stiffened.

After a pause, Em said, 'Sorry, I shouldn't have mentioned it.'

She shouldn't have, although it wouldn't have been a problem if Jules's memories hadn't taken the direction they had earlier.

'It was a long time ago, Jules,' Em reminded her. 'You need to forgive yourself.'

'Seven years,' Jules murmured. 'Daisy was almost thirteen. Old enough to fall in love for the first time.'

'Which she did, with Joe, and who'd have dreamt back then that it would last the way it did? All those long hot summers together at the lake, him coming with us to Kesterly each Christmas . . .'

Jules's heart felt as though something harsh and relentless was trying to push through it. She wanted the conversation to end. Em would understand if she said so, but the hurdle was down, there was no halting the memories as they spilled into forbidden territory, treading over it as though there was nothing painful about it all, when just about everything was . . .

It wouldn't have happened if Em had been in Chicago when Jules and Daisy arrived that summer; or if Kian and the grannies had come on the same flight. Not that she was blaming anyone else; the guilt lay entirely with her, she would never pretend otherwise. It was simply that if fate hadn't separated them all at that time, then nothing unusual would have happened during those first sultry, strangely surreal days of the visit.

Since Em and Don had already gone ahead to the lake to open up the house, Jules and Daisy had stayed with Em's father-in-law, Gray, and his new wife, Esther, along with Em's children, Mattie and Oscar, until Kian and the grannies flew in to join them. It was during that time, when the air was so still and humid it was an effort to move, and when home felt like it belonged to another world, that Daisy had first met the great love of her life.

'Mum, this is Joe,' Daisy told her, holding on to the boy's hand and looking so sparklingly happy that Jules could hear Kian saying, 'She really is all things Bright and beautiful.'

'Hello Joe,' Jules said, understanding immediately why Daisy was so drawn to him. He might only be thirteen, but he was already almost as tall as Jules, and was so handsome in his all-American physical way that he must surely have been making a lot of young girls' hearts flip over. 'It's good to meet you.'

'To meet you too,' he said, politely. 'Daisy's been telling me all about the Mermaid. It sounds really cool.' He had clear, intelligent eyes, an erratically deepening voice and the kind of smile that was both shy and engaging.

'Joe's coming to the lake with us,' Daisy informed her. 'Mattie rang Auntie Em this morning to check it was OK, and it is.'

Amused by how fast this budding romance was blooming, Jules said to Joe, 'Have you been out to the lake before?'

'Not that lake,' he replied. 'My grandparents have a place further south in Indiana, we go there sometimes. Usually at Passover and Thanksgiving.'

Passover. So he was Jewish, which, for no fathomable reason, made Jules like him more. 'Where do you live, Joe?' she asked.

'Mum, I told you yesterday,' Daisy chided. 'He lives three blocks away, and goes to the same school as Oscar.'

'Of course, I'm sorry.' Daisy had indeed told her yesterday, when she'd returned from seeing a movie with Mattie and Oscar and been able to talk about nothing but Joe who'd gone with them.

'You should see him, Mum, he is like totally dropdead and you know I don't ever say that about anyone unless it's true.'

'No, you don't,' Jules had smiled. 'So do you think he's interested in you?'

Daisy blushed. 'Mattie says he is, and even Oscar reckons there's something . . . Oh Mum, I wish we weren't going to the lake. I mean, I'm glad we are because we always love it there, but I've just met him and I might never see him again after the end of this week, or not until we come back next year and by then he'll have forgotten all about me.'

Sympathising with her adolescent angst, Jules pulled her into an embrace. 'I don't think anyone could forget you, my darling.'

'Oh Mum, you would say that, but it might come as a shock to you to know that I'm not special to everyone else the way I am to you and Dad and the grannies.'

'And Auntie Bridget and Uncle Danny, Auntie Ruthie and Uncle Connor, Auntie Terry and Finn, Uncle Pete, Bob and Cheryl . . .'

'Mum stop, it's not the same and you know it. They've known me all my life and I've only just met Joe.'

'Do you have any plans to see him again before we leave?'

Daisy twinkled mischievously. 'He's invited us to his house tomorrow. They've got a pool, so we can swim.'

'Did you tell him you have a beach?'

'Mattie did, but it's not a competition, Mum.'

'Sorry.'

'Mattie says she doesn't think he has a girlfriend, but Oscar's going to find out to make sure. Oh please don't let him already have someone. I'll just die if he has. But guess what, he's really interested in loads of things the same as me, and we're into all the same music. Oh yes, and he's made films at school, not like we make, more kind of factual stuff, although we do them too, like our film about the moor, and the other one we did about the history of Kesterly. His dad's a doctor, but that's not what he wants to do when he's older. He's going to be a lawyer, he says, and he reckons it's dead cool that I want to get into directing. Apparently there are some really good places in New York for that, he's going to find out more about them for me.'

'Wow,' Jules laughed, 'is there anything you haven't discussed yet?'

Laughing too, Daisy threw her arms around her mother's neck and carried on talking about Joe, repeating herself over and over the way she did when talking to Stephie, and clearly thrilling and rejoicing and swooning at all the new and wonderful sensations fizzing about inside her.

It was the evening after the announcement that Joe would be joining them at the lake, during a cocktail party at a neighbour's house, that Esther introduced Jules to Nicholas, Joe's father.

As Jules looked into the man's unsettling dark eyes, a deeper, wiser, far more knowing version of Joe's, she felt something shift in the normal calm of her demeanour. They shook hands and it was as though a quietly powerful charge was passing between them, fusing a connection that was both shocking and intriguing. She wasn't sure she'd ever experienced anything like this before, and wasn't entirely comfortable with it, but it would have appeared rude to move away.

'Nicholas is a heart surgeon,' Esther was telling her, and Jules almost embarrassed herself by saying, 'Well, a man who can so obviously break them should be able to repair them.'

After Esther left them they talked for just a few minutes about where she was from, how infrequently he got to Europe, and how long he'd lived in Chicago, before moving on to mingle with the other guests. Though she didn't look his way again, she continued to feel his presence, and wondered if he felt hers too.

'It would seem,' he said, coming to join her on the terrace later, 'that my son's fascination with your daughter has got him an invite to the lake.'

Jules was watching Daisy, sitting on the grass with Em's children and Joe, sensing her attraction to the young lad as deeply as she was now sensing her own to the father.

She took a small sip of her Martini. He was so close he was almost touching her. She listened to the murmur of American voices around her and felt as though she was in a movie where the colours were blurred and the sound was hushed. Nothing about the setting seemed real, apart from him and her and what was happening between them.

Things like this weren't supposed to happen when you were forty and happily married.

'Do you think she feels the same way?' he asked softly.

Jules understood the nuance of the question, and nodded.

'I believe they're arranging to get together again tomorrow,' he said. 'Do you have any objection?'

Keeping her eyes on Daisy, she took another sip of

her drink. 'Do you know where they're planning to go?'

'Somewhere we're not invited, I'm sure.' He smiled. 'Do you have any plans yourself?'

Her breath caught as she felt the answer forming in ways that went beyond words.

They met at his home the following afternoon. She stayed for almost four hours making love with a man she didn't know, had no intention of ever getting to know, but allowing him to do things to her that no one had ever done before. She was insatiable; she didn't want it to stop. They hardly talked; words were of no interest; all that mattered were the acts of love that wasn't love at all.

She couldn't remember later how often she'd thought of Kian during those hours, if she'd even thought about him at all; she only knew that she couldn't get him out of her mind afterwards. It was as though he was invisibly there, watching her, accusing her, berating her for the betrayal. She felt so ashamed it was making her want to claw and tear at her own skin as though to remove every last memory of Nicholas's touch.

What had driven her? How could she have done it when she loved her husband so much she'd rather have died than do anything to hurt him? How was she going to face him with this guilt? How could she bear to see the hurt and bewilderment in his eyes, the shock, anger; his love turning to disgust and distrust? She felt so appalled and wretched, yet even as her conscience tormented her, her body, as though it had a life of its own, continued to thrill to the intensity of those stolen hours.

'Is everything OK?' Kian asked a few days later, as they began the three-hour drive to the lake. 'You haven't seemed yourself since I arrived.'

'I'm fine,' she assured him, reaching for his hand, 'it's just the heat of the city. I'll be glad to get somewhere cooler.'

His eyes flicked to the rear-view mirror, where the grannies were dozing in the seats behind them and Daisy and Joe were playing something on a console at the far back.

Jules couldn't look at the boy without feeling a terrible weight inside her. Thank God his father hadn't accepted Esther's invitation to join them too.

'There's plenty of room,' Esther had told him down the phone, 'and we'd love to have you along.'

Jules hadn't been able to hear his reply.

'Sure, I understand,' Esther said in the end. 'Be sure to send her my love. We can't wait for the wedding.' After putting the phone down she said to Jules, 'He's getting married at the end of next month to a very good friend of mine, Corinna Linus. It's good to see him happy; his first wife's death hit him hard.'

Jules realised that the tightness in her chest was far closer to jealousy than the relief she should have felt to learn he was involved with somebody else. She shut the emotion down quickly. It didn't belong with her, had no place in her life at all. She wondered how hard he might be struggling with his own conscience, if it was anything like the way she was suffering with hers.

She'd made sure not to be there that morning when he'd come to drop Joe at Gray and Esther's. If Kian were to see them together he'd know right away. She felt everyone would, which was why she never mentioned him, or listened particularly attentively if someone else did, in case she somehow gave herself away.

'Our little girl's besotted,' Kian smiled as they stopped at a rest area to break the journey.

'So's he,' Jules murmured, watching the youngsters following the grannies into the low, red-brick buildings to get snacks and cold drinks. Em's kids were already inside with Esther and Gray.

Not ready to be alone with Kian, Jules pushed the car door open. 'It'll seem rude if we don't go in too,' she said.

'You're right,' he agreed, and turning off the engine he followed her out into the blazing heat.

In the end, because she had to tell someone, Jules waited until she and Em were on one of their early-morning walks around the lake, a long way from the house, and confided everything that had happened.

Em's shock was apparent, as was her sympathy for how hard Jules was being on herself. 'Sometimes things get out of control,' she tried to soothe, 'I know, because it almost happened to me once.'

'With Nicholas?' Jules cried aghast.

'No, not with Nicholas. It doesn't matter who with, it was a long time ago, and I've put it out of my mind now, which is exactly what you must do.'

Sighing, Jules turned to gaze at the water where early swimmers, sailboats and skiers were shimmering like apparitions in the misty sunlight. 'I want to,' she said, 'more than anything, but it means lying to Kian and I don't know if I can do that.'

'Listen to me,' Em said firmly, 'I promise you, no

good will ever come from telling him. In fact, in my opinion, it's the most selfish thing you could do. You're the one who made the mistake, so you're the one who has to live with it. Not him. He's happy; he loves you more than his own life, so why the hell would you do anything to spoil that when you've got no intention of seeing Nicholas again . . .' She stopped. 'Please tell me you haven't.'

'God no,' Jules exclaimed. 'Do you think I'm crazy?'

Em eyed her warily. 'Possibly, for doing it,' she admitted. 'Crazier still if you start trying to ease your conscience with a confession.'

'I've never had secrets from Kian before.'

'So, you have one now, and the reason you're keeping it is for his sake, not yours. You can't go destroying what you two have for something that doesn't even mean anything. And what about Daisy? Have you thought about how it's going to affect her if you decide to break her daddy's heart?'

Jules continued to gaze at the water, feeling nothing but guilt, and the brutal truth of Em's words.

'The choice is yours, Jules,' Em said softly. 'You can either devastate the people you love most in the world, or you can put it out of your mind and start forgiving yourself.'

Jules almost smiled. 'That's not going to be easy.'

'Maybe not, but let me tell you this, no one goes through life without doing at least one thing they regret, they wouldn't be human if they did. So for God's sake, put your family first and let your conscience get over itself – and now we need to change the subject, because Daisy and Joe are about twenty yards away.'

'Hey Mum! Hey Auntie Em,' Daisy called out as she and Joe jogged past in their trainers and luminous Lycra. 'See you're doing a great job of burning off all that wine you had last night.'

'Thanks for the reminder,' Jules retorted wryly. 'Are you going to the café?'

'That's the plan,' Joe told her. 'See you there?'

'Keep a table for us.' Laughing as he suddenly scooped Daisy up and began running with her towards the water's edge, she said, 'Why, of all people, did it have to be his father?'

Em sighed sympathetically. 'This is just a holiday romance. Trouble is, you thought you could have one too.'

With a sardonic smile Jules pressed a fist into Em's arm. 'You're right. I have to keep this to myself,' she said decisively. 'I can see that now.'

'Good.'

'Thanks for listening.'

'Isn't that what friends are for? We'll talk about it more later, if you like, but for now, call Kian and invite him to come and join us for coffee.'

Jules did, and her heart burned with painful emotions to hear the relief and eagerness in his voice. He had no idea why she'd been shutting him out these last few days, but this was sounding as though she might finally be letting him back in again, and she wanted to weep for how happy it was making him.

Chapter Seven

'Hi, it's good to see you,' Andee smiled, as Jules joined her in a window booth at the Seafront Café.

Jules's nerves were tight, her head ached as she greeted Fliss, the café's owner, and ordered a decaff Americano.

'A latte for me,' Andee told Fliss.

After jotting the order down Fliss said to Jules, 'How are you, sweetie? Haven't seen you in a while.'

'I'm fine,' Jules replied, knowing Fliss's concern was real, though she was undoubtedly curious about what was behind this meeting with the ex-detective Andee Lawrence, particularly with Amelia Quentin's release on the horizon.

Apart from another couple seated close to the counter Jules and Andee were the only customers inside the café; with the weather being so warm the tables on the pavement outside were full of tourists, in spite of the traffic fumes.

'I'm guessing,' Jules said, bracing herself, 'that a date's been set.'

Andee nodded. 'It's the twenty-ninth, the end of next week, a little earlier than I'd expected.'

Jules kept her eyes down as she struggled with how wretched this news was making her feel, how cheated and vengeful, frustrated, helpless, furious beyond any words. It would do no more good to try and express her feelings than it would to continue feeling them, so she attempted to stuff them back into the darkness they'd sprung from. 'Do you have any idea,' she said to Andee, 'why she's coming back here, why she's even being allowed to?'

Andee shook her head. 'I'm afraid not, but if you're worried . . . If you'd like me to talk to someone . . . She won't be allowed to come near you. It'll be one of the conditions . . .'

Jules's head came up. 'Do you think I need protecting?' she asked sharply.

Andee held her gaze.

Jules turned to the window, looking across the street at the crowded beach where a Punch and Judy show was under way, kids were riding donkeys, families were splashing about in the waves. Normal life, oblivion, except everyone had a story. Probably not one like hers. 'I'll be fine,' she said quietly. After a while her eyes returned to Andee. 'She can't do any more to me than she already has.'

Andee sat back in her seat as Fliss delivered their coffees.

'A couple of pastries on the house,' Fliss announced. 'You look like you could do with feeding up,' she told Jules.

After she'd gone, seeming to sense that they needed to ease away from Amelia Quentin for a while, Andee said, 'How's your mother?'

Jules sipped her coffee and stared into it as she put it down again. 'The same,' she replied. 'There, but not, if you know what I mean.' She looked up. 'How's yours?' she asked, struggling to remember what she knew of Andee's mother.

Andee's eyes danced. 'She's cruising at the moment, with my husband's mother.'

Jules nodded. 'It makes a big difference when both sides of the family get along,' she commented, thinking of how close her and Kian's mothers had always been. 'Your mother-in-law is Carol Farnham, the old mayor's wife, isn't she?'

'That's right.'

'How is she?'

'OK. She still misses Dougie, but I guess that's to be expected. They were very close and married a long time.'

'The whole town misses Dougie. He's the best mayor we ever had. I expect you hear that a lot.'

Andee smiled. 'He enjoyed working with Kian, I know that. Do you remember how excited they used to get about their projects? We'd hear all about them every time we came to Kesterly on holiday, and I remember my kids forever begging to go to Daisy's shows, or be in one of her films if they could.'

Making herself smile, Jules said, 'Were they ever?'

'A couple of times. Small parts.' Moving away from Daisy, Andee said cheerfully, 'We were all at the reopening of the old cinema. Do you remember that?'

Jules did. 'Everyone was allowed in for free that day,' she reminisced, 'and the film was . . . What was the film?'

'Bend It Like Beckham.'

'That's right, and a couple of the cast came to add a bit of glitz to the occasion. It was quite a party after.'

'One of Kian's and Dougie's many strong points, parties.'

'I hear Dougie even stage-managed his own funeral.'

Andee's eyebrows rose in surprise. 'You weren't there?' Then remembering, 'No, of course not. Sorry.'

Jules swallowed and picked up her coffee again. 'So is your name Farnham, now you're married?' she asked after a moment.

'Yes, but I still tend to use Lawrence.'

Jules tried imagining not using Kian's name, but it wasn't somewhere she wanted to go so she let it drop. 'Does it feel different to be married after you were living together for so long?' she asked curiously.

Andee shrugged. 'I suppose it did, at first. It felt quite romantic, in fact, but now it's . . . I guess the same as it always was.'

Jules frowned. 'That sounds . . .' She shook her head. 'Sorry, it's none of my business.'

'It's fine. I know I sound disillusioned, and I suppose in a way I am, but not because of Martin. He's a great husband and father, generous, attentive, wanting to make up for leaving me when he did . . . The trouble is, I can't help wondering . . . Well, I suppose what life would have been like if I'd taken up with someone else during the time we were apart.'

'Were you apart for long?'

'A couple of years.'

'And did you meet anyone else in that time?'

Andee's eyes drifted as she nodded. 'Yes, as a matter

of fact I did. It wasn't serious, but I think it could have been if Martin hadn't come back on the scene.'

'Do you ever see this person now?'

'We run into each other now and again at various functions. It's a small town.'

Jules couldn't deny that. There wasn't anyone in Kesterly who didn't know what had happened to her. Most of the country knew about that. 'Is it awkward?'

'A little. To be honest, it still feels like unfinished business, which is crazy when I'm married to someone else. What do I think I'm going to do, have an affair?'

Jules regarded her closely. 'Would you, if you had the chance?' she dared to ask.

Andee smiled as she shrugged. 'In my dreams, maybe, but I wouldn't want to hurt either of them, or myself, so I guess the answer has to be no.' Seeming to shake it off, she said, 'How about you? Have you ever . . . ? No, you and Kian were always so close . . .'

Jules's heart contracted. 'Yes, we were,' she said quietly, 'but I almost ruined it all once with a moment of madness. I've never been able to forgive myself for it. Sometimes I even wonder if what happened later was my punishment. It was how it felt for a long time, but I don't think it works like that, does it?' She wasn't sure about that, but it was hard to be sure about anything now.

'Did Kian know about the . . . "moment of madness"?'

Jules shook her head. 'No, I never told him, but it changed things between us anyway. It was like, because I knew I couldn't be trusted, I no longer knew if I could trust him. That's crazy, isn't it, but it's how it was. It made me love him more too, like I wanted to protect him, and I was terrified I was going to lose him . . . Sometimes I felt so desperate when I looked at him. It was very muddled. I guess I was a bit of a basket case, although I think, on the surface, I seemed fine to everyone else.'

'Do you know if he was ever unfaithful?'

'I don't think so. I used to wish he would be, in the hope it might make me feel better, but I don't think he ever went past the flirting stage. Even that changed after I . . .' She broke off, suddenly not wanting to go any further, and yet the words were there, needing to be spoken, and there was nothing she could do to stop them. 'I got pregnant,' she said shakily. 'We'd always found it so hard to conceive, me and Kian, and then, after that one encounter I found I . . .' She swallowed hard. 'I had no idea which of them was the father.'

Andee's eyes were dark with feeling. 'So what did you do?' she asked gently.

'Actually, I didn't have to do anything, because I miscarried. I guess that was a blessing, but it was still my baby, and it might have been Kian's . . . Of course he thought it was, so he was as devastated as I was when I lost it.' Her heart burned with all the anguish and deceit she'd felt at the time. She couldn't think now how she'd managed to get through it, but somehow she had. 'I let him grieve for a child that might not have been his,' she said dully. 'I don't know if you understand how that makes me feel, even now.'

'I can only imagine,' Andee whispered truthfully.

'He thought it was the reason for my depression, and I suppose it was, but mostly it was about deceiving him. He didn't deserve that, and yet he didn't deserve to be hurt either.' She took a breath. 'I sometimes wonder . . .'

When she didn't elaborate Andee simply waited, allowing her to decide whether she wanted to continue.

'You remember Joe, Daisy's American boyfriend?' Jules said in the end.

Andee nodded. 'Of course.'

'It was his father that I . . . So I sometimes wonder, if Joe hadn't stayed in our lives, would I have found it easier to put it all behind me? Not that I ever saw him. We never met again after that day . . . He was tactfully somewhere else whenever Kian and I were in Chicago, and he never came to England with Joe. Of course Daisy stayed with him and his wife during her visits to the States, and on a couple of occasions, when she was younger and she and Joe were first together, Kian would fly over with her for the weekend, so he'd stay there too.'

'That must have been hard for you.'

'I hated it, but what could I do? Daisy and Joe were besotted with one another. I kept telling myself it would burn itself out as they got older, but it never did. They spent every summer together, usually with us at Em's lake house, and every Christmas here in Kesterly, at the Mermaid. The half-terms in between were either in Chicago, Kesterly, or sometimes for a special treat someone would take them to New York or London. There was no point trying to split them up, having an ocean between them was already taking care of the physical distance, but they never allowed it to be a problem. And the way kids use social media these days, it's like most of them have virtual relationships anyway.

It could even be said that they spend more time together online, FaceTiming, instant messaging, texting, or whatever, than if they were in the same town, or even the same room. I'm not sure how old they were when they started to talk about getting married, probably only fourteen or fifteen. It was crazy, a kind of dream with no real understanding of what it all meant, so we didn't take it seriously. On the other hand I used to worry about there being a wedding and what it would be like to see Nicholas again.'

'Did you want to see him?'

'I guess there's no point in denying that a part of me did, but I dreaded it too. If they did end up together it would become harder than ever to avoid him . . .' Her voice ran dry as all the useless worrying faded back into the waste of time it had been. 'Joe's coming here in a couple of weeks,' she said.

Andee's eyes narrowed. 'I take it you've told him about Amelia's imminent release?'

Jules nodded. Her eyes were distant, her thoughts spiralling downwards into a very dark place. The only way to rescue them was to think of Daisy and the way she lit up the world with her laughter, her kindness, her sense of fairness and determination to see good in everyone, even Amelia Quentin . . .

Jules flinched; everything kept coming back to the Quentin girl. It seemed impossible to escape Amelia no matter how hard she tried, but even if she managed it there was always the guilt of Jules's betrayal . . .

'There's definitely something wrong, Mum, I can tell,' Daisy insisted, skipping backwards against the wind so she could see her mother's face. 'If something's upsetting you then you must either tackle it, or put it out of your mind. It never does any good to let it fester. So now, what's getting to you? You know you can tell me anything. I won't be shocked.'

Smiling, Jules raised a hand to shield her eyes from the winter sun. Her darling leggy daughter, who was growing into a stunning young woman with her father's wayward blonde curls, violet-blue eyes and irrepressible good humour, was never backward in throwing out a challenge.

'All that's bothering me right now,' Jules declared, 'is working out the staff rota over Christmas, and will we get all the deliveries on time.'

'Pfft!' Daisy scoffed. 'You never stress over stuff like that. Anyway, it's Misty's job, so sorry, not buying it.'

Amused by her certainty, Jules said, 'OK, I'm wondering if Dad's bitten off more than he can chew with this new pleasure-cruise project.'

'Sorry, still not doing it for me. Dad's always biting off more than he can chew but when does it ever not work out? Shall I tell you what I think it is?'

In spite of the fear that Daisy might actually know, Jules made her eyes twinkle.

Daisy said, 'OK, here goes. You're worrying about me and Joe and how our relationship has gone on to the next level, but honestly, you shouldn't, because there's nothing to worry about.'

Jules's eyebrows rose. In her opinion there was plenty to worry about where that relationship was concerned, not least how long it might be before Daisy left them to go to the States. However, all she said was, 'Well that's good to hear,' and grabbing Daisy's arm she steered her away from a slimy pile of seaweed.

'Look at it this way,' Daisy continued. 'You and Dad are soulmates, right?'

Since Jules had always thought so, she wasn't going to deny it now, when they'd surely come good again one day, please God. 'Yes, we are,' she confirmed.

'So that's just like me and Joe. All that's different is that we met when we were younger, and we live in different countries, which actually makes it even more meant-to-be if you think about it.'

Jules didn't argue, since there was every chance Daisy was right. She was sixteen now, Joe was seventeen, and Jules and Kian had long ago given up telling themselves that the friendship, which had become a fully intimate relationship back in the summer (though Kian didn't know that), wouldn't last.

'We're using contraception,' Daisy assured her, 'if that's what's worrying you.'

'I'd assumed you were.'

Daisy grinned. 'It's just amazing, Mum. I mean, I had no idea anything could feel like that. He's so . . .'

'My darling, love you as I do and happy for you as I am, I really don't need the details.'

With a choke of laughter, Daisy said, 'OK, so here's the big question, are you going to let him sleep in my room when he comes for Christmas?'

Jules's eyes narrowed playfully. 'Why don't you ask Dad that question?'

Daisy collapsed into a groan. 'Mum!'

'What?'

'He'll say no.'

'Are you sure?'

Daisy tilted her head as she considered it. 'I guess I just have to go about it in the right way,' she decided. 'If I remind him of how young Romeo and Juliet were when they fell in love . . .'

'Not a good idea. Think how it ended.'

Daisy bubbled with laughter. 'OK, so how about I ask him how old you were when you first got it together. How old were you, by the way?'

'Old enough.'

'You mean legally? So am I.'

'Not in the States.'

'But we won't be in the States.'

'I'm not sure that counts in Joe's case. Under American law you're still a minor.'

'You're just confusing things now. I need you on my side, Mum, so tell me you don't object.'

'I'm fine with it, but how do you think he's going to like sharing you with Ruby and the mermaids?' Though the mermaid collection was much pared down these days, and certainly more tastefully displayed, neither it nor Ruby had moved out altogether.

'He *loves* Ruby and the mermaids,' Daisy insisted. 'Did I tell you that he's promised to take me to Copenhagen to see the Little Mermaid one of these days?'

'Did you tell him your grannies took you when you were ten?'

'No, because I didn't want to spoil it. By the way, are you going over to Granny Marsha's later? Oh hang on, who's this?' and taking out her mobile she checked her texts. 'Two from Stephie, one from Dean wanting to know . . .' Whatever had been asked she didn't share as she rapidly sent messages back. 'Great. So where were we? Oh, I know . . .'

'Is that your phone again?'

Daisy was already reading the next text. 'Cool,' she muttered as she dealt with it. 'About six of us are going to be here for breakfast tomorrow,' she informed her mother. 'There's this film project we're working on for college . . . Oh yes, and Stephie's auntie's got three tickets for her, me and Dean to go and see the Kaiser Chiefs in Birmingham while Joe's here, so we need Dad to find out if he can get an extra one.'

'I'm sure he'll know someone. He usually does.' Jules's eyes returned to Daisy's phone as another text arrived.

'Oh, how sweet,' Daisy smiled as she read it. 'It's from this girl at the gym who . . . Oh my God, I forgot to tell you about her. You'll never guess who it is.'

'Probably not,' Jules conceded.

Laughing, Daisy said, 'It's only Naughty Amelia Jane. Do you remember her? I barely do, but she says she definitely remembers us and that was what I called her the first time we met. Apparently she knew who I was the minute she saw me.'

Conjuring an image of the serious little girl with mussed hair and awful manners, Jules said, 'Gosh, I'd forgotten all about her, it's been so long. Where did you say you'd seen her?'

'At the gym. We had a good laugh about me calling her Naughty Amelia Jane. Can you believe her remembering that? I didn't have a clue what she was talking about when she introduced herself that way. "Hi

Daisy," she said, "I'm Naughty Amelia Jane. Do you remember me?"'

Both amused and curious, Jules said, 'What's she doing now, did she say?'

'No. We only spoke for a few minutes, but she asked me to say hi to you.'

Since Daisy was engrossed in sending a text back to Amelia, Jules simply said, 'I guess you can tell her hi from me when you next see her. Did she happen to mention her mother?'

Daisy shook her head. 'Like I said, we didn't talk for long. I was about to go into a class and she was on her way out, I think.'

Jules nodded. She wasn't sure why Amelia Quentin's sudden reappearance in their lives wasn't feeling good. Perhaps it was because she'd long felt bad about not doing more to befriend the girl's mother. She wondered how the years had treated her, if she and her husband were still together. And what sort of changes had time wrought on the daughter? All for the good, she hoped.

As Daisy finished her text, Jules said, 'Are we still going to a Zumba class tonight?'

'Yes, definitely,' Daisy assured her. 'Stephie's coming too. Oh no, sorry I forgot. That's tomorrow. Tonight I promised I'd go for a run with Dad before Stephie and Dean come over. Do you mind?'

'No, of course not.' She did, but only because she hadn't been invited to run with them. 'Where are you going?'

'I'm not sure yet. Probably along the promenade and up round the old town. Listen, I'd better go, I'm supposed to be FaceTiming with Joe in five minutes. I'll send him your love and tell him you're cool about

146

us sharing a bed,' and after treating her mother to a boisterous hug she took off across the beach to the pub.

As Jules watched her go she was aware of a strange mix of emotions pulling her from sadness to pride, to joy and hope; she even felt a twinge of loneliness. There was a time when the three of them, she, Daisy and Kian, had done everything together, walks, runs, gym, the Performing Arts shows, charity events . . . Of course it was only to be expected that things would change as Daisy grew up and became more independent; she just couldn't help feeling that events were moving beyond her grasp.

Pulling her coat more tightly around her, she turned to walk on towards the cliffs. It was a grey, blustery day, with slender shards of sunlight escaping the belligerent clouds, and a lively tide hurling itself against the rocks. There was so much going round in her mind, issues with the pub, concerns about her mother, Daisy's future with Joe, but always uppermost in her thoughts was how much she missed her closeness with Kian. She knew he missed it too, and yet they never discussed it. If they tried, and she ended up confessing what she'd done, she was sure it would push them even further apart and she just couldn't bear that to happen.

Realising her phone was ringing, she tugged it from her pocket and seeing it was him she felt a rush of teenage flutters. 'Hi,' she said, speaking up over the wind, 'is everything OK?'

'Sure. What are you doing out there on your own?'

Turning to look at the pub, she said, 'Just finishing up the walk Daisy and I started. Where are you?'

'Bedroom window.'

Spotting him, she waved and smiled as he waved back. 'What are you doing?'

'Just sorting out a few things before Daisy and I set off on a run. Has she brought the uni in America thing up with you yet?'

'No, she hasn't.' It was coming, they both knew it, and were dreading it, but they'd resolved not to stand in her way.

'OK, I thought it might have been what you were talking about. If not, I'll keep bracing myself.'

Deciding not to mention the sleeping arrangements over Christmas, she told him to have a good run and rang off to take a call from Aileen.

'I'm at your mother's,' Aileen told her. 'She's crying because she thinks she hasn't seen you for weeks. I keep reminding her that you were here this morning, but I'm afraid it's not making a difference.'

'I'll be right there,' Jules promised, and clicking off the line she headed back across the beach.

'Do you want me to take you?' Kian offered when she explained where she was going.

'No, it's fine. I could be there for a while and you don't want to miss your run.'

He nodded, and watched her pick up her car keys.

It wasn't until she was halfway to Temple Fields that she realised she should probably have accepted the offer. He'd wanted her to, she could sense it now, but it was already too late. This was yet another example of how they just weren't in sync with one another any more.

'I'm sorry,' Jules said as Andee thanked Fliss for their second coffees. 'I'm talking too much, something I haven't done in a long time.' Her eyes sparked with irony. 'I guess I need to get out more.'

Andee smiled. 'It's good to hear you talking about Kian and Daisy. I wondered if you were able to.'

'I'm not, usually.'

Andee nodded her understanding. 'The text you just mentioned, that Daisy received from Amelia after running into her at the gym, did you ever see it?'

Jules thought. 'No, I don't think so. I only remember Daisy saying it was sweet. Actually, most of her texts were, until they started to seem . . .' She shook her head, not quite sure how to express it. 'Something I remember very clearly, I don't know if I told you this before, but it was the first time she came to the pub. Not as a child, with her parents, but as a friend of Daisy's. It was really quite . . . odd.'

'Mum!' Daisy shouted down the stairs. 'Amelia's just arrived. Can you send her up when she comes in?'

Glancing up from the new iPad ordering system she was testing at the bar, Jules looked out of the window and spotted a young woman coming across the garden with a large bag clutched closely to her chest. Since her head was down her face was masked by the fall of her mousy hair, but it was plain to see, in spite of her voluminous brown coat, that she was neither tall nor particularly slender.

To Jules's surprise as she reached the door – open for Kian to bring in logs – it suddenly slammed shut in her face.

Wondering where on earth the gust had come from, Jules hurried to let her in. 'I'm sorry, there's usually a doorstop there,' she apologised, ushering the girl inside. 'Are you OK?'

'Yes, I'm fine,' she answered, tucking her hair behind one ear and seeming less interested in being abruptly shut out than in studying her surroundings.

Jules watched her lichen-green eyes, set slightly too close together and fringed by pale lashes and eyebrows. Her complexion was fair and freckled, her cheekbones prominent, and her mouth wide and delicate.

'This isn't how I remember it,' Amelia murmured, sounding vaguely piqued.

'There have been some changes since you were last here,' Jules told her with a smile. 'How are you, Amelia? I'm Jules, Daisy's mum.'

As Amelia's eyes came to hers bearing not even the hint of a smile, Jules was reminded of the three-year-old child who'd been hit in the face by the table-skittles ball.

'You're not like I remember you either,' Amelia stated, making it neither an insult nor a compliment, 'but I guess I only saw you a couple of times.'

'And you were so young I'm surprised you remember me at all. Have you been living in London all this time?'

Amelia nodded. 'Sort of,' she replied, looking around again. 'In my mind this place was bigger and darker . . . I remember the fireplace. I had a dream once that I fell into it.'

Startled, Jules said, 'Well I hope the fire wasn't lit at the time.'

Amelia frowned, apparently taking the poor joke seriously. 'I can't remember, but it was a weird dream to have. I think Daisy pushed me in, but it could have been anyone.'

Not quite sure how to respond to that, Jules said, 'So, what a coincidence you running into Daisy at the gym. Have you been a member there for long?'

'No, I just joined a few weeks ago. You belong too, don't you?'

Assuming Daisy must have mentioned it, Jules said, 'I do, but I don't manage to go anywhere near as often as I'd like.' The sudden eruption of angry voices upstairs made them both glance at the ceiling.

'That'll be Stephie and Dean,' Jules smiled fondly. 'Don't worry, it'll all be over before you get there.'

'I'm not worried,' Amelia assured her.

With slightly raised eyebrows Jules walked the girl towards the bar.

'So how are your parents?' she asked. 'It's been a very long time since I last saw them.'

'Daddy's fine, thank you,' came the airy reply. 'Always busy, so I don't get to see him much. I'm afraid I can't tell you about Mummy; she left us when I was about nine and she's never been in touch since.'

Stunned, as much by the girl's apparent indifference as by the news itself, Jules said, 'I'm sorry to hear that. Do you know where she is now?'

Amelia shrugged. 'I guess she doesn't want to be found.' She was still looking around the bar, apparently inspecting it for only she knew what. 'Who did the paintings?' she asked. 'They're quite good.'

'They're all by local artists,' Jules told her. 'Daisy, Stephie and Dean put on a couple of exhibitions each year, usually at the town hall, and those that don't sell are given a few months on display here.'

Amelia nodded. 'She's got some sort of theatre company, hasn't she?' 'I saw the sign as I drove in, *The Hope Cove Performing Arts Society.*'

'It's not just theatre,' Jules replied, 'they make a lot of films as well, and stage concerts and dances and charity events. There's not much they aren't into.'

Amelia nodded again. 'Sweet,' she murmured, turning around as the pub door opened.

Seeing Tina, Stephie's mother, Jules lit up with relief – she'd worked hard enough with this girl for one day and was happy to be rescued. 'Tina, meet Amelia,' she announced cheerfully as the plump, pretty redhead finished a call. 'Amelia, this is Stephie's mother.'

'Nice to meet you, Amelia,' Tina smiled warmly. 'Are you new around here?'

'Not really,' Amelia replied.

Catching Tina's surprise at the shortness, Jules said to Amelia, 'Well I expect you want to go and join the others now. It's lovely seeing you again. Just follow the sound of voices and you'll find them.'

Amelia glanced at the stairs. 'Thank you,' she said quietly. 'It's lovely seeing you again too, Mrs Bright.'

'Oh, please call me Jules. Everyone does.'

'Jules,' Amelia repeated, as though finding the name unusual, and tossing her hair over one shoulder she wandered off in the direction she was being shown.

'So why did you find it odd?' Andee asked curiously as she put down her coffee. 'I mean, from what you've just described, I can think of several ways in which it

152

qualifies, but I'm interested to hear what you have to say.'

'Well, to begin with it was the door slamming in her face as she arrived,' Jules replied. 'There was no wind that day, not a breath of it, and no one came out of the kitchen to cause a draught, but if you'd heard the slam . . . It was hard enough to rattle the windows. It wasn't until later that I wondered if it was Ruby, and I think it probably was.'

Andee frowned. 'Ruby?'

In a sardonic tone, Jules said, 'Ruby the ghost. She lived with us the entire time we were at the pub.'

Surprised, but apparently deciding to go with it, Andee asked, 'So why did you think it was her?'

Jules shrugged. 'It was just a feeling . . . Actually, I sometimes wonder if she was behind another incident, years before, when a table-skittles ball seemed to acquire a life of its own and hit Amelia in the face. OK, I know how crazy it sounds, but I keep wondering if Ruby was able to sense something about the girl that the rest of us couldn't. Although, I have to admit, I could never warm to her, even as a child. She was spoiled rotten, that much was clear, but not in a normal, loving way, more in a "give her anything and shut her up" kind of way, and there was a look about her . . . Well, all I can say is think Chucky.'

Andee's eyebrows shot up.

'OK, she wasn't ugly like that,' Jules admitted, 'she was just colourless, stary-eyed, like she was seeing right through you and thinking horrible thoughts. Really strange for a girl of that age.'

Andee didn't disagree. 'Were there any other Ruby-type incidents?' she wondered.

Jules nodded slowly. 'Actually, there was one, after the door slam at the pub, when she came to have lunch with us one Sunday and a jug of scalding hot gravy ended up in her lap. She was so angry I thought she was going to smash the jug against the wall, or even throw it at someone. If she'd known who to blame, she might have, but even if not all ghosts are invisible, which was what she once said to Daisy, Ruby is.'

After a while, Andee said, 'So do you think it *was* a coincidence, her running into Daisy at the gym?'

Jules shook her head. 'No, I don't, but whether she had any specific plans in mind when she first came back, I've no idea. Nor can I tell you why she decided to come when she did. There must have been ample opportunities to befriend Daisy over the years, presuming she was visiting Crofton Park with her father. If she did, we never saw them, and when she did start coming to the pub, after meeting up with Daisy, she almost never talked about her father or anything else to do with her life.'

'But you know now that she'd been asked to leave several schools, junior and senior, and that she'd always had a problem making, or keeping friends?'

'Oh yes, we know that now. Actually, I knew it before, because her mother told me back when Amelia was no older than seven. Then it turned out that Stephie's cousin was at one of the schools Amelia had been excluded from and she had plenty of stories about the kind of things the girl got up to. They were horrible, even cruel some of them, especially where small animals or even birds were concerned. She'd use their innards, or beaks or tails to play sick jokes on other children. And apparently she had a very divisive nature, you know, always trying to come between friends, making up lies about people and trying to turn them against one another. When Stephie told me all this she and I, Dean too, tried to persuade Daisy to stop seeing the girl, but Daisy wouldn't listen. She felt sorry for her and kept insisting that we'd all be different and even a bit weird if we didn't have parents who loved us or friends who cared.' As tears welled in her eyes, Andee reached over to squeeze her hand.

'I'm sorry,' Andee whispered, 'I didn't mean to put you through it all again.'

Jules shook her head. 'I'm fine,' she assured her. 'It's not like I don't think about it every minute of every day, seeing, knowing what I should have done differently, wishing to God that I had . . .'

After a while, Andee asked, 'When did you find out the truth about her mother?'

Jules's eyes went down. 'At the same time that everyone else did,' she replied, 'but it made no difference, it was too late by then and I've heard other rumours since, that . . .' She took a breath. 'Let's just say it wouldn't surprise me if they're true.' She looked at Andee. 'Have you heard them?'

Andee nodded. 'And like you, I wouldn't be surprised if they're true.'

With a sigh, Jules said, 'I had the urge once to send Olivia Quentin details about the women's refuge. I wish I had, things might have turned out very differently if she'd come to us.'

'They might have, but you don't know that for certain, so I hope you're not blaming yourself.'

'Not blaming, exactly, but it goes to show how important it is to act on worthy instincts, even if you end up being told to mind your own business.'

Conceding the point, Andee said, 'So Stephie and Dean didn't like the girl . . .'

'None of Daisy's friends did, it was only Daisy who had time for her.'

'What about Joe? What did he think of her?'

'The same as the rest of us, although obviously he saw a lot less of her. He definitely took against her when she started trying to come between him and Daisy . . . The way she did that . . .' Jules shuddered. 'We should have done something about her then. We tried, of course, but there was never any changing Daisy's mind about someone she saw as an underdog, and as far as she was concerned Amelia was absolutely that . . .'

'Mum, look at this,' Daisy said, passing over her phone to Jules.

Wiping her hands, Jules took the mobile and frowned at the photo that had come with a text saying, *What do you think?*

'Is that Amelia?' Jules asked, knowing it was and wishing it wasn't.

'She's had her hair cut and coloured just like mine,' Daisy stated in a mock how-lovely sort of way. 'I don't know whether to be flattered, or spooked.'

Knowing exactly how she felt, Jules said, 'Well at least it suits her, sort of.'

Daisy took the phone back. 'I'll tell her you said that, she always likes to know what you think.'

Hoping that wasn't true, Jules carried on with the evening meal she was preparing, expecting to be asked at any minute if Amelia could join them, and wishing she could think of a way to say no that wouldn't earn her a lecture from Daisy on how important it was to be open-hearted and tolerant.

'Ah, here she is again,' Daisy declared, opening up a new text. '*Your mum's so lovely. Please tell her thank you for what she said. You're very lucky to have her.*'

Covering her real feelings with a twinkle, Jules said, 'And don't you forget it, young lady.'

'As if you'd ever let me,' Daisy shot back, and putting the phone down she returned to her iPad to carry on instant messaging with Joe. 'Oh no,' she groaned, 'he's having to change his flight and come later, because of a flaming football game.'

Only half listening, Jules said, 'Is that such a disaster?'

'It is for us. We don't get to spend enough time together as it is. I really miss him when he's not here.' Picking up the phone as it bleeped with another text, she said, 'Amelia again. *Did you get my last message? Just wondering because I haven't heard back.*' She sighed wearily. 'What does she want me to say?'

Jules popped a leg of lamb in the oven. It was the middle of a sunny Saturday afternoon in October with only a few customers left over from a hectic lunchtime downstairs, and a group of forty-something ladies starting to turn up for a birthday tea in the library. Later, with a local jazz band due to play in the function room, and most of the pub tables booked out for one of Marco's special Italian evenings, Jules, Kian and Daisy had all offered to help out where they were most needed.

Reading another text, Daisy said, 'Oh, that's brilliant. Stephie's saying she can come and lend a hand tonight if we need her, and she's pretty sure Dean will be able to get away too.'

'Angels, the pair of them,' Jules smiled. 'Talk to Misty, I'm sure she'll jump at the offer.'

A few minutes later, Daisy said, 'OK, so I've told Amelia that I know how lucky I am to have such a fabulous mum and I'm really happy to share you. Would you like to have her as a daughter?'

Jules's eyebrows rose.

Daisy swallowed a laugh. 'You are so transparent, and mean. Poor Amelia doesn't have anyone . . .'

'Let's not go there again. I'm afraid I can't feel as sorry for the girl as you do, which probably makes me a really wicked person, but I never claimed to be a saint. Now, when exactly is Joe arriving, so Dad or I can schedule in an airport run?'

'He's going to let me know as soon as the flights are confirmed.'

Looking up from her supper preparations, Jules realised Daisy was watching her, head propped on her hands. 'What?' she prompted.

'I'm just thinking.'

'About anything in particular?'

'Well, yes, I guess so. I mean, you know me and Joe are going to end up together, right?'

Jules cocked an eyebrow. 'I kind of had a feeling.'

Smiling, Daisy said, 'The trouble is, I don't know if

I want to go and live in the States. I mean, I do, obviously, to be with him, but it's going to mean leaving you and Dad and the grannies and everyone . . .' As tears filled her eyes Jules went to embrace her.

'You don't have to make any decisions yet,' she reminded her. 'There's plenty of time.'

'Except there isn't. I mean, I already know I want to go to uni here, either in Bristol or Exeter, which means I've already chosen you and Dad over him, and I feel so bad about it because I know he was really hoping I'd try to get into the same uni as him.'

'I'm sure he understands that you don't feel ready to leave your roots yet . . .'

'Of course he does. You know what he's like, he understands everything and never puts on any pressure, but I know he's afraid that I'll end up not wanting to leave England at all.'

'Then maybe he could come here when he's got his degree?'

Daisy shook her head. 'We've talked about that, but the law's different here, so his qualifications wouldn't work, and anyway he'd never get the kind of high-powered job in Britain that he would in the States.'

'If he was in London he might.'

'But his dad's got loads of connections over there that could help him get started with a really big firm.'

Of course Nicholas would have.

Since Daisy was still looking torn, Jules said, 'Listen, you'll work something out when you have to. And in the meantime you shouldn't get upset about it. Dad and I understand that you'll be flying the nest one of these days, and it's only right that you should.' She didn't add that it was going to break their hearts and suck all the life out of their home when it happened; that was a truth, a dread, Daisy never needed to know.

Gazing up into her eyes, Daisy said, 'I can't imagine ever wanting to leave you.'

Feeling the words curling lovingly around her heart, Jules smiled as she said, 'That's because you're still only seventeen and the time hasn't come for you to leave yet. When it does, believe me, it'll feel right, and Dad and I will support you in whatever you decide.'

With a twinkle Daisy said, 'It's no wonder all my friends would love to have you two as parents. You're so cool, and wise and easy-going and crazy – that's Dad, obviously, although he's not as crazy as he used to be, is he? I mean, he's still like really out there, and he gets involved in everything we do, but . . .' She shrugged. 'He's kind of different in a way. Still the best dad in the entire world, but different.'

Knowing she was to blame for the way a light had gone out in Kian four years ago, Jules turned away to hide her guilt and dismay. She might never have told him how she'd betrayed him, but he obviously knew that something had changed between them, and because of it the light he'd lost then had never really come back again.

Off went Daisy's phone with another text. 'Ah, it's about the charity walk next Sunday,' she announced. 'Did you register yet?'

'I did, and I need to pick up our T-shirts on Monday. I ordered thirty, is that enough?'

'I think so, but I'll check to make sure. Everyone wants to do it. Can we increase if we have to?'

'I'm sure we can.'

'Great. And our group's supporting Granny Marsha and the Alzheimer's Society. Do you think she'll be able to manage the walk herself? When I asked her she said right away that she wanted to, but half an hour later she'd forgotten all about it. Anyway, I think ten miles is too far for her,' Daisy added, reading another text. 'Right, Amelia's saying she'd LOVE to have you as a mother.'

Rolling her eyes, Jules looked up as Kian came in.

'Ah ha, everything that's Bright and beautiful in my world,' he declared, going to plant a kiss on Daisy's head. 'What are you up to?' Though he was looking at Jules, he didn't approach her, and because she wasn't sure what to do either, she ended up turning away.

'Just stuff,' Daisy answered. 'Are you coming on the charity walk with us next Sunday?'

'Sure, if I'm invited.'

'Did you register him, Mum?'

'No,' Jules replied, guiltily, 'but I will. How come you're back so early?' she asked Kian. 'We weren't expecting you until five.'

'Blasted Land Rover broke down,' he grumbled, going to put the kettle on. 'Can't do a safari without one, so mapping the new routes will have to wait. What news from Joe? Is he still arriving next Friday, as planned?'

'No, he's got a football game, so he'll be here on the Monday or Tuesday. You know he can drive now, don't you? He's even got his own car.'

'Which means can he borrow one while he's here?' Kian stated. 'We'll see, because it's a bit different driving in England to driving in the States. For a start, can he handle a stick shift?'

Daisy shrugged.

'OK, I'll give him a couple of lessons and take it from there. Anyone else want tea?'

'Not for me, I'm going to take a shower,' Daisy replied, still reading from her phone as she got to her feet. 'Great, Misty deffo wants Stephie and Dean to come in tonight, oh and Amelia's asking what we're all doing. I guess I should invite her?'

'Tell her you're working so it won't be much fun for her,' Jules advised.

'I don't think she'll mind about that. The alternative is probably being at home on her own.'

'Is her dad ever there?' Kian wondered.

'I guess, sometimes.'

'But otherwise she stays in that great big house all on her own?'

Daisy shrugged. 'There's a housekeeper and other staff around, although I don't think they live in. It sounds like an amazing place with its own indoor pool and stables and everything. I don't think she's short of things to do. I'll warn her that we're all working, but say that she's welcome to come over anyway. Actually, I don't think I invited her on the charity walk. I should probably do that. Oh, and we'll be able to see her new hair.'

'New hair?' Kian echoed.

Since Daisy had already gone, Jules said, 'She's had it cut short, curled and dyed blonde. Guess who that makes her look like?'

Kian's eyebrows rose. Then dismissing it, he said, 'Girls that age are always copying each other.'

Unable to deny that, Jules said, 'You really don't have a problem with Amelia, do you?'

He seemed baffled as he threw out his hands. 'Like Daisy, I feel sorry for her. You can see how lonely she is.'

Yes, Jules could see that, nevertheless she still couldn't summon the same sort of compassion for the girl that Kian and Daisy so easily managed. Nor could Aileen, who was at the pub later when Amelia turned up, looking so much like Daisy from the back that Aileen had already embraced her before realising her mistake.

'What's that all about?' she murmured to Jules, as Amelia, apparently thrilled with the success of her new look, went to perch on a stool at the end of the bar.

'I've no idea,' Jules murmured back as Stephie came to join them.

'You'll never guess what she just said to me,' Stephie whispered furiously. 'She only said that Joe *asked* her to cut her hair like Daisy's.'

Jules's eyes widened in shock.

'That is such bullshit,' Stephie seethed. 'He'd never do that, not in a million years. She is in such a fantasy world. I mean, apart from anything else there's no way he'd even have her number to get in touch and ask . . . Unless,' she added accusingly as Dean turned up beside her, '*you* gave her Joe's number. I heard her asking you for it the other day . . .'

'Yeah, and I really gave it to her,' Dean retorted sarcastically. 'What the hell do you take me for?'

'Well we all know that you'd love it if the weirdo

managed to split up Joe and Daisy so you could get a look-in.'

With a derisive sneer, Dean said, 'You don't know anything, Stephie, least of all what goes on between me and Daisy.'

'That's what you think,' Stephie muttered, as he walked away.

Used to their spats, Jules said, 'I thought he was over his crush on Daisy, and he and Joe always seem to get on so well.'

Stephie shrugged. 'I guess they do, on the surface, but that doesn't mean Dean's given up hope. Anyway, I hear Daisy's invited the weirdo to join us for the walk next Sunday?'

Aileen groaned. 'Just please don't leave her with me,' she implored. 'I never know what to say to her.'

'She's not interested in us,' Stephie told her. 'She's only interested in Daisy. And Joe, apparently, but he won't be here in time.'

'I'm not sure Amelia's coming either,' Jules informed them. 'The last I heard, she's going to be in London next weekend.'

'But of course she wasn't,' Jules said to Andee as they strolled along the promenade on the way to their cars. 'She turned up on the day of the walk, along with the rest of our group, bright and breezy, raring to go, with a T-shirt she'd had made up specially. Can you imagine my shock when I saw what she'd had printed on the back? *In Memory of Jules Bright*, in great big black letters.'

Andee glanced at her sideways. 'So what did you do?'

'I guess we made ourselves accept that there had been some confusion somewhere along the line and got on with the walk. You know, she didn't apologise or even seem particularly embarrassed about it, nor did she take the T-shirt off or cover it up. She just marched along there in front of me, making sure I could see it, until in the end Kian got so annoyed that he took off his own T-shirt and insisted she put it on.'

'Did she mind?'

'If she did she never said so. She just carried on walking with Daisy, arms linked as though trying to keep out the rest of Daisy's friends, while I followed with Aileen and the others. There were quite a lot of women from the refuge with us that day, raising money for their own cause, and here's what Amelia said to Daisy about them after the walk . . .'

'They're such a bunch of losers those women, don't you think? They ought to learn to stand up for themselves.'

Overhearing, Jules spun round in a fury, cutting right across Daisy as she said, 'Amelia, you have no idea what most of those women have been through, and I hope you never find out.' Even as she spoke the words she wondered how wrong she might be. After all, given what she remembered about Amelia's parents it was quite possible the girl knew more about domestic abuse than most.

Flushing as she shrugged, Amelia said, 'I was just saying, that's all. I didn't mean to cause any offence.'

Softening her tone, Jules said, 'Well it would have if any of them had heard you.'

Coming to join them, and apparently unaware of the tension, Stephie said, 'Hey Daze, what time will you and Joe be getting back from the airport tomorrow?'

Relaxing, Daisy said, 'I'll check with Dad, but it should be around midday.'

Amelia turned accusingly to her. 'You didn't tell me Joe was coming tomorrow. I thought he was coming on Tuesday.'

Daisy and Stephie glanced at one another. 'He managed to get an earlier flight,' Daisy informed her.

'And what's it to you anyway?' Stephie wanted to know.

Looking as though she'd been slapped, Amelia said to Daisy, 'Sorry, but I didn't think we had any secrets from each other.'

As Stephie gasped Daisy shrugged uncomfortably. 'It wasn't a secret. I guess the subject just didn't come up.'

'What is she on?' Stephie muttered, as Amelia turned back to the car park where bottles of water were disappearing fast and blisters were being exposed to the air.

'Why on earth would she be so hurt that you didn't tell her Joe was coming?' Jules asked a few minutes later as Amelia drove off in her swanky sports car without saying goodbye.

Daisy shook her head. 'I've no idea.'

Stephie said, 'I wonder what he'll think of her new hair when he sees it. You know what she's hoping for, don't you, Daze? She's hoping he'll take one look at her and think wow, what the hell am I doing with the genuine article when I can have a full-on fruitcake fake?'

As they laughed, Jules took out her phone to read a text. *Sorry for what I said about the women. Didn't mean to upset you. Axxx*

'She can only have got around the corner by now,' Daisy remarked when Jules showed her the message. 'She must be feeling really bad, poor thing. I'll text and ask if she'd like to get together while Joe's here so she'll know I'm not trying to keep secrets, or whatever she's thinking, and frankly that has to be anyone's guess.'

As it turned out Amelia spent the following two weeks in London, and no one heard a word from her until she returned, three days after Joe had gone back to the States.

'So do you think she was deliberately avoiding him?' Andee asked.

'Who knows, but if she was it definitely wasn't the case when Joe came back at Christmas with Em and her family. Amelia joined us that year while her father went skiing. She hated skiing, she said, she'd rather spend the whole time on her own in the house than have to go and be with all his boring friends.'

'Knowing what we do now,' Andee commented, 'it was no doubt a relief to them all that she decided not to go.'

'You mean because of the way she would make mischief and try to cause arguments? I'm sure you're right.'

'So what happened when she came to you?' Andee prompted.

'Well, to begin with she was quite helpful and

seemed really glad to be with us, but then she started flirting with Joe, so outrageously that none of us quite knew how to handle it. If it had been a regular sort of flirting it might have been easier, but she didn't seem to know the meaning of subtlety, or modesty . . .'

'Do you fancy me now?' Amelia teased Joe, fluffing out her pretty blonde curls and batting her eyelids. 'Don't I look just like Daisy?' In truth, with her pale skin and freckles, plump cheeks and close-set eyes she was a sad, even pathetic caricature of Daisy.

'It's cool,' Joe mumbled awkwardly. 'Where is Daisy, does anyone know?'

'She was downstairs playing pool with Mattie, Oscar and Dean the last time I saw her,' Jules replied.

'I'll come and look for her with you,' Amelia offered, linking his arm as he started to leave the kitchen. 'We could always go via one of the bedrooms.'

As Jules turned round in shock, Joe quickly tried to detach himself.

'It's OK, I'm good,' he told Amelia, obviously seriously annoyed by the suggestion.

'But I want to come too,' Amelia pouted. 'Please let me *come*, Joe.'

Joe's confused dark eyes went desperately to Jules.

'Amelia, can you give me a hand here,' Jules said, not making it a question.

'Oh no, it's fine,' Amelia responded, 'I'm sure you can manage, and I need to help Joe find Daisy. Of course,' she said to Joe, 'I know I'm not as pretty as she is, but I promise you I have other things going for me.'

Before Jules could step in again Joe said, 'Daisy and I have things we need to discuss. We'll catch up with you later, OK?'

Amelia looked crushed. 'But Daisy doesn't have any secrets from me,' she protested, 'so she really won't mind if I'm there too, and I love listening to you talk. The American accent really does it for me.'

'Amelia,' Jules said firmly, 'please let go of Joe and come and give me a hand.'

With a curious little shrug, as though suddenly fine about doing as she was told, Amelia breezed back to the table and sank down on a chair. 'So what do you want me to do?' she enquired, picking up the salt and pepper pots.

As Jules started to answer, her mother and Em came in from their walk on the beach.

'Oh God, not her,' Amelia sighed under her breath.

Jules glared at her, shock robbing her of an immediate response. 'Please tell me I didn't just hear you correctly,' she finally demanded.

Amelia's expression was bland. 'I didn't say anything,' she insisted. 'Hi Em, hi Marsha, did you have a good walk?'

Ignoring her, Em said to Jules, 'Does Amelia have a problem with someone?'

'No, not at all,' Amelia assured her. 'I think Marsha's really sweet. I was just repeating the sort of thing Stephie says when she sees Marsha coming.'

Stunned as much by the outrageousness of the lie as its clumsiness, Jules's eyes went to Em, who was clearly equally shocked. However, Jules really didn't want to get into a scene with the girl while her mother was there, so deciding to let it go she turned to Marsha, whose wind-reddened cheeks were shining as brightly as her watery eyes.

'Em and I are going for a walk,' Marsha informed her.

Jules smiled sadly, though she was relieved that her mother seemed to know who Em was now, which hadn't been the case when Em had first arrived.

'You've got a friend called Em,' she'd told Jules as Em had embraced her warmly. 'Lovely girl, she is. Just like a sister to you.'

'This is her, Mum, but she's all grown up now.'

Marsha had simply smiled and patted Em's hand.

Now, Jules said gently, 'You've just come back from a walk, so would you like a cup of tea?'

Marsha blinked.

'I'll make it,' Amelia offered, springing to her feet.

'It's OK,' Jules said, putting a hand out to stop her. 'Why don't you go downstairs now and find the others?'

'Ah ha, so I'm dismissed?'

Jules's eyes narrowed.

'Daisy,' Marsha murmured, but to Jules's relief she wasn't looking at Amelia, she was looking at Jules.

'Sit down, Mum,' Jules urged. 'I'll put the kettle on and Amelia, perhaps you could go and ask someone in the kitchen if they have some cakes or scones to go with our tea?'

'On my way,' Amelia trilled, and with a little wave she took herself off, presumably to do as she was told.

Going to close the door behind her, Em said, 'What's the matter with the girl? Is she always like that?'

Jules shrugged and shook her head. 'We've never had her to stay for this long before. If I'd known she was going to behave like this . . . You should have heard her with Joe just now. I guess you realise the hair is all about trying to look like Daisy.'

'Obviously, and Daisy enjoys having her as a friend?'

'I'm not sure enjoy is the right word. She puts up with her because no one else will, including her family, apparently.'

Sighing, Em sank down at the table and gently eased a knife from Marsha's hand.

With a smile Jules said, 'If you'd seen Joe's face . . . He looked petrified, poor guy, and I don't imagine there's much that scares him these days.'

Em grudgingly smiled too. 'He's a great guy. I've grown very fond of him over the years.'

Thinking of the many vacations they'd all spent together, Jules said, 'I actually feel he's a member of the family now, and apparently his father and step-mother say the same about Daisy.'

'I can confirm that. They adore her. It's just a shame you never get to see her with them. OK, we won't go there, but I just need to know, are things any better with Kian these days?'

Jules's lips flattened. 'They're not any worse,' she admitted, 'but even after all this time we're still not back to the way we were before.'

'So no chance of another baby?'

Jules's heart contracted as she glanced at her mother. Since it was clear that Marsha was in a world of her own, she said, 'We're still making love, if that's what you mean. Maybe not as often as we used to, but when

171

you've been married as long as we have . . . Is it the same for you?' She really needed Em to say yes, and when Em nodded she felt a huge rush of relief.

'Jules, are we going for a walk?' Marsha asked, getting to her feet.

'You've just come back,' Jules told her, 'and we're about to have a cup of tea.'

Marsha blinked and sat down again. 'Where's Aileen?'

'She went to pick up some things from the farm store with Kian and Don,' Em told her. 'In fact, they're probably back by now, so they'll be down in the bar.'

Marsha looked at her hands, and as a fat tear plopped on to them Jules suddenly felt like crying too. 'What is it, Mum?' she asked, going to put her arms around her.

'I'm a silly old fool,' Marsha whispered brokenly. 'I don't ever seem to know what I'm doing or what's going on, and I'm such a burden for you . . .'

'No, you're not a burden,' Jules protested, 'we love you and we'll always be here for you, so you mustn't worry about anything.'

'No, mustn't worry,' Marsha echoed distantly. 'That's what Daddy always says, mustn't worry. Will he be here soon?'

Jules looked at Em helplessly. There was no point trying to explain something to someone who'd lost the ability to process it.

'In Amelia's case I wonder if she ever even had the ability in the first place,' Jules was saying to Andee as they reached her car alongside a row of beach huts.

'She certainly didn't seem to operate the same way as everyone else.'

'So I take it nothing ever came of the flirtation with Joe?'

'Not in the way she wanted, that's for sure, because it's what prompted Daisy to cool it with her in the end. It didn't happen that Christmas, although I know Daisy was a bit freaked out by the way she was carrying on and she definitely didn't like the way Amelia kept walking into her room without knocking, especially when Joe was there. Anyway, when the new year came and everyone went their separate ways we didn't hear from Amelia again until the end of January. She was in London, apparently, with her father, and a boyfriend we'd never heard anything about until suddenly, she couldn't seem to text about anything else.'

'Did you ever meet him?'

'No. To be honest, we weren't even sure he existed. She just kept sending Daisy messages about how fantastic he was, and how wonderful it was to be in love, and how she couldn't wait to bring him to Kesterly.'

'But she never did.'

Jules shook her head.

'Did she ever send photos? They're all so mad about Instagram and selfies and so on these days.'

'No photos that we ever saw. When she finally showed up again she said she'd broken up with him because he was getting too serious, and she'd rather be here with Daisy and everyone, than in London where she hated it.'

'How did Daisy react to that?'

'She seemed OK with it at first, but then Amelia started to get clingier than ever, wanting to go everywhere Daisy went, be involved in everything Daisy did . . . She even used to wait outside the college to offer Daisy a lift home at the end of the day, which Daisy accepted at first, but then Stephie didn't want to get into the car any more, so Daisy decided she wouldn't either.'

'Was Amelia upset by that?'

'Was she ever. She came to see me in a terrible rage, telling me I didn't know what Stephie was like, that she was a liar, and that she'd been saying evil things about Daisy behind her back and Daisy ought to be warned . . . She ranted on and on until finally I had to ask her to leave.'

'So that was when Daisy stopped seeing her?'

'Not quite. She carried on for a while, even though Stephie and the others made it clear that they didn't want her around. It was when Joe came at Easter and Amelia started making moves on him again that Daisy finally told her that they needed to cool it.'

'I'm sorry, but I have to say this,' Daisy told Amelia as gently as she could. 'The way you are with Joe . . . I mean, it's kind of embarrassing, and it's not really the way you should be with someone else's boyfriend.'

Amelia regarded her with bewildered, yet hostile eyes. 'So what do you want me to do?' she snapped. 'I mean, if you don't want to share Joe, I get it, but I want you to know, I'd be happy to share him with you if he were mine.'

'But that's just weird,' Daisy protested. 'Surely you can see that.'

Amelia's face remained cold and pinched as she stared at her.

Daisy looked at her mother, apparently lost for what to say next.

Since she was there because Daisy had felt anxious about handling the situation on her own, Jules said, 'Amelia, what Daisy's trying to say is that you could both probably do with some space from each other for a while.'

'But why?' Amelia demanded. 'I don't feel as though I need any space.'

'Well, I'm afraid Daisy does.'

'It's not that I don't like you,' Daisy quickly added, 'it's just that things have become kind of a bit intense, and I've got loads of college work to get through . . .'

'I can help you with that. You're taking the same subjects as I did.'

Daisy looked at her mother again. They both knew that wasn't true, but neither of them attempted to challenge it.

'It's OK, Joe's helping Daisy while he's here,' Jules told her, 'and she's doing pretty well anyway. There's just a lot of it.'

'Please, don't be upset,' Daisy urged. 'It's not like I'm saying I never want to see you. We can still get together, just not as often, and you don't need to text me every day, or call up, we can just, you know, cool it a bit.'

Looking as injured and incensed as she clearly felt, Amelia said, 'You don't know the first thing about friendship, do you? Everyone else laughs about you behind your back, they think you're pathetic . . . If it weren't for me they'd have nothing to do with you . . .'

'Amelia,' Jules interrupted.

Rounding on her, Amelia cried, 'And I'm the one who tells everyone it's rubbish about your husband having affairs all over the place. They all gossip about you, making things up . . .'

'*Amelia*,' Jules shouted over her. 'It's time for you to leave.'

'Don't worry, I'm going,' Amelia raged, starting for the door. 'But you'll be sorry about this. You know my dad's a really important lawyer, and no way will he allow anyone to get away with treating me the way you have.'

Chapter Eight

Jules was at home now, sitting at the kitchen table with the answerphone flashing on the counter top behind her and her thoughts still hopelessly trapped in the past. Andee had wanted to come with her, had obviously been concerned about leaving her on her own after their talk, but Jules had insisted she was fine.

She wasn't, of course, but nor was she Andee's problem. She'd taken up enough of the ex-detective's time, and though she couldn't stop this journey now she'd begun, she felt instinctively that she needed to go on alone.

Of course Amelia's threat about her father had been so absurd that neither she nor Daisy had taken any notice of it. However, what she'd said about Kian had upset Daisy a lot.

'You don't believe her, do you Mum?' Daisy had cried worriedly as the door slammed behind Amelia. 'You know what a liar she is, and Dad would never . . . I mean, it's just not the way he is.'

'Dad would never what?' Kian demanded, coming into the kitchen. When neither of them answered he said, 'What's going on? And what was all the shouting about just now?'

'It was Amelia,' Daisy explained. 'She got upset because I told her I didn't want to see so much of her. To get back at us she . . .' She glanced awkwardly at Jules.

'She said,' Jules continued, 'that you were having affairs all over the place . . .'

Kian frowned.

'And we know it's not true,' Daisy jumped in, 'because we know what a liar she is.'

There was a horrible silence as Kian stared at Jules. 'Did you believe her?' he said coldly.

'No, of course not,' Jules retorted, though a part of her had, or had maybe wanted to if only to ease her own conscience.

'So why are we even having the discussion?' he demanded.

'We're not!' Daisy exclaimed. 'I mean, we were, but only to say what a meddling liar she is, and how she's always trying to make trouble. For God's sake, she's doing it now between you two, and you're letting her. So stop. Both of you.'

Seeing how tense Kian remained, Jules decided to back down first.

'You're right,' she said to Daisy, 'we should know better than to allow her to manipulate us like that.'

'Maybe she wouldn't be able to if you didn't have a problem with trust,' Kian commented acidly.

'I don't have a problem with trust,' she protested. 'I've already said I didn't believe her, so can we leave it at that?'

'Come on Dad, Joe's going to be back any minute with Dean and we don't want them walking into the middle of a domestic.'

Never able to resist his daughter, Kian allowed her to take him down to the bar while Jules stood at the kitchen window, staring out at the estuary and doing her best not to weep for all she'd spoiled with one random act of selfishness.

They hadn't heard from Amelia for months after Daisy's little chat with her, no texts or Facebook messages, no phone calls or emails. At first the silence had surprised, even unnerved, them a little; was she plotting some terrible revenge, watching them from the shadows, digging up some awful dirt that even they knew nothing about? Maybe she was trying to persuade her father to bring some fantastic lawsuit against them.

In the end it became a bit of a joke, especially with Stephie and Dean, but Daisy, typically, worried about how much Amelia might be hurting, so she began sending texts urging Amelia to let her know how she was. She even invited her to the pub if she was around.

Finally, after a few weeks, she received a text saying, *Life hectic here in London, too busy to get together. Ax*

Satisfied that Amelia was moving on with her life, and apparently not spending nearly as much time as Daisy and Jules reliving that awful break-up scene, Daisy put it out of her mind and became so immersed in exams, the trip to California she and Joe were planning for the summer, the shooting of a short comedy film Stephie and Dean had written and all the other things that filled her teenage world that she all but forgot about Amelia.

As did Jules. Amelia's life might be hectic, but so was hers, especially with her mother needing so much more attention now. She was going downhill so fast that Jules and Kian decided to move her over to the pub, in spite of her protests. She really couldn't cope on her own. In fact, she was so bewildered or distressed most of the time that she was alarming the neighbours and even fighting off the carers who came to help her shower and dress in the morning, thinking they were there to harm her.

So Jules and Kian settled her into the room next to Daisy's, with Jules taking on the care herself, often assisted by Aileen, while Daisy spent what little spare time she had taking her granny for walks on the beach, or going through old photograph albums with her. Marsha always loved having Daisy around; Daisy could make her laugh in a way no one else could, although she often confused her with Jules, when she'd tell her how happy she was that she'd met Kian and brought all those lovely Irish people into their lives.

'They'll keep us safe,' she would tell Daisy. 'They're good people and I'm not afraid of them, though I probably ought to be.'

Or she'd pat Daisy's hand and say, 'You'll have a baby one day, you wait and see.'

'I'm that baby, Granny,' Daisy would tell her, 'but I'm all grown up now.'

Marsha usually blinked at her in a kindly way as she said, 'Of course, you're Daisy, you're Daddy's all things Bright and beautiful.'

Those were the good days; the bad days could be beyond distressing, when Marsha screamed and choked and soiled herself in fear of only she knew what. Kian generally took charge on those occasions, partly because he had the physical strength to deal with her, and because he seemed to have a knack for calming her.

There was so much going on in their lives around that time that when, in late July, Daisy received a text from Amelia, Jules read it and said, 'Who's A?'

Daisy rolled her eyes. 'Duh! Amelia,' she replied.

Frowning, Jules returned to the message. *OMG, have found out where my mother is. In bits. Don't know what to do. At Crofton Park. Please come. Ax*

Jules looked at Daisy.

Daisy shrugged.

'Are you going to go?' Jules asked, willing her to say no.

'Go where?' Kian wanted to know, glancing up from the paper.

Jules passed him Daisy's mobile.

As he read the message Daisy said to Jules, 'I have to go. I mean, finding her mother . . . It's going to be a major thing for her.'

Jules didn't doubt that, but with Amelia's track record of lying . . . 'When was the last time you heard from her?' she asked carefully.

Daisy shrugged. 'Ages ago, but what's that got to do with anything?'

Jules wasn't sure. 'You're about to go to California with Joe,' she reminded her, 'so do you really want to get involved in this when you can't be there for her after today?'

Daisy threw out her hands. 'I don't see how I can

181

turn her down,' she cried. 'If she's found her mother, and she's asking me to go and see her . . .'

'I understand that you want to be supportive . . .'

'Of course I do, because I can't imagine what it would be like to grow up without you, to not have you there for me every step of the way, knowing what I'm thinking – which is really annoying, by the way – to care and love and all that rubbish, in spite of everything . . . That's what mothers do, and she had so little of that. In fact, I reckon it could have been us rejecting her that pushed her into looking for her mum and now she's found her she needs to share it with us, and ask our advice.'

Jules stared at her hard. 'So what are you going to tell her?' she asked.

'I've no idea until I find out where her mother is, and what the circumstances are. Mum, I can't just ignore her. It would be so mean.'

'Of course, I'm just thinking . . .' What was she thinking?

'Do you think I should go, Dad?'

'I don't see why not,' he replied, glancing at Jules. 'In fact, I can drop you if you like. I'm meeting Geoff Peters at the Castle in half an hour and it's on the way.'

'Great,' Daisy cried, giving him a hug, 'I'll get my bag,' and off she went to her room, already texting Amelia to let her know she was coming.

'What's the matter?' Kian asked Jules as she stood staring after Daisy.

Jules's eyes went to his. 'Will you pick her up on your way back?' she asked.

'Sure, if she's ready to leave. If not, Amelia will probably bring her.'

Yes, of course, Amelia had a car – so why hadn't she offered to come and collect Daisy?

By seven that evening Daisy still wasn't back. Jules had tried calling and texting, but she was constantly directed to voicemail, and so far there had been no texts back.

'This just isn't like her,' she said anxiously to Kian. 'She's always got her phone on. Tell me again what she said when you rang to ask if she wanted a lift home.'

Finishing an email, he replied, 'Just that Amelia would bring her later.'

'Is that all?'

'That's all.'

'How did she sound?'

'What do you mean, how did she sound?'

'Was she upset, in a rush, laughing . . . ?'

He shrugged. 'She sounded normal.'

Still not quite satisfied, Jules forced herself to carry on checking the invoices in front of her, needing to get them approved by the morning.

Half an hour later she tried Daisy again.

'Her battery must be flat,' Kian decided, getting up to pour them both a drink.

It was possible, it happened, but Amelia must have a charger, or if she didn't, she'd surely let Daisy use her phone.

Sending a text to Stephie to ask if she had Amelia's number, Jules said, 'I hope they haven't gone off on some crazy mission to confront the mother.'

With raised eyebrows, Kian said, 'If they have, it's not likely to end well.'

Jules threw him a look.

Sighing, he picked up his own phone. 'I might still have her father's number,' he said. 'I guess he could be at the house. If not, he should be able to give us Amelia's number.'

As Jules watched him scroll and dial, she was doing her best not to overreact, but her imagination was taking her to such terrible places that she was finding it hard to make herself think straight.

Taking a breath, she reminded herself that Daisy was a young adult now, independent, sensible and considerate, so there was bound to be a simple explanation for this silence.

Finding himself connected to Quentin's voicemail, Kian said, 'Hey, Anton, Kian Bright here, at the Mermaid in Kesterly. I dropped Daisy at Crofton Park earlier to meet Amelia, and we thought she'd be back by now. If you can shed any light on where they might be will you give us a call? Or text me Amelia's number?' In spite of the lightness of his tone Jules could tell he was starting to worry now too.

'From the ringtone,' he said, 'it sounds like Quentin's abroad.'

Jules snatched up her phone as it beeped with a text.

It was from Stephie. *Sorry, don't have it. Everything OK?*

Not sure, Jules texted back, *Daisy went up there this pm and hasn't come back yet.*

A moment later Stephie rang. 'How come she went up there?' she demanded. 'I thought she didn't want any more to do with her.'

After explaining about the texts earlier, Jules said, 'I'm afraid they might have gone off to confront the mother, except surely Daisy would have let me know, and anyway she should still have been back by now. She's flying to the States in the morning and she hasn't finished packing.'

'There'll be a reasonable explanation,' Stephie assured her firmly. 'God knows what it is, but we'll find out soon enough. Meantime, I'll try Dean to find out if he has Amelia's number.'

As she rang off Jules had to force herself to breathe steadily.

Glancing at the time, Kian said, 'Maybe we should take a drive up there. OK, I know Daisy might not appreciate us crashing in . . .'

Jules was on her feet. 'I just need to check on Mum.'

'I'll get someone up from the bar to stay with her while we're gone,' Kian said, and picking up his keys he made for the stairs.

After finding her mother dozing in front of the TV, Jules ran down to the bar, passing Romana, a sweet Polish girl who helped in the pub, on her way up to sit with Marsha.

It took her a while to get through the garden tables with so many people around that she knew, but eventually she found Kian in the car park with two of his cousins, Finn and Liam.

'We're going to tag along,' Finn told her, 'just in case we have to go searching the pubs in the village. It'll be easier if there are more of us.'

Jules didn't argue, or allow herself to engage with how anxious she was feeling, she simply climbed into the Range Rover and waited for Kian to start the engine.

Throughout the twenty-minute drive they scanned

every inch of the roadside for any signs of a break-down, or a hitch-hiker, or anything at all that might speak of Daisy, but the densely clustered wilderness beyond the lay-bys and ditches offered no more than shadowy glimpses of this impenetrable stretch of moor. They checked every passing car in case someone was giving Daisy a lift back to town; they even pulled over to examine an old trainer that Kian spotted in a pothole.

By the time they arrived at Crofton Park Jules was clutching her phone so hard her hands ached. While the rational side of her continued to insist there was a perfectly logical explanation for why Daisy wasn't in touch, there was another side that couldn't see anything logical about this at all.

Jumping out of the car as they came to a stop at the gates she went to ring the entryphone, trying to peer through the tiny cracks in the metal-studded wood to see into the grounds beyond. It wasn't possible to make out any more than a sliver of roughly tarmacked driveway.

As Kian joined her she rang the bell again. 'Someone has to be home,' she muttered impatiently. 'There are staff. Do they live in?'

'I've no idea,' he replied, signalling to Finn and Liam to come and give him a leg-up. Using their hands as a foothold he hoisted himself to the top of the gates and looked around. 'Daisy!' he shouted. 'Daisy, are you in there?'

The only answer was the sweetly melodic sound of birds singing and the hum of distant traffic.

'Can you see anyone?' Finn asked.

Kian shook his head.

'What about Amelia's car?' Jules wanted to know.

Again he shook his head. 'I can't see anything past the trees apart from the roof of the house.'

As he came down again Jules jabbed a finger to the bell and held it there.

'They must have gone off to find the mother,' Kian stated.

'Or they're in the village somewhere,' Finn suggested. 'Liam and I'll go check it out.'

Jules's heart leapt as her mobile rang, and thudded with hope when she saw it was Stephie again. 'Have you heard from her?' she gasped. *Please, please say that you have. Please. Please.*

'No, nothing,' Stephie replied. 'Have you?'

'No. We're at Amelia's now, but there's no sign of them. Kian, call Anton Quentin again and ask if he knows where Amelia's mother is.'

As Kian made the call, Jules said to Stephie, 'I take it Dean didn't have the number?'

'I'm still waiting to hear from him. I guess his parents have got him on some religious love-in. You know, I reckon her phone's run out of battery.'

'It's possible,' Jules replied, clutching at the straw like a fading lifeline. 'I should go. I'll call as soon as we've found her.'

As she rang off Kian said, 'I still can't get through to Quentin, so I left another message,' and clicking on the line again he said, abruptly, 'Danny. What's up?' His eyes went to Jules. 'No idea, mate, that's what we're trying to find out. Yeah, we're up at Crofton Park now. Finn and Liam have just gone to check the village . . . OK, thanks. Let me know if you . . . Right, good.' As he rang off he clicked on to take another call. 'Ma? Are you OK?'

'What's going on?' Jules heard Aileen shout down the line. 'Where's our Daisy?'

'I'm not sure, Ma,' he replied, looking paler than Jules could bear, 'we're trying to find her. I guess you didn't hear from her?'

'Not since this morning. I thought she'd broken off with that Quentin girl.'

'She came to help her with a . . . situation. It'll all be sorted out, so don't you worry. There's another call coming in now and it might be her.' As he checked the ID he shook his head at Jules and said, 'Hey, Terry. How are you doing?'

Jules's phone was ringing now. It was Ruthie, followed by Bridget, followed by Trish and Steve . . . Word was spreading like wildfire; everyone wanted to know if it was true that Daisy was missing and to be told what they could do to help.

Though Jules knew they all meant well, she wished to God they'd stop calling, because their concern was pushing her right to the brink of all-out panic.

Mummy! Mummy! Help me, please . . . The screams tore silently through the night, seeming as real to her as the terrible fear in her heart.

Shaking her head to try and stop the voices, she listened as Kian barked into his phone. 'Finn? What news? Did you find her?' As he listened to the reply his eyes remained bleak and Jules wanted to scream in frustration. 'No sign of her so far in the village,' he told Jules. 'Let's take a drive round to see if there's a back way in.'

After following a track that hugged the perimeter wall they eventually came to another set of gates as impenetrable as those at the front, though smaller. Once again Jules tried the bell, but couldn't even tell if it was working since there was no confirming buzzer, nor did it elicit a response.

Suddenly she said to Kian, 'I think we should call the police.'

Pushing a hand through his hair he said, shakily, 'She's almost eighteen, and Amelia's twenty-one. No one's going to take anything seriously until they've been gone for at least forty-eight hours.'

'But if we tell them she's supposed to be getting a flight tomorrow . . .'

'That might do it,' he conceded. 'And if we could tell them where the mother is . . .'

'Well we can't,' Jules broke in furiously, 'and that's what's really bothering me. I think the girl was lying again, and if I'm right then why did she want to see Daisy, and where the hell are they now?'

By the time they returned to the pub the estuary was basking in the kind of molten-gold sunset that made everything and everyone seem vaguely surreal. Jules could only wish she was in a dream as she and Kian found most of their friends and family waiting for the good news they didn't have.

'It's not that late,' someone said as they passed, 'I'll lay money she's back here any minute.'

'It's not like her to make her parents worry,' Jules heard someone else commenting. 'She's always such a considerate girl.'

'Has anyone spoken to her boyfriend?'

'He's in the States. He probably doesn't even know.'

'Is it true Amelia's mother upped and left her when she was a child?'

'Poor thing.'

'Daisy's always been such a good friend to her.'

'Daisy's good to everyone. She's like her parents in that respect. Can never do enough for you.'

'Did anyone ask around the village to see if they knew where Amelia's mother was these days?'

'We did, me and Liam,' Finn answered, 'but we couldn't find anyone.'

As Aileen took Jules's icy hands, she said firmly, 'Let's go upstairs where it's a bit quieter.'

Turning to Kian, Jules said, 'How much longer did the police say we should wait?'

White-faced and tense, he said, 'A couple more hours. If she isn't back, or we haven't heard from her by then, I'll call someone higher up to see if I can get some action.'

As her head went down and he pulled her into his arms she longed for everyone else to leave. She didn't want them all here for this reason; they were making everything feel so much more serious and foreboding.

'Stephie's just arrived,' Kian whispered into her hair.

Jules turned round and seeing Stephie surrounded by most of the Performing Arts Society, she had a hard job holding back tears.

'We weren't sure if there was anything we could do,' Stephie said, embracing Jules, 'so we thought we'd come over and find out.'

'Thanks, but I don't think there's anything for the

moment,' Jules replied. 'It's a bit of a waiting game, I'm afraid. Any word from Dean?'

'Still nothing. I'm sure she's all right,' Stephie insisted, though Jules could see how worried she was.

'Of course,' Jules smiled. 'Maybe they've seen Amelia's mother, and things are going so well that Daisy doesn't like to interrupt . . .' Turning to Kian she said, 'We should check the hospital in case there's been an accident.'

'I did that half an hour ago,' Danny told them, swaggering in from outside, 'nothing then, but it's always worth checking again.'

Kian made the call and received the same response that Danny had.

'Mary-Jane's got her car,' Stephie announced, 'so we could drive up to Amelia's again to see if they're back yet.'

Realising they were desperate to do something, Jules waved them on and took the drink Misty was pushing into her hand. She watched Kian try to take the top off a pint and realised he was finding it as difficult to swallow as she knew she would if she tried. She hated seeing him like that, felt angry with him for it. She needed him to be his usual self, laughing, joking and so confident that Daisy would be back any minute that he could down his drink in one go, put the glass on the bar and order another.

'Come on,' Aileen whispered, 'we ought to go check on your mother.'

They found Romana watching the TV alone.

'She wanted to go to her room,' Romana explained, 'so I helped her there and she was fast asleep when I looked in a few minutes ago.'

After thanking the girl, Jules went with Aileen to Marsha's room, and felt an awful weight come over her to see her slumped so awkwardly in an armchair, her knees gaping and yoghurt stains down her front. She looked so pathetic and undignified, so not the woman she used to be.

'She needs putting to bed,' Aileen said gently. 'I'll see to it, don't you worry.'

Though she'd normally have insisted on doing it herself, or at least helping, Jules left Aileen to it and wandered along the hall into Daisy's room. Though it was no longer the child's underwater emporium it used to be, there were still a number of mermaids around, along with giant daisies in tall glass vases, posters on the sea-foam walls from various Performing Arts productions, and cleverly assembled montages of photographs of Daisy with Joe, or Kian, or her grannies. There were dozens more with her friends, and even more from across the years with her mother. The shot that had pride of place on a special table, along with various gifts from Joe and Ruby's shoe, was one of her and Jules laughing fit to burst during one long hot summer at the lake.

Stepping over the open suitcase on the floor, she went to sit on the bed and taking out her phone she called Daisy's number again. 'Hey, sweetheart,' she said hoarsely into the voicemail, 'I know you're probably trying to get hold of me and can't for some reason, but don't stop trying, OK? I'm keeping my phone with me, so's Dad, and we can always come and get you.' She sat quietly for a moment, not wanting to ring off, but not sure what else to say. 'I hope you haven't run into any difficulties with Amelia's mother, presuming that's where you've gone . . . She always seemed such a sweet lady the couple of times I saw her. Anyway, call me as soon as you can and let's get you home. I can see from your suitcase that you've hardly made a start on your packing . . .'

As her voice trailed off she ended the call and buried her face in her hands. She hadn't heard any imagined screams in a while and couldn't be sure whether that was good or bad. Maybe it simply meant that her mind had gone into shutdown, except it hadn't because she was still being tormented by the most terrible fears.

Hearing a message drop into Daisy's mailbox, Jules went to sit at the laptop. Since Daisy had never been secretive, it was easy to see that her most recent emails and social-media messages were from Joe, wondering where she was and why he hadn't heard from her all day.

Stop freaking me out, Daisy Daze, tell me you're def still coming tomorrow.

OK, reckon you're having some kind of techno breakdown over there, so just to let you know I'll be at O'Hare to collect you tomorrow as arranged. Tickets to California booked for next Tuesday. Great news, my cousin Wendy and her husband can put us up in SF, and one of Dad's ex-patients has the heart (ha ha, OK not funny) to give us his summer house for a week in Monterey. How lucky are we? Still trying to get tickets for Buena Vista Social Club at the Hollywood Bowl. Should be amazing if we can get them. Going to send you all this by text now in the hope your phone's still working. LYM Jx

LYM – love you madly.

Jules only knew that because Daisy had told her.

Wondering if she should message Joe to let him know there might be a delay in Daisy's arrival, she checked to see if he was online right now. He didn't seem to be, but she started to type anyway.

Hi Joe, it's Jules here. I'm afraid Daisy's gone off on some mad mission with Amelia to find Amelia's mother and she hasn't come back yet. Actually, we're getting a bit worried in case they've broken down somewhere and can't find a signal to call for help . . .

Looking at the words she saw how pathetic they were, even delusional, because even if there wasn't a signal a passer-by would surely have stopped by now to offer assistance, or a lift . . .

Oh God, if they'd got into a stranger's car . . .

Feeling her head starting to spin, she turned away from the computer and looked around the room again. Spotting Ruby's shoe she took it from its special place and held it close to her heart.

'Where is she, Ruby?' she whispered desperately. 'Please give me a clue if you can, or just let me know that she's all right.'

Looking up as the door opened, she froze at the expression on Kian's face. 'What is it?' she gasped, getting to her feet. 'What's happened?'

'Anton Quentin just rang from Italy,' he said roughly. 'Apparently Amelia's mother died twelve years ago.'

Jules's heart tripped in shock. This wasn't making any sense. Amelia had said she'd left . . . 'But how can she . . . ? Are you saying . . . ?'

He shook his head. 'I don't know what I'm saying, except that it can't be where Daisy and Amelia have gone.'

194

Chapter Nine

It was both alarming and reassuring how quickly the police came after Kian called them again. At first there was only one uniformed officer, who introduced himself as Barry Britten. Later two detectives arrived, DS Alan Field, an older man with a rugged complexion and yellowish eyes; and acting DC Leo Johnson, a fresh-faced lad with a shock of red hair and sunburned cheeks.

Field began by asking Jules and Kian to talk them through everything, going back to how the two girls knew each other, while Johnson took notes.

Jules made sure to miss nothing out, describing Amelia's oddness of character, the reasons they'd felt Daisy had needed to cool the friendship, right through to the text Daisy had received that day saying that Amelia had found her mother.

'But now you're told that the mother's dead?' Field prompted.

'I called Amelia's father,' Kian replied, 'and when I explained about the text he said that couldn't be possible because Amelia's mother died twelve years ago.'

Jules said, 'I'm afraid she lies all the time, and in

this instance, I think it was a sure-fire way of persuading Daisy to go to her house – and of getting her away from me.'

The detective's eyebrows rose. 'Why would she want to get her away from you?'

'Because she wouldn't want to discuss finding her mother in front of me. She probably guessed I'd see through her in a way Daisy might not. Our daughter can be very trusting, she likes to see the best in people.'

Field was frowning. 'Could it be possible that Amelia doesn't know her mother's dead?' he suggested.

Jules started to answer and stopped. The possibility hadn't even occurred to her.

Appearing just as thrown, Kian said, 'That still wouldn't make her alive and able to be found.'

Conceding this with a nod, Field said, 'Perhaps you could let us have the father's number.'

After reading it out to the younger detective, Kian said, 'He's in Italy at the moment, on holiday.'

'Perhaps the girls are on their way to join him?'

Jules wanted to strike the man. 'I just told you, Daisy is due to fly to the States tomorrow,' she said through her teeth.

Appearing unfazed by her manner, Field said, 'Another possibility is that the message Daisy received today was some sort of code that only the girls understand.'

Jules stared at him so fiercely it hurt her eyes. Where the hell was he coming from? Hadn't he heard anything they'd just told him? The girls were estranged, they didn't have codes.

Moving on, Field said, 'OK, let's say it's not a code and that Amelia Quentin is aware that her mother's dead – what do you think her real reason could be for wanting to see your daughter?'

Jules's heart twisted with dread as she looked at Kian. 'We don't know for certain,' she answered brokenly, 'but I'm afraid she's planning some kind of punishment for the rejection.'

Field frowned. 'Does Amelia Quentin have a history of punishing people?'

'I don't know,' Jules replied, 'but she does have a history of lying and causing trouble and of doing things . . .' Her voice caught on a sob. She didn't want to repeat what she'd heard about the small animals and birds when the girl was a child, but she had to.

Field's expression darkened as he listened, until finally he said, 'You've already been up to the Quentin family home, you say, and there was nobody there?'

'We couldn't get an answer when we rang the entry-phone,' Jules reminded him, 'which isn't the same as nobody being there.'

Biting out the words, Kian said, 'Maybe if you were to go and check we'd know for certain if anybody's there.'

'Someone already has,' Field informed them, 'and like you they received no reply.'

Kian's temper flared. 'And that's it!' he cried. 'Because no one answers the door, you just assume that no one's there.'

'Not necessarily,' Field countered, 'but we have no evidence at this stage to say that anything unusual or untoward has occurred . . .'

Jules leapt to her feet. 'I've just told you what kind of girl we're dealing with. We know she lied to get my daughter to go and see her . . .'

'But how do you know that your daughter wasn't a part of the lie?'

'What the hell are you talking about?' Kian demanded. 'I don't get why you're not believing us.'

'It's not that I don't believe you,' Field corrected, 'it's simply that in my experience the parents are often the last to know what their children are up to . . .'

'And in my experience of our daughter we are NEVER the last to know,' Kian thundered. 'What the hell is it with you? Can't you see how worried we are? Do you think we're putting it on for attention, or something? Next thing you'll be telling us is that she's been groomed by some jihadi group and run off to Syria . . .'

'At this stage I wouldn't rule anything out,' Field responded mildly, 'but given their backgrounds and ethnicity I grant you the jihadi scenario is unlikely. What wouldn't be unusual is for two girls to concoct a plan to go off and meet a couple of boys together, or . . .'

'Daisy has a boyfriend,' Jules cut across him. 'His name is Joe Masters, he lives in the United States and as I've already told you she is due to fly over there tomorrow morning to see him. There is absolutely no way in the world she would deliberately miss the flight . . .'

'And she hasn't yet,' Field pointed out reasonably. 'It is quite possible she'll come home tonight and be ready to go at whatever time . . .'

'What's the fucking matter with you?' Kian raged, banging a fist on the table. 'Instead of sitting here trying to tell us we don't know our own daughter, why don't you go up there and break the bloody door down if necessary to find out if she's in that house?'

Eyeing him with some distaste, Field said, 'We'd need a warrant to search the place, and at this moment in time we have no grounds for an application. All we know is that you dropped your daughter outside the gates at around three o'clock this afternoon, meaning *you* were the last one to see her . . .'

Jules reeled as Kian turned white.

'I hope to God you're not trying to suggest I had anything to do with this,' Kian seethed.

Field's penetrating stare remained on him as he said, 'I'm simply trying to get the facts straight. You say you dropped her at the gates, but didn't wait to see if she went in. So, presuming that's true, for all we know Amelia Quentin came out and they drove off somewhere.'

'Like where, for Christ's sake?' Kian fumed. 'To see a mother who's apparently dead?'

'As I've already mentioned, it could have been a ploy . . .'

Jules clapped her hands to her head as Kian snatched up his phone. 'We need to get our Danny on this,' he growled.

'Who's Danny?' the detective enquired.

'My cousin. He won't have a problem getting in there.'

'Illegally.'

Losing it altogether, Kian yelled, 'For fuck's sake, she's been tricked into going somewhere she wouldn't normally go, on the eve of a trip to the States with her boyfriend, she isn't answering her bloody phone, what more do you want?'

'We're simply trying to establish . . .'

'I don't give a fuck what you're trying to establish.

I want my daughter back here *tonigh*t, and if you aren't going to make it happen then I bloody well will.'

'Mr Bright,' Field called after him as Kian stormed off, 'I must warn you that taking the law into your own hands can have serious consequences.'

Kian wasn't listening; he was already charging down the stairs to see Danny.

'And I must warn *you*,' Jules hissed at Field as she made to follow Kian, 'if anything happens to our daughter that could have been prevented, *you* are the one who'll be facing serious consequences.'

The pub was still crowded when Jules got downstairs, but there was no sign of Kian or Danny.

She found them outside in the car park surrounded by a group of Danny's cohorts, already planning their break-in at Crofton Park.

'You stay here, Kian,' Danny instructed, 'you don't want the law coming back on you for this. The rest of us can handle it.'

'No way am I staying here,' Kian growled. 'She's my daughter . . .'

'I'm coming too,' Jules insisted.

'Listen, the pair of you . . .' Danny broke off as he spotted Field returning to his car. 'Scum,' he spat, loud enough for the detective to hear.

Field made no response, simply got into the Ford Focus and headed out to the main road.

'Mr and Mrs Bright,' a voice called out from behind them.

They turned to find the younger detective beckoning them over to a marked police car where he was standing with the young officer who'd arrived at the pub first.

Going over to them, Jules said coldly, 'Yes?'

After glancing at his colleague, Leo Johnson said, 'Is there a chance, if we call Mr Quentin, that he'll tell us how to gain access to the house?'

Momentarily thrown after such a hostile meeting with Field, Jules called Kian over. She repeated Johnson's question and saw his own surprise register.

'Well?' she prompted.

'Yeah, I guess there is,' Kian replied, clearly thinking it through. 'I mean, why wouldn't he?'

'Precisely,' Johnson responded, 'and that way, if we go in, no crime's been committed because we have the owner's permission to be there.'

Jules and Kian looked at one another, taking a moment to register that these officers at least were on their side.

'I'll make the call,' Kian stated.

'No, I'll do it,' Johnson interrupted. 'It'll have more authority coming from the police.'

Not arguing, Jules and Kian watched him step away, still thrown by this sudden cooperation, but welcoming it nonetheless.

'What was it with that bloke Field?' Kian demanded of the uniformed officer. 'It was like he didn't believe a word we said.'

'Let's put it this way,' Barry Britten responded, turning down the volume of his two-way radio, 'he's been at it a long time and he's seen a lot of kids get their parents all worked up over nothing.'

Kian snarled, 'Still no reason to treat us like a pair of liars, or to damn well insinuate that I'm in some way involved in my own daughter's disappearance.'

'I'm afraid parents sometimes are,' Britten reminded him.

'Well it's not the case with us,' Kian barked. 'I don't want him here again. No way is he ever crossing my threshold . . .'

'Don't worry, he's very close to retirement.'

'OK,' Johnson announced, clicking off the line as he came back to them, 'he's given me a code for the gates and a number for the caretaker who's got keys to the house.'

'So what's the score?' Danny wanted to know, coming to join them.

'We're going up there,' Kian told him, 'and the police are going in.'

Danny cocked a look at Barry Britten. 'That's my man,' he muttered, making it plain that this wasn't the first time the two men had met.

'I think it's best if you wait here,' Johnson cautioned. 'What we're doing isn't strictly official and if . . .'

'But you've got Quentin's permission,' Kian pointed out.

'Agreed, but it hasn't been signed off back at the station. If it comes out that we went in there and took a bunch of you with us . . .'

'We'll wait outside,' Jules told him. 'We don't have to go in,' she explained to Kian, 'we just need to be there to bring her home.'

An hour and a half later Kian and Jules, along with Danny and several others, were standing in the moonlight outside Crofton Park watching the marked police car coming back along the drive towards them.

202

Jules's heart was in her mouth. *They had to have found Daisy, they just had to.* There were three people in the vehicle, but it soon became clear that the third person was the caretaker who'd come to open the place up for them.

Leo Johnson was shaking his head as he got out of the car. 'No one there,' he told them. 'No lights on anywhere, no cars in the drive. The place is deserted.'

Desperate and frustrated, Jules turned to Kian, willing him to do something, anything, but he was as helpless as she was.

'Can you think of anywhere else they might have gone?' Johnson asked, as Britten saw the caretaker back to his car.

Jules shook her head, her heart jolting as her phone rang. Seeing who it was, she almost didn't answer. 'It's Joe, her boyfriend,' she said brokenly. 'He'll be wondering why he can't get hold of her.' *Oh dear God this wasn't happening. Please, please, it couldn't be real.*

'I'll talk to him,' Kian told her, taking the mobile.

As he walked away from the group, Johnson said to Jules, 'If you haven't done it already you should contact Daisy's friends to ask if they can shed any light on where she and Amelia might have gone.'

Jules nodded. 'Of course, but I can promise you, if they knew they'd already have spoken up.'

Danny said, 'Are you going to start a search for them? We can get the girl's car registration number from her father . . .'

'We will,' Johnson assured him, 'but at the moment this still isn't official . . .'

'You're kidding me,' Danny cried. 'What the hell does it take . . . ?'

'They're seventeen and twenty-one,' Johnson reminded him.

'And one of them got the other here under false pretences. Surely to God that means something.'

'I'm on your side,' Johnson broke in, 'but we haven't seen the text . . .'

'Are you saying we're lying?' Danny exploded.

'No, of course not, I'm just trying to explain how it's looking back at the station, especially with Field on the case. Kids are taking off all the time without telling anyone where they're going . . . If Daisy was younger, or mentally or physically challenged in some way, or if Amelia had a history of violence . . .'

'Maybe she has,' Jules cut in forcefully. 'We've heard things . . . We need to check. She might even have a police record.'

Johnson was shaking his head. 'A check was run on both girls as soon as your call came in, nothing on either.'

Kian rejoined them. 'What's happening?' he asked, handing Jules back her phone.

'Fuck all as far as I can tell,' Danny snarled.

'How's Joe?' Jules wanted to know.

'Worried. He wants to come over, but I told him to stay put for now, at least until we know she's missed the flight.'

Unable to let herself even think of it, Jules watched Barry Britten punch in the code to close the gates. 'You can't stop looking for her,' she begged him, 'please, she has to be somewhere and we need to find her.'

*   *   *

It was just before eight the next morning, following the worst night of Kian's and Jules's lives, that they saw acting DC Leo Johnson arrive at the pub. PC Barry Britten was with him, but remained in the car while Johnson went into the bar where he found at least two dozen people, who'd clearly been there all night, waiting for news. After acknowledging them, but not engaging with their hostility, he followed Kian and Jules upstairs to the flat.

'I'm presuming,' he began a little hesitantly when they were in the kitchen, 'that you haven't heard anything overnight?'

Kian's eyes were glassy with fatigue, his jaw tight with stress. 'If we had we'd have let you know,' he responded tersely.

'No, we haven't,' Jules said more gently. If he was the best they could get on their side, he was certainly better than no one.

'So are you going to continue the search today,' Kian demanded, 'or is she still not important enough to be considered at risk?'

'We should be on our way to Heathrow by now,' Jules added brokenly. For Daisy not to have come back in time for the flight meant there was no evading the fact that something was seriously wrong.

Johnson's eyes were full of pity as he said, 'Have you checked to see if her passport is still here?'

Jules looked away as she nodded. 'Yes, it's still here,' she mumbled. This felt like the worst imaginable nightmare, one she desperately needed to wake up from if only she knew how.

'I don't want you to think nothing is being done,'

Johnson continued kindly. 'Barry, the PC you met last night, and I are hoping to go back to the Quentins' house at some point today to carry out a more thorough search, and Amelia's car registration number has been circulated throughout the Dean Valley force.'

'And if she's taken Daisy out of the area?' Kian prompted, checking his mobile as it rang. His eyes went to Jules as, with a brief shake of his head, he clicked on. 'Dougie, what can I do for you?' he said abruptly.

Dougie? The mayor?

As Kian listened he put a hand to his head, and for one awful moment Jules thought he was going to cry. 'That's great, thanks mate,' he managed in the end. 'We really appreciate it. Yeah, Jules is here, I'll tell her.'

After ringing off he said, 'He got the call about Daisy an hour ago . . . He's working on getting us all the police cooperation we need . . .' As his voice fractured to nothing Jules put her hands over her face.

'This is good news,' Johnson said quietly. 'With the right sort of manpower and resources it shouldn't take us long to find her.'

He was almost at the door before Jules remembered to thank him. 'Did you call the mayor?' she asked.

He coloured slightly. 'Not personally, but I spoke to someone who has his direct number. He's a good bloke, I was hoping he'd make a difference.'

Jules's mind wasn't working properly; she couldn't think what to say when she was once again trying to process the fact that this was about Daisy and the fact that *she hadn't come home all night*.

'You should have a family liaison officer soon,'

Johnson told them, 'and you should prepare for more questions . . .'

'Not from the bloke who was here last night,' Kian protested. 'I don't want him here again.'

'Field's a good detective,' Johnson assured him, 'just a bit jaded now he's coming to the end.'

'Then let him go and be jaded with somebody else,' Jules retorted. 'We want someone who actually believes there's a problem, who cares about finding my daughter . . .'

'We all care about that,' Johnson promised, turning as Barry Britten came into the room.

'I'm the FLO,' Britten told him. 'Field's outside in his car waiting for you to go with him to the Quentins' place.' To Jules and Kian he said, 'From now on it's my job to keep you informed of everything that's happening, but I need to bring myself up to speed with what's going on at the station. Give me five minutes and I'll know more.'

As both officers left Kian turned away, pushing a hand roughly through his hair. Jules watched him absently while listening to the voices downstairs. She should go and tell the others that they had police support now, that they weren't being left to their own devices after all. She didn't move. It was as though a giant hole was opening up inside her. It was making her feel sick. They were turning into one of the families they saw on the news, the parents who spoke to their children's abductors through the media, begging them not to harm them and let them come home. She didn't want this to be happening. She had to make it go away and bring their world back to normal.

'Marco rustled you up some breakfast,' Aileen announced, carrying in a tray of eggs and bacon. 'You need to keep up your strength.'

Kian didn't turn around; Jules simply looked at it as though she had no idea what it was.

After making fresh coffee and preparing another tray for Marsha, Aileen said, 'I'll go and see to your mother. She's probably awake by now.'

Jules tried to think about her mother, what she needed, how she might be this morning, but she couldn't get her thoughts to make any sense. She said to Kian, 'We should go and look for her ourselves.'

Taking out his phone he started to dial.

'Who are you calling?'

'Quentin. No way should he be allowed to carry on sitting there in Italy while his daughter's playing God only knows what kind of games with Daisy . . . Anton, it's Kian Bright. There's still no sign of them and we're worried out of . . .' As Quentin broke in Jules watched Kian's face turning white. Suddenly he shouted, 'You can't be fucking serious. Of course I gave the police your number . . . I don't give a fuck what it's . . . No, you listen to me, you supercilious bastard, your daughter tricked mine into going to meet her . . . Yes, that *is* what happened. I was here, I saw the text. She said she'd found her mother . . .'

Jules snatched the phone. 'Does Amelia know her mother's dead?' she shouted down the line.

'Of course she knows,' Quentin snapped back, 'which is why it's nonsense for her to have said she'd found her.'

'Well that *is* what she said, I saw the text myself, so what the hell is going on, *Mr* Quentin?'

'How the hell am I supposed to know when I'm here and they're there . . .'

'Except they're *not here*,' Jules raged. 'Amelia's taken Daisy off somewhere and we need to know where that might be.'

'As far as I'm aware the police are looking, so what more do you think I can do?'

'Have you given the police the addresses of your other properties?'

'Not yet, but I will when they ask.'

'We need to know now,' she barked, rummaging for a pen.

'I'm afraid it's not convenient right now. We're about to go out for the day,' and the line went dead.

Jules stared at the phone, dumbfounded. Had that really just happened? Had he truly treated her like some irritating mosquito he was trying to bat out of the way when he knew how distressed she was? 'He hung up on me,' she told Kian. 'That bastard just told me he was going out for the day . . .'

As Barry Britten returned, Kian said, 'You need to speak to Anton Quentin, get the addresses of his other properties . . .'

'Don't worry, it'll be done,' Britten assured them.

'But when?' Jules cried furiously. 'You should already have that information, and that monster of a man should be made to come back here . . . Jesus Christ, this is a shambles. Just because she's seventeen doesn't mean she's any less vulnerable . . . She's just a child, my child, my baby . . .' As she started to break down Kian pulled her into his arms.

'We've got to try and stop making things worse for ourselves,' he said gently. 'I know it's hard, but there could still be a reasonable explanation . . .'

Jules pushed him away. 'Then give me one,' she challenged hysterically. 'Tell me something, anything, that even begins to make sense . . .'

'We're exploring a number of possibilities,' Britten interrupted, 'and there really isn't any reason to start looking on the black side yet.'

'Yet?' she echoed wildly. 'So when do we actually start? What is it precisely that triggers the black side, if taking my daughter under false pretences isn't enough?'

From the door Aileen said, 'I'm sorry, Jules, but you need to keep your voice down. Your mother can hear and she thinks someone's here to harm her.'

Turning away, Jules closed her eyes as she tried to force down the raging swirl of emotions. She longed to go to her mother, not to calm her, but to shake her back to her normal self so she could seek comfort and reassurance, hear her say everything would be all right, because she was going to make it so. She didn't understand what was happening to the people she loved. Where were they? Who was taking them away? Her mother couldn't come back, but Daisy could, and would . . . It was just going to take time and patience . . . She needed to trust the police, to remind herself that they dealt with cases like this all the time. But how could she believe in them when the detective leading the search had practically accused Kian of being involved in the disappearance?

There were so many prejudices, mistakes, delays, and all the time Daisy was being held somewhere by Amelia who was very probably not right in the head . . .

It was around lunchtime when the mayor himself arrived to check on progress. The pub was closed, the bar staff were outside turning people away, though of course they let Dougie through, while the kitchen staff rustled up coffee and food for the family and friends who were still there. It largely went untouched.

As Kian talked to the mayor Jules wandered back upstairs, avoiding Daisy's room where a forensic team was going through everything. She didn't look out of the windows, either, to where a dozen or more officers and several of Daisy's friends were combing the beach. Heaven only knew what they were looking for, when everyone knew that she'd gone to Amelia's and hadn't come back.

They'd been told to expect further questioning, but it hadn't happened yet. She might actually welcome retelling what she knew in case she'd somehow missed a vital piece of information, though she dreaded how it was going to be for Kian. Would they try once again to twist things around to make him look, feel, even behave, as though he had something to hide? No one who knew him would ever suspect him of trying to harm his daughter, but DS Alan Field didn't know him, nor did DS Alan Field care how devastating his questions and insinuations might be in his quest to get this inconvenient *misper* as he no doubt called a missing person, out of the way before his retirement.

Kian would be seen as collateral damage.

Unless Daisy turned up right now, unharmed, unafraid, and bursting to tell the craziest story of what had gone wrong, where they'd been, why it hadn't been possible to get in touch.

Joe came through on her FaceTime as the forensic team was leaving.

For one irrational moment Jules allowed herself to think that he was going to tell her that Daisy had got the flight after all.

'I'm sorry, there's still no news,' she had to confess. 'The police are taking it more seriously now, or so we're told, but I'm not sure exactly what that means.'

'I need to be there,' he said gruffly. His dark, velvety eyes looked sore and scared, his complexion the palest she'd ever seen it.

'Just wait a while,' she cautioned. 'She could turn up at any minute and if she does everything will go back to normal and we'll get her on the next flight.'

'I guess no one's heard from Amelia?' he ventured.

'Not that I'm aware of. Her father was very difficult with me earlier . . .'

'Do you think he knows where they are?'

'I've no idea, but I'm sure the police have spoken to him by now, so if he does . . .' She was losing track of her thoughts.

'You look beat,' he told her. 'How's Kian holding up?'

'We're OK, but we'll be glad when it's all resolved and we can put it behind us.'

'Sure. I'll second that. I'm going crazy here. I just don't get what's happening.'

'None of us do.' She turned away from the camera.

'I think someone's just arrived downstairs. I should go and see who it is.'

'Let me know if it's her, won't you?'

'Of course. If it is, I'll get her to ring you herself.'

It wasn't Daisy. It was a detective by the name of Hassan Ansari who asked to speak to Kian alone.

When the interview was over Kian came to find Jules in the kitchen. 'He took my phone,' he said shakily. 'He questioned me about the call I made to Daisy yesterday afternoon when I asked if she wanted a lift home. He wanted to know where I thought she was when she answered. I said I assumed she was at Amelia's, where I'd dropped her, but I had no way of knowing that for certain. So he asked if I was sure that was all we discussed?' He looked so dazed that Jules could tell he was losing all sense of reality.

'Did they say why they wanted your phone?' she prompted gently.

He looked at her blankly, then said, 'I should have asked. I didn't think . . . Maybe they'll be able to trace where she was when she took the call . . . Can they do that?'

'I don't know. Maybe.'

This was tying them up in so many knots, tearing them apart in ways they could find very hard to repair if it didn't stop soon.

At the sound of someone climbing the stairs they stopped talking, and watched Danny come into the kitchen.

'Stephie and her parents have just turned up,' he

told them. 'Apparently Dean hasn't been home all night either.'

As a jolt of confusion hit her, Jules turned to Kian.

'Do they know where he is?' Kian asked.

'I don't think they know what to make of it at the moment.'

'If he's with her she'll be all right,' Jules broke in hopefully. 'Dean would never let anything happen to her.'

Taking his own comfort from that, Kian said, 'He's a good kid. He's like a brother to her.'

'I should speak to his parents.' Jules went to the phone. 'They'll be as worried as we are . . .'

Not entirely sure what she was going to say to them, Jules waited for someone to pick up at the Foggartys' home, but no one did. 'Maybe they're on their way here,' she murmured, hanging up and going to the window. There were no police on the beach now; they were either walking around the garden or over inspecting the weir.

She was about to turn away when a Ford Focus swept in from the main road with two more cars following on behind. Her heart started to burn with a terrible mix of hope and terror. *They'd found Daisy. They'd brought her home. It had to be that.*

'She's here,' she cried, and pushing past Danny she tore down the stairs, across the bar and out to the garden. Kian was right behind her, and almost ran into her as she came to a sudden stop.

Where was Daisy? There were only police officers in plain clothes and uniforms getting out of the cars.

DS Alan Field came forward. He appeared no

friendlier today than he had last night; if anything the grimness of his expression was making her take a step back. She felt panic, denial, an urge to run, to throw herself at his feet, anything to stop him confirming what his eyes were already telling her.

'Mr and Mrs Bright,' he said quietly, 'I'm afraid . . .'

'Have you found her?' Kian broke in roughly.

Field looked at him. 'I'm sorry to tell you, sir . . .'

Jules's head started to spin. She couldn't hear what he was saying. His voice was drowning in a gulf of horror. 'Where is she?' she cried, stumbling towards him. 'What have you done with her?'

His voice dipped away as he answered, and came back as he said, '. . . made two arrests . . .'

She stared at him wildly. 'Tell me she's still alive!' she growled. 'Say it *now*. Kian, make him say it.'

No one moved. No one spoke.

Jules looked around, up at the moor, across the sky. 'No!' she screamed. 'No! No! No! No! I want my baby! Daisy, where are you?'

Aileen and Bridget rushed to catch her as she slumped to her knees, and Kian sank down on a bench, his legs unable to hold him.

Jules looked at Field. Her voice was trapped inside her, but she forced it out, needing to make him hear her. 'It's not her,' she tried to shout. 'Kian, you have to tell them, they've got it wrong.'

Still no one moved, or spoke; all they could do was look at her with heartbreak in their eyes as a terrible, unbearable silence fell over the bay, so terrible and so unbearable that it was no silence at all.

Chapter Ten

Jules was still sitting quietly at the kitchen table at her home in the Risings, vaguely hearing the postman rattling the letter box and the distant sound of a barking dog. The phone had rung several times, but she hadn't answered. She'd simply allowed her memories to carry her back to the times before that terrible day, to when she'd known how truly wonderful it was to be a mother, a woman who sang and danced, laughed and cried in all the normal ways. She'd been so blessed, had known so much happiness, and had tried to help others in any way she could, until one day nothing had made sense any more.

As the clouds darkened outside she could feel the deep, unrelenting claws of loss curling through her like an incurable disease. Her memories were sharp and brutal now, ugly and cruel, yet they were unreliable and skittish too, skimming over events as though afraid to stay too long in one place in case it cracked wide open and pulled her right in to drown.

It was the day after the police had found Daisy's body, in a stable at Crofton Park, that Kian had gone with Danny to identify her. They'd advised Jules not to go, the injuries would make the experience too distressing, they said, and because she was still unable to accept it was Daisy she had stayed at home. Such was her denial that she'd even tried to carry on as normal, preparing breakfast, taking her mother for a scheduled check-up with the psychiatrist, until Em had stepped in and taken over.

She had no clear recollection now of Em's arrival, she only knew that her friend had been there throughout those hellish days as the pub garden and beach filled with flowers and candles and toys, and Jules had stared at them as though she had no idea how they had got there, or what she was going to do with them. Joe had flown over too, with his father. Seeing Nicholas had meant nothing, and yet everything, for she was afraid he might be the reason she was being punished. Em tried to talk her out of that, but Jules was careful never to be alone with him. She didn't want to break down and end up saying things that would help no one, least of all her. The cruellest irony was the way Kian seemed to take so much comfort in Nicholas's presence; they'd clearly struck up a good friendship over the years that Kian had spent time in Chicago with Daisy.

Joe was so devastated it wasn't easy to know what to say to him. He might be over six feet tall with a true sportsman's physique and all the bluff confidence of a youngster, but that didn't mean he had no need of being held and soothed like the child he still was. Jules spent many hours in Daisy's room with him, listening to him talking about her, trying to come to terms with something that made no sense, and dreading the day he would leave and she would lose him too.

The funeral undid them all. It was impossible for anyone to hold themselves together as they tried singing 'All Things Bright and Beautiful'. Jules knew that she would never forget the wretchedness of Kian's sobs as he sank to his knees, unable to support his grief. It simply wasn't possible for any of them to think of a world without Daisy in it. There was nothing bright or beautiful about that, there was only darkness and anger and the evil that had stolen her from them.

As time went on Jules stopped talking about her, even to Kian. She held her grief so tightly in her heart that sometimes it seemed to stop beating. She found it hard to look at those who'd loved Daisy the most; it was as though they were turning into shadows, losing themselves in the emptiness that had taken over their world. Nothing mattered any more; there was no point to anything when life, in the shape of a plain girl with an insanely malicious heart, could so randomly and cruelly snatch it away.

Amelia and Dean had been arrested at the scene of the crime and were later charged with joint-enterprise murder.

Dean had been a part of it. Daisy's dear friend who'd been like a brother to her, like a son to Kian and Jules. He hadn't tried to save her. Instead he'd raped her and taken part in the attack that had ended her life.

Could that really be true? Surely someone had made a terrible mistake. This wasn't the Dean they knew and loved.

It shocked everyone, even the press, when Dean was remanded in custody and Amelia was released on bail. It was virtually unheard of for anyone to get bail on a murder charge, so why was she a special case? What made her so much less of a risk to society when everyone knew that she'd sent the text that had tricked Daisy into going to her house? And the post-mortem had shown that every one of the fifteen frenzied stab wounds had been inflicted by the same left hand.

Amelia was left-handed. Dean was not.

The answer, of course, was that Amelia's father was connected in the places that mattered. As a lawyer himself he could call on, and afford, the best of his colleagues, while the Foggartys had to rely on legal aid.

'I don't expect your forgiveness, or your under-standing,' Dean's mother, Gemma, had said when Jules and Kian finally agreed to see her, 'I just want you to know what Dean has told me, and what he will say in court.'

Neither Jules nor Kian spoke, simply regarded her tormented, swollen face and waited for her to continue. *Where was her God now?* Jules wondered. *What good had he done her?*

'Amelia tricked Dean into going there too,' Gemma began. 'When he arrived Daisy was already in the stable tied up with coarse string and tape over her mouth. She couldn't move, or speak, but he could see how terrified she was, and knew she was begging him to help her. He tried, but Amelia leapt in front of him and started . . .' She put a trembling hand to her head as she took a breath. 'She started cutting Daisy with a knife, and telling Dean if he didn't back off it would only get worse. Then she threatened to kill Daisy unless he . . . forced himself on her. She kept saying she knew he wanted to do it, that it was all he ever dreamed about, so here was his chance. He begged her to put the knife down, kept telling her she was wrong, but she wouldn't listen. In the end she started cutting Daisy again, and Daisy screamed so hard that the tape came off her mouth and she pleaded with him to do as Amelia said, anything to make her stop.'

Jules's eyes closed as the depth of Daisy's fear and panic engulfed her. She could see, even feel the knife sliding into her tender skin, the blood oozing out, thick and red . . . Then her beloved friend raped her . . .

Gemma Foggarty said, 'When it was over he thought she would let them go, but she didn't, so he tried to escape to raise the alarm, but Amelia . . .' Her eyes went to Jules, showing how reluctant she was to give the detail.

'Go on,' Jules whispered raggedly.

Visibly steeling herself, Gemma said, 'Amelia stabbed her so hard, in the leg, that he didn't dare to try leaving again. He kept telling himself she'd let them go eventually, or he'd find a way to overpower her . . .'

'But he didn't,' Kian said dully.

Gemma's eyes went down. 'No,' she murmured, 'he didn't, but no one is sorrier about that than he is.'

Kian asked, 'Has he told the police all this?'

'Of course, but Amelia's telling a different story. She says it was all his idea and that she knew nothing about what he was planning when he persuaded her to trick Daisy into going to Crofton Park that day.'

'The wounds were inflicted by a left hand,' Kian reminded her.

'She's saying that Dean did that deliberately, because

he knew she was left-handed. Please, you have to know he'd never harm Daisy. She meant the world to him. He's so devastated and traumatised by what's happened that he's not really fighting. He seems to have lost himself . . . I don't know what to do to help him.'

Though Jules felt pity, and was even willing to believe Dean's story, she had no idea how to help him either.

Kian said, 'Where's your husband? Why didn't he come with you?'

Gemma's eyes filled with tears. 'He can't face you,' she answered brokenly. 'He's too ashamed, too distraught . . . He prays all the time, we both do, but I'm afraid our son is going to need more than prayers to get him through this.'

Knowing she was right, Jules could find nothing to say.

'Does he think Amelia always meant to kill her?' Kian asked. 'That getting him to rape Daisy was only a part of her . . . intention?'

Gemma shrugged helplessly. 'I don't think he has any idea what was going through the girl's mind . . . He said that it all got out of hand when it became clear she wasn't going to let them go. Daisy began screaming at Amelia that she was a crazy bitch, a liar, a freak . . . He could see the effect it was having on Amelia, so he tried to make Daisy stop, but she wouldn't, or couldn't. She was hysterical, beyond his reach. Then suddenly Amelia began stabbing her . . . Dean tried grabbing her hands, but her strength . . . He says it was impossible to get hold of her . . . He did in the end, but by then it was . . . it was too late . . .'

221

Jules turned away as Kian covered his face with his hands.

'I'm sorry, I'm so, so sorry,' Gemma wept desperately.

Eventually Kian said, 'What happened once he realised . . . ? Why didn't he run away then?'

She shook her head. 'He doesn't know, but I think he must have been in shock. He says he was terrified she was intending to kill him too, she had the knife pointed at him, and she was covered in blood . . . They both were. She said she was going to tell everyone that he'd carried out the attack, that he'd tried to rape her too, but she'd managed to get away . . .' Gemma broke down again. 'They've charged him with murder, but I know in my heart that he'd never harm Daisy. She was the sister he never had. He loved being here with you and your family . . . You meant the world to him, all of you.'

And where were you all that time, Jules wanted to ask, but didn't.

It was two months after Gemma's visit that Misty and her team reopened the pub. It was either that or lay everyone off, and Jules and Kian didn't want to put their loyal staff out of work. They didn't go down to the bar themselves, the way they used to; they either stayed in the flat, or came and went via the back door. Their lives were in limbo as they waited for the trial to begin. They rarely spoke about it, even though it was all that occupied their minds. When the lawyers were in touch they had no choice but to go over everything they knew again; the rest of the time they simply waited and tried to grieve and did their best to keep themselves together.

Sometimes, when it got too much to bear, Jules took herself out to the moor where she'd howl and rant with the pain of the loss, or berate herself for not reacting to Daisy's screams. She'd heard them, while it was happening. With a mother's instinct she'd known her child was in trouble and needed her, but she hadn't been able to find her.

All the time she wrangled with her conscience she'd hold tightly to Ruby's shoe, wanting to believe that Ruby was taking care of Daisy, wherever they were now.

'Ruby, please tell her I love her,' she'd whisper wretchedly. 'Tell her I miss her and I'm sorry with all my heart that I didn't come to save her.'

Ruby never gave a sign of having heard; it was as though she'd left them too.

With Marsha's condition deteriorating, Aileen moved into one of the pub's guest rooms so she could be on hand to help, but they all knew that it was also because she was finding it hard to be on her own. She missed Daisy every bit as much as Jules and Kian; losing her angel had changed her from the bubbly, wry, looking-on-the-Bright-side woman she used to be, to someone who was as injured and broken as her son. Like Jules, she sometimes envied Marsha's oblivion; surely it was better to have forgotten Daisy than to have to live with the knowledge of what had happened to her.

During those long, bitter months as they waited for the trial to begin there was never any sign of Amelia, though Anton Quentin visited Crofton Park towards the end of March. No one seemed to know if Amelia was with him, she hadn't been spotted, but Jules felt convinced she was there. She could feel her presence seeping across the moor, pouring down the hillside, spreading about the bay like a poison. She was a dark, invisible force in the guise of an ordinary girl, come to exacerbate their torment, intensify their grief.

And it was to get even worse, for they received a letter one morning around that time informing them that the charge of murder had been reduced to Voluntary Manslaughter with Provocation.

Voluntary Manslaughter *with Provocation*.

The blow was so harsh that neither Jules nor Kian, nor any of their friends and family, could find a way to deal with it. It was unthinkable that Daisy might have contributed in any way to her own death; it was such a cruel and wicked twist in this appalling nightmare that Jules knew if someone were to put a knife in her hand at that moment she'd plunge it straight into Amelia Quentin's heart and gladly watch her die.

The first she knew of Kian's visit to the Quentin residence was when DC Leo Johnson got in touch to warn them, as gently as possible, that they could be arrested if they went near the Quentins again.

'What were you thinking, going there in the first place?' Jules demanded as Kian punched a fist into the wall.

'I don't know,' he answered savagely. 'I guess I just couldn't take any more. I had to do something . . . I needed them to know what they've done. I needed to call her a murderer to her face, so that she'll go into that courtroom knowing that *I know* what she did and that there was *no provocation*, because Daisy was tied up. She was defenceless, a victim, and that crazy bitch stabbed her fifteen fucking times. Nothing Daisy did could have provoked that kind of attack, and let's not forget that Daisy went there out of kindness because that lying . . . scheming . . .'

'It's OK, it's OK,' Jules tried to soothe as he broke down. 'I understand why you did it, of course I do . . . Just tell me what happened. Did you see her? Did they let you in?'

He shook his head. 'Her father came to the gate with a bloody shotgun. Can you believe that? He brought a fucking gun with him and told me he'd use it if I ever came near his property or his daughter again.'

Jules was horrified, incredulous. 'He threatened you,' she gasped. 'He actually *threatened* you when he must know what you're going through? Jesus Christ, what kind of man is he?'

'They're not like us, Jules, I can tell you that much.'

Still fuming, she cried, 'If I thought it would do any good I'd send Danny and his friends up there right now to show him just how much respect we have for his property and his daughter.'

'Do it!' Aileen growled from the door. 'Our Danny will know how to make it happen without that bastard having a clue what hit him.'

Though Jules and Kian were sorely tempted, they were painfully aware that any sort of attack on the Quentins at this time would inevitably come back on them.

'What else did he say while you were there?' Aileen asked Kian.

He started to answer, then stopped and shook his head.

'What did he say?' Jules prompted.

'It doesn't matter . . . It won't do any good . . .'

'I *want* to know.'

'OK, if you have to hear it . . . He started going on about Daisy bringing things on herself, that we'd spoiled her, hadn't ever taught her how to treat people decently, and the way she led Amelia on, letting her think she was a friend . . . Mum, don't,' he pleaded as Aileen began to sob. 'You shouldn't be listening to this . . .'

'I'm sorry,' Jules cut in, 'it's my fault. I made him tell us . . . Aileen, please. Come and sit down. I'll make us a cup of tea . . .'

'Don't worry, I'll have myself together in a minute,' Aileen promised, 'it's just that I can't bear to think of what our dear, sweet angel went through, and now for those wicked people to try and make out it was her own fault . . . What kind of god do they answer to, that's what I want to know, because I'm praying to mine that it's a vengeful one.'

'It's not about God, it's about connections and belonging to the right club . . .'

'That's right,' Aileen snarled, 'they're all in on it, even the people who are supposed to be prosecuting, or they wouldn't have let the charge be reduced. Everyone knows that the murder was premeditated; the text she sent proves it. She even warned you, the day she walked out of here, that you'd be sorry. So how can anyone in their right minds accuse Daisy of provoking what happened?'

Since it was a question they had no answer for, and could still hardly believe they were asking, Jules and

Kian simply shook their heads and fell back into the silence of loss and torment that they endured each day.

Sitting alone now in front of her lava-log fireplace with misty sunrays strobing the hearth, Jules was remembering how keenly everyone had assured her that the trial would bring closure. 'Once it's all over,' they'd said, 'and that monstrous girl is behind bars you'll be able to move on.'

No one had mentioned Dean, it was as though it was impossible to make any sense of his involvement, and Jules had to admit she hardly knew what she felt about it either. Something else no one mentioned – or perhaps they hadn't known – was what a harrowing ordeal it would be to sit in the courtroom every day, listening to the evidence while looking at Amelia Quentin, and be unable to stop herself seeing over, and over, what she had done to Daisy. The contorted face, the savagery, the demented stabbing, the screams, and the blood, *Daisy's blood* . . . To others it might not seem likely that this ordinary-looking, po-faced girl with mousy brown hair and nervous eyes could commit such a violent atrocity, but Jules knew what evil lay behind that fake demeanour.

Though they weren't surprised to find cameras and reporters outside the Crown Court when they arrived on the first day, the media presence felt invasive, to the point of humiliating. Jules clung tightly to Kian's and Joe's arms as they passed through the large rotating doors, while Aileen, Em, Gordon and Danny kept in close behind.

Dickon Bruce, the prosecuting QC, came to find them

in the main lobby. He was a burly man in his late fifties with wiry grey hair and a voice so thickly plummy that it wasn't always easy to understand him. 'DS Field won't be giving evidence,' he informed them, while glancing through the papers he was carrying. 'DC Leo Johnson will be taking the stand in his place.'

During the several times they'd met Dickon Bruce over recent weeks none of them had found it possible to warm to him, mainly because his voice was so like Anton Quentin's. It wasn't helped by the fact that he barely looked at them as he spoke, and that he seemed to feel more inconvenienced by this trial than determined to make sure justice was served. If Jules and Kian had had the power to sack him they would have done so, but they didn't get to choose who represented the state; that singular privilege belonged to the Crown Prosecution Service, the same service that had allowed the charge to be reduced from murder to manslaughter *with provocation*.

Dickon's junior, Laura Cosgrove, a woman of around fifty, was friendlier, albeit in a brusque, slightly dismissive way.

It was fifteen minutes before the trial was due to begin that an angel in the guise of Andee Lawrence had found them in the court's annexed cafeteria and come to introduce herself. She was a tall woman with lustrous dark hair clipped tightly back from her oval face, and compelling aquamarine eyes behind dark-rimmed glasses.

After taking Jules and Kian to a separate table, she said, 'Dougie Farnham, the mayor, asked me to come. He's my children's grandfather on their father's side.

I'm actually with the Met, but my kids and I are here on holiday at the moment and Dougie felt you might need some impartial moral support.'

The mention of the mayor's name along with a kind face seemed to Jules like a spark of light trying to break through at the end of the darkest tunnel.

'You mean a lot to Dougie,' Andee told them softly, 'and Daisy did too . . . Actually, my kids knew Daisy from the holidays they spent here, they went to a lot of her shows, so they're also very keen for me to support you in any way I can. It'll be unofficial, of course, and if you feel you don't need anyone . . .'

'No, we need someone,' Jules broke in hastily.

The warmth of Andee's smile felt like the familiar chords of a beloved melody playing straight into Jules's heart; she instinctively knew that this woman was someone they could trust, who really did mean to be there for them. 'There seems to be a lot going on that we don't really understand,' Jules admitted. 'Of course we've asked, but we never get any straight answers.'

'Such as?' Andee prompted.

'Well, like reducing the charge to Voluntary Manslaughter – with Provocation. Why, how, did that happen?'

'It'll be because the defence have either shown evidence, or have provided persuasive argument, to convince the CPS that Manslaughter with Provocation is the more accurate charge. I'm afraid I can't tell you what evidence or argument was put forward, but obviously it'll come out in the trial – and make no mistake, that charge can also carry a life sentence.'

'But not necessarily,' Kian stated.

'No, not necessarily.'

Jules said, 'We're starting to feel more like the criminals than the victims.'

Andee nodded sympathetically. 'Dougie was afraid that might happen, which is why he asked me to meet you. I've had some experience of how tough these situations can be on families.' She glanced at her watch. 'We don't have a lot of time now, but any questions that come up during the day, anything you don't understand or need to be sure about, make a note and we'll meet later to go through it.'

Jules and Kian looked round as someone called their names from the cafeteria door.

'Your barrister will be wanting to talk to you before the trial begins,' Andee explained. 'Dickon Bruce is leading?'

Kian nodded. 'Is he good?'

'I've never been in court with him, but he has a lot of experience and a reasonable track record. I'm sure it won't come as any surprise that no expense has been spared for Amelia's defence, the reduced charge is already evidence of their influence, but by all accounts Dickon Bruce is no lightweight. Oh, one small piece of advice before you go, avoid the press as much as you can . . . Do you have a spokesperson?'

'Daisy's boyfriend wants to take it on,' Kian told her.

'Where is he?'

'Over there with the others. He's trying to be strong for us all, but he's just a boy really, and I don't think he's any closer to getting over it than we are.'

'It'll be good for him to feel useful.'

Glad to have her own instinct confirmed, Jules said, 'The court's going to be quite full of our friends and family.'

Andee smiled. 'It's good that you have their support. It'll mean a lot over the coming days, and don't be afraid to lean. It's what they're here for.'

As they prepared to go to the barrister, Jules turned back and looked into Andee's unusual eyes. 'Thank you for coming,' she said softly. 'I hope this doesn't put too much of a burden on you, but I feel better already just knowing you're here.'

Their first sight of Amelia Quentin, already seated in the dock when Jules and Kian arrived in the courtroom, made Jules feel sick to her soul. The girl looked nothing like Daisy now. Gone were the blonde curls and rosy cheeks; her hair was its usual lank and mousy sadness, while her grey woollen dress appeared at least two sizes too big for her. She couldn't have looked more pathetic or vulnerable if she'd been half her age and truly innocent. Without uttering a word she was managing to portray the image of a wretched, lonely young woman who really shouldn't be where she was, *so please let me go home where I belong*.

Then her eyes met Jules's.

The moment was so fleeting that anyone else might have missed it, but Jules felt it like a physical force. There was no misunderstanding the burn of Amelia's gaze that conveyed triumph, even pleasure, and no remorse at all.

I warned you you'd be sorry.

Feeling herself breaking into a sweat, Jules clenched

her hands tightly and silently swore that no matter what happened in this court, that girl was going to pay the full price for what she'd done.

Sitting beside Amelia in a navy suit and dark red tie, Dean kept his head down throughout the lengthy process of the jury being sworn in, looking up only once when it was plain to see how very afraid he was. His parents were in court, but they avoided eye contact with everyone, and like their son, kept their heads down as the trial got under way.

The first day was mostly taken up with the prosecutor's opening statement. It was rambling, unemotional, and often hard to follow, until he began describing what the jury would hear from the pathologist. At that point Jules found herself getting up and leaving. The detail was too graphic, and she didn't need to hear it twice. When the pathologist took the stand would be enough, she could hear the details then of how many times Daisy had been stabbed before the actual blow that had caused her death, and how deeply the raffia string had cut into her wrists as she'd struggled to break free. She'd suffered horribly, both mentally and physically, Jules knew that. It was the detail of the injuries, along with the memory of what he'd seen when identifying the body, that kept Kian awake at night, tormenting him to the point of madness at times.

As she walked along the corridor she turned at the sound of the courtroom door opening, hoping it would be Kian, but it was a young woman with a shock of red hair and a concerned expression.

'Mrs Bright? Are you OK?' she asked kindly.

'Yes, I'm fine, thank you,' Jules replied, feeling sure

she recognised the woman, though unable to place her for the moment.

'Heather Hancock,' she announced, holding out a hand to shake. '*Kesterly Gazette*. I've been trying to get hold of you. We'd be very interested in getting a . . .' She swung round, almost guiltily, as the courtroom door opened again and Andee Lawrence came through.

'Everything OK?' Andee asked, looking from Jules to the reporter and back.

For some reason Jules couldn't think what to say.

Taking her arm, Andee threw a knowing look Heather Hancock's way and led Jules along the echoey marble hall. 'I saw her follow you,' she said quietly, 'and guessed you might welcome a rescue.'

'Thanks,' Jules murmured. 'They're everywhere. You wouldn't believe how much money we've been offered by some of the nationals . . .'

Andee's eyebrows arched. 'I probably would,' she said sardonically.

Jules looked on down the corridor to where a couple of gowned barristers were talking quietly to a woman in a pink suit. She didn't know what to say or do; was still finding it hard to connect with the fact that she was even inside this building, never mind playing such a major part in one of its dramas.

'Would you rather be alone?' Andee asked softly.

Jules thought about it and shook her head.

Leading the way back to the cafeteria, Andee ordered two coffees while Jules found a corner table with no windows and no one else seated nearby.

It surprised her afterwards to realise how easily she and Andee had fallen into conversation, talking about things that had nothing to do with the trial, as if they'd somehow disconnected from where they were and why. They were like old friends doing no more than catching up. They discussed where in Kesterly Jules was from; where Andee's family lived; the fact that Jules's mother had Alzheimer's; how Andee's children, both younger than Daisy, had appeared as extras in one of Daisy's films. Jules admitted how worried she was about Kian, and Andee confided that her children's father – the mayor's son – had left her two years ago to go and live his own life.

They'd bonded over that time in a way that pleased Em no end when she heard about it later. She was constantly worrying about how lonely Jules seemed in spite of their regular phone calls, and being surrounded by family and friends. She never really talked to anyone, apart from Em, but Em couldn't be there all the time. Jules needed someone closer to home; better still, Andee was someone who hadn't known and loved Daisy as they had, so she could be detached in a way that was rational and necessary.

Anton Quentin was called to the stand on the second day.

Jules was once again sitting with Em one side of her and Joe the other. The night before she'd held Joe in her arms as he'd wept like a baby, wishing she could find a way to comfort him, but what could she say?

'I'm getting counselling, back in the States,' he'd confessed. 'Dad thought it would be a good idea, and I guess he's right.'

'Is that why you came, because the counsellor

thought the trial would help you to gain closure?' Jules asked softly.

He nodded. 'But I wanted to be here anyway. It would seem wrong to be so far away while it was happening. I know it won't bring her back, nothing's ever going to do that, but it makes me feel closer to her to be here, with you, and I just can't stand the thought that after this trial I won't have a reason to come any more.'

'You'll always be welcome,' Jules assured him, while knowing that in time he would move on, find someone else and build a new life.

How it made her heart ache to think of that, to imagine what might have been, should have been, and now never would. Daisy had been so brutally cheated. It simply wasn't right that she was no longer in the world, able to pursue her dreams and live her life. No one had the right to take that from her, and yet Amelia Quentin had decided that she did.

Unlike Joe, the rest of them wouldn't be able to move on or find anyone else; there would never be any replacing Daisy, or forgetting, or creating new dreams. There would only be the lives that had been shattered that day and still lay in forlorn, hopeless pieces around them.

Now, she glanced past Joe to Kian, who was murmuring something to Gordon, Em's husband. Aileen looked her way and gave a watery smile of encouragement. Aileen was surrounded by her sisters, nieces and nephews – the whole clan, who'd love nothing more than to take justice into their own hands right now and dispense with the lawyers. Misty was back at the Mermaid taking care of Marsha. They'd decided to close the pub during the trial.

Jules desperately wanted to be sitting with Kian. Though they hardly touched, or even spoke much about what was happening, she needed to feel him next to her, to take what strength she could from the love that still existed between them, even though it couldn't seem to find its way through to where it should be. She wondered if he felt as desperate to sit with her. If he did, he was showing no sign of it.

'Mr Quentin, did your daughter know that her mother was dead prior to the text she sent to the deceased on July 14th?' Dickon Bruce asked.

With no hesitation, Quentin said, 'No, she didn't.'

Jules's eyes flew wide with shock. Beside her she felt Em and Joe tense. How could that abominable man, a lawyer himself, take an oath to tell the truth and nothing but the truth, then stand there and lie?

'So her mother had been dead for twelve years and during all that time your daughter believed she was still alive?' the barrister asked incredulously.

Quentin touched a shaky hand to his forehead. 'I didn't realise until all this happened that Amelia had rejected the truth and created her own story.'

'I see. So you told her, when she was nine, that her mother was dead?'

Glancing at his daughter, Quentin said, 'I admit, I might not have used that word, which I realise now was a mistake.'

Allowing a moment to pass, the barrister said, 'Can you explain why your daughter claimed to have found her mother in the text she sent to Daisy Bright?'

Quentin's eyes flicked to the defence team, as though expecting an interruption. When none came he said, 'She'd found a woman with the same name and age as my wife, living in Cornwall, I believe.'

The barrister nodded. 'So Amelia assumed this person was her mother?'

'I think it was what she wanted to believe. She's an only child who's missed out on a mother's loving care. The loss created a very big gap in her life.'

Much like the one your daughter's created in ours, Jules wanted to shout into his lying face.

Feeling Em's hand slide into hers, Jules gave it a squeeze and kept her eyes on Quentin.

'Sir, can you tell us where *you* were on July 14th last year?'

'I was in Italy with my partner and her children.'

'On holiday?'

'Correct.'

'But Amelia wasn't with you?'

'She didn't want to come.'

'Do you know why?'

'She said she wanted to sort things out with Daisy, and try to become friends with her again. She'd always been very fond of Daisy, had come to think of her as a sister in a way, and she adored Daisy's mother. I saw a difference in her when she started spending time with them. She seemed happier, more light-hearted, as if she'd finally found what she was looking for. It's why she was so heartbroken when they told her she was no longer welcome in their home.'

Jules didn't look at the jury; she didn't have to to know how effective those words were.

'Would it be correct to say that your daughter fell into a depression after she was rejected by the deceased and her mother?'

'Yes, it would.'

Dickon Bruce turned to the defence team as he asked, 'Do we have any medical records to back this up?'

Appearing slightly strained, Quentin answered the question. 'My daughter didn't want to see anyone, and I wasn't inclined to force it.'

Bruce nodded, as though he'd expected as much. 'And would you say that she was still in a similar state when she sent the text to Daisy, saying she'd found her mother?'

A defence barrister objected, 'My Lord, the witness isn't qualified . . .'

'Quite . . .' the judge responded.

Unperturbed, Dickon Bruce said, 'Did you have any idea what excuse your daughter was going to give to get Daisy to see her?'

'No, none.'

'But you did know she was intending to contact Daisy?'

'I did, because she'd told me. Not only that, she'd asked if she could bring Daisy to Italy with her should things work out. Of course, I said Daisy would be very welcome.'

Jules was feeling sick. Beside her Joe was muttering through his teeth, 'I don't believe this BS. Daisy was coming to the States, for God's sake. No way would she have gone to Italy.'

The fantasy, fabrication, ambiguity and outright lies spun on and on throughout the day, until even Jules began to wonder what she believed.

'Mr Quentin, will you please tell the court how your wife died?' Dickon requested towards the end.

'Relevance, my lord?' the defence demanded.

The judge waved the prosecutor on.

Forced to answer, Quentin said, 'My wife drowned in a boating accident.' A moment passed before he added, 'We've never been sure whether or not it was suicide.'

As a murmur of shocked sympathy threaded around the room, Jules and Em looked at one another. Had Quentin added that as a genuine concern of the time, or to paint his daughter's loss in a more tragic light?

'I don't understand,' Jules said to Andee later, 'why the prosecutor let Quentin off so lightly.'

Andee looked baffled too. 'All I can think is that he has a strategy,' she replied.

The following day, or perhaps it was the day after that, it was hard for Jules to be sure about everything now, Dean was called to the stand. His voice and hand shook so badly as he was sworn in that Jules felt sure each and every juror was finding it impossible not to be moved. For her part, all she could see was the small boy who used to tell jokes that weren't funny in front of an audience of strangers, who all laughed simply because he did. The boy who came alive when he was with them and shut down when she drove him home. The boy who'd loved Daisy like a brother, and who'd quietly accepted her relationship with Joe when they all knew he was in love with her himself.

She desperately didn't want him to be a monster,

someone who had tricked and deceived them all over so many years . . . That couldn't be him. He was no rapist who'd added to Daisy's suffering at the end.

Dean began by explaining how Amelia had sent him a text on July 14th inviting him to her house where she had a big surprise waiting. He texted back to remind her that he didn't have a car, and he wanted to know what kind of surprise. She didn't tell him, but she did offer to come and pick him up. It was around five o'clock by the time they got to Crofton Park, but when Amelia drove in through the gates instead of taking him to the house she drove on through the grounds for about half a mile, until they reached a dilapidated barn where she parked her car. After closing and padlocking the barn doors she led him over to a stable block, so he assumed she was about to show off a new horse.

'And that was when you came upon Daisy?' the lawyer prompted.

He nodded and sobbed on a breath.

'Can you tell us how she was when you found her?'

'She – she was . . . half lying, half sitting on the floor, crying, and tied up by her hands to a metal hook in the wall.'

'What did you do when you saw her like that?'

'I started to run to her, but Amelia jumped in front of me with a knife. I asked her what the hell she was doing. I told her she had to let Daisy go, but she said if I came any closer it would be the worse for Daisy. I couldn't believe she meant to harm her really, but when I went forward she jabbed the knife into Daisy's cheek. Daisy started crying again. She couldn't speak because of the tape on her mouth, but she could make sounds and I knew she was begging me to help her. I wanted to, more than anything, but I was afraid if I went to her that Amelia would cut her again.'

'So what happened next?'

'It went on like that for what seemed like ages, me begging Amelia to let Daisy go and Amelia telling me to shut up or I'd spoil the fun.'

After allowing that to settle, the lawyer continued. 'OK. Please tell us what happened when Daisy's father rang to offer her a lift home.'

Dean's eyes went briefly to Kian. 'Amelia got her to answer the call and to make sure she sounded normal when she told him she'd get a lift later.'

'Is that what Daisy did?'

He nodded. 'Yes.'

'Just like that?'

'Amelia had the knife next to Daisy's eye. She said she'd cut it out if Daisy didn't do as she was told.'

Jules froze inside. *Had she cut Daisy's eyes out?* She didn't know, and nor did she want to know in case it was true. She looked along the row to Kian, but his head was down. He'd gone to the mortuary; was the fact that she had no eyes what haunted him so cruelly?

It couldn't be. That sort of detail would be known to everyone by now, there would have been no escaping it. The press would never have let it go.

'Tell us about the rape, Mr Foggarty,' the lawyer said. 'How did it come about? Was it something you and Amelia Quentin discussed beforehand, making it a part of the plan?'

'No, no it wasn't like that at all.'

241

He looked so stricken, so ashamed and terrified as, in his description of the rape, he used the very words his mother had when she'd come to see Jules, that it truly wasn't hard to believe him.

Aware of Joe sitting next to her, and how hard this part must be for him, Jules tucked his hand through her arm. What kind of effect was this going to have on the rest of his life? On everyone's lives?

Dean's cross-examination took up most of the afternoon, and by the end of it Jules had to wonder if even his parents still believed him.

Dickon Bruce took apart everything he'd said, from the text Amelia sent asking him to come because she had a surprise – where was the text now, he'd never been able to produce it – right through to the rape itself.

'It was what you'd always wanted, wasn't it?' Bruce accused scathingly. 'We know this, because we know you were obsessed with Daisy Bright. You even had a Facebook page dedicated to a delusional romance with her.'

Dean hung his head in shame.

'My Lord, members of the jury, you will see on the screens in front of you a sample from the hundred or more postings detailing romantic assignations the accused claims to have had with Daisy, or Danni, as he calls her here. We can all see who it really is. There is no mistaking the deceased in the thousand or more photographs also posted on this page.' To Dean he said, 'Some of them date back to when you were small children together. Many of the more recent shots, which are on the screens now, were originally of Daisy looking very happy and in love with her real boyfriend, Joe. However, we see no sign of Joe, because his image has been very cleverly replaced with shots of Guy, as the accused chose to call himself on this site. Some attempts, as we see, are rather amateurish, but others could almost be the genuine article.'

Dean's humiliation was hard to watch; harder still was discovering what he'd been hiding all these years. A crush, yes, they'd all known about that, but to have taken things so far . . .

'You have even,' the lawyer continued, 'written about your fantasies as if they were reality, describing to your eager followers the taste of Daisy's – Danni's – kiss, the feel of her breasts, right up to the taking of her virginity.'

Joe was so tense by now that Jules tightened her hold on his hand to try and calm him. 'Remember, it's not true,' she whispered. 'He never did any of those things.'

'In his head he did,' Joe growled, 'and that's bad enough. The guy's sick.'

'. . . and here,' the lawyer was saying, 'is a post claiming that Danni enjoyed rough sex and you were happy to give it to her. "The rougher the better, she loves to pretend I'm raping her, very happy to oblige. Totally awesome."'

Jules's eyes closed. Her heart was like a clenched fist in her chest, trying to ward off any more. So Daisy had been betrayed, brutalised and shown no mercy at all at the end by one of her closest friends.

* * *

When it came time for Amelia to perform – for that was what she did on the stand, perform – it was no easier to bear. In many ways it was far worse.

She lied, wept and whispered her way through her lawyer's questions, glancing occasionally at the jury, or up at the judge, but mostly she stared at Samia Henshawe QC, an elegant, self-assured woman with a kindly voice and exotic eyes, who was taking her carefully through the friendship she'd built up with Daisy and how much it had meant to her.

Were Jules not hearing it with her own ears she'd never have believed anyone capable of lying so convincingly, especially in a court of law. In halting, breathy tones Amelia described days she'd spent with Daisy that Jules knew had never occurred, much less in the way she was claiming. There had been no shopping trips, just the two of them, with Amelia spending hundreds, sometimes a thousand or more pounds on Daisy, any more than there had been sleepovers at Crofton Park with midnight picnics and long, secret chats about the boys they fancied, or the film company they were going to start when Daisy left college (which Amelia would finance), or how eager Daisy was to help Amelia to find her mum.

'So when you sent the text telling Daisy you'd actually found your mother,' Samia Henshawe said gently, 'you totally believed Daisy would be thrilled for you and want to discuss what, if anything, you should do about it?'

'That's right,' Amelia replied meekly.

'And when Daisy came did she have any thoughts on it?'

244

Amelia's eyes went down as she shook her head. 'Not really. I mean, she did, but not like I was expecting.'

'Please tell us what she said.'

Amelia shrugged nervously. 'She got angry with me. She said I was insane for always trying to find my mum when it was obvious my mum didn't want to know me.'

Looking injured for her, Henshawe said, 'This must have come as quite a shock, when she'd always been so supportive over the matter before?'

Amelia nodded. 'Yes, it was. I didn't know what to say. I really thought she was going to help me, but she kept going on about me being a loser and how no one liked me so why did I think my mum was going to be any different?'

Henshawe frowned. 'So some pretty hurtful stuff?'

'Yes.'

'Did you ask her to stop?'

'I'm not sure . . . I was so upset . . . I was crying and asking her why she was being so mean . . .'

'Had she ever been like it before?'

'Not very often.'

'So she had been like it before?'

'Only once or twice when she said things to humiliate me in front of other people, or she'd call me a stalker who needed to get a life.'

From the public gallery Stephie yelled, 'Because you are a stalker, you lying bitch.'

Stephie's mother yanked her back to her seat as the judge called for order.

'One more interruption like that and I'll have you removed,' he warned Stephie.

Everyone turned back to Amelia, whose eyes were swimming in tears.

Very gently, Samia Henshawe said, 'I won't ask you to repeat any more of the things Daisy Bright said to humiliate you, or how you felt when she accused you of being a stalker. I'll just ask if you forgave her for this cruelty?'

'Of course,' Amelia whispered, 'because mostly she was lovely and kind and I really, really wanted to be her friend.'

'Why? What was it about her that drew you to her?'

'Well, I suppose because she was popular, there was always something going on around her . . . She had this performing arts society, and everyone always wanted to be involved.'

'Was that Daisy's only attraction for you?'

Amelia appeared flummoxed for a moment, until apparently catching on she said, 'There was her mum, too. She was always really lovely to me. I used to think, if I had a mother, I'd want her to be just like Daisy's mum.'

'So you came to think of them as a second family?'

'Yes, definitely.'

Appearing moved by that, Samia Henshawe allowed a moment for it to sink in with the jury.

Jules was staring hard at Amelia, willing her to look her way, but Amelia simply kept her head down in her convincingly puppy-whipped way.

'She's told so many lies already,' Em murmured, 'that I'm almost afraid to hear what's coming next.'

Feeling much the same way, Jules glanced along the line to Kian again. His eyes came to hers and he shook his head, clearly as stunned as she was by the false and yet appallingly believable picture being painted of their innocent daughter.

Resuming, Samia Henshawe said, 'Let's return to July 14th and how Dean Foggarty came to be in the stable with you and Daisy.'

Joe growled, 'She hasn't even asked how come they were *in* the stables.'

'It'll be taken care of on the cross,' Jules assured him, confident that it would be.

'Did you invite Dean to visit you that day?' Henshawe asked.

Amelia shook her head. 'Not exactly. I mean, I'd told him before that he was welcome at any time, but I had no idea he was planning on coming that day.'

'So what happened? Did he just show up?'

'Yes.'

'You hadn't sent a text telling him you had a surprise for him?'

'No, definitely not.'

Jules glanced at Dean, and the bitter look on his face was enough to convince her that Amelia was lying about that too.

But where was the text?

'What happened when he arrived?' Henshawe asked. 'What were you and Daisy doing?'

'I was sitting on a straw bale, crying, and Daisy was telling me to grow up and pull myself together. Dean came in and asked what was going on, so Daisy told him I was making a fool of myself over my mother.'

'And what did Dean say to that?'

247

'I can't remember him saying anything. He just kind of looked at me, and then at Daisy.'

'Did you ask him why he'd come? Or even how he'd got there?'

'I didn't get the chance, because he called Daisy outside to talk to her. I couldn't hear what they were saying, but when he came in he told me Daisy was on the phone to her dad saying she didn't need a lift home because I would take her later.'

'Were you OK with that? She'd been pretty horrible to you, so I expect you were keen for her to go.'

'I was and I wasn't. I mean, I didn't want her to go on being horrible to me, but I still really wanted to be her friend and I thought that if she stayed we could work things out.'

'But that isn't what happened?'

Amelia shook her head miserably. 'No, it isn't.'

'So tell us what did.'

Her breath shuddered on a sob as she said, 'It was while Daisy was on the phone to her dad that Dean started saying that she shouldn't have been so mean to me. He said she always got away with things, and it was time she got her comeuppance. I didn't know what he was talking about at first, but when Daisy came back he suddenly grabbed a ball of raffia string and twisted it around her hands. Then he pushed her on to the floor and attached the string to a hook in the wall. Daisy was screaming at us that we were both crazy and we should let her go, but Dean was already tearing off her jeans. She tried to kick him away, so he told me to grab her legs. I didn't want to, but I was afraid of what he would do to me if I didn't.'

'So you held her legs?'

'As best I could, but she was going berserk and I wasn't strong enough.'

'So you threatened her with a knife?'

Amelia nodded dolefully.

'Where did the knife come from?'

'I ran back to the house to get it.'

'With the intention of using it?'

'No, definitely not. It was only to make her lie still for Dean.'

'And did it work?'

'Yes, it did.'

'Did you cut her before he raped her?'

'Yes, but only by accident. She moved suddenly, and the knife went into her face.'

'So you didn't purposely injure her?'

'No.'

'Jesus Christ,' Joe seethed.

'What happened next?' the lawyer asked.

'She kept shouting and screaming and calling us names, especially me. She said I was a waste of space and I should do everyone a favour and stab myself because no one wanted me as a friend. Dean kept telling me to shut her up. They were both shouting at me, so loudly and angrily . . . I didn't know what to do . . . I was so scared and confused . . . I just . . . It was like I wasn't myself any more . . .'

'This is when you started to stab her?'

'No, no. I didn't stab her. It was Dean. He grabbed the knife from me and just went berserk.'

'But the wounds were caused by a left-handed person. Dean is right-handed.'

'I don't know about that. I only know that he did it with his left hand.'

'You noticed at the time that he was using his left hand?'

'I think so. I mean, yes, I did.'

'And you didn't try to stop him?'

'I couldn't. He was too strong for me and I'd never been in a situation like that before. It was terrifying . . . I couldn't think straight . . . I just knew I wanted him to stop, but I didn't know how to make him.'

'So when did he stop?'

'It must have been when he realised Daisy wasn't shouting or fighting any more.'

'Did he say anything to you then?'

She nodded. 'He looked at me and said, "What the fuck have you done? You're a bloody mental case."'

'And what did you say to that?'

'I don't think I answered. I was so shocked. I couldn't believe what had happened.'

Unable to take any more, Jules collected her bag and went to find the nearest Ladies. Never in her life had she imagined having to suffer anything like the scene she had just witnessed. That the girl could be allowed to stand there lying through her teeth, twisting one fact after another, trying to turn herself into the victim rather than the manipulating, cold-blooded killer that she actually was, was enough to turn Jules herself into a killer too, if it was the only way justice could be done.

Em found her as she was splashing cold water on her face. 'It's over for today,' she said, handing Jules a wad of paper towels. 'I'm not sure what we're going to do now, we're all so shell-shocked by that pack of lies. Surely to God the jury saw through it.'

'I don't know that they did,' Jules answered roughly. Her throat was parched; her face was so white and strained across the fine bones it seemed likely to tear apart with grief. 'Where's Kian?'

'He was talking to Andee as I left. We should probably go and find him.'

Much later that evening they were all sitting in the pub bar sipping the drinks Misty had served, and picking at the food rustled up by Marco. Everyone was there: Daisy's friends and their parents, the entire Kesterly contingent of Kian's family, Joe, Em and her husband, even Andee Lawrence and Dougie, the mayor.

They talked around everything that had been said that day, how easy it was going to be to pick holes in it, how certain it was that Dickon Bruce would show Amelia and her father to be nothing but liars.

'What that girl hasn't told us yet,' Andee said quietly to Jules as she was leaving, 'is why, when she had a knife in her hand, didn't she use it on Dean to save Daisy? In fact, nothing she said is adding up, from how Dean just happened to turn up, to running off to the house to fetch a knife . . . Why didn't she just raise the alarm while she was gone? If she knew what Dean was intending, and she's already said that she did, any normal person would have gone straight for the phone. So, whatever the jury might be thinking tonight, I'm fully confident that by this time tomorrow everything will have turned on its head.'

* * *

The following day's cross-examination didn't follow the pattern anyone was expecting. To begin with, Jules and Kian had imagined Dickon Bruce tearing Amelia's lies about her friendship with Daisy to shreds, but it wasn't even he who asked the questions, it was Laura Cosgrove.

'Where did you meet the deceased?' she asked.

'At the Kesterly gym.'

'Did you become friends right away?'

'Yes, we did.'

'And how long ago was this first meeting?'

'About two and a half years.'

'So roughly eighteen months before Daisy was brutally hacked to death?'

As Jules flinched and Amelia's eyes narrowed, there was a protest from the defence that the judge seemed to ignore.

Directed to answer the question, Amelia dropped her head and spoke so softly that the judge asked her to repeat it. 'That's correct,' she said, managing to sound shaky and picked on.

From there Laura Cosgrove moved on to the afternoon of July 14th, when Amelia had sent the text to Daisy. Apparently she had no interest in dates or detail of the fictitious shopping sprees; saw no importance in how often Daisy had stayed over at Crofton Park, which was never, nor did she ask Amelia to tell the court exactly what she and Daisy had discussed during their conversations about Amelia's mother. Jules knew very well that the conversations had never taken place; if they had, Daisy would have told her.

Lies, lies and more lies. How could anyone do it? Clearly swearing an oath meant nothing to that family.

'When you sent the text about finding your mother,' Cosgrove asked, 'did you expect Daisy to reply right away?'

'Yes, I thought she would.'

'Because she was a kind and sensitive friend?'

'Most of the time, yes.'

'So she did reply and she came to see you?'

'That's right.'

'When she arrived, did you go into the house first, or straight to the stables?'

'Straight to the stables.'

Why did you go to the stables? You have to ask her why.

Cosgrove said, 'I believe the stables are some distance from the house. Did you drive Daisy there, or did you walk?'

'I drove.'

'And had Daisy ever been to the stables before?'

'Yes, a few times, we even camped out there once, after my dad had sold the horses.'

As Jules's mouth fell open Stephie shouted, 'You are such a liar!'

The judge's head came up. 'I've already warned you once,' he said crossly, and moments later a bailiff was escorting a fuming, crying Stephie from the court.

Jules was watching Amelia, wondering how it felt to lie with such a flagrant disregard of the fact that people in the room *knew* she was lying. Including her father. There had never been any camping out, and as far as Jules was aware there had never been any horses either – or none that had ever been mentioned to her and Daisy.

'You told us yesterday,' Laura Cosgrove continued,

'that Daisy wasn't as sympathetic to the discovery of your mother's whereabouts as you'd expected her to be.'

'No, she wasn't.'

'Could this be because you hadn't actually found out where your mother was?'

Amelia's face hardened. 'I thought I had,' she stated coldly.

'Because you'd tracked down someone living in Cornwall with the same name and who was the same age?'

'That's right.'

Jules waited for Cosgrove to tell her that the police hadn't found anyone who'd met the criteria when they'd carried out their own search, but all she said was, 'I believe you knew from the age of nine that your mother was dead, but you decided, perhaps in your teens, maybe even later, that a mysterious disappearance would evoke more sympathy and interest than the plain truth.'

Amelia's eyes flashed as she stiffened. 'That's not true,' she replied, glancing at her father.

Cosgrove moved on. 'Dean Foggarty claims that Daisy was already tied up when he arrived at the stables. Is *that* true?'

'No, it isn't. I wouldn't have been able to do that. Daisy was taller and stronger than me. She could easily have fought me off. Anyway, I had no reason to tie her up.'

'You had plenty of reason if it was your intention to kill her . . .'

'My Lord . . .'

'Quite.'

Unapologetic, Cosgrove said, 'She wouldn't have been able to fight you off if you were threatening her with a knife.'

'Where's the question?' Samia Henshawe demanded.

'Were you able to tie Daisy up because you were threatening her with a knife?' Cosgrove rephrased.

'I didn't tie her up. Dean did, when he came.'

Jules looked at Dean. The intensity of his loathing as he stared at Amelia made it clear to Jules, and maybe the jury, that the girl was still lying, but it was her word against his.

'OK, so let's go back to the text you sent Dean telling him you had a surprise for him. Would I be correct in thinking that Daisy was the surprise?'

'No. I mean, I didn't send Dean a text.'

Cosgrove said, 'Did you know about Dean's Facebook page, the one we've seen here in the court?'

'No, that was the first time I saw it.'

Cosgrove appeared surprised. 'Really? Are you sure that previous knowledge of this page wasn't what persuaded you to urge Dean to rape Daisy Bright?'

'Yes, I'm sure.'

'But you knew from reading the page, didn't you, that it was what he wanted?'

'Yes, but . . . I mean, I never saw the page, so no.'

'Yes or no?'

'No.'

Surely to God someone had checked her computer.

Jules asked Andee during a recess, 'Wouldn't someone have checked her computer?'

'Yes,' Andee assured her, 'and apparently she did view the page, several times.'

'So why didn't the prosecutor pursue it?'

Andee shook her head in bewilderment as she said, 'It's a question I'd like answered myself. Perhaps she'll get round to it this afternoon.'

'You say,' Laura Cosgrove declared, 'that you went to the main house to fetch a knife.'

Amelia simply looked at the lawyer. Clearly she'd been schooled only to answer if there was a question.

'I know I'm asking myself,' Cosgrove continued, 'and I'm sure the jury is too, why on earth you didn't seize this opportunity to raise the alarm?'

Amelia's eyes went down as her breath caught on a sob. 'I – I don't know,' she stammered. 'I wish I had . . . I just wasn't thinking straight.'

'But you claimed to know that Dean was about to rape your friend, that seems pretty clear to me. So why didn't you raise the alarm?'

'I – I'm sorry. I know I should have. I wish I had.'

'So we're agreed that you didn't put a stop to what was happening when you could have? Instead, you held a knife to Daisy's face while . . .'

'No, no I didn't do that.'

'But you've already told the court that you did.'

'But not in the way you're making it sound. I didn't want her to be hurt . . .'

'So what did you want?'

'I don't know. I – it all happened so fast . . .'

'Isn't it true that you tricked Daisy into coming to see you with the sole purpose of seeking revenge for the way she and her mother had rejected you several months before? You planned the whole thing, Amelia . . .'

Amelia was throwing panicked looks her father's way. 'I know how it must seem,' she protested, 'but I swear it's not how it happened. I really cared for Daisy. I'd never want anything bad to happen to her . . .'

'And yet according to your own testimony you stood by while she was stabbed no fewer than fifteen times . . .'

'I didn't stand by . . .'

'Then what did you do?'

'I – I can't remember. I – I was shouting at him to stop. I tried to grab him, but he was too strong.'

Cosgrove eyed her coldly.

Amelia eyed her back.

'It was you who carried out the stabbing, wasn't it?' Cosgrove said quietly.

Amelia's eyes flashed. 'No! It was him,' she cried, pointing at Dean.

'With his left hand?'

'I don't know. If you say so.'

Cosgrove's manner remained chill. 'What I say, Amelia, is that it was your left hand that carried out the stabbings, it was *you* who lost control, not Dean Foggarty . . .'

Henshawe was on her feet, but Laura Cosgrove was already saying, 'No more questions, my Lord,' and with a flourish of her gown she retook her seat.

The other part of the trial that had always remained in Jules's mind was the judge's summing-up.

'When you go away to make your deliberations,' he told the jury, 'I would ask you not to forget at any point that an innocent young girl lost her life that day.

I think this fact has been somewhat overlooked at times during the past few days, but it is why we are here. I will remind you again that the charge is joint enterprise, so it is your job to decide whether Amelia Quentin and Dean Foggarty conspired to cause harm to Daisy Bright that resulted in her death. But even if you decide there was no conspiracy, the fact that they were both present at the killing can render them each as guilty as the other.'

He'd said much more, but that was the part that had stayed with Jules and Kian. It had encouraged them to believe that the judge, at least, was on their side.

The jury came back into court far sooner than anyone expected. It was impossible to know whether this was a good sign, or not, but Kian and his mother were optimistic.

Jules had no idea how she felt; all she knew was that no matter what the verdict turned out to be, it was never going to bring Daisy back.

It was only when the foreman declared them both to be, 'Guilty as charged,' and a buzz of surprise threaded through the court, that she realised she was losing her grip on the world.

As Joe clutched her in an embrace she watched Dean sobbing and looking around for his parents. She saw them, hunched and broken, helping to hold one another up as they made their way to the door. They would probably be allowed a few minutes with their son before he was taken back to prison to await sentencing.

Jules's heart was breaking for them; she didn't want

to believe he was guilty any more than they did, but there was no getting away from the Facebook page and all it implied.

Next to him Amelia was as white as a sheet and staring at her father in a state of abject shock. She clearly hadn't expected this, and by the look of him, nor had he. They must have told themselves, had perhaps even been assured by their lawyers, that she would walk away from her crime, that being who they were, with the contacts they had, the law could be made to work in her favour.

They knew now that when it came to taking the life of an innocent girl, they were no more special in the eyes of a jury than anyone else.

That ought to have been an end to it; the guilty verdict should have brought the closure they so desperately needed, and maybe it would have if the sentencing hadn't made such a mockery of it, had even seemed to trivialise Daisy's life.

For the premeditated – and in Jules's and Kian's book it had always been premeditated – killing of their precious only child, the judge, who they'd thought was on their side, had decided that Amelia Quentin need only be sentenced to five years in prison.

The old boys' network might not have achieved the verdict they'd wanted, but in the light of that failure the sentencing was no doubt being viewed as a triumph.

It was Dean's punishment that came as the biggest shock. The judge's comments were scathing as he accused the boy of plotting everything, most particularly the rape.

'Whether it was the intention to end Daisy Bright's life after committing this appalling act we will probably never know,' he stated gravely, 'but it did end, and so the sentence I am going to impose on you, Dean Foggarty, is for ten years.' *Ten years*, twice as long as Amelia.

Jules watched as they were taken away. She had no idea how Amelia was feeling, she only hoped it was terrified and ashamed and as guilty as she undoubtedly was. As for Dean, though she still couldn't make herself believe that he'd deliberately harmed Daisy, she still couldn't forget the Facebook page.

'Are you OK?' Kian asked as they left the court.

Jules shook her head. She had no idea how she was feeling. All she knew was that this wasn't an end to it. It couldn't be, because there was simply no way that they or their daughter had received proper justice from this court.

Chapter Eleven

Amelia didn't write to Jules from prison, which was just as well because Jules would have torn the letter to shreds rather than read a single word her daughter's murderer had to say.

Dean wrote during the first week of his sentence, covering page after page with the detail of what had happened that day, swearing that everything had taken place the way he'd told his mother, and the court. He was sure, he said, that Amelia had erased the text from his phone while he was holding Daisy after it had happened, sobbing his heart out and trying to will her back to life.

I loved Daisy more than anyone else in the world, he wrote in a careful, almost childlike hand, *she meant everything to me. That stupid Facebook page was all a front. Daisy knew about it, because we made it up together. I can see now that we got carried away and went too far, but it felt like a joke at the time. We had no idea it would backfire the way it did. She knew I was gay, she was the only one I ever told, and we thought, stupidly I can see that now, that if I made it easy for my parents to find the page they wouldn't suspect how I really am. They have really strong views about homosexuals, and I was afraid of what they might do if they found out. Daisy said I should tell them anyway, that she'd come with me if I wanted her to, and if they threw me out I could always come and live with you.*

I miss her so much, and I hate myself more each day for not being able to save her from the evil that calls itself Amelia. I deserve to be where I am just for that.

I swear I didn't rape her, Jules, at least not in the sense everyone means it. I truly believed, so did Daisy, that if I made myself do as Amelia said she'd let Daisy go, but it turned out she was lying. There's something horribly wrong with her, as frenzied and out of control as she seemed while she was attacking Daisy, it was like she was enjoying it. I just know that she'd planned it all, from the lie about her mother, to getting me there, to trying to frame me for what she did. She's a maniac, a psychopath, she shouldn't ever be allowed to go free.

I hope this letter hasn't upset you too much, but I feel desperate for you to know that you were never wrong about me. I always loved Daisy more than anyone, and I always will.

Jules had wept a lot over that letter. She still had it somewhere, but she hadn't looked at it in a long time, although she'd answered it to let Dean know that she believed him.

I showed your letter to a detective we've become friendly with, she told him, *her name's Andee Lawrence. She gave it to a lawyer who wasn't involved in the case, but apparently without any new evidence there can't be a new trial. I know you weren't asking for that, but I'm sure you must have been hoping. If anything changes of course I will do my best to support you, and if it's any consolation meanwhile, Kian believes you too, and so does the detective who read the letter.*

He'd written again, telling her how much her words had meant to him, and letting her know that his parents, on the advice of their spiritual leader, had moved away from Kesterly. They were in Leicester, apparently, but Dean didn't pass on an address and Jules didn't write back to ask for one. She saw nothing to be gained from remaining in touch any more, it would be painful for them all, and do nothing to help them move on.

And so here she was two years later, looking back on the time that had passed in a blur of grief, anger, despair and such desperate longing for her precious girl that she often had no idea how she got through the day. Her life was so different now, so removed from the exhilaration of love and dreams she'd shared with Daisy, the highs and lows of a normal existence, that she sometimes wondered if she was still the same person. Perhaps she wasn't. Maybe she really had morphed into somebody else; after all she could no longer call herself a mother, or a wife. In truth she wasn't sure what she could call herself, apart from a daughter, even though her mother didn't always recognise her. And a friend, she mustn't forget that. She still had Em, albeit some four thousand miles away, and now there was Andee too.

Andee had stayed in touch after the trial, ringing often and visiting several times after she and her children moved to Kesterly when she joined the Dean Valley force. Eventually, the demands of her new job had meant that she and Jules saw less and less of each other. Jules understood that, and in some ways she was glad of it, for Andee was a reminder of that terrible time.

It was after Kian's first suicide attempt that Em and Aileen had persuaded her that it was time to move out of the pub.

'You don't have to make a decision about selling right away,' Em had said gently. 'Misty and Marco are more than capable of running things, but living here, surrounded by so many memories, is too hard, not only for Kian, but for you too.'

So Jules, with Aileen's help, had found the house she was in now, which was probably not far enough away from the pub, or the coast, but it was as far as she'd been able to make herself go. It was crazy to think that she still needed to be on hand for Daisy, but it was how she felt. She simply couldn't abandon everything and start all over again as though Daisy had never existed.

Oddly, one of the most heartbreaking parts of leaving the Mermaid had been forcing herself to let go of Ruby. Though there'd been no sign of her since Daisy had gone, no flickering of lights, random bursts of the burglar alarm, or mysterious movements of her little shoe, Jules still spoke to her in her mind, while clutching the shoe to her heart. She truly believed that Ruby was passing messages to Daisy, doing all she could to keep them connected, and even if that weren't the case, it made her feel better to do it.

'Do you think I should take the shoe with me?' she

asked Misty a few days before she was due to leave.

'Why not, if you want to?' Misty replied. 'I think she belongs with you.'

'But this is her home. What if she doesn't want to leave?'

In the end she decided to give the shoe pride of place on a mantlepiece in the library, and Misty had promised never to move it. So, if it ever disappeared, or turned up somewhere else in the pub, they would know Ruby was back.

Though Kian had agreed that moving was the right decision, Jules could tell that his mind was hardly on what she was saying. There was always a glazed, faraway look in his eyes these days, as though he wasn't in the present, but constantly staring into the past. It made it all but impossible to reach him.

'I'm sorry,' he said to Jules the day before their departure, 'but I won't be coming with you.'

Jules looked up in shock, praying she hadn't heard right, even though she'd half expected it.

'We can't be together any more,' he told her sadly. 'We both know it, and it's time to admit it.'

Going to him, her eyes swimming in tears, she cupped his face in her hands as she said, 'I still love you, Kian.'

'I still love you too,' he said, 'but things haven't been . . . You know what I'm saying . . . It had changed before, and now, every time I look at you all I can see is Daisy, and I know it's the same for you when you look at me.'

She couldn't deny it: it wrenched at her so painfully at times that she'd almost stopped looking at him. 'So are we going to let Amelia Quentin destroy everything?' she asked brokenly.

His voice was toneless, resigned, not even bitter as he said, 'She already has. So it's best if I go to Ireland with Mum. We'll help you to settle Marsha into the care home first, of course . . .'

Jules took a step back. 'You've been discussing this without me?' she accused, hurt and shocked.

He shook his head. 'You've known Mum's plans for a while. I haven't told her yet that I intend to go with her.'

Though she wanted to beg him to change his mind, to not give up on them and come with her to the new house, she knew in her heart that it had to be this way if they were going to stand a chance of surviving. So, resting her head on his shoulder, she said, 'I don't know if I can bear it without you.'

Wrapping her in his arms, he whispered, 'It's going to be hard for me too. You've always been my rock, the one I never thought I could be without, but now . . . Watching you suffer . . . Knowing how terrible and hopeless you feel . . . I'm sorry, I wish I was stronger, that I could be here for you to lean on, but I'm not the man I was before this happened, and I don't think I ever will be again.'

So she'd moved into the Risings and he'd gone with his mother to Ireland.

The second time he tried to take his life was on the third anniversary of Daisy's death. Jules already knew from Aileen that he was still a long way from being able to pull himself together, since he barely spoke or ate, almost never left the house, or agreed to visitors; some days he didn't even get out of bed.

Aileen had rung Jules as soon as she'd realised Kian was missing. She was hoping, praying, that he might be on his way to Kesterly to spend the anniversary with his wife, but if he was he'd never mentioned the intention to Jules.

By the time Aileen rang off the emergency services had already found him; someone had seen his car going off the road into a ravine and had immediately reported it. He was airlifted to hospital and everyone agreed, it was nothing short of a miracle that he'd survived.

Clearly he wasn't meant to die, even if he thought he was.

'I don't know when he started blaming himself,' Aileen whispered shakily to Jules, as they sat waiting for him to come round. 'He just started coming out with it one day, saying he shouldn't have taken her to that house, that he should have gone back there to pick her up, if he had she'd still be alive . . .'

Jules didn't admit how many times she'd had the same thoughts, how often she ran them through her mind with happier, life-saving conclusions, though not a part of her blamed Kian for what had happened. He couldn't possibly have known what Amelia was doing to Daisy when he'd spoken to her on the phone; no one could, because no normal person's mind worked that way.

Except hers had. She'd heard Daisy screaming and she'd made herself believe it was her overactive imagination.

Since Kian's accident that everyone knew was a suicide attempt, though no one called it that, he had withdrawn even more deeply into himself. No one mentioned Daisy any more. The way he flinched on hearing her name, as though they'd struck him, made everyone feel so bad that they'd decided it was best to respect his need for silence. Fortunately one of Aileen's neighbours was a GP who kept a close eye on him, and also put Aileen in touch with a psychiatrist. However, Kian didn't want to engage with anyone. His only wish was to be left alone. He couldn't even seem to help himself in order to relieve the strain on his mother, who had aged terribly over the past three years.

So had Jules, she could feel it in her heart and her bones, in the way she moved and even thought; and she could definitely see it in the way she looked. Her eyes were bruised and shadowed by grief, the droop of her mouth made her look as unhappy as she constantly was, the grey in her hair was a reminder of everything she needed to forget, yet would never be able to. Maybe, after more years had gone by, she would find it easier to smile again, or be able to go for hours at a time without thinking about her precious girl and wondering what she'd be like now, whether she'd be in the States with Joe, making it big as a director in Hollywood or New York, becoming a mother herself.

Knowing it was never going to happen had been the hardest truth to accept. She still hadn't managed it, none of them had. Their lives remained in pieces while Amelia Quentin was being allowed to start hers all over again, or pick up where she'd left off – or choose some other unsuspecting, generous-hearted girl to befriend and butcher.

* * *

'Jules, is that you?'

The line was crackling, the voice was a long way away, but Jules knew instantly who it was. 'Yes, it's me,' she shouted with a rare smile. 'How are you, Stephie? Where are you?'

'I'm on an island called Ko Lanta, just off Thailand. I caught up with my emails this morning. I can't believe the bitch is being released?'

Sinking down at the table, Jules said, 'I'm afraid so, even earlier than we expected. Your mum told you?'

'Yes, she did. Everyone did. This is all such an effing stitch-up! Everyone's in on it, even the bloody parole board it seems. It's just not right, Jules. That nutjob is a total psycho. She's not safe to be on the streets.'

Though Jules might agree, all she could say was, 'There's nothing we can do, apart from stay out of her way. Did you hear she's going back to Crofton Park?'

'What! You have to be kidding me. Why the hell would she want to go there after . . . ? Jesus Christ, she is *seriously* sick. Can you stop her?'

'I don't think so, but I'm told she won't be allowed to come near me.'

'Too bloody right she shouldn't. So when does she come out?'

'This Friday, apparently.'

'That soon? But it's OK, I should be able to get back by then.'

Jules's eyes flew open. 'What are you talking about? You've hardly been gone a month . . .'

'I don't care. No way am I letting you stay there on your own while that psycho bitch is around. What the f . . . is everyone thinking, letting her go back to Crofton Park?'

'It'll be fine, Stephie, I promise. She doesn't scare me, so please, you mustn't break off your trip . . .'

'Have you been in touch with Joe? Does he know about this?'

'Yes, he does. He starts his European tour in a couple of weeks, so he'll be here . . .'

'That's great. I'll message him as soon as I'm off the phone. And what about Kian? How's he taken it?'

'No one's told him yet. His mother and I thought it was best that he didn't know. It won't help him.'

'Mm, maybe not. Jesus Christ, if that bitch only knew the damage she's done . . . Even if she did she wouldn't care. I bet Kian's family have had something to say about her early release, which is why I don't get her wanting to go back to Crofton Park. She's met Danny, she's got to know that no one wants her around . . . I guess she doesn't care about that either. Anyway, I'll text or phone as soon as I've booked my flight . . .'

'Stephie . . .'

'Jules! If you have the time please get my room ready, because no matter what you say I'm coming home,' and before Jules could protest any further the line went dead.

Hanging up her end, Jules had no idea whether she wanted to laugh or cry. She loved Stephie so much and knowing she was coming, that she actually *wanted* to come, was so moving and uplifting that she felt almost afraid of how much it mattered.

Of course, she should have told Stephie herself about the release, and she would have had she not guessed that Stephie would react this way. She was twenty-one now and needed to get on with her life as much as the rest of them. This year out of uni was supposed to be helping her to do that, though Jules knew that her mother, Tina, was still worried. This was the third university course Stephie had abandoned, and she still had no idea what she wanted to do with her future.

Please get my room ready because I'm coming home.

How wonderful it felt to know that Stephie thought of this as her home, which it kind of had been since she'd started her attempts at uni. With her problematic older brother, his equally problematic wife and two small children taking up all the extra space in Stephie's parents' house, Stephie herself had asked Jules if she could rent a room with her whenever she came back to Kesterly. Jules had been delighted, but of course had never charged Stephie a penny, and had made sure, before sealing the deal, that Tina didn't think she was trying to use her daughter to replace Daisy.

What Tina thought was that she'd love to come and live with Jules from time to time too, it would be as good as a month in a spa in comparison to all the goings-on in their house.

'You think when they grow up that they'll go away and leave you alone,' she'd complained, before realising who she was talking to.

'It's OK,' Jules assured her, 'I know it's not always easy being a parent, and just as long as you don't think I'm trying to be that for Stephie . . .'

'What I think is that you'll enjoy spending time together. It might even help you both to heal.'

So that was what they'd done for the past couple of

years, house-shared whenever Stephie was in Kesterly, and it was odd, in fact totally unexpected, how being with Stephie often helped Jules to bear things a little better. Stephie spoke about Daisy as freely as if she might walk in the door at any minute. No one else ever did that, apart from Jules when she was with Stephie. Of course they shed tears together too, and talked about all the terrible things they hoped were happening to Amelia, and how desperately they dreaded them happening to Dean.

Occasionally she and Steph would make the two-mile drive down the hill to Hope Cove, where they'd scattered Daisy's ashes on the beach; or they'd post songs, or film links, or anything they felt would be of interest to Daisy on her Facebook page. It was surprising, and moving, how many of Daisy's friends still did the same, especially around the time of her birthday or anniversary of her death. *Hey, Daisy Daze, thought you'd love this singer. Take a look at these guys, Daze, amazing dancers, don't know how they do it. This made me think of you, and how much we all still miss you.*

Jules was at her computer now, intending to get on with some work, but wondering what Daisy would say about her killer going free so soon after the girl had ripped their lives apart.

Are you going to haunt her? she typed into an email to Daisy that only she would see. *Will you and Ruby scare her literally to death? Do you want revenge? You were never the sort to wish ill on others, nor was I, but I have to admit I am now.*

She paused in her typing and took a steadying breath. It had been a while since she'd last written to

Daisy and doing it now was making her feel light-headed, as if she were losing a sense of where she was. It didn't matter; what was important to her was how this sort of communication seemed to create a more tangible connection than simply thinking the words in her head.

I often wonder if you can see what her life is like in prison? Do the other inmates make her life hell? Is she damaged now – I should say even more damaged than before? What is her father doing? Will he come back to Crofton Park too? It sullies the feel of the moor even to think of them being here. They're like the enemy on the hill, great big mounds of toxic waste that we need to get rid of.

Realising she was allowing her hatred to get the better of her she went to the fridge, poured herself a glass of wine and settled down to begin again.

Can you see Daddy, my darling? How's he doing? Is there a way you can help to cheer him up? I miss him almost as much as I miss you.

With a smile hovering over her lips, she went on, *Did you watch me finding a flight for you the other day so you could go and join Stephie on her travels? I didn't pay for it, of course, I'm not that nutty yet! What did you think of the tops and shorts I picked out for you to take with you? I could especially see you in the lime and turquoise sundress, and those gorgeous sparkly gladiator sandals. I'm not sure if they're still all the rage, but they were so eye-catching that I couldn't stop myself putting them in the basket. You know, I almost heard Daddy reminding me that you need to take sunblock. Do you remember how he used to go on about your delicate skin and how you need to protect it? Knowing him, he'd have taken the flight to Bangkok with you to make sure you got there safely, the way he used to when you flew to Chicago to see Joe.*

I wonder if you can see what they're all up to now in the States. You know that Joe was late starting college. He took what happened very badly, worse I think than I realised, but I was so busy trying to cope with me and Daddy and the grannies . . . His father put him into therapy. I think it helped, because he's just finished studying for the Bachelor's degree he needs to get into law school. He told me in one of his emails that he's feeling confident that things are finally on course. Do you know if he's found another girlfriend yet? Do you mind if he has? I think I would, but of course I'd have to get over it. He's going to be here soon. I'm anxious about him running into Amelia, or going to seek her out. What's he going to do, confront her and tell her how she's devastated our lives? She already knows that and I really don't think she cares.

She stopped typing again and drank more wine. She was feeling better, calmer, as though something was lifting itself from her heart and allowing her to breathe more easily. It was often like that when she wrote to Daisy; it was as though her daughter still had the power to bring light into her life.

Chapter Twelve

Amelia's big day had arrived. The release was happening right there, on the TV screen, in all its repugnant glory.

'We're expecting her at any minute,' a reporter from the local news was saying over a wide shot of the open prison's bizarrely hospitable entrance, with its jaunty flower beds and helpful signage. 'As you can see some friends have turned up to greet her . . .'

'What friends? She never had any friends before,' Stephie spat in disgust. 'So where the hell have that lot suddenly come from?'

Having no answer for that Jules and Andee continued to watch, waiting for Amelia to appear from the black hole of the facility.

'. . . one of the friends was telling us earlier,' the reporter continued, 'that they were looking forward to the coming-out party later.'

As Jules flinched, the news anchor said from the studio, 'Coming out? That makes her sound like some kind of debutante about to be presented to the Queen.'

'Indeed,' the reporter retorted drily.

The camera suddenly swung round as a stretch

limousine pulled up in front of the prison. On the screen a chauffeur, complete with cap and grey suit, got out and went to open a rear door. A lithe, handsome young man in a leather jacket and faded denim jeans emerged.

'WTF?' Stephie hissed incredulously as the waiting women surrounded him.

'Any idea who that is?' the anchor asked the reporter.

'None,' the reporter replied, 'but it would appear Amelia Quentin's going to be leaving prison in style.'

'I feel sick,' Stephie muttered.

Feeling much the same way, Jules glanced at Andee, then back at the screen as the reporter cried in a burst of excitement, 'Here she is. Yes, it's definitely her. The girl who killed Kesterly's beloved Daisy Bright.'

Jules's stomach churned again and as Amelia came further into shot she felt her blood running cold.

'My God,' Stephie murmured in appalled amazement.

Amelia didn't look like someone who'd spent the past two years suffering all kinds of hardship behind prison bars. Dressed as she was, in a chic apple-green dress, black low heels and a colourful silk scarf, she looked more like a young sophisticate leaving an expensive department store or exclusive spa than an ex-convict vacating a penal institute. Her mousy hair was styled in an elegant boyish cut, and her normally pasty skin was enlivened with a subtle but effective application of make-up.

'Amelia! A word for the local news,' the reporter shouted, as the waiting friends gathered around the girl.

Amelia didn't look up. She simply continued to accept her friends' boisterous welcome as though there were no cameras present at all.

'You have to wonder how this is going down with her victim's family?' the news anchor commented.

Jules and Andee looked at one another, neither of them knowing what to say, while Stephie glared at the screen as though she might smash it.

'I'm getting the feeling that there's something stage-managed about this,' Andee commented, as the limousine drew alongside the celebrating group and the young man opened a door for Amelia to get in.

'Amelia! Do you have anything to say to Daisy Bright's family?' a reporter shouted.

Amelia stopped and looked up.

The camera zoomed in and as her face filled the screen Jules felt the bile of loathing rise in her throat. It was as though the girl was looking straight at her.

'I want them to know,' Amelia said softly, 'that I'm very sorry for what happened to Daisy, and that I forgive them for the way they've treated me, and that I bear no ill will.'

Stephie gasped as Jules stared at the screen in stunned disbelief.

'What's next, Amelia?' someone else shouted.

'I'm still considering my options,' she replied modestly.

'Is it true you're writing a book?' someone else asked.

'Will it be a work of fiction?' the local reporter called out scathingly.

Before Amelia could reply the young man took her by the elbow and handed her into the car.

As it swept away, leaving the street empty but for the press, the local reporter stepped in front of the camera to continue her piece. 'So, Amelia Quentin is now out of prison and, we're told, on her way back to her home on Exmoor.'

'Have we heard anything from the Bright family?' the anchor asked.

'No, no comment from them so far,' came the reply.

'OK, thanks Beth. Now, for more breaking news . . .'

The screen changed and Stephie hit the remote, plunging them into a silence of stunned anger and bewilderment.

'What the hell was that?' Stephie cried, slapping her hands to her head. 'She's carrying on like she's some kind of victim, or bloody celebrity, when everyone knows *she did it.*'

Looking at Jules, Andee said, 'I have a horrible feeling she's trying to pull you into some sort of mind game, so whatever you do, please don't respond.'

'I have no intention of it,' Jules assured her, glancing at the phone as it rang. 'It'll be one of Kian's family,' she decided. 'I'll call them back.'

'That bloke who was with her,' Stephie snorted. 'Who the heck is he, is what I want to know. And the limousine, and all those trampy-looking females. Where the hell did they come from?'

'There was no sign of her father,' Jules commented.

'I noticed that,' Andee responded. 'So will he be joining in the "coming-out" celebrations, I wonder?'

Was the girl really going to have a party? It felt like such an insult, such a slap in the face, that Jules had to put it out of her mind. Andee was right, she mustn't engage.

She checked her mobile as it bleeped with a text.

'It's from Joe,' she announced, 'wanting to know if "it's" out yet.' After quickly texting back she said to Stephie, 'I wonder if Dean saw it. I don't suppose he will have. It's so wrong that she should be walking free now and he isn't.'

'She's making me feel so violent I hardly know what to do with myself,' Stephie growled.

Getting to her feet, Jules said, 'Let's try to focus on something else, shall we? The last thing we need is to obsess about her,' as if she'd been doing anything else these past three years.

Though they tried talking about other things, and actually succeeded for a while, the way the phone kept ringing and texts flooded in was a constant reminder of what they were trying to forget. It seemed everyone Jules knew had either seen or heard about the release and wanted to sympathise, or express their outrage, or offer whatever support Jules might feel she needed.

'I know Stephie's with you now,' Danny growled in his deep, gravelly way, 'but if you feel that's not enough I'm happy to send someone to sit outside and watch the place, make sure she doesn't come anywhere near you.'

'It's fine, Danny, honestly,' Jules assured him. 'It's not as though she's ever threatened me and she's sure to be subjected to all sorts of restrictions, so the chances are we won't see her at all.'

'Let's hope that's the truth, because we definitely don't want her anywhere round here. Have you spoken to Aileen today?'

'Not yet. We're still not intending to tell Kian, so I hope you . . .'

'It's OK, he's not going to hear it from me. I don't think he can handle it. I just want to make sure you can, that's all.'

'If I feel I can't, I promise I'll be in touch.'

'You do that. Oh, and before you go, the smarmy bastard who turned up in the limo, do you know him?'

'I've never seen him before.'

'Well, if I'm right about who he is . . . I'm making some enquiries, so I'll let you know. You've got my number, if you're worried about anything use it, any time day or night, phone's always on.'

Three days later Jules was in her mother's room at Greensleeves, watching Marsha's anguished eyes darting about the room as if trying to find an escape.

'It's only me, Mum,' she said for the fifth or sixth time. 'You remember me, don't you?'

'Nurse!' Marsha croaked weakly. 'Nurse!'

Since this was Marsha's routine response to most things Jules knew it was doubtful anyone would come, though she couldn't help wishing someone would. The carers were a friendly bunch and most stopped for a chat when they could. However, they were busy with afternoon tea right now, and getting those who weren't bed-bound from the lounges to the dining room could be like trying to herd cats.

'Amelia Quentin's out, you know,' she said to her mother. 'I keep thinking she's going to get in touch with me, but I haven't heard anything from her.'

Marsha's gaze was focused on nothing now. She

wasn't listening; for all Jules knew she couldn't even hear.

'She doesn't know where I live,' Jules ran on, 'so she's not likely to drop round.'

She wondered what she'd do if Amelia did appear. She knew what she'd like to do.

Marsha burped and a line of drool ran down her chin.

Wiping it away with a tissue, Jules said, 'Do you remember Daisy? Your granddaughter, Daisy?'

Marsha turned her head away.

Aware of an awful frustration building, Jules suddenly exclaimed, 'It's all right for you, isn't it? You just sit here in your own little world with everyone taking care of you, bringing you food, changing your clothes, wiping your bloody nose . . . You don't give a damn about anything that's happening around you. You couldn't care less, could you?'

'Nurse!' Marsha mumbled. 'Nurse.'

'Listen to me,' Jules snapped, grabbing her hand. 'I'm going out of my mind here wondering what to do, or say, or even think. Stephie's trying to help, but she can't talk about anything else either, and my phone hardly stops ringing. "Have you seen her?" "Do you know if she's definitely at Crofton Park?" "I swear I caught sight of her in Bar 4 One the other night." Why do people think I want to know about her? I just want to forget she exists, pretend she never even came into our lives, but how the hell am I going to do that when she robbed us of the most precious thing we ever had?'

Marsha was cowering away, trying to tug her hand free.

'Stop it, Mum, just stop,' Jules cried helplessly. 'You know who I am and you know I'd never hurt you, so for God's sake stop being like this.'

'Nurse,' Marsha whimpered.

'Nobody's coming,' Jules tried not to shout, 'do you hear me? No one's listening to you apart from me, and I don't know what the hell to do with you.'

Marsha was starting to shake; tears were filling her eyes.

Beside herself, Jules shot to her feet. 'I have to go,' she sobbed. 'I can't stay here with you today,' and pressing a kiss to Marsha's head she made for the door.

'Jules,' Marsha muttered. 'Where's Jules?'

'Oh Mum, I'm here. Why can't you see it's me?'

'Is everything OK in here?'

Jules turned to find Malinda, one of the nurses, regarding her worriedly.

'I'm sorry,' Jules mumbled, 'I'm not coping so well with her today. I need to go.'

'Of course,' Malinda said kindly. 'She'll be fine here with us. We've got a nice cup of tea on the way, Marsha, and I expect you'll want a slice of the lovely carrot cake someone brought in . . .'

Weighted with guilt and self-loathing Jules took off along the corridor, promising herself she'd come back later when she'd managed to get a grip – and thanking God for the angels who cared for her mother so much better than she ever could.

Jules had no idea what she was doing here, what kind of madness had made her turn her car in this direction when she'd left Greensleeves. She only knew that she hadn't wanted to go home, or into town, or anywhere that might have actually made some sort of sense.

As if this did.

She was parked in the shade of a sprawling sycamore tree diagonally opposite the black wooden gates to Crofton Park. The gates she and Kian had tried so desperately to get through the night Daisy was murdered.

She sat motionless, expressionless, staring at the stillness and trying not to torment herself with images of Kian blithely dropping Daisy off and driving away. It could have happened yesterday, or last week, or maybe she was plucking it from a dream.

If only.

Sunlight was streaking through the trees that spilled over the Park's walls, casting dappled pools amongst the shadows in the street. Jules barely noticed. Since Daisy had gone nature had lost its lustre; all pleasures, along with hope and understanding, had fallen away like autumn leaves to be trampled, turned to mulch in a sodden ditch.

Amelia Quentin belonged in a ditch, one so deep and clogged that she would never have been able to find her way out. Instead she was behind those walls enjoying the luxury of her father's home, tasting the heady delights of freedom, soaking up the promise of a future that held all the options she was apparently going to take some time to consider.

Hatred, resentment, the need to hurt, even destroy the girl, were burning holes all the way through Jules.

Why should Amelia Quentin have the right to anything at all after what she'd done? If she'd belonged to any other family she'd have been charged with murder and so would be serving a mandatory life sentence now. There'd have been no easy open prison, no privileges, or early release, and God knew she wouldn't have been able to stage that appalling show she'd put on for the cameras last week.

Jules wondered bitterly if Amelia ever thought about Daisy, and if she did how she felt. Dismissive? Triumphant? Was she capable of guilt or remorse?

I forgive them for the way they treated me and bear them no ill will.

Jules's head went down as longing for Daisy overwhelmed her. How could anyone measure the depth of pain and suffering of someone being frenziedly hacked to death? How long had it taken? Had Amelia been sure Daisy was dead before she stopped, or had she simply run out of strength?

She wanted to ask Amelia why she thought she'd had the right to take Daisy's life. What sense of entitlement, outrage, self-pity even, had made her force Daisy, and her family, to pay such a terrible price for such a small offence?

Whatever the answers, the girl would never have been able to justify what she'd done, so maybe Jules didn't want to ask after all. She only wanted to make Amelia pay . . .

Hearing a motorbike approaching she glanced in her wing mirror and watched it pass, expecting it to carry on around the bend. Instead it slowed to a halt as it reached the Park gates.

Sinking lower in her seat she kept her eyes on the rider as he took off his helmet, shook out his hair and used a booted foot to press the entryphone bell. It was the young man who'd met Amelia from prison.

Come to be paid for his part in the show? Or was he really a friend?

A few moments later the gates slid apart, and he roared off along the drive.

By the time the engine noise died the gates were closing again. There had been plenty of time for Jules to follow, had she wanted to, but she wasn't ready for a confrontation yet. She wasn't sure if she'd ever be, if it was even what she wanted, but knowing how long the gates took to close felt like useful information to tuck away.

She should have left then, should have taken herself home to try and clear her head, or back to Greensleeves to check on her mother, but for some reason she stayed where she was.

Several minutes ticked by, a couple of cars swept past, the birds continued to sing, and a squirrel darted across the top of the gates to disappear into the trees. Everything was so perfect, so tranquil. No one would ever have guessed that a killer was in the vicinity, hidden like a predator in the bush, or an odourless poison in the air.

Jules suddenly noticed that the gates were starting to open again.

Quickly ducking into the shade of the passenger seat, she watched as an open-topped BMW with Amelia at the wheel and the young man beside her swept out into the lane and on around the bend.

Immediately starting her car, Jules crunched it into gear and took off after them. She had no idea why she was doing this, what she hoped to gain by it, she simply felt compelled to follow, as if their destination might in some way provide her with information she needed to know.

Fifteen minutes later, as they turned left off the moor into the upper reaches of Kesterly, Jules's heart rose into her mouth. They were heading down the hill towards the Risings. Surely to God they weren't intending to drop in on her? Was Stephie there? What would she do if she opened the door and found her best friend's killer in the porch?

It would terrify her.

It was already terrifying Jules, until the BMW sailed on down the hill and she remembered that Amelia didn't know where she lived.

Or she shouldn't, but how could anyone be sure about that?

It was when they reached the bottom of the hill, where the road curved around to the right to carry on along the coast into Kesterly, that Jules realised where Amelia and her passenger were going.

She could hardly believe it, couldn't even bear the thought of it. The brazenness, the sheer horror of such gall was stifling her breath. They were out of sight now, because they'd already taken the spur road to the left, the one that led straight into the heart of Hope Cove.

Driving on past, she pulled into a layby and dropped her head on to the steering wheel. She felt nauseous, panicked, like she wanted to scream or yell or bang her fists into Amelia's hateful face – or stab a knife into the very heart of her.

How could she? What kind of sick person could go to the home of the girl she'd killed as though she might actually be welcome, or as if it were some kind of fond trip down memory lane? What the hell was wrong with the girl? What was she trying to prove? No normal person would even think about going into the cove, never mind actually set foot in it after the chaos and heartbreak they'd caused there.

There was no doubt in Jules's mind that Misty and Marco would throw the pair straight out again, but she took out her mobile anyway, intending to call Misty, until she realised she didn't want anyone to know that she'd been following Amelia. For the same reason she couldn't call Andee either, to ask about Amelia's parole conditions. And though she was sorely tempted to involve Danny she quickly reminded herself that nothing good would come of it if she did.

Besides, if anyone was going to avenge Daisy's killing it would be her.

In the end, deciding she needed to go home to steady herself, she turned the car around and started back up the hill. She hadn't got far when her mobile rang, and seeing it was Stephie she clicked on.

'Hi, are you still with your mum?' Stephie asked.

'No, I'm on my way back. I should be there in a couple of minutes. Is everything OK? You sound worried.'

'Do I? No, no I'm fine. Well, no I'm not actually. I've just been online and there's something . . . Well, there's something here that you ought to see.'

* * *

Hey all you sizzly peeps, party time at my place. Everyone invited. If anyone in touch with Daisy's mum pls tell her would love to see her. Dates and times to follow. AQ x

Jules looked at Andee, whom she'd called right after Stephie had shown her the post.

Andee was shaking her head in disbelief. 'If I hadn't seen this with my own eyes . . .' she murmured.

Still inwardly reeling at the tone of the message, never mind what it said, or where Stephie had found it, Jules pushed an unsteady hand through her hair.

'It's putting it on Daisy's Facebook page that's really getting me,' Stephie raged. 'How dare the bitch go anywhere near it? It's like having filth poured over something lovely and pure.'

To Andee Jules said, 'She surely can't believe I'd go, so what's this really about?'

'I've no idea,' Andee replied. 'Her mind doesn't seem to work along the same lines as most, but she's definitely trying to engage you in something.'

'She's totally schizo,' Stephie snorted. 'Have you read what she said to Janey Field, who told her she'd rather hang herself than go anywhere near her? She actually said, "I'm sure I can help with that ☺."'

Jules turned to Andee again. 'Is this breaking the terms of her parole, going on to Daisy's Facebook page?'

'I'm not sure,' Andee replied, 'but I can check.'

'Did you hear she went to the Mermaid yesterday?' Stephie asked Andee.

Andee's eyebrows rose in shock.

'She didn't even get through the door,' Jules told her. 'It wasn't only Misty who barred the way, a few of the regulars were there so she realised pretty quickly that she was making a mistake.'

Andee frowned as she thought. 'Like you,' she said, 'I'm asking myself what this is really about. Not just this bizarre invitation, but why did she choose to come back here at all?'

'And why,' Stephie cut in, 'stage that ludicrous display outside the prison with a bunch of fake friends and a bloke who can only be interested in her money, or there's something wrong with him too. I mean, who in their right minds gets involved with a convicted killer?'

'According to Danny,' Jules said, 'he's the brother of someone she was in prison with. We're guessing that most of the friends are similarly related.'

'I wonder,' Andee said very gently to Jules, 'if it's time to close down Daisy's Facebook page?'

Jules immediately felt a surge of resistance. 'It would feel like a victory for her if we did,' she replied. It would also feel like closing off another part of Daisy, and she'd had to close off so much already.

'It would be one less way for her to get to you,' Andee pointed out.

'We can always defriend her,' Stephie piped up. 'And there has to be a way of taking that post down. I'll ask Joe, he's sure to know.'

All eyes went to the laptop as another post bleeped its arrival.

Hey peeps, me again. Someone pls tell Daisy's mum that we were watching her on CCTV yesterday. Sad. She should come to the party. It might cheer her up to have some fun.

Andee frowned. 'What CCTV?' She turned to Jules. 'Where were you yesterday?'

Realising she had to come clean, Jules said, 'I drove up there.'

Stephie's eyes widened as Andee regarded her darkly.

'I know it was a crazy thing to do,' Jules admitted, 'I can't even really say why I did it. I guess I needed to know for sure if she was there.'

'Did you try to go in?'

'No, of course not. I sat outside for a while.' She looked from Andee to Stephie and back again. 'It was a bad day,' she explained. 'I wasn't thinking straight . . .'

'The next time you feel like doing that,' Stephie cut in, 'call me first and I'll come with you.'

'It would be best not to go at all,' Andee cautioned. 'Look, I understand this isn't an easy time, emotions are fraught, nerves are in shreds, but engaging with her on any level will only make things worse.'

Jules turned away, her insides clenched with frustration and fury, while the need to lash out at the girl, to crush her with a whole lot more than rejection, made her head thump with its power.

'Jules?' Andee said carefully.

Realising Andee was sensing something, Jules forced herself to sound calm as she replied, 'You're right, of course, we need to give Crofton Park a wide berth, and maybe it is a good idea to close down the Facebook page.'

Stephie was regarding her uncertainly.

'Just do it,' Jules told her. 'Then maybe you can private message everyone from your own account to explain why it's not there any more.'

Following her into the kitchen, Andee said, 'You

shouldn't be having to deal with this. Have you thought about going away for a while?'

Being in such a turmoil, so dislocated from anything that made sense, or felt right, even sounded right in her own mind, it took a moment for Jules to register the words. When she did her eyes sparked with anger. 'She's done enough already,' she snapped, 'I'm not allowing her to push me out of my own home.'

'That's not how it would be . . .'

'It's the way she would see it. I would too. No, I'm sorry, if anyone's going to leave this place I can promise you this, it'll be her, not me.'

Chapter Thirteen

'Jules, it's Aileen. How are you, dear?'

'I'm fine,' Jules replied, lifted by the sound of her mother-in-law's voice, just because she loved her. 'How about you?'

'Oh, you know how it is. Over my cold, but I've got myself a niggling pain in the back to take its place. It'll go. It's not why I'm ringing.'

Jules guessed as much. 'Is Kian OK?' she asked, always her first concern.

'Sure, as OK as he can be, but I'm afraid someone's told him she's out. Don't ask me who, but with that telly thing we heard about and everyone knowing, it was bound to reach him sooner or later.'

Of course. She should have thought of that. 'How's he taken it?'

'To be honest, he didn't say much, but I heard him on the phone to our Danny last night.'

'Saying what?'

'I didn't catch a lot of it, but he was definitely asking Danny to look out for you. Do you reckon that girl means you some harm, Jules? Is that why she's back there?'

'I think she's trying to mess with my head,' Jules admitted, 'but as for anything else . . .' Her eyes flicked across the street to the closed gates of Crofton Park. Thank God Aileen couldn't see where she was, but presumably Amelia could. 'Don't let's talk about her,' she said, turning aside. 'Tell me about Kian.'

Aileen didn't need much encouragement, so it wasn't long before Jules knew that Kian had started to help his second cousin Cullum on the building sites, and he'd been to see Father Michael a couple of times lately, although Aileen didn't know what they'd discussed. 'I don't think he's doing the confessional, or has settled down to some praying,' Aileen ran on ruefully, 'but he's got a lot of questions he still wants answering, so I'm guessing he's testing the Good Lord through our long-suffering priest.'

Jules couldn't be sure whether she was finding it hard, or easy, to picture her shattered husband sitting down with a man of God to demand reasons for why he'd had to lose his daughter, especially in such a senseless and brutal way, or even why he'd had to lose her at all. All she knew was that her heart was filling with his confusion and pain, and all the love she still felt for him. She missed him so much that sometimes it was almost as hard to bear as losing Daisy, but it still did no good for them even to speak on the phone. They couldn't go more than a few minutes without mentioning her, or, even if they did manage not to, she was so powerfully there they simply ran out of words. How sad and hard it was that they couldn't bear each other's pain.

Eventually, she said, 'It's good to know that he's going out. Be sure to send him my love, won't you?'

'Oh, and he'll be sending his too,' Aileen responded. 'Can I tell him you're coping all right with her being around?'

Jules looked over to where the CCTV camera was partially hidden in a tree. 'Yes, you can tell him that,' she replied, and after promising to be in touch again soon she switched off the phone.

A few minutes later she got out of the car, walked across the street and stared up at the lens.

If Amelia was watching at her end they'd be in eye-to-eye contact now.

Did Amelia feel afraid, or at least unnerved by these unusual visits from her victim's mother? This was the third one Jules had made in as many days, each time parking in the same spot under the sycamore, and crossing from time to time to go and stare up at the camera.

With a small twist of her mouth, that might have been a smile, she turned from the camera and walked back to the car.

If this wasn't throwing doubt on her sanity, she didn't know what would. A mother, torn apart by grief, crushed by the system that had robbed her of proper justice, traumatised by the proximity of her nemesis, besieged by Facebook posts and attempted visits to her old home . . . How, in the light of all she'd been subjected to, could it come as a surprise to anyone that she'd lost all sense of reason? And if she had no sense of reason, how on earth could she be held accountable for her actions?

Maybe she'd be tried for Voluntary Manslaughter – With Provocation.

* * *

Stephie was going to be away for two nights. She'd rented a car so she could drive up north to visit Dean in prison, and was planning to drop in on his parents on the way back, if they were up for seeing her. After that she'd arranged to spend the night at a hotel near Heathrow in order to be handy for picking up Joe and his friend when they flew in the next morning.

This small house was going to seem quite crowded with all four of them bustling about in it, something Jules had no idea if she was ready for, or was even looking forward to. She felt sure she must be, given her fondness for Stephie and Joe, but lately she'd seemed so out of kilter with her feelings, as if they weren't really hers, that it wasn't always easy to know what was actually going on in her mind. All she could say for certain was that in the wake of Stephie's departure she was aware of a swamping loneliness trying to drag her into its endless murky depths.

However, she'd made plans for this evening that should, in their own strange way, rescue her from the worst of it.

It was just after eight when she got into her car and drove into Kesterly. A dark mass of cloud was swirling in from the horizon as she reached the seafront, dimming the evening light, and making the Victorian promenade appear like a faded postcard of its original era. She'd heard on the forecast that there might be rain later; it seemed they were right.

After parking in the multi-storey close to the marina, she crossed the busy main road and headed into the old town's pedestrian area. Here the streets were cobbled and crooked, with quaint Dickensianstyle shopfronts, quirky restaurants and plenty of cafés with bistro tables and parasols spilling out of their bi-fold doors on to plant-studded courtyards. It was the part of town Daisy had always loved to come to with her friends, and where Jules and Kian had enjoyed many nights out too – and where, tonight, Amelia was 'meeting up with the girls' at Fruit of the Vine Wine Bar.

Jules knew this because she'd begun visiting Amelia's Facebook page. She'd discovered that Amelia was using it to make public just about everything she was doing. *Manicure at K's Tue 3 pm; hair at Jessica's Wed 5 pm; Ollie back from London tonight, going to movie,* Fifty Shades of Grey, *anyone seen it yet? Party at Mel's, what's everyone wearing? Anyone fancy some shopping tomorrow?*

To read her entries anyone would think she was like any other girl of her age, mostly interested in herself, her boyfriend and having a good time. There was nothing about being a killer, or a person of no conscience, or someone who'd carry out a deadly revenge if anyone wronged her.

Jules had started to wonder if Amelia was advertising her movements on Facebook especially for her benefit. Though the girl's warped mind was impossible to read, it seemed like the perverse kind of thing she'd do, either wanting to rub Jules's face in the fact that Daisy could no longer do these things, or to taunt Jules into following her.

So far Jules had done no more than walk into the nail bar a few minutes after Amelia to make an appointment of her own. Since she hadn't glanced Amelia's way it wasn't possible to know if Amelia had spotted her, but Jules liked to think she had. Later, she'd rung to cancel the appointment, making the call while waiting for a 'friend' outside the cinema that was showing *Fifty Shades of Grey*.

Although Amelia hadn't taken long to spot her – under the hanging flower baskets at the centre of the plaza – she'd quickly turned away and gazed laughingly up into her boyfriend's eyes while clinging to his arm. *Oh, she was so happy and in love, and with her whole lovely, privileged life unrolling like a carpet of fresh, vibrant daisies in front of her.*

She apparently chose not to be aware of the mutterings around her, some of them so loud that even Jules, standing fifty feet away, could hear them: *There she is, over there. The one who killed Daisy Bright. I don't know how she's got the nerve to show her face around here. Hope she's not sitting anywhere near us, we'll have to move if she does.*

Of course Jules was recognised too; at least a dozen old friends came up to ask how she was and to say how good it was to see her out and about, as if this were the first time they'd seen her since Daisy's murder. For some it was. No one mentioned Amelia, clearly not wanting to bring Jules's attention to the fact that her daughter's killer was in the vicinity; a couple even tried to persuade her to abandon her plans for the film and go and have a drink with them.

Declining the offer, she simply went home and after she and Stephie had finished watching the start of a new drama series on TV, she'd made a last check of the day on Amelia's Facebook page. Finding nothing new, she closed down her laptop and took herself to bed and the gruesomely vivid dreams she'd been having lately about Amelia Quentin.

A lot of blood, sweet revenge and endless tears.

Now, as Jules pushed through the crowd of youngsters outside Fruit of the Vine, she was looking around for Amelia and saw her almost immediately, sitting on a stool at the bar, surrounded by a gaggle of her ex-con girlfriends. Had she been interested Jules might have noticed their cheap spray tans, tattoos, piercings and mega-lashes, but she wasn't looking at them. She was staring straight at Amelia, who was swaying around on her stool while waving her glass in the air and slurring something that Jules couldn't hear, although it seemed to be some sort of toast.

Maybe this was the first time Amelia had ever been the real centre of attention. Did she realise they were probably more interested in her money than they were in her?

It didn't take long for one of the friends to notice Jules, and after treating her to a long, slit-eyed look up and down she dug Amelia in the ribs and nodded Jules's way. Amelia peered over her shoulder, seeming vaguely irritated until, realising who was watching her, she turned right around on her stool and met Jules's stare.

Her eyes were mocking, challenging and narrowed with interest.

Having achieved what she'd come for, Jules broke the stare and left.

The forecast storm started around ten that night, long after Jules had returned home, and was still battering the windows by the time she went to bed at eleven. Unable to sleep, she lay in the darkness listening to the frantic clanging of the wind chimes Stephie had brought back from Thailand, as fierce gusts swung them wildly to and fro.

Stephie had texted earlier to say that she was feeling a bit down after her visit with Dean, although she'd tried not to show it while she was there.

Saw Mrs Foggarty, but Mr F was away on some sort of retreat. She looks terrible. Hard talking to her. Apparently he's in an even worse state. Feel desperately sorry for them. Driving to Heathrow now. No idea what I'm going to do with myself until Joe's flight gets in but I guess I'll find something. How's everything your end? Sxxx

Everything's fine here, Jules had texted back. *Sad that seeing Dean upset you. Thinking of him where he is upsets me too. I can imagine what it's doing to his parents. We'll talk when you get home. Jx*

Poor Stephie had lost her two closest friends thanks to Amelia, and was still, three years on, struggling to find her way without them. She was directionless, lonely, and though not friendless exactly, she still hadn't connected with anyone who was coming close to filling the void left by Daisy and Dean.

Turning on to her side Jules continued to stare into the darkness, thinking about Dean and how wrong it was that he was still in prison while Amelia had been allowed to go free. Was there anything she could do about that? Maybe his parents already had it in hand. If they did, she hoped it was with lawyers, because she didn't imagine that God held much sway with the parole board.

It wasn't long before her head was spinning with so many fears and worries that she wasn't sure at first if the banging she heard downstairs was real, or something she'd imagined.

Was someone knocking at the door?

Her heart tightened with alarm as the banging started again.

It was definitely someone at the door, but who on earth could it be at this time of night?

Throwing back the sheet, she moved silently through the darkness into Stephie's room and peered down to the garden and pull-in drive. There was no moon, but a nearby street lamp was casting a greyish glow over her car and what little she could see of the porch. There was no sign of anyone, but the wind chimes had stopped, she realised, so they'd either fallen or someone had taken them down.

Concerned that they'd been annoying a neighbour who'd come to complain, she ran downstairs ready to apologise. As she reached the front door she jumped violently as someone banged on the back door.

Quickly moving through to the kitchen, she shouted, 'Who is it?'

The only reply was a rowdy blast of wind that sent a dustbin crashing to the ground.

'Who is it?' she called out again.

Still no answer.

'Danny?' she shouted, knowing it wouldn't be him, but needing it to be.

No more knocking. No footsteps either.

She stayed where she was between the hall and kitchen, hands clenched tightly together as she listened, waited and prayed that whoever it was had gone away.

Surely to God it couldn't be Amelia?

Maybe her ex-con friends were helping her to play a sick joke.

Minutes ticked by.

Knowing she couldn't return to bed until she'd checked there was no one outside, she moved carefully towards the dining-room window, inched back a curtain . . . and almost screamed as a face loomed towards her.

Belatedly realising it was her reflection, she pressed a hand to her chest and wondered if she should phone Danny.

She continued to wait in the darkness, trying to hear the sound of movements or voices above the storm.

Nothing happened, until suddenly the letter box creaked open.

She spun round.

'Jules?' a voice whispered down the hall.

Horrified, Jules took a step back. 'Who is it?' she shouted, praying it was Stephie come home unexpectedly and had lost her keys.

'It's me, Amelia. Can I come in?'

Shocked into silence, Jules stayed where she was. *Amelia Quentin was here, in the dead of night, asking to be let in? Was she completely out of her mind?*

Didn't she already know the answer to that?

'Jules. I'm soaked right through and I need to talk to you.'

'Go away,' Jules shouted. 'I don't know what you're trying to achieve . . .'

'I promise I won't stay long . . .'

'Go right now or I'm calling the police.'

'You don't understand. I know you think I mean you harm, but I swear I don't. I just want to talk.'

'I'm not interested in anything you have to say . . .'

'I know you hate me, and I don't blame you, but if we could just talk . . . Five minutes, I promise I won't stay any longer . . .'

'You have to be crazy if you think . . .'

'But you want to talk to me, I know you do.'

'You don't know anything.'

'So why are you following me?'

Jules felt the air leave her lungs. The only answer she had for that was so complex and visceral that even she barely understood it.

'I think it's because you see me as a connection to Daisy,' Amelia told her, still speaking through the letter box. 'And I am, because no matter what she will always bind us together . . .'

'Get out of here,' Jules seethed, 'or I swear you'll regret you ever . . .'

'I already regret everything, so you can't make me regret any more.'

'You're lying.'

'Jules, I'm soaked and freezing, please let me in.'

Jules remained where she was.

More minutes ticked by. The letter box stayed open.

'How did you get here?' Jules shouted. 'How do you even know where I live?'

'My car's at the end of the street. I thought you were still living at the Mermaid, it's why I went there the other day. I expected you to follow me in . . .'

'Answer the question, *how did you find out where I live*?'

'One of my friends is from the Temple Fields estate. She asked around over there and in the end someone told her.'

'Who told her?'

'I don't know, I didn't ask.'

Having no choice but to let that go, Jules said, 'Do you realise the trouble you could be in for coming here, not only with the authorities, but with Kian's family?'

'No one will know unless you tell them.'

Shocked, Jules said, 'I have no intention of keeping your secrets. You need to leave this minute and don't even think about coming back.'

Amelia said nothing.

Jules waited.

The letter box closed.

Time passed. It was impossible to know what was going on outside without opening the door.

'Amelia?' Jules called out.

Nothing.

'Amelia, are you there?'

When there was still no response, Jules tiptoed into the sitting room to peer out of the window. No sign of anyone in the street, but the girl could have reached her car by now, or maybe she was still sheltering in the porch.

After waiting another few minutes Jules returned to the hall, checked that the chain was firmly in place and cracked open the door.

'I'm still here,' Amelia told her.

Jules stared at her wildly, hardly knowing what she was feeling beyond shock and an overwhelming urge to commit a brutally violent act. *How dare this girl come here? How did she have the nerve to stand there facing her victim's mother as though she might actually be welcome?*

Amelia shrugged, almost coyly. Her sodden hair was plastered to her skull, her face was streaked with mascara and her dress was like tissue stuck to her skin. Were it anyone else Jules would have hurried them inside to get dry; given who it was, all she could think about was the gun she should have allowed Danny to give her.

Amelia raised her hands to show they were empty. 'No phone, no anything,' she said calmly. 'Definitely no knife,' she added with a smile.

'For God's sake . . .'

'Sorry, sorry, bad joke. I didn't mean it.'

She really wasn't like other people.

'What exactly do you want?' Jules demanded harshly.

'Just to talk,' Amelia replied. 'I swear, nothing more than that.'

'Why on earth do you think I'd want to talk to you?'

'I guess because I was the last one to see her alive.'

Stunned, Jules cried, 'Which is precisely why I don't want you anywhere near me.' As she tried to slam the door, Amelia quickly jammed a foot in the way.

'Then why are you following me?' she challenged. 'You *do* want to talk to me . . .'

'Get away from here,' Jules cut in savagely.

'I swear I'm not going to hurt you. If I did, I'd be straight back to prison, and I can promise you I have no intention of ever going back there.'

'You should never have been allowed out. You murdered my daughter. Anyone else would be serving a life sentence . . .'

'We don't have to do this on the doorstep. If you'd just let me in . . .'

'In the middle of the night? Do you think I'm crazy? You've seen me outside your house enough times, you could have spoken to me then . . .'

'I wanted to, but Ollie kept saying you probably had a gun.'

Startled by that, Jules said, 'Maybe he was right.'

Amelia let go of the door and it slammed hard. 'I get that you'd probably like to kill me,' she shouted.

'There's no probably involved,' Jules shouted back, 'which is why you should go, right now.'

Amelia was still speaking. 'It's just that someone like you . . . It's not who you are.'

'Don't make assumptions, Amelia, we're none of us who we used to be, thanks to you.'

'Can you accept that I might have changed too?'

'No, I can't. I'll never be able to do that.'

After a moment Amelia said, 'If we're going to carry on talking here, I think I'll sit down.'

Flabbergasted, Jules waited before cracking open the door. To her amazement Amelia had dropped to the ground and crossed her legs.

'I haven't agreed to talk,' Jules hissed. 'There's nothing you can say that will change anything . . .'

'I know that, and it's not what I'm trying to do. I just want to explain to you how it was for me . . .'

'Do you seriously think I care how it was for you?'

Amelia's head went down.

'All I care about is that you get yourself as far away from here as you possibly can and don't ever come back. And I don't only mean my house, I mean Kesterly.'

Amelia's head stayed down and moments later Jules realised she was crying. 'No one ever wants to listen,' she sobbed. 'It's like I don't matter to anyone . . .'

'Stop it!' Jules seethed furiously. 'Self-pity isn't going to work on me.'

Amelia's head snapped up, her teary eyes flashing with temper. 'Why is Daisy the only one who ever counts?' she cried. 'I've got feelings too, but no one ever wants to think about that.'

'After what you did . . .'

'Let me tell you about it. Please. No one knows what it was really like, because no one else was there . . .'

'What about Dean? Are you forgetting him? You tricked him into being there, just like you tricked Daisy, and now she's dead and he's in prison for something *you* did. That's what happened to two innocent people who fell for your lies.'

'But I'm not lying now, I swear it. I just want to talk to you.'

But I'm not lying now? An admission that she had been before?

Jules slammed the door in her face.

'Jules, please,' Amelia begged. 'It's starting to rain again.'

Closing her eyes in frustration, Jules let her head fall back against the wall. She couldn't let the girl in; it was crazy even to consider it, and yet they couldn't stay here all night, talking through a closed door. She should just ignore her now, go back to bed and pretend she'd gone.

'I know you're still there,' Amelia said softly.

Wondering if she was losing her mind, or even dreaming this madness, Jules stormed through to the kitchen, hid the knife block in a cupboard, and secreted the sharpest one in the table drawer. She thought of calling Andee. Even at this late hour Andee would want to know that Amelia had turned up. She'd tell her that under no circumstances should she let the girl in. She'd probably even send the police . . .

Was that what Jules wanted?

Danny would still be up, probably even out somewhere, but if she asked him to come . . .

Crazy as it was, she didn't want Danny terrorising Amelia – that was her right and privilege.

Minutes later, still hardly able to believe she was doing it, she let Amelia walk ahead of her into the kitchen where she gave her towels and told her to sit down.

'Not there,' she barked, as Amelia went to sit in front of the table drawer. 'Here.' She was pointing to the other side of the table, and kept an eye on Amelia as she did as she was told.

'You don't have to be scared,' Amelia said, dabbing her face with a towel.

'Really? You're a convicted killer,' Jules reminded her.

Amelia simply looked at her.

Feeling suddenly weak, Jules sank down in a chair.

Amelia was glancing around the room, reminding Jules of the first time she'd come to the pub to meet

Daisy, when she'd seemed to drink everything in as though . . . As though what? What had been in her mind then? 'So this is where you live?' she said.

Jules didn't bother to answer.

'It's different to before.'

Still Jules only looked at her.

'Where's Kian? Someone said he left you.'

Jules tensed, ready to attack her with words, but before she could get them out Amelia was saying, 'You didn't understand what it was like for me when you shut me out. I didn't have anyone to turn to. You and Daisy were my only friends. You meant everything to me. I was happy when I was with you, I felt as though I mattered to someone, then suddenly you didn't want me any more and that was that. You had each other and I had no one.'

Jules stared at her, unmoved, and unable to credit the bid for sympathy. 'No matter how badly your feelings were hurt,' she retorted, 'you surely can't think it excuses what you did? You . . .'

'I was angry, upset!' Amelia cried. 'I couldn't think about anything else . . . I didn't go out for months, I had nowhere to go and no one to talk to . . .'

'You have a father . . .'

'He doesn't listen. No one does, not to me. I've always been on my own . . . I make friends, but then they end up pushing me away . . .' Her head went down as tears, real or fake, fell on to the towel she was holding. 'You and Daisy were always the nicest to me,' she exclaimed. 'I kept wishing I was a part of your family . . . Then suddenly one day, Daisy told me I wasn't welcome any more.' Her mouth twisted as she tried to stop herself crying. 'You used to listen to me,' she sobbed. 'You were the only one who ever really did that. I kept wishing you were my mother, I even convinced myself sometimes that you were.'

'But I hardly knew you . . .'

'Yes you did. You understood me in a way no one else . . .'

'No! That isn't true. Whatever you were telling yourself, then or now, I wasn't – I'm not – the person you seem to think . . .'

'Yes you are. I know you care about me . . .'

'For God's sake! You know what you did to my daughter, so how on earth can you think I care about you? I despise you, I want to see you back in prison paying for your crime . . .'

'So ring the police. Tell them I'm here.'

Jules met her steely gaze, knowing she should do exactly that, and not entirely sure why she wasn't moving. 'It's time for you to go,' she said bitterly.

'But I want to stay here with you.'

Alarm raced across Jules's heart. The girl sounded so pathetic, so convinced even that it might actually be possible . . .

'Don't worry, I know you don't want me,' Amelia ran on wretchedly, 'and I understand that you'll never be able to forgive me, but whether you like it or not you're the mother I should have had, would have had, if things had been different.'

Wondering how on earth she'd come to that conclusion, Jules said, 'You had a mother. I'm sorry that she died.'

Amelia turned her head away.

Cautiously, Jules said, 'Did you know she was dead when you and Daisy first met?'

After a while Amelia said, 'I kept telling myself it wasn't true, but I knew it was really. Maybe she deserved to die.' She turned to Jules, her eyes seeming to flash a challenge.

Jules blinked. 'Why on earth would you say that?' she asked, appalled.

Amelia shrugged. 'Maybe some people do.'

Jules had no idea what to say.

'Daddy told me once that she'd committed suicide. If she did, it just goes to show how much I meant to her. Nothing. She'd rather be dead than stay with me. Not that I care. She should have learned to swim.'

In spite of reminding herself that she wasn't in any way equipped to deal with this, Jules said, 'You must have had some counselling when you were young, or even when you were in prison.'

Amelia shrugged. 'Some, not much. Anyway, I know I'm different, I don't need anyone to tell me that.'

'But a lot of people lose a parent when they're young and it doesn't turn them . . . Doesn't make them do what you did.'

Amelia's eyes narrowed. 'It wasn't my mother's death that made me do it,' she said, 'it was *you*. You're to blame for what happened to Daisy, not me. If you hadn't made her push me away . . .'

Jules rose to her feet. 'You need to go, *right* now,' she seethed. 'Get out of my house . . .'

'But you need to take some responsibility,' Amelia cried.

Snatching the knife from the drawer, Jules pointed

it straight at her. 'Get out now, or I swear to God I'll use this.'

Amelia stared at the blade.

Jules stared at Amelia, shaking, breathing raggedly.

'See, we're not so very different, you and me,' Amelia said drily. 'You want to do the same to me as I did to Daisy, so how you're feeling now, that's how I felt . . .' She jumped as Jules plunged the knife into the table so hard the force jarred her whole body.

Their eyes met, Jules's glittering with hatred; Amelia's showing only surprise.

In the end Amelia got slowly to her feet.

Watching her, Jules tried to pull the knife free.

It was stuck.

Amelia looked at it.

Jules was still watching her.

'All I wanted,' Amelia said, 'was for us to be friends.'

'Go away,' Jules said darkly, 'just go away and don't ever come near me again.'

Putting down the towel, Amelia looked her straight in the eye as she stated, 'My dad believes that we're not all one thing, and I think he's right. I might have killed someone, but I can do good things too.'

'If that's true, then confess, take the sentence you deserve, and let Dean go free.'

Amelia's eyes turned flinty. 'I'm not going back to prison, not for anyone.'

'But it's where you belong.'

Amelia tossed her head. 'I should have known it would work out like this,' she declared, 'that I'd push you even further away, but at least I tried. I've found it in my heart to forgive you for what you did to me, but it seems you can't find it in yours to forgive me.'

Jules regarded her incredulously. 'You need help,' she told her forcefully. 'Get it, please, before you hurt someone else.'

Amelia turned away and started for the door. As she reached it she looked back. 'I'm having a party,' she announced. 'Will you come?'

Dumbfounded that she could even ask, never mind think she might get a positive reply, Jules said, 'I'd rather use this knife on you than ever see you again. I hope that's clear enough for you. We will never be friends and nothing you say or do will ever change that.'

Amelia regarded her intently. 'Aren't you afraid of what I might do to repay you for that?' she asked, sounding genuinely intrigued.

'Whatever you do, you can never hurt me as much as you have already, so no, I'm not afraid of you.'

Amelia's eyebrows rose. 'But you should be,' she murmured, and leaving the threat hanging she walked along the hall and closed the front door behind her.

For several minutes after she'd gone Jules remained where she was, holding the knife, leaning on it, hands trembling, heart thudding as she absorbed the relief of being alone again, the shock of what had just happened.

She couldn't understand what had made her let the girl in. What had she been thinking, expecting? Some sort of closure? Was she losing her mind? The way she'd been behaving lately suggested she was.

Collapsing into a chair she dropped her head in her

hands and began to sob uncontrollably. She'd sat across the table from Daisy's killer and had allowed her to speak, to attempt to justify her actions, and all Amelia had done was try to blame her, Jules, for driving her to stab Daisy fifteen times until she was dead. She was clearly mentally disturbed, probably even clinically insane. She had no moral compass, no understanding of people or kindness or right and wrong. Even now, after the time she'd spent in prison, she seemed to have no comprehension of how serious her crime had been, or how devastating the consequences remained.

She shouldn't be walking the streets. She was still a danger to society; a ticking time bomb, a toxic explosion that anything or anyone could set off at any time. Why hadn't anyone realised that? What had happened during her assessment? How had she managed to persuade a panel that she was remorseful, ready to start life again, and above all sane?

We're not all one thing. I might have killed someone, but I can do good things too, as if killing someone was no more serious than bumping into them in the street, or forgetting their birthday. And what sort of good things? Did she even understand what good was? Or regret? Or compassion? Or shame? She'd seemed to understand that by coming here she was risking being sent back to prison; didn't she realise that issuing threats would guarantee it?

Jules lifted her head and looked at the phone, knowing she should call the police. They would probably come right away, would want to know everything that had happened, and why on earth Jules had let her in the door. She could tell them how Amelia had virtually confessed to committing murder; that she'd intended to do it all along. If Amelia ended up denying it, it would be her word against Jules's, and they'd surely believe Jules – or would they? She had no proof of Amelia even being here, let alone of what she'd said. Hearsay, they'd call it. Whereas Amelia could show them tapes of Jules Bright sitting outside the walls of Crofton Park, walking up to the camera and staring in. Amelia had witnesses who'd confirm that Jules had turned up at the wine bar, stared at Amelia and walked away, as though she herself was issuing some sort of threat . . .

No, she wasn't going to tell anyone what had happened. With her head being where it had been lately, there was too much that she couldn't properly explain. They'd think she was losing her grip, that she shouldn't be left alone at any time, that *she* might be a danger to Amelia rather than the other way round. And they'd be right about that, because she *was* a danger to Amelia: she just hadn't figured out yet exactly what she was going to do.

Chapter Fourteen

When the phone rang just after ten the next morning, Jules felt sure it would be Stephie or Joe letting her know they were on their way. She wanted them to come quickly, to distract her from the anguish and fear she'd woken with and remind her that there were normal, decent people in the world.

To her amazement it was neither Stephie nor Joe at the other end of the line. When she realised who it was she sank down on the edge of the bed, overcome by too much feeling.

'Are you OK?' Kian asked softly.

It took her a moment to say, 'Yes, yes I'm fine. How are you?'

'I'm good.' His voice was low, intimate, wrapping itself around her like a veil of tenderness.

Why was he ringing now?

Through the relief and surprise a stab of fear suddenly struck. 'Is your mother . . . ?'

'She's OK. Sends her love.'

She allowed his calmness to reach her, yet she still felt afraid of why he might be calling. Everything frightened her these days. 'It's good to hear you,' she told him. 'You sound . . .' How did he sound, from the little he'd said? Like his old self? No matter how hard she might wish for it, he'd never be that again. Neither of them would.

'It's good to hear you too,' he said. 'I miss you.'

A rush of unsteadying emotion stole her voice. He missed her. Did he have any idea how much she missed him?

She felt a sudden urge to tell him about Amelia's visit last night and how badly it had unnerved her, but of course she couldn't. It would upset and worry him and there was nothing he could do.

There was a smile in his voice as he announced, 'I'm coming over.'

Her mind whirled. How she'd longed to hear those words, to see him, to hold him and feel his strength returning to restore them both. Could she dare to hope? 'Are you sure?' she asked shakily. 'I mean, I . . . I – I'm not sure what I'm trying to say.'

'That you want me to come?'

'Of course. How could you even doubt it? I'm just . . . I . . .' She was suddenly crying so hard that the words wouldn't come. She hadn't realised until now just how desperately she needed him, hadn't allowed herself to feel it, even think of it, although it was always there.

'Hey, hey,' he soothed gently, and his tone reminded her of all the times he'd tried to comfort her in the past, and succeeded. 'It's going to be OK.'

Was it? How could it be? Yet if he came, and he was feeling stronger, everything would feel different, maybe even better. They could be a couple again, lean on one another, come to terms with this cruelly confusing world; decide on what sort of future they could share.

'I shouldn't have left you on your own,' he said huskily. 'I didn't want to, I just didn't know how . . .' He swallowed hard. 'I'm sorry I let you down . . .'

'No, don't be sorry. It wasn't your fault. We didn't know how to be with one another, what to do, where to turn . . . I still don't know, but if you're sure, if you think you're ready, I want you to come.'

'I'm ready. I knew I would be one of these days; I just didn't want to promise anything until I was sure I could carry it through. And I don't want to take anything for granted.'

'Such as? You know I'm here for you.'

'Yes, but we need to talk, to make decisions that won't be easy. We can't go on putting them off.'

Suddenly afraid of what he might mean, she said, 'Do you want us to be together again? It's what I want, more than anything, but if you feel the memories are going to get in the way . . .'

'It's what I want too,' he assured her. 'We'll learn how to deal with the memories and everything that comes with them.'

He really was sounding like his old self, more capable, more positive and ready to restart their lives.

Please God let that be true.

'Tell me,' he said after a pause, 'have you seen anything of her?'

Though her first thought was of Daisy, she knew he meant Amelia, and all the softness inside her turned to stone. 'Yes, I have,' she admitted.

317

'So she's wandering around freely?' He didn't sound bitter, but she knew he must be feeling it as deeply as she did.

'I'm afraid so,' she replied.

'It shouldn't be happening.'

'I know.'

After a while he dropped the subject, leaving it to fester until they were ready to pick it up again. 'Mum tells me Stephie's with you,' he said.

'She will be later. She's bringing Joe and his friend from the airport.'

'Joe and his friend?'

'They're travelling around Europe for a month before starting their law degrees. Kesterly's their first stop.'

He took a moment to digest this. 'How long are they staying?'

'I'm not sure.'

'OK.' Whatever he thought of Joe's visit he didn't say, but she felt sure he'd be pleased to see the boy, in spite of how painful it would be.

'I'll call again when I've booked a flight,' he told her. 'Danny can pick me up.'

'I don't mind coming . . .'

'You'll have a houseful of guests, and I need to talk to Dan before I see you.'

She didn't object. She was still trying to make herself believe he would soon be with her.

For a while she listened to him breathing, imagining his face, his eyes, his laughter that had always been so ready to gather everyone up in its joy.

'Did you ring off yet?' he asked.

'No, I'm still here.'

'It's going to be all right,' he said quietly. 'Everything will be taken care of, I promise,' and a moment later the line went dead.

By the time Stephie turned up with Joe and his friend, Ethan, Jules was so ready to see them that she tore open the front door and ran straight into Joe's arms. He'd grown so much, had become, if it were possible, more handsome than ever, and even more powerfully built. How come young American men seemed to grow so much bigger than everyone else?

'He's a god, isn't he?' Stephie teased, as Jules drew back to admire his day-old stubble and intense black eyes. The grief was still there, but his confidence was back. 'I've been swooning all the way home,' Stephie added.

Jules laughed as Joe said, 'So that's why you were driving on the wrong side of the road,' and cupping Jules's face in his hands, he gazed into her eyes. 'I knew it was going to be good to see you, just not this good,' he declared.

Loving the quirk of his smile and roguish drop of dark hair over one eye, Jules couldn't help thinking of how thrilled Daisy would have been with him, how much in love. 'I have some good news,' she told him, 'but first, are you going to introduce me?'

Turning to his blond-haired, blue-eyed friend who was almost as tall and athletically built, Joe said, 'This here is Ethan Calder, fellow law student and all-round great guy, provided you don't get on the wrong side of him on a football field.'

Clocking the way Stephie was flushing as she looked at Ethan, Jules took the boy's large hand in both of hers and shook it warmly. 'I'm so glad you came,' she told him. 'I know we're a bit off the beaten track down here in Kesterly, but we'll do our best to make sure you enjoy your stay.'

'It's real good to be here,' he assured her. 'I've heard such a lot about you folks, so I've been looking forward to meeting you all.'

'We've been drawing up plans of where to go, what to do,' Stephie told her excitedly. 'Joe wants to show Ethan all our old haunts, including the Mermaid, and we're hoping, if you've got time, you'll come too.'

'Oh, you don't want me there,' Jules protested, feeling instantly resistant to sharing their memories with an outsider. But it had to be a good thing, she told herself firmly. After all, she hardly wanted Stephie and Joe to avoid, much less deny, the joy Daisy had brought to their young lives, especially when their companion seemed so good-natured.

'That's just where you're wrong,' Joe was insisting as he went to unload the car. 'The main reason for coming here is to spend time with you, and the only way you're off the hook on that is if you can convince me you're just not up for spending time with us.'

Enjoying the way Ethan was encouraging her to say yes, Jules said, 'We'll see how things go, because as it turns out you're not going to be my only visitors over the next few days.'

They were all immediately interested.

Feeling her heart bubbling over, Jules announced, 'Kian's coming,' and she almost wanted to laugh at how girlishly excited that made her feel. To Joe she added, 'That's my good news, by the way.'

'It sure is good news,' he responded warmly. 'I was wondering if we might put Ireland on our tour, but if he's coming here . . . You are going to just love this guy,' he informed Ethan. 'I know I've told you about him, but meeting him in person . . .'

Deciding now wasn't the time to remind Joe that Kian was no longer the man he used to be, Jules put an arm round Stephie's shoulders as they led the way inside. 'Ethan's pretty cute,' she commented in a whisper.

'Get out of here,' Stephie muttered in mock astonishment.

Jules laughed.

'I'll go sort the coffee,' Stephie told her, 'if you want to show the guys where they're sleeping.'

A few minutes later, after leaving Joe and Ethan to freshen up, Jules returned to the kitchen to find Stephie standing over the coffee while checking her mobile.

'Great, we've got tickets for Sunday's concert on the beach,' she declared, putting the phone down. 'So when's Kian coming? I'm sure we can get a ticket for him too, if he's interested. Does this mean he's feeling better?'

'That's what he said,' Jules replied, starting to unpack the cookies Marco had sent up from the pub to welcome the boys. 'He's going to let me know when he's booked his flight, but I imagine he'll be here by the weekend.'

'Is Aileen coming too?'

'He didn't mention it, so I'm guessing not.'

Stephie nodded thoughtfully. 'And did he say anything about *her*?' she wanted to know, leaving no doubt with her tone who she was referring to.

Swallowing drily, Jules said, 'Not much. How about Joe, has he mentioned her at all?'

Stephie glanced at the stairs and went to close the door. 'He didn't want me to tell you, but he's threatening to go and see her,' she confided.

Jules's eyes widened with alarm.

'He says,' Stephie continued, 'that someone needs to persuade her to – I quote – get the hell out of here, and if she doesn't want to go willingly he'll show her exactly why it would be a mistake to stay.'

Jules frowned. 'What does he mean by that?'

Stephie shrugged. 'But he's right, she can't stay around here. Kesterly's your home, yours and Kian's, and it's not as if she doesn't have anywhere else to go. Coming back here was like sticking two fingers up to you two, and no way should she be allowed to get away with that. What happened to the table, by the way?'

Jules glanced at the deep gouge she'd made while working the knife free. 'Oh, nothing,' she said dismissively. 'Shall we have coffee outside? It's warm enough now the sun's out again.'

Over the next twenty-four hours Jules watched the youngsters coming and going, enjoying their wit and energy and envying their ability to talk so freely about Daisy. Sometimes it felt as though Daisy might be about to walk in the door, or even chirp in with an anecdote of her own. It hurt terribly, and yet it was uplifting too. They never seemed to notice how little she contributed to the conversations, or if they did, they presumably took her silence for encouragement, even approval of their stories. They were right to do so, for she loved hearing about the funny, or amazing, or even the sad things they remembered. Most of these were incidents she hadn't known about at the time, but it was easy to picture Daisy at the heart of them. Ethan was a great listener, she discovered. He showed no signs of impatience, or boredom, or even discomfort; if anything, he seemed as taken with the memories as he was with their first excursion to Hope Cove and the Mermaid.

Jules didn't go with them. Instead she went to visit her mother, and told her all about her visitors and waiting for Kian to call, and how she was doing her best not to think about Amelia.

'You don't even know who she is, do you?' she murmured, smoothing her mother's hair and feeling nothing but thankful that she didn't.

'Nurse,' Marsha mumbled.

'Shall I let you into a secret?' Jules whispered.

Marsha's eyes drifted about their sockets.

'You won't tell anyone, will you? No, of course you won't. I threatened the Quentin girl with a knife the other night, and I'm sorry now that I didn't use it. I would have if I'd thought I could get away with it. That makes me as bad as her, doesn't it? I don't care, because I really do wish she was dead. If it would bring Daisy back I wouldn't think twice; nor would Kian, or anyone else. It's like she's taking up Daisy's place in the world, or dancing on Daisy's grave, and that shouldn't be allowed.'

After leaving the care home she'd gone to meet Stephie, Joe and Ethan at a gallery in town, where one of Andee's friends was holding an exhibition for local photographers. Though Jules spent some time chatting with Andee and took pleasure in reintroducing her to Joe, she didn't mention anything about Amelia and was glad that Andee didn't bring her up either.

In fact, no one had spoken about the girl since Stephie had warned Jules that Joe was intending to persuade her to 'get the hell' out of the area. She wondered if they were visiting Amelia's Facebook page. She was, so she knew that the party was still on for next Saturday night, and that everyone was still invited. She just hoped that Joe and Stephie didn't know anything about it, because nothing good could possibly come of it if they decided to go.

'Any word from Kian?' Joe asked, as he and Jules watched the sea spray breaking like glittering crystals over the rocks below.

'Not yet,' Jules replied. 'I thought there would have been by now. I hope it doesn't mean he's changed his mind about coming.' Though her heart twisted with the dread of it, she knew she had to prepare herself for the worst, hard as that would be.

Clearly genuinely concerned, Joe said, 'Do you think he will?'

Her eyes wandered out to the far horizon, where ships were passing like ghosts in the shimmering summer haze. 'I'm not sure,' she said honestly. 'It could be he thought he was ready, but when the time came to leave he found himself unable to face it.'

'Have you tried calling him?'

'Not yet. I don't want to pressure him, but I will if I don't hear soon.' She turned to him and smiled. He met her eyes and smiled too as she stroked the tumbling hair from his face. How proud she felt of him, as though he were her very own son.

'Thanks for coming,' she said softly. 'I know it can't be easy for you being here, but it's meant a lot to me, seeing you.'

'It's meant a lot to me too,' he assured her.

She had no trouble believing him. She could feel their bond as though it were physically wrapping itself around them.

'I still think about her all the time,' he confessed. 'I don't mean in an obsessive, needy sort of way, I think I'm past that now, but I don't ever want to forget how special she was.'

Though she loved him for still caring so deeply, she said, 'You're young, with your whole life ahead of you, and she'd be the first to tell you to live it.'

'I know, and I promise I intend to, but it felt kind of important to come here. I thought it might give me some sort of closure.' He paused, as he considered whether that had been the right thing to say. 'What I'm getting,' he said, 'is a sense of something that feels . . .' He shrugged as he struggled for words. 'For as long as I can remember you've been like family, so it feels kind of right to remember her with you because you loved her as much as I did, and still miss her every day the way I do.'

Feeling for his confusion, Jules said, 'Maybe that's the closure you need. To reconnect with us, and feel close to her by being here, so that when the time comes to leave you'll feel ready to say a proper goodbye.'

Though he considered this, it wasn't long before he was shaking his head. 'I don't think I'll ever feel ready for that.'

Certain he would, in time, Jules said, 'What about other girls? Have you met anyone since . . . ?'

His head went down as he shook it again. 'No one that means anything,' he replied. After a while he added, 'I guess that sounds arrogant, cruel even, but having something like this happen . . . It changes you and not always in a good way. I still feel angry . . . I mean, I thought I'd managed to get over it, but when you told me the bitch was coming out . . . I just can't get my head round the fact that she's being allowed to go on with her life when she'd hardly even begun to pay for what she did. It's not right. We didn't receive justice for Daisy. We only found out how some people get what they deserve and others just don't.'

As the words resonated deeply within her, Jules turned her eyes back to the horizon. Wasn't that the truth? Some people did get what they deserved, while others didn't, and who, she wanted to know, got to make the decisions? Who was responsible for the diabolical selection of life's winners and losers? And how did they, the losers, carry on living with a winner flaunting her good fortune in their faces?

It was on Sunday afternoon, while Stephie, Joe and Ethan were at a concert on the beach, that Jules received a call from Andee asking if she was all right.

'Yes, I'm fine,' Jules assured her, curiously, worriedly

– why was Andee asking out of the blue like this? Had something happened? 'Is there any reason I shouldn't be?' she enquired cautiously.

Andee's tone was casual. 'No, not really. I was just wondering if you'd heard from Kian?'

Surprised by the interest, Jules said, 'As a matter of fact I was hoping you'd be him.'

'So he's here, in Kesterly?'

'No, not yet. Why?'

After a pause Andee said, 'Can you hold for a moment? Don't go away, I'll be right back.'

As she waited Jules checked her mobile for messages just in case she'd missed a text from Kian, but she hadn't – and trying not to think about how awful it was going to be if he'd decided to cancel, she got up from her computer and went to check on the lamb she was slow-roasting for dinner.

'We'll be back by seven at the latest,' Stephie had promised as she and the others had headed for the door.

'Are you sure you won't join us?' Ethan had pressed.

'I'm sure,' Jules had responded as Joe came to hug her. 'Are you OK?' she whispered. He'd seemed quite down since getting up this morning, or maybe distracted was a better word, and she had the feeling he'd rather not have been going to the concert either.

'I'm cool,' he insisted. 'Just kind of, you know . . .'

Understanding that was the best she was going to get while the others were listening, she hugged him again and felt worried as she watched him go. Something was on his mind, that much was clear, and she couldn't help wondering if he was trying to work himself up to telling her that it would soon be time for him to go. She was already dreading it, especially now that Stephie had accepted his and Ethan's invitation to travel with them. The house was going to seem horribly empty and silent – unless Kian kept to his word and came.

'Are you still there?' Andee asked, coming back on the line.

'Still here,' Jules confirmed. 'Is everything OK?'

'I'm not sure. One of my old colleagues at the station contacted me just now to say that Amelia Quentin's father has . . .' To someone else she said, 'It's OK, I'll be right there, just give me a minute.' Coming back to Jules she continued, 'Apparently Amelia was supposed to be throwing a party at Crofton Park last night, but it was called off at the last minute because no one could find her.'

Startled, Jules said, 'What do you mean, no one could find her?'

'That's what I was told, and now her father's contacted the police demanding they mount a search.'

Jules's head was starting to spin. 'When was she last seen?' she asked.

'I believe it was sometime on Friday, but I don't have the details. I only know that the father is insisting the police question you and Kian . . .'

'What!' Jules broke in furiously. 'How dare he? Kian's not even in the country, and what the hell does he think *I've* done with his precious daughter?'

'I've no idea.' Andee took a breath. 'I'm sorry to ask, but I take it you haven't seen her in the last forty-eight hours?'

'No, I haven't.'

'What about Stephie and Joe? Do you know if they've had any contact?'

Thinking instantly of Joe's sombre mood this morning, and how he'd told Stephie he was going to get Amelia to leave Kesterly, Jules quickly skipped over it as she said, 'I shouldn't think so. We tend to try and forget she exists.' Surely to God Joe hadn't found a way of making the girl disappear? Even if he had, he couldn't have done it alone, and the others hadn't seemed anything but their normal selves earlier . . . 'Am I to expect a visit from the police?' she demanded.

'Not at this stage. It's why I got a call asking me to be in touch, so it doesn't seem official. She hasn't been gone long enough for that, and I'm sure she'll show up before the cavalry's brought in. Listen, I'm sorry, I have to go; I'm in the middle of a family party. I'll get back to you if I hear any more.'

Fraught with all sorts of foreboding, Jules immediately connected to Stephie's number.

'Hey Jules,' Stephie shouted over the music. 'Did you change your mind and decide to come?'

'No. I need to ask you something. Can you hear me?'

'Just about. Is everything OK?'

'I don't know. I've just heard that Amelia's disappeared.'

There was a beat of shocked silence before Stephie exclaimed, 'You mean like in *disappeared*?'

'Apparently no one knows where she is.'

'You're kidding me! Did someone off her, do you think? If they did, let me shake their hand.'

Flinching, though relieved that Stephie was taking it this way since it suggested she had nothing to hide, Jules said, 'I've no idea what's happened to her, but apparently her father is trying to persuade the police to talk to me and Kian.'

'What! I don't believe it. How do you know?'

'Andee rang a few minutes ago. She asked if you guys might have seen Amelia recently. I said you hadn't, but . . . Have you?'

'No, at least not in person, but we've been checking out her Facebook page and all the stuff about her party. We even thought about going to try and screw it up for her, but we decided against it in the end.'

'So you went to see a movie last night?' That was what they'd told her, and she'd had no reason to doubt them until Andee had called.

'*Fast and Furious 7*. Listen, I'll tell you what's happened to the evil that calls itself Amelia, she's run off somewhere with all her ex-con buddies, and with any luck she'll never come back.'

Hoping that was true, Jules said, 'I should go. I'll call again if there's any more news, otherwise see you here around seven.'

After ringing off she stood staring at the phone, trying to gather her scattered thoughts. The girl hadn't really disappeared; she was hiding out somewhere, either to get her father's attention, or maybe Jules's. So far she was succeeding, but what Jules couldn't get out of her mind was what Kian had said at the end of his last call.

'*It's going to be all right. Everything will be taken care of, I promise.*'

Grabbing the phone, she pressed in Aileen's number.

'Hi, it's me,' she said when her mother-in-law answered. 'Is everything OK with you?'

'I think so, pet. How about with you?'

'Yes, I'm fine. Enjoying having the kids around. It livens things up a bit.'

'Oh, I'm sure it does. They keep us all young, so they do. I told Kian they'd do him the power of good, and I'm hoping you're ringing to tell me I'm right.'

Feeling her throat turning dry, Jules said, 'Isn't he with you?'

'With me? Heavens no. He left here yesterday morning. Could hardly wait to get on the plane. Don't tell me he hasn't been in touch with you yet?'

Jules was trying to stay calm. 'No, he hasn't. So I'm guessing he's with Danny.'

'He said they had some business to sort out, so I'd say your guess is right. He should have let you know he was back.'

'Yes, he should,' and after assuring Aileen that she'd call again as soon as she'd found him, she wasted no time in calling Kian.

'I've just spoken to your mother,' she told his voice-mail, 'so I know you're back. Please call me as soon as you get this.'

A moment later she was leaving a message for Danny. 'Is Kian with you?' she demanded heatedly. 'I've just spoken to Aileen, so I know he took a flight yesterday morning. What's going on, Danny? Why have I just received a call from Andee Lawrence about Amelia Quentin? You need to call me back, and you need to do it now.'

After ringing off she tried Finn, Bob Stafford, Danny's mother, Bridget, Uncle Pete, Liam, Connor and Ruthie, but no one admitted to knowing where Danny was, or to having seen or heard from Kian in the last twenty-four hours.

'You sound worried,' Ruthie told her bluntly. 'So what's going on?'

'I'm not sure,' Jules replied. 'All I know is that Amelia Quentin's father has reported her missing, and now I can't find Danny or Kian.'

'Jesus,' Ruthie muttered under her breath. 'Do you think . . . ?'

'I don't know what to think, and I won't until one of them gets in touch with me. So if you do know where they are, or if anyone else does . . .'

'Just you leave it with me,' Ruthie interrupted, and the line went dead.

Chapter Fifteen

It was around lunchtime the following day that Andee rang again.

'There's still no sign of Amelia,' she told Jules, 'so the police are on their way to talk to you.'

Having heard nothing from Kian, Danny or Ruthie, Jules did her best to sound indignant, which she thought seemed the right attitude in the circumstances. 'What on earth do they think I might know?' she demanded hotly.

'The answer to that is probably nothing; they just have to follow procedure. If you want me to come, I will, but obviously there won't be anything I can do, apart from listen and maybe explain or advise in some way after they've gone.'

Jules didn't need any time to consider. 'I'd like you to be here,' she told her.

'OK. I'll call and let them know and get there as soon as I can. Actually, you know one of them. Leo Johnson?'

Remembering him as the young detective who'd taken Daisy's disappearance seriously from the start, Jules said, 'Do they have any theories yet on where Amelia might be?'

'Not that they've shared with me. Try not to worry, this is simply routine . . .'

'Because her father's insisting on it?'

'Partly, but also because they'd be failing in their duty if they didn't interview you.'

After ringing off Jules went to find Joe and Ethan in the garden. 'The police are on their way,' she informed them.

They immediately looked up from their laptops.

'Apparently they still haven't found her,' she explained.

'Did you get hold of Kian yet?' Joe asked, his mind clearly going along the same lines as hers.

She shook her head.

'Do the police know he's not in Ireland?'

'I'm not sure. Where's Stephie?'

'Right here,' Stephie replied, stepping out of the door behind her. 'So she's still missing?'

Jules's head was throbbing; her expression was as grim as the foreboding in her heart as she pictured all kinds of terrible scenarios. Not that Amelia didn't deserve any one of them, but if Kian was involved . . . 'Apparently,' she said. 'I should call Ruthie.'

Going back inside she got to her mobile just as it started to ring. Seeing it was Aileen she quickly clicked on. 'Have you heard from him?' she asked in a rush.

'No,' Aileen replied. 'But I've just spoken to our Bridget. So the Quentin girl's done a disappearing act?'

Unsurprised that the news had travelled, Jules said, 'It would seem so.'

'Mary, Mother of God,' Aileen muttered. 'What are

they thinking? They can't be taking the law into their own hands . . .'

Chilled by the voicing of her own fear, Jules said, 'We don't know anything yet. Did Kian tell you what sort of business he had to sort out with Danny?'

'No, I just assumed . . . Well, it doesn't matter what I assumed, what does is where the heck they are now and what they might have done with that girl. If they've done anything, and I'm not saying they have, but the coincidence . . . It doesn't look good, Jules, and why aren't they answering their phones, either of them? Have you asked yourself that?'

Jules had, far too many times, and the lack of an answer was getting her more worked up than ever. 'I need to call Ruthie,' she said shortly. 'She gave me the impression yesterday that she might be able to find out where they are.'

Moments later Ruthie was saying, 'I felt sure one of the cousins would know, but if they do they're not saying, and frankly I'm not convinced that they do.'

'Well they have to be somewhere,' Jules snapped frustratedly, 'and once the police find out that Kian's not in Ireland, if they haven't already, and that Danny, who presumably collected him from the airport yesterday, has vanished too, you can imagine what conclusions they'll jump to. The very same conclusions as I'm jumping to myself.'

'I have to admit the coincidence is bothering us all,' Ruthie informed her, 'but there could still be a perfectly good explanation . . .'

'If you can come up with one then please let me know in the next few minutes,' Jules cut in, 'because the police are about to turn up here and I'd like to be able to tell them that whatever's happened to Amelia Quentin has nothing to do with the Brights.'

As she put the phone down she felt Joe's arm slip comfortingly around her, and because she needed to lean on someone for a moment she didn't pull away. 'It'll be fine,' she told him, as much to convince herself as him. 'I'm not sure how yet, but we'll work it out.'

Giving her a squeeze he said, 'Just tell us what you need us to do.'

'It's enough that you're here. I expect the police will want to talk to you too . . .' Her eyes closed as the implications of what this could mean for Joe and Ethan dawned on her.

'Don't worry about us, we'll be fine,' he insisted when she voiced her fear. 'We haven't done anything, so no way are we going to end up with some sort of guilt by association if there's . . .'

Not wanting to remind him about Dean and joint enterprise, she said, 'But if it stops you going to college . . .'

'It won't, whatever *it* is, and as we don't know that yet, we should just keep a lid on it and remember that none of us has anything to hide.'

Only wishing that were true, Jules turned away and stiffened as someone knocked on the door. Stephie and Ethan came in from the garden.

'I expect it's them,' Stephie said edgily. 'I'll go let them in.'

Praying it would turn out to be Kian, or at the very least Danny, Jules waited with Joe and Ethan, watching and listening, and trying not to show how wretched she felt when Andee came into the kitchen followed by DC Leo Johnson and a slight woman in her mid-twenties who, perversely, looked vaguely like a darker version of Amelia.

'I'm DC Jemma Payne,' the young woman told her. 'Please just call me Jemma, or Jem.'

Jules attempted a smile, and after introducing Joe and Ethan she suggested they go through to the sitting room. 'I'm guessing she hasn't turned up yet,' she said, perching on the edge of an armchair while Andee took the other and the detectives settled on the sofa. The youngsters squatted on the floor in front of Jules as though trying to protect her.

'I'm afraid not,' Leo replied as Jemma took out a notebook. He glanced at Andee who'd once been his superior officer, but she wasn't looking his way.

'When was she last seen?' Stephie asked.

'As far as we know it was on Friday evening about half past nine,' Leo replied.

'Where?' Joe wanted to know.

'At home. Apparently her boyfriend went into town with a few of their friends around that time, but Amelia stayed behind.'

'And she'd gone by the time he got back?' Stephie prompted.

'We're still trying to establish that.'

'But surely her boyfriend must know if she was there when he got home,' Stephie pointed out.

Leo smiled pleasantly. 'I'm supposed to be the one asking questions,' he reminded her.

Flushing, Stephie said, 'If you ask me she decided to dump him and did a runner.'

Leaving him and the ex-con friends with access to the house? Jules was thinking. It didn't seem likely.

'Have you had any contact with her since she was released from prison?' Leo Johnson asked Stephie.

Stephie's face tightened as she shook her head. 'No thanks,' she spat.

'How about you guys?' he asked Joe and Ethan.

'None whatsoever,' Joe replied. 'She's got to be the last person I'd want any contact with.'

'And yet you're here, in Kesterly, only weeks after her release?'

Joe reddened. 'Coincidence,' he responded. 'I was always coming now, prior to taking a trip round Europe. When I booked I had no idea she'd be around by the time I got here.'

Seeming to accept that, Leo said to Jules, 'How about you, Mrs Bright? Have you had any contact with Amelia since she came out of prison?'

Jules's eyes darted to Andee as she prepared to lie.

'Of course she hasn't,' Stephie piped up crossly. 'You know what that psycho did to Daisy, so no way would Jules want anything to do with her.'

Leo regarded Stephie for a few moments before returning his attention to Jules. 'How about your husband?' he asked. 'Do you know if he's had any contact with Amelia?'

'Not as far as I'm aware,' Jules replied steadily.

'Is he still in Ireland?'

'He was the last time I spoke to him.'

'Which was when?'

'On Wednesday of last week.'

'And you say, or Stephie here says, that you haven't seen or spoken to Amelia at all in the last few weeks?'

Jules's throat turned dry.

Leo Johnson waited.

Silence seemed to crack the air.

When Jules still didn't answer Stephie turned to look at her.

'Have you?' Leo prompted.

'No,' Jules finally managed.

As Leo's eyes went down Jules knew instantly that she'd made a mistake. 'That's not actually true, is it?' he said, looking at her again.

Sensing Joe bristling, Jules put a hand on his shoulder as she said, 'Why do you say that?'

'Because there's CCTV footage of you parked outside Crofton Park,' Leo told her gravely. 'It also shows you walking up to the camera and staring into it before driving after Amelia when she left the property.'

From the corner of her eye Jules saw Joe's disbelief, while Andee gazed at her in dismay.

'We also have reason to believe that you followed Amelia to Fruit of the Vine Wine Bar last Thursday evening,' Leo continued.

Belligerently, Joe demanded, 'Exactly where are you going with this?'

Benignly, Leo said, 'I'm just trying to establish what sort of contact Mrs Bright has had with Amelia Quentin during the past few weeks, but most particularly over recent days.' To Jules he added, 'Did the two of you engage in conversation at the wine bar?'

'She needs a lawyer,' Joe broke in hotly.

'It's all right,' Jules assured him. 'No, we didn't speak at the wine bar,' she told Leo, 'or while I was parked outside her house.'

Curiously, Leo said, 'Can I ask *why* you were parked outside her house?'

Jules swallowed hard, and felt almost feverish as she replied, 'It's hard to explain . . . I wasn't there to do anything, I guess I just wanted to show her that I wasn't afraid of her, or maybe I wanted to frighten her, to let her know that even if the system had decided she'd paid for her crime, as far as I was concerned . . .' Suddenly realising where she was taking herself, she came to a stop.

Clearly registering the unspoken words, Leo said, 'Where were you on Friday evening, after nine thirty?'

'I was here,' Jules replied.

'We all were,' Stephie put in.

Knowing that wasn't true, Jules said, 'No, sweetheart, you guys went down to the Mermaid for something to eat.'

'Yes, but we were back by nine thirty.'

'It was closer to ten thirty,' Jules told her gently, realising Stephie was trying to give her an alibi.

'And what about Saturday?' Leo asked. 'Can you give us an account of your movements that day?'

'Um, yes, I think so. In the morning I went to the care home to see my mother. After that I met Misty Knowles, who runs the Mermaid, at the Seafront Café for lunch. I guess I got home around four and then I was here for the rest of the time.'

'Alone?'

'No, we were here,' Joe answered.

'All evening?'

'Yes, all evening.'

'No, you went to the cinema on Saturday evening,' Jules reminded him. Didn't they realise that lying to protect her was going to end them up in more trouble than they needed?

Everyone looked at Jemma Payne as her mobile started to ring.

After checking who it was she murmured something to Leo and left the room.

Taking out his own notebook, Leo turned back to Jules. 'I'm presuming the staff at the care home will confirm that you were there on Saturday morning?' he asked.

'They will.'

'Same goes for Misty Knowles and Fliss at the Seafront?'

'Fliss wasn't in on Saturday. Vince was running things, and there were a few other staff around. I can probably give you their names.'

After glancing at Andee he changed course with a question Jules really hadn't been expecting. 'Did Amelia Quentin come here last Tuesday evening?' he asked.

Tensing to her core as all eyes came to her, Jules had no choice but to admit it.

Stephie turned to her open-mouthed.

Cutting her off with a raised hand, Jules waited for Leo to continue.

'Did you speak to her?' he wanted to know.

'Yes, I did.'

'So you let her in?'

'Eventually.' Sensing the others' incredulity, she added, 'She wouldn't go away and I . . . I can't really say why I ended up opening the door.'

'Are you sure you didn't invite her here?'

'Perfectly sure. I kept trying to make her go away, but she wouldn't.'

'I'm sure you know the conditions of her release, so didn't it occur to you to call the police, or her probation officer?'

'Yes, but . . . I guess I didn't feel threatened.'

He seemed puzzled by that. 'So what did you feel?'

'All sorts of things. Angry. Outraged. The kind of things you'd expect someone to feel when their daughter's killer turns up at the door.'

Passing over the sarcasm, he said, 'So after you let her in, what did you talk about?'

'Her mother and father. How she felt when Daisy told her they needed a break from each other . . .'

Leo waited for her to continue.

Suspecting Amelia had told her boyfriend, or another friend, everything that had been said while she was here, Jules said, 'I'm not sure what she hoped to gain from coming to see me, but I can tell you this, she as good as admitted to killing Daisy. I realise it's my word against hers, but there's never been any doubt in my mind, and this time she didn't deny it.'

The youngsters were staring at her again.

'Is that when you threatened her with a knife?' Johnson asked quietly.

Into a shocked silence, Jules said, 'No, that happened

after she tried to blame me for what she did to Daisy.'

'She blamed *you*?' Stephie cried in disgust.

Jules continued to look at Leo. 'I ended up plunging the knife into the table,' she told him. 'You can see the mark it left.'

Leo was about to speak again when Jemma Payne called him into the hall.

As the door closed behind him Jules looked at Andee, while feeling the strain of the others' confusion as they watched her. 'I don't know where she is,' she told Andee earnestly.

Appearing to believe her, Andee said, 'Why on earth didn't you tell someone she'd been here?'

Jules shook her head. 'I guess I didn't want the fuss, or anyone to find out I'd been stalking her.'

'You weren't stalking,' Stephie protested.

'I think that's the way the law would see it,' Jules corrected her.

'I reckon she's gone into hiding to try and cause trouble for you,' Joe declared decisively. 'She's obviously told her friends what happened when she came here, so now they're . . .' He broke off as the door opened and Leo and Jemma came back into the room.

Seeing how worried they looked, Jules immediately thought of Kian, and felt her insides turning to liquid.

Remaining standing, Leo looked directly at her as he said, 'We know that your husband was on a flight out of Dublin into Bristol on Saturday morning.'

Jules managed to return his gaze.

'Do you know where he is now?' he asked solemnly.

Trying to swallow, she said, 'I'm afraid not.'

'Are you sure?'

'I'm sure.'

'How about his cousin, Danny Bright? We're told Danny collected your husband from the airport and it seems no one's seen either of them since.'

'I've tried calling them,' Jules admitted, 'but they haven't rung back.'

Leo glanced at Andee. 'The call Jemma just took,' he said gruffly, returning his eyes to Jules, 'was to inform us that a body's been found on the rocks down by Porlock weir.'

As the words hit Jules like a blow the room started to spin. She was barely aware of what everyone was saying; it was as though they were all talking at once, while Andee only looked at her.

'Mrs Bright,' Leo said, stepping forward, 'I am arresting you on suspicion of . . .'

'For heaven's sake, Leo,' Andee cut in angrily, 'you know better than that. Unless someone's already identified the body?' Her eyes flashed the challenge.

Leo was forced to admit that no one had.

'Then I suggest you get a few more facts together before you start making arrests.' She was on her feet, leaving the young detectives in no doubt that she was showing them the door.

As they left Jules made herself look at the others. It was clear no one knew what to say. She felt so wretched, so afraid, that she wanted to run and run as though she might end up in another land, another life that had nothing to do with it all.

Instead, she went to her phone and rang Kian.

'You have to call me,' she told his voicemail, angrily, brokenly. 'The police have just tried to arrest me.

They've found a body, Kian . . . For God's sake, what the hell is going on?'

Within an hour of the detectives leaving, news came through that the body found at Porlock weir was a young male, still unidentified, but believed to belong to a Devonshire lad who'd left a goodbye note for his parents.

Though it seemed wrong to feel relief at someone else's tragedy, Jules couldn't help the way she almost collapsed with it when Andee received the call.

'I think me being here wasn't helpful for Leo,' Andee admitted. 'He doesn't normally make mistakes.'

'I knew it couldn't be her,' Stephie declared, sounding sorry that it wasn't.

Since it still didn't provide any answers to where Kian and Danny might be, or Amelia, Jules was soon pacing again, leaving Joe and Ethan to man the landline as calls started flooding in from curious friends and the press, while Stephie drove over to see her parents and put their minds at rest.

'They must surely know when she left the house,' Jules commented to Andee. 'The CCTV would show it.'

'Only if she left via an exit where there are cameras,' Andee pointed out.

'So she could still be on the property?' This was too much like when Daisy was missing for Jules not to feel edgy and afraid.

'I doubt it. They'll have carried out a thorough search before coming here, particularly in light of what happened before.'

It was during the late afternoon when Anton Quentin, looking as smoothly arrogant as ever, appeared on a news bulletin declaring himself fully convinced that members of the Bright family were holding his daughter hostage and very probably meant her harm. 'I'm afraid I can't go into any more detail at this time,' he continued in his insufferably superior way, 'but I can tell you that we have incontrovertible evidence to back up our claims.'

'What sort of evidence?' Jules cried.

'He's probably talking about the CCTV,' Andee reminded her.

'And the fact that I threatened her with a knife,' Jules added. 'And stalked her and lied to the police when they asked if I'd seen her.'

'He probably won't know about that,' Andee assured her.

By early evening, having heard the news, virtually every member of Kesterly's Bright family was crowded into Jules's small kitchen-cum-sitting room. Half of them had already been questioned by the police, while the other half were expecting to be at any time. It didn't take Jules long to believe that not one of them knew where Kian and Danny might be, not that they'd have been likely to give them up to the police if they did, but she could tell that they were as worried about the way things were looking as she was.

'I can't see them hurting her,' Ruthie declared for the umpteenth time. 'Even if she does deserve it.'

'They'll be making her see that she's got to move away from here,' Finn told them. 'She should never have been allowed to come back, not after what she did.'

'I can't believe she had the nerve to anyway,' Bridget stated hotly to Jules. 'I've always said she's not right in the head, and it seems she just wants to go on proving it.'

'What if they don't have her?' Liam piped up.

Everyone gawped at him in amazement.

'If they don't,' Ruthie said, 'maybe you'd like to tell us where else they might be.'

Since neither Liam, nor anyone else, had an answer for that they fell silent, until Stephie said to Jules, 'Is Andee coming back here tonight?'

'I don't think so,' Jules replied. 'Unless we hear something, I suppose.'

'What's getting me,' Bridget mused, 'is how long does it take to persuade the girl that she's not wanted around here? No one's seen her since Friday night . . .'

'And Kian didn't fly in until Saturday morning,' Joe put in keenly, 'so he couldn't have been involved in anything before that, unless Danny somehow got to her on his own on Friday, hid her away somewhere, then went to the airport for Kian.'

'No one's actually said that she disappeared on Friday night,' Stephie reminded them, 'they only said it was the last time she was seen. If she slept alone and got up early on Saturday morning . . . What time did Kian's plane get in?'

Quickly going online to check, Ethan said, 'Eleven a.m.'

Stephie grimaced. 'By the time they got back here from the airport it would have been at least half past twelve. Someone would have been bound to see her before that, if she was still at Crofton Park, so I'm not sure my little theory is helping us.'

Round and round, back and forth, only questions,

no answers and several phone calls from Aileen, who was as mad as a trapped bee and threatening to sort out Amelia Quentin herself if the boys hadn't already managed it. 'She's been nothing but trouble for this family,' she ranted furiously, 'and I for one have had enough of it.'

'You're making it sound as though she's to blame for going missing,' Bridget pointed out.

'And so she is,' Aileen snapped at her sister on the speakerphone. 'If she hadn't done what she did to our Daisy we wouldn't any of us be in the positions we're in now, including her, so yes, she's to blame for whatever's happening to her. I just hope it's good and final and she doesn't come bothering any of us again.'

Checking her mobile as it rang, Jules's heart lurched to see it was Andee. 'What news?' she asked, clicking on.

Andee's answer was so unexpected that it turned her horribly light-headed.

'Are you sure?' she murmured, as everyone looked at her.

'I'm sure.'

Jules's mind was buzzing. She wasn't dreaming this, she was awake, it was real. Still not fully breathing, she managed to say, 'Tell me, is she . . . ?' She couldn't finish the question.

Andee understood. 'She's unharmed, and on her way back to Crofton Park.'

Jules relayed the information to the others, and said, 'So where was she?'

'I don't know yet,' Andee replied, 'but I can tell you

that Kian, Danny and another man have been taken into custody.'

'Oh God,' Jules muttered, pressing a hand to her head. *Where was this going to end? What the hell had he been thinking?* 'What other man?' she asked hoarsely.

'I don't have a name, but as soon as I do I'll get back to you.'

As she rang off Jules looked at the others, feeling the strain of their concern and needing them to leave as she tried to think what to do. She didn't want this to be happening. She wanted her life to be normal and calm, unafflicted by tragedy, undarkened by fear.

No matter what happened to Kian, nothing was ever going to be as bad as what had happened to Daisy.

And so began the second longest night of her life as they watched the news, waited for calls and tried to work out who the other man could be.

'It has to be someone Danny hired to lure her out of the house,' Finn decided. 'You know, like a private detective, or someone down at his club who needed a few bob.'

'I wonder where they were holding her,' Stephie ventured. 'In a dungeon, I hope.'

Unable to stop herself damning Kian for being so reckless and stupid, Jules eventually went upstairs to lie down. She felt exhausted, drained, ready to give up on everything, as if there was anything left to give up on. How could she have believed that Kian was ready to restart their lives and try to put the past behind them, when she knew that good fortune had turned its face from them three years ago? They'd had all the happiness that was going to be theirs with their lottery win, the Mermaid, and most of all Daisy. Now all they had to look forward to was the time Kian would spend in prison for his part in this madness – and very probably another breakdown, this time hers.

'Jules? Are you awake?' Stephie whispered, putting her head round the door. 'I've brought you some tea.'

Surprised to realise she'd been sleeping, Jules rolled on to her back and looked at the bedside clock. Ten past eight. In the morning? It must be, or it would read twenty ten. She'd slept all night? That was something she hardly ever did.

Suddenly swamped by the awful reality of what was happening in her life, she closed her eyes, as though she could shut it all out again.

'They're saying on the news,' Stephie said, coming to sit on the bed, 'that no one's been charged with anything yet, but there should be some sort of announcement in the next couple of hours.'

'Has Andee rung?' Jules asked, checking her phone.

No calls on her mobile since Aileen had rung last evening. 'Is everyone still here?' she said, forcing herself to sit up.

'Terry and Finn had to leave, but everyone else is. Joe's taking orders for breakfast if anyone wants it. Marco sent supplies from the pub last night.'

Remembering how Misty and Marco had kept them all fed when they'd waited for news of Daisy, Jules mumbled, 'That was good of him.'

What the hell was happening to her life? Why was everything so out of control?

After forcing herself up and into the shower, she went downstairs to join the others who were all busy on their phones with texts and emails, or glued to the news. She was greeted lovingly, tenderly, treated almost like an invalid, and she had to admit she felt like one.

'Anything yet on who the other man might be?' she asked as Joe put a strong coffee in her hand.

'Finn's going to call if he finds anything out at Danny's club,' Bridget told her.

Not sure that it even mattered, Jules drank her coffee, looked at Joe and felt an absurd rush of tears suddenly stinging her eyes. Turning away, she went to the back door and stepped out into the garden. In spite of the sunshine and joyful birdsong it was going to be a long, horrible day, with more long, horrible days to come, and she wasn't sure she had the energy to get through them.

'Fancy going for a walk?' Joe murmured, coming up behind her.

Leaning into him as he put an arm around her, she had to fight back the tears again before she could speak. It simply wasn't fair that her daughter was no longer a part of this wonderful young man's life. They'd have been so happy together, had always seemed meant for one another, so what foul, evil demon had thought to use Amelia Quentin to smash it all apart? The same foul, evil demon that had driven Kian to abduct the murdering lunatic; to try and wreak some sort of vengeance for what she'd done to his precious girl?

A while later she and Joe were strolling through the surf of West Beach, watching their bare feet in the clear water, while listening to the screech of gulls as they soared and dived around the bay. The heat was intense, but since there was no sand here, only stones, there weren't many people around, just a couple of dog-walkers, and a young family having fun flying a kite. It sent Jules's mind back to the summer Joe and Daisy had flown a kite from a boat on Lake Max, and ended up capsizing. How they'd laughed and teased one another afterwards, seeming to need no one but each other to complete the perfect world they were in.

'Are you OK?' Joe asked softly.

'Fine,' she assured him.

'Thinking of Kian?'

'Daisy, actually.' She wondered why she found it so easy to be honest with him, and if she ought really to spare his feelings.

His voice was throaty, broken as he said, 'You know what scares me? It's the thought that one day you won't feel like my family any more.'

Taking his hands in hers she turned him to her, and said, 'I can promise you this, when that time comes it won't matter, because years will have passed and you'll have a family of your own.'

His face was strained as he turned to the horizon.

Jules spoke very gently. 'Stephie told me you were planning to set off for Paris in a few days. I want you to go, Joe, please. You can't allow what's happening to Kian to hold you back. He wouldn't want that, nor would Daisy and nor do I.'

After holding her gaze he let his head fall forward, coming to rest on hers.

'Live your life,' she whispered. 'There's more happiness waiting for you, I swear it, and if you ever want to share it with us we'll always be here for you.'

Gathering her into his arms he held her tightly as he wept, letting grief roll from his heart to try and make way for the future he feared.

In the end, with their arms linked, they walked back to the car and paused for a moment to gaze along the coast to where the Mermaid's roof and chimneys were glinting tantalisingly amongst the trees.

'Do you never go there?' he asked, turning to look at her.

She shook her head. 'Our story there has ended. It wouldn't be right to try and step into someone else's.'

His smile was faint. 'Ruby did,' he reminded her.

Jules's head tilted to one side. 'Yes, Ruby did, and I sometimes wonder if she misses us, or did she leave with Daisy.'

'Maybe they're both still there.'

Jules shook her head. 'I don't think so.'

He started to say more, but stopped as her mobile rang.

Seeing who it was, she felt such a jolt in her heart that she almost dropped the phone. 'It's Kian,' she murmured and quickly clicked on. 'Where are you?' she demanded. 'Are you OK?'

'I'm fine,' he assured her, sounding tired, but not as shattered as she might have expected. 'Are you?'

'I'm worried about you. What's happening?'

'They're just signing me out.'

'Signing you out?' She looked at Joe in bewilderment. 'Do you mean they're letting you go?' Could she dare to believe it? It didn't seem to make any sense.

'I'll explain everything when I get there. I've only got euros so are you OK to pay for the taxi?'

'Of course. I can come and get you . . .'

'No, taxi's here now so I won't be long.'

'Is Danny coming too?'

'No, it's a bit more complicated for him, so I'm not sure when they'll let him go.'

'But they will? His mother will want to know.'

'Like I said, I'll tell you everything when I get there.'

Chapter Sixteen

Watching the taxi coming along the street and pulling up outside the house was like watching a dream unfold. It was hard for Jules to make herself accept it was happening, that Kian really was here at last, while at the same time it was as though he'd never gone away. Time seemed to contract, distance itself, disappear; all the love, grief and confusion that had kept them apart now seemed to be drawing them together.

Going to him, aware of the others watching from the window, she realised he'd always been here, in her heart, and like Daisy would never leave. Emotions overwhelmed her as he stepped on to the street, his tousled blond curls as familiar as if they were her own, his violet-blue eyes showing tiredness, pain, but most of all relief and love as they locked to hers.

Wrapping his arms around her he held her so tightly she could hardly breathe, but she held him the same way. It felt so right, so reassuring, even exhilarating, as though her body was returning to where it had always belonged. She could feel that he'd lost weight, but he smelled so wonderfully, magically like himself that she began to laugh through her tears. All this time of being alone, of doing her best to stay strong and courageous, she'd only been a shadowy, fractured part of herself. Without him and Daisy she'd lost her real purpose, had forgotten how to function fully, no longer feeling that she was even properly alive.

Gazing deeply into his eyes she saw a flicker of the old humour returning, and felt her heart stirring with relief and hope. He was through the worst of it, had found himself again and in so doing had come back to find her.

Please God she was reading this correctly.

'The house looks full,' he murmured wryly as he glanced at the faces crowded at the window. 'What do you say we get back in the cab and run away?'

Knowing he was only half joking, she said, 'If Danny were here to explain what the heck is going on, I'd say let's do it and don't look back.'

Grimacing, he stood aside as she paid the driver, then gazed at her proudly, teasingly, as she linked his arm ready to re-enter the house. They were like newly-weds coming home as they sailed down the path.

If only that were true. The chance to start over again.

The next few minutes turned into a rowdy, back-slapping melee, with more hugs for the women than most had enjoyed in a while, and a hearty embrace for Joe, who'd grown a full four inches since the last time Kian had seen him.

'My boy,' Kian whispered roughly as he clutched Joe's shoulders and gazed incredulously into his eyes. 'Look what's happened to you. You've become a man.'

'That's what he tells everyone,' Ethan teased as Joe introduced him. 'Take it from me, it's all surface.'

Laughing, Kian greeted Ethan warmly, before turning back to Stephie and drinking her in all over again. 'You're a beautiful young lady,' he told her tenderly. 'I always knew you would be.'

Everyone was thinking of Daisy in that moment, but no one mentioned her as Stephie threw herself at him, weeping as she laughed. 'It's so good to see you, Kian. I really missed you. We all did.'

'I missed you too,' he assured her, 'but it was thinking of you all that kept me going.'

'Are you tired?' Bridget queried, peering at him knowingly. 'You look like you could do with a wash.'

'And a shave,' he agreed. 'They don't have much in the way of facilities down at Kesterly nick.'

Knowing they wouldn't be able to wait for him to freshen up, Jules led him to the sofa, perched on the arm next to him and waited for the others to settle. 'This better be good,' she informed him, as Joe passed him a cold beer, 'because if you're off to prison, or Danny is . . .'

'Where is Danny?' Bridget wanted to know. 'Why didn't they let him go at the same time as you?'

'Because he's a bit more involved in it than I am,' Kian admitted.

'Oh, well wouldn't that be typical,' she clucked knowingly. 'And who the hell is the other bloke they've been going on about, that's what I want to know?'

'That's a good question,' Kian replied, reaching for Jules's hand and entwining their fingers. 'I have to be honest, I wouldn't have recognised him when I saw him, he's changed that much . . . I guess we all have, in our ways, but what's happened to him . . .'

'Who *is* he?' Bridget pressed. 'We need to know who you're talking about.'

'They're not naming him in the press yet, but it's Dean's dad, Gavin Foggarty,' Kian told them.

Everyone's eyes widened in amazement.

'You mean the Archangel Foggarty?' Bridget murmured in bewilderment.

Kian nodded. 'That's him.'

'I thought they'd moved up north,' Terry said.

'They did,' Stephie told her.

'So what happened?' Liam wanted to know. 'Don't tell me, he came back after the girl . . .'

'. . . and who can bloody blame him,' Bridget snorted, 'when his son's serving a sentence he didn't deserve and that bitch who stitched him up is walking round free as a bird?'

'We need to let Kian tell it,' Jules reminded them.

All eyes returned to Kian, and Jules couldn't help smiling secretly to herself as she felt her husband warming to his audience and beginning to speak in the melodic, natural storyteller's way that she knew so well, drawing them all in so that they might almost have been through the past few days with him.

'Kian, my man, it's good to see you,' Danny cried, emerging through the airport crowd to wrap his cousin in a boisterous hug. 'You're looking good, mate. Better than good, but I'm afraid we've got a problem.'

Just like that, no preamble, no chatty wander out to the car first, just straight in with 'we've got a problem.'

Warily, Kian said, 'What sort of a problem?'

Danny was buzzing. 'A big one, but you're not to worry, we'll sort it.'

Kian regarded his cousin's round, rugged face with all its scars and ruddy good looks, and tried to remember a time when there hadn't been a problem. 'You know why I'm here,' he said darkly, 'and I don't need anything going wrong . . .'

'Nothing will, cross my heart. We've just got this bit of business to deal with, then everything'll happen the way it's supposed to. Come on, let's get you to the car, I'll explain on the way.'

Minutes later they were exiting the airport complex and heading south on the A38 towards the Somerset border. This was a journey Kian knew well, and had even been looking forward to – now he wasn't so sure. 'I need to let Jules know I'm here,' he stated, turning on his phone.

Danny's hand came out to stop him. 'Not yet,' he cautioned. 'I need to tell you what's happened first.'

Not liking the sound of that, Kian said, 'Tell me Jules is all right. Nothing's . . .'

'Jules is good. She's fine, nothing to do with her, it's just she'll expect to see you right away if you call and like I said, there's this bit of business we need to sort.'

Kian said, 'Dan, if you've got yourself into some kind of trouble . . .'

'Don't worry, I've got most of it sorted already, but well, it's like this . . .'

Kian noticed his hands tightening on the steering wheel, while his head kept turning towards Kian and back.

'I got a call on Thursday night,' he began. 'I swear I thought it was a joke, I mean he was the last person I was expecting to hear from, I didn't even know he had my number, not that it's a secret, but he's hardly the sort . . .'

'Who are we talking about?' Kian cut in evenly.

'Gavin Foggarty, Dean's old man,' was the surprising reply.

Danny glanced at Kian again, registered the restrained shock and hurried on. 'Honest to God, he calls up out of the blue, like we was old mates or something, and asks for a favour. He didn't call it a favour, he said help, and when he tells me what he needs help with . . . Well, like I said, I thought it was a joke, but it turns out he was deadly serious, and when I got to thinking about it, I thought, yeah, why not give the poor bastard a hand? His one and only's rotting away in that prison for something we all know he didn't do, and the only one who can change that is the Quentin bitch.'

The mention of Dean's name had been enough to liquefy Kian's insides; knowing now that Amelia Quentin was in some way involved was making him wish he'd stayed in Ireland.

Shaking off the echoes of screams, and images of terrible stabbings into the most precious flesh that ever existed, he said, 'What's happened? And whatever it is, does Jules know about it?'

'Good God no!' Danny exclaimed. 'No one knows, and they can't, not yet anyway, because we haven't finished sorting it out. I thought it would be done before you got here, but things haven't gone quite the way we expected and I thought . . . Well, I said to myself, if anyone can handle this our Kian can.'

Certain he didn't want to handle anything, Kian said, 'Go on.'

Danny's glance was part hopeful, part grateful. 'So, it's like this,' he continued. 'Gavin had this plan, well that's a bit generous because it wasn't any sort of a plan at all, but the basic idea was sound. He wanted me to help him get to the girl so he could persuade her to tell the truth about Dean, so his lad can go free. Obviously I had no problem with that, why would I when none of us is happy about what happened to the boy, and I thought, at the same time we were having a chat with her I could do my bit in persuading her to get the hell out of Dodge, so to speak.'

Kian's eyes turned to the passing countryside, seeing only a blur, feeling far too much as he realised where this was going. 'So you've had a chat with her?' he prompted.

'We have, a few times, and I'm afraid it's not going well.'

Wishing he didn't have to ask, Kian said, 'How are you getting her to speak to you at all?'

'Ah, well, that's where the difficult part comes in, and to be honest, I don't think I should tell you too much about that, because you weren't involved and you wouldn't have wanted to be, knowing you, so it's best we keep it that you didn't know anything until you got here this morning . . .'

'Which is true . . .'

'Which is true, so you can't have been a part of taking her . . .'

Kian's head came round. '*Taking* her? What the hell's that supposed to mean?'

'What do you think it means? We took her from her house . . .'

'Jesus Christ, Danny!'

'Cool it. It needed to be done.'

'Says who?'

'Who cares, it's happened, we've got her, move on . . .'

'How the hell did you get in? That place is a fortress . . .'

'Not for my boys. They figured out a way in and out that couldn't be detected, waited till they knew she was inside on her own, then delivered her to me and Gavin for our little chat.'

Kian's eyes closed. Danny was right, he really didn't want to know how they'd done it; this scant detail was already too much.

'The problem we've got now,' Danny ran on, 'is that she's still refusing to admit it was all down to her, and Dean played no part. I swear to God, if I was running the show I'd have let her go by now, but Gavin's having none of it. He's not letting her go anywhere until he's got what he came for, and if he doesn't get it he says he's going to kill her.'

Kian's eyes widened with alarm. 'He doesn't mean that,' he murmured.

'You haven't seen him. The guy's lost it. He doesn't care what happens to the girl, or to him, he just wants his son out of prison with his name cleared. And here's the real rub, he's managed to get himself a gun.'

Kian turned to him incredulously.

Danny's hands went up. 'Don't ask me where it came from, I swear it had nothing to do with me. I had no idea he even had it until after my guys delivered the girl . . .'

'Delivered her where?'

'Foggarty's old house on Felham Street. You know the one, on its own at the far end of the lane, behind those iron gates . . .'

'Yes, I know it. Didn't he sell it when they moved?'

'I guess not. Maybe it belongs to his church, they do that, them sort, don't they, have communal property? Or some of them do, I don't know . . . Anyway, that's where they are now, and he's saying if anyone turns up, other than you and me, he's going to use the gun before they can get inside.'

Stunned by just about everything he was hearing, Kian found himself saying, 'Are you sure the gun's loaded?'

Danny's head swung round. 'Do I want to find out the hard way?' he demanded meaningfully.

Accepting that he obviously didn't, Kian tried to make himself think rationally, as if there were anything rational about this at all, and he definitely didn't think there was. In fact, it was totally stark raving crazy. Yet, on the other hand, how could he not understand Foggarty's desperation? Hadn't he frequently imagined himself in the exact same position, doing anything, trying everything to make sense of what had happened? And if it would bring Daisy back to him, wouldn't he want to force Amelia Quentin to speak the truth?

'Kian, the bloke's a nutter,' Danny was telling him. 'He's not listening to anyone, and like I said, he's not caring what happens either. I've been trying to talk him down . . .'

'When exactly did you take her?' Kian interrupted, needing to get things straight in his mind.

Speeding up as they joined the M5, Danny said, 'It was last night, about nine. I wasn't there myself, I thought it was best not to be . . .'

'Did anyone hurt her?'

'No, not at all. I mean, I guess she wasn't any too thrilled about being tied up and gagged, but she's none the worse for it. Mad as hell, but I suppose that was only to be expected.'

Moving past that, Kian said, 'Has anyone reported her missing yet?'

'Not that I'm aware of. As soon as anyone does one of my guys will notify me.'

'At which point you intend to do what?'

'I have to be honest, I've no idea. Actually, I thought that was where you could come in.'

Feeling a painful throbbing in his temples, Kian pressed his fingers to his eyes to try and ease it. It wasn't that he felt any sense of protection towards the Quentin girl, quite the reverse. She could rot in hell as far as he was concerned, he just didn't want to be a part of sending her there. 'If Foggarty's got a gun we should be calling the police right now,' he stated.

'That's just it, it's because he's got a gun that we can't. Unless you want to risk him using it the minute they show up. If you ask me he's crazy enough to shoot us all.'

'If we ring the cops now, while he's alone with her . . .'

'He'll shoot her the instant he sees anyone but us, or that's what he says. Not that I have a problem with it, but if it gets out that I was involved in taking her . . .'

Wishing he didn't care about any of it, Kian said, 'So what's supposed to happen now? We go back there and . . . what?'

'And you use your expert diplomatic skills to persuade her to give Foggarty what he wants. Or, just as good, you talk him into letting her go. Either way we get out of there in one piece.'

Having no such confidence in his fantasy diplomatic skills, Kian said, 'Or we wait until the bloke's asleep and get the gun away from him?'

Danny nodded eagerly. 'That's definitely an option too,' he agreed. 'Yep, I'm liking the sound of that.'

Still not liking the sound of anything, Kian turned to stare out of the window again. Though he desperately wanted to call Jules, certain she'd handle this far better than he could, he was afraid that if he involved her something would end up going horribly wrong, for which she could pay the price.

By the time they arrived in Kesterly, taking a lot of back roads to get to the shady suburb of Risley where Felham Street meandered through a scant woodland to a handful of large, gated residences at the end of the cul-de-sac, Kian had already received two texts from his mother wanting to know if he'd arrived safely.

'Give it a while before you text back,' Danny advised, as they pulled up in front of the Foggartys' Victorian-Gothic manse. 'It shouldn't be long before we get this sorted, then you can send all the texts and make all the calls you want.'

Convinced they were handling this all wrong, but unable to come up with an alternative plan, Kian got out of the car and followed Danny to the gabled front door. In the entry hall they were greeted by an ominous painting of the Good Lord gazing solemnly down from the cross; a sad, despairing observer of the wrongdoings taking place under this roof. Kian averted his eyes and looked around. There were no windows and so much dark wood panelling that they were only able to take in the oppressive gloom of the place when Danny turned on a light.

'Dean used to live here?' Kian murmured incredulously. It was no wonder the boy had spent so much time at the Mermaid. If he'd known Dean's home was as bad as this he'd have tried to adopt him.

'They're up there,' Danny whispered, pointing towards a solid oak staircase. 'Or they were when I left. With any luck he'll have talked her round by now and they've gone. I'll go find out.'

As Kian watched his cousin climb the stairs he felt sickened, unsettled by the horrifying prospect of being under the same roof as his daughter's killer. Unless something had changed while Danny was away the girl was up there right now, being held hostage by a man who hated her every bit as much as he did. The bizarre, unthinkable reality of it was affecting him deeply, threatening to unleash all the hatred and rage he'd struggled so hard to control since his daughter died.

He turned his eyes from the stairs, as though this might in some way detach him from the evil instincts he could feel seeping into his soul. He made himself focus on the stench of must and something else he couldn't – didn't want to – define. He began asking himself what the heck sort of a life poor Dean had led, growing up here. It was as though he'd swapped one prison cell for another, and yet that wasn't true, because at least he'd been able to come and go from this one. His parents had never tried to stop him being friends with Daisy, or taking part in all their projects. And maybe this place hadn't been as bad when the family was actually here – after all they'd been gone for over two years now, and by the look of it no one had been inside – or outside – since.

Hearing the sound of voices from above, he felt his heart contract. Apparently Foggarty at least was still here, so presumably the girl was too. He tried to make himself think straight. It had never entered his mind that he'd walk into something like this the minute he got back to Kesterly. In fact, if he'd had any idea it was happening he'd never have come. However, he was here now, and there was no way he could leave Danny to deal with things alone when he was clearly in over his head with Foggarty. And his cousin's motives, though skewed, couldn't really be faulted, since the reason he wanted Amelia Quentin gone from Kesterly was more for Kian and Jules than himself – and didn't they all want the girl to be paying a real price for what she'd done, and Dean to be freed?

So whether he liked it or not, he was going to have to do whatever it took to bring about an outcome that didn't end them up in prison, or worse, and the sooner he got on with it the sooner he could get out of here and home to Jules.

*　*　*

It was Saturday evening, the sun was starting to go down and what remained of the light was making it through the trees to cast warped and eerie shadows over the Victorian manse.

Kian was in the kitchen, where he and Danny had made coffee and sandwiches an hour ago with the supplies Danny had got one of his people to bring in. Whether Amelia or Foggarty had eaten, Kian had no idea; he'd simply watched Danny carry up a tray and come back down a few minutes later, empty-handed.

He hadn't been up there himself; Foggarty had to think, apparently, and would let them know when he was ready to talk.

'This is crazy,' he muttered to Danny. 'Does he reckon we're going to sit here all night like a pair of morons waiting for bloody Godot?'

'Who?' Danny asked.

Kian waved it away. 'If he won't talk, then I can't see how the hell we're going to get out of this.'

'I've already said that to him,' Danny responded, 'trouble is, I don't know how much he's hearing. He's just sitting there with his gun, mumbling some sort of shit . . . Maybe he's praying . . .'

'And what's she doing?'

'Sitting on the bed watching him.'

'Doesn't she need to use the bathroom?'

'He lets her, but he goes in with her.'

Kian's eyes closed in disgust.

Foggarty had their phones up there with him; like fools they'd handed them over when he'd sent down instructions for them to take out the batteries and bring them upstairs unless they wanted something to happen to Amelia. In any sane world Kian would have told him to do what the hell he liked to the girl; the problem was they clearly weren't in a sane world, and he didn't want Foggarty's actions hanging around his conscience as he and Jules tried to get on with their lives.

'I'm going up there,' he declared, getting abruptly to his feet.

Danny shrugged. 'Just don't make him mad,' he warned, 'or we're all going to end up sorry.'

Wondering if Jules knew he was in Kesterly yet, and angered by how worried his mother would be that he hadn't texted back, Kian climbed the stairs two at a time.

'Foggarty! Open this door,' he shouted, hammering it with the side of his fist. 'There are other ways of achieving what you want, this is only going to end you up in trouble.' So much for his diplomatic skills, but what the hell was he supposed to say?

What was he going to do to the girl when he saw her?

'She knows what she has to do,' Foggarty called back. 'Once she's given us the confession we can all go home.'

Biting back his exasperation, Kian cried, 'Come on, man, you've got to know things don't work like that. No one's going to act on something you've forced out of her. It's called coercion . . .'

'I know what it's called, but I'm not leaving here until she's admitted she's a liar, and nor is she.'

'Right, so we all sit and wait . . .'

'The Lord is my protector, he will make right the wrongs that have been done to me and my son.'

Before he could stop himself, Kian said, 'He hasn't even put right the wrongs done to his own son.'

'That's what you think, but it's happening all the time. The world is paying. Look around you and see how it is paying.'

'Whatever God's doing, his word is clear in the Bible, thou shalt not kill, so put down the gun, Gavin . . .'

'It is also written an eye for an eye.'

Realising there was no point getting into some half-cocked theological exchange that was going to end them up precisely nowhere, Kian said, 'So she confesses, you take it to the police, and all they're going to do is lock you up for holding her hostage. Can you see that, Gavin? Is this making sense to you?'

'Nothing makes sense about this, Kian, and you know it. You've lost your daughter, my son's in prison for something he didn't do, and the only one who committed a crime was *her*.'

Picturing him jabbing the gun towards Amelia, or at the very least glaring at her as she shrank away, or maybe glared back, Kian said, 'Listen, mate, I'm no happier than you are that she's walking free, but what you're doing here, it's not going to change things. They'll just . . .'

'They'll change for me. I want to hear her admit she did it, that she framed my son and made him hurt someone he loved . . .' His voice faltered. 'He'd never have wanted to hurt Daisy, everyone knows that . . . This evil rotten specimen of humanity has ruined Dean's life, mine and yours too. Don't you at the very least want to see her back behind bars paying for what she did?'

'Of course I do, and we'll try to make it happen, but this isn't the way.' How true those words were. He needed to hang on to them, use them to quash all his baser instincts. He was a good man, a decent man who'd never harmed anyone in his life. He wasn't going to let his hatred of Amelia Quentin turn him into something, someone he wasn't.

Gavin shouted, 'Then tell me what is the way. Tell me how you're going to right the wrongs without God's help.'

Kian looked round as Danny came to join him on the landing. 'I don't understand,' he called to Foggarty, 'are you saying that you've got God's help now?'

Danny nodded, as Foggarty declared, 'The Lord is assisting and guiding me to seek the vengeance that should be mine.'

Kian grimaced at Danny. With that kind of logic how the hell was he ever going to reason with the bloke?

'I've been round and round this a dozen times already,' Danny murmured. 'He's not listening, or understanding, or even connecting with anything beyond whatever shite he's got going on in his head.'

Clutching at straws, Kian said, 'Do you know where his wife is? Maybe she can talk him round?'

'Do you know how to get hold of her?'

Kian didn't.

Danny shrugged. 'For all we know she's in on this, although he hasn't received any calls as far as I know and he hasn't mentioned her at all.'

Pulling Danny back down the stairs, Kian said, 'All we can do is wait for him to fall asleep and grab the gun then.'

Danny's eyebrows shot up. 'Easy. Question is, how are we going to know he's asleep if we're not in the room?' He was clearly expecting an answer.

'Don't look at me,' Kian exclaimed, 'I can't see through bloody doors any more than you can.'

'So how about coming up with some solutions instead of more bloody problems?' Danny growled. 'I don't want to be stuck here any more than you do, but the alternative is to walk out and leave him to it. We can do that, if you like. It makes no odds to me if he blows her brains out . . .'

'If it didn't you'd have already gone.'

'I stayed put so you could take advantage of the situation if you wanted to. If you don't . . .'

Kian's hand went up. 'Stop,' he cut in sharply. 'This is getting us about as far as arguing with him, so here's what we're going to do. We're going to get that confession from her, give it to him to do whatever the hell he wants with it and then we're all going home.'

Danny snorted. *'We're* going to get the confession?' he repeated incredulously. 'And exactly how are we going to do that when he won't even let us in the room?'

'We'll have to make him let us.'

'How?'

'You're an Irishman, aren't you? By *talking* him into it.'

And so began a charm offensive that went on through that day and the next, by which time they'd both yielded to exhaustion more than once, run the gamut of every imaginable approach in their persuasion from begging to cajoling to threatening and all the way back again, and still, as far as they knew, Gavin hadn't slept. The bloke was clearly on something; or his Special Connections were keeping him alert. Exactly what Amelia was doing they could only guess; having heard nothing from her they couldn't even be sure she was still there, although there didn't seem any point to Foggarty staying put if he no longer had his hostage.

It was as dawn began rolling in through the open windows on Monday morning, fresh and fragrant and alive with birdsong, that Foggarty thumped the floor, a signal for one of them to go up there.

Danny went, and was back a few minutes later with his hands in the air and Foggarty, holding the gun, right behind him.

'Jesus Christ,' Kian muttered, springing to his feet and raising his own hands. 'What's going on?' he asked, looking from Danny to Foggarty and back again. He could see right away what Danny had meant about Foggarty losing it. Despite the man's evident exhaustion there was a wildness about him, an almost feral light in his desperately haunted eyes, that seemed close to the point of explosion.

Telling Danny to sit down, and keeping the gun trained on him, Foggarty said to Kian, 'OK. Go and talk to her. She's sleeping now, be there when she wakes up. Let's see how she can stand up to the father of her other victim.'

Kian glanced at Danny. Apparently his cousin was the new hostage.

By the time Kian reached the top of the stairs his head was spinning with tiredness and a desperate need to make himself think straight so he could handle this properly. He'd lost count of how many hours they'd been here, had practically even forgotten why he was in Kesterly.

'It's going to be all right,' he'd told Jules the last time they'd spoken. 'Everything will be taken care of, I promise,' and now, depending on how much she knew, he could only imagine what conclusions she was coming to.

The room was dark and stuffy, smelled of sweat, food and old wood. It took a moment for Kian's eyes to adjust, to register the thickly brocaded curtains edged by gleaming bands of sunlight, the walls of fading posters, most from Hope Cove Performing Arts Society productions; *The Magic Roundabout; Tears of My Fellows; One Night in Hector's Heaven; Around Town in Eight and a Half Jokes*. He remembered them all, and the sudden swell of grief made him feel disoriented and nauseous.

There was a large crucifix hanging over the single, iron-framed bed; a muscular yet forlorn-looking Christ gazed down on the wretched creature below.

And she was wretched. Her hair was a tangled nest, her eyes were rimmed in old make-up; her mouth was set in a tight defiant pinch.

'Yes I did it,' she hissed at Kian before he could speak, 'but nothing you or anyone else says is going to make me give that madman a confession.'

Kian's eyes closed as bile rose up from the darkest depths of his soul. This was the girl who'd destroyed his precious daughter, who'd ended her life so violently and needlessly that she should never have seen this side of freedom again. Why didn't he just call the police and let Foggarty do his worst? She didn't deserve to live; she didn't even deserve to speak, after all the lies she'd told.

Looking at her, he forced himself to say, 'I don't want to be here any more than you do, but neither of us is going anywhere unless you own up to what you did.'

'I just told you,' she raged.

'I know what you told me, but your father's a lawyer, so I'm sure you know that nothing you say now will be usable against you. You will still have got away with murder. I don't know how that makes you feel, but frankly I don't care how you feel. You're not like the rest of us. No one with normal compassion and a functioning conscience would even want to hurt someone who'd never done them any harm . . .'

'But she did,' Amelia cried savagely, 'and who ever talked to *her* about compassion and conscience? Who tried to make her care about what she'd done to me?'

Regarding her with as much contempt as disbelief that she still didn't seem to get it, he said, 'I'm not wasting my time on you. I want you out of my life for good, and that's what's going to happen. Once we leave here you'll be history for this town and for my family . . .'

'You can't make me leave . . .'

'Don't tell me what I can and can't do. Just listen to what I'm telling you. As soon as you've given Gavin Foggarty the confession he wants I'll call the police myself and tell them to come and get you. There won't be anything they can do with the confession; it's not admissible because it will have been extracted under duress. So all you have to do is pick up that pen and paper there and write the words that will corroborate Dean's story. Let Gavin read how you tricked his son and Daisy into going to Crofton Park that day, how you planned the whole thing right down to everything you were going to tell the police, and how you lied in court, then you'll be free to carry on your life however and wherever you please.'

Her eyes were slits of suspicion; she was making no move to carry out his instructions.

Suddenly he could hear Daisy's voice calling to him, from a great and terrible distance.

Daddy, Daddy, please help me.

He closed his eyes, but he could still see her lying on the ground, helpless, terrified, and this girl's maniacal face looming over her, twisted, sallow, spattered in blood. She was crazed, out of control, loving what she was doing, panting, seething, raising her hand time after time . . .

Knowing the only safe course was for him to leave the room right now, he turned abruptly for the door. 'I'm calling the police,' he told her, 'and if Gavin shoots you before they get here, do me a favour and go straight to hell.'

'Wait!' she called after him.

He stopped, but didn't turn back.

'Why are you here and not Jules?' she demanded.

Puzzled by the question, he said, 'What difference does it make?'

She shrugged. 'I just thought . . . Does she know what you're doing?'

He didn't answer.

Finally she said, 'Why are you still here?'

He turned to look at her.

'You could have walked out at any time and left me alone with Gavin,' she challenged, 'but instead you're staying, and the only reason you're doing that is because you don't want him to hurt me.'

Kian's sudden snarl made her draw back. There were so many things he wanted to say to that, so much hatred and venom he'd like to scald her with, but in the end all he did was turn away.

'I'll do what you want on one condition,' she said as he reached the door.

He didn't respond, but nor did he leave.

'If Jules will agree to see me so we can repair our friendship, I'll write the confession.'

'My God! What on earth did you say to that?' Stephie cried, as Kian took another sip of his beer and tried to hide his tiredness.

'You surely didn't agree to it,' Bridget protested. 'Delusional bitch, thinking she can set out conditions.'

'He must have gone for it,' Liam put in, 'or he'd still be there.'

Jules's heart turned over as Kian's eyes found hers. 'I didn't say anything at all,' he told her. 'I just carried on out the door, closed it behind me and went downstairs. When I got there I found Gavin fast asleep on the sofa and Danny standing out in the garden, aiming the gun.'

'At what?' Bridget demanded.

'At nothing.'

Frowning, Joe said, 'So it was all over? You called the police, they came and now here you are?'

'Not quite. We decided to let Gavin sleep for a while, and by the time he woke up it turned out Amelia had written the confession.'

Stephie's jaw dropped as Jules blinked.

'She wrote it?' Joe responded incredulously.

Kian nodded. 'She handed it to Gavin when he went upstairs, warned him that she'd tell the police he'd forced it out of her, and said she wanted to go home.'

As everyone frowned or gaped in amazement, Terry said, 'So what happened then?'

Kian shrugged. 'We knew the police were looking for her by now, so there was only one thing we could do. We called them, they came, we were arrested and she was taken to wherever they took her.'

'So what made them let you go?' Jules wanted to know.

'I'm guessing she gave a statement that confirmed what I'd already told them, that I wasn't involved in snatching her, and flight records would show that I wasn't even in the country when it happened.'

'So they were satisfied that the only reason you didn't call them the minute you found out what was going on was because Gavin had a gun?'

Kian shrugged again. 'They didn't tell me much, but according to the duty solicitor that's about the size of it.'

'What's going to happen to Gavin now?' Joe asked.

Before Kian could answer Bridget jumped in crossly. 'Never mind him,' she cried, 'what about our Danny? He's going down again, isn't he? They'll throw away the bloody key this time. Well, serves the silly bugger right, is what I say. He's like his father, never did know how to stay out of trouble.'

'Don't be too hard on him,' Kian countered, 'remember, the only reason he did it was to try and help Gavin get Dean's name cleared, so technically that makes him the good guy. And as barmy as Gavin might be, every one of us understands what drove him to do what he did.'

Sobered by that, they were quiet for a while, each caught in their thoughts of Daisy and the torment they'd been through since losing her.

Jules looked at Kian, and as their eyes met she could see his tiredness.

'It was a pity,' Bridget said, 'that you didn't manage to persuade the girl to stop darkening our doorsteps. Why doesn't she get that she's not wanted around here?'

'I think she gets it,' Stephie answered, 'but she just doesn't care.'

Kian got to his feet. 'If you'll forgive me,' he said, 'I need to shower and shave and spend some time alone with my wife.'

Chapter Seventeen

Over the next couple of days Jules and Kian deliberately put Amelia Quentin out of their minds, not
wanting her, or anything about her, to spoil the time
they had left with the youngsters before they took off
on their European travels. It was uplifting for them all
to discover just how much they enjoyed being with
one another, though there were many tears too. Most
important of all, they found, was the fact that the time
was proving as cathartic as it was special.

'I'm going to miss them when they've gone,' Kian
sighed, as he and Jules got ready for bed the night
before the others were due to leave for Paris. 'It feels
strange to think that by this time tomorrow it'll only
be us in the house.'

Teasingly, Jules said, 'Do you wish you were going
with them?'

He considered it. 'Let's just say I wouldn't mind
being in Paris,' he decided, 'but only with you. They
need time to themselves now, and so do we.'

Not arguing with that, she slipped into bed beside him
and settled against his shoulder as he put an arm around
her. 'I still can't believe they've dismissed the charges

against Danny,' she commented. 'One minute he's getting the book thrown at him, the next we hear he's down the pub with his mates like nothing ever happened.'

Equally mystified, Kian said, 'No doubt we'll get the full story soon enough, but that lawyer Andee Lawrence got for him, what was her name?'

'Helen Hall.'

'That's right. Well, she's obviously the business. It's a shame we didn't have her on our side two years ago, things might have turned out very different if we had. Anyway, at least they let Gavin out too, even if he isn't walking away scot-free. Silly sod, he knew all along that they wouldn't be able to use the confession, but he had to have it. Let's just hope it doesn't end up costing him his freedom. That would be a bitter irony, wouldn't it: instead of freeing Dean he gets himself banged up instead?'

'It would indeed,' Jules agreed, 'but when I spoke to Gemma, Dean's mum, earlier, she said Helen Hall had told her to take Gavin for a psychiatric assessment. If they can prove that the stress of everything has unhinged him, he'll probably be recommended for counselling rather than anything more serious.'

'Helen Hall's working for the Foggartys, is she? Well, I guess that's some good news for them. What we need to hear now is that Dean's on his way home, but I guess that's not going to happen any time soon.'

Sighing, Jules said, 'I wonder if Dean knows yet what his father did. Poor Gavin, he's obviously suffered horribly over everything, and we had no idea.'

'Could we have done anything if we had known? We haven't been in great shape ourselves.'

Sobered by the truth of that, Jules said, 'Do you think we are now?'

He gave it some thought and nodded slowly. 'We're getting there,' he decided. 'There's still a way to go, but no one ever said the journey would be short or easy.'

She curled her fingers round his. 'Once the kids have gone . . . Well, we've got a lot to talk about, you and me. So much that I hardly know where to begin.'

Dropping a kiss on her head, he said, 'Then allow me.'

She turned to look at him. 'That sounds as though you're ready to get started.'

'That could be true,' he conceded, 'because there's a lot I want to say, though none of it matters more than how sorry I am for everything I've put you through.'

Surprised and saddened, she said, 'You've got nothing to apologise for . . .'

'Oh but I have. What I tried to do to myself, the way I handled things so badly . . .'

'Wasn't your fault. Oh Kian, you have to know that I understand how hard it was for you . . .'

'For you too . . .'

'But we all handle things differently.'

'I should have been there for you. You needed me, more than you ever have, and I let you down.' Kian sighed deeply.

'No you didn't. What you did was try to cope with your grief, to make some sense of what happened, and because there was no sense to it, it wasn't possible for either of us to know which way to turn.'

'You didn't fall apart . . .'

'Yes I did, in my own way. I withdrew from everyone. I didn't want to see or speak to anyone in case they mentioned her, or in case they didn't. No one, even you, would have been able to do or say the right thing, so in a way it was a relief when you went to Ireland with your mother.'

Shaking his head sadly, he said, 'There's her, too. I put too much on her. She's not getting any younger . . .'

'But she's your mother. She wouldn't have wanted it any other way. I know that from being a mother myself.'

Hugging her to him, he said, 'And you were so wonderful at it. No child could have asked for more . . .'

'It was you she adored.'

'It was both of us. We were blessed, that's for sure.'

'Until Amelia Quentin came along.' With a shaky sigh, she said, 'I wonder if she'd have turned out differently if her mother had lived.'

'I guess we'll never know the answer to that, but you remember, when she was small, and her mother was still around, there was always something . . . strange about her.'

Remembering it only too well, Jules said, 'Why did fate send her our way? I've asked myself that a thousand times. What did we do that was so evil that we had to be punished like that?'

'We didn't do anything, because that's not how it works. Bad things happen to good people, and just as often good things happen to bad people. We have no say over it; all we can do is choose how we respond to what is thrown at us, and for a long time I was definitely choosing the wrong way.'

Curious, she said, 'Does that mean you feel differently now?'

'Mm, I guess it does. Not that it doesn't hurt any more, or I don't long for my girl every minute of every day, or feel empty inside when something happens I want to share with her. But I've come to realise, with some help from Father Michael, that only by *accepting* that it's happened am I ever going to start getting over it.'

Intrigued to know more, she said, 'So you were talking to Father Michael about things?'

'I kind of found myself doing it without even realising it was happening. He's an easy man to talk to and he said a lot of things that, after I thought about them, seemed to make sense. He made me understand how resisting, instead of accepting, just causes more pain and keeps us all locked up inside our grief.'

Feeling drawn to this new understanding, Jules said, 'Did you tell him about your suicide attempts?'

He nodded grimly. 'I feel so ashamed now,' he whispered shakily. 'To think of what I put you through . . . I wasn't in my right mind . . .'

'None of us were. How could anyone expect us to be?' After a beat she said, 'I've been so afraid you'd try again and manage to succeed.'

Turning to her, he said, 'It's never going to happen, I swear it. We might not have Daisy any more, but after talking things through with Father Michael he's made me see how much I still have to live for, and just about all of that is wrapped up in you. I don't know how I lost sight of it, but I do know that I never will again.'

Gazing deeply, tenderly into his troubled eyes, she said, 'Do you think Father Michael would talk to me too, if you asked him? He sounds so wise.'

'I know he would, because he's said so. Catholic priests have got themselves a bad rap these days, but he's definitely one of the good ones.' Tilting her mouth up to his, he kissed her softly. 'Do you remember on the phone, before I left Ireland,' he said, 'that I promised everything was going to be all right, that it would all be taken care of?'

She nodded, ready to hear whatever it was now she felt sure it had nothing to do with Amelia Quentin.

'Well, I've got a proposal for you,' he began. 'If you don't think it'll work, or if it's not what you want, we can always bin it and try something else, but whatever we do, it's time we started moving our lives forward, don't you agree?'

'Of course,' she murmured, bringing his hand to her cheek. 'Just please let it be together.'

Sounding surprised, he said, 'Of course we'll be together, as long as it's what you want.'

'There's nothing I want more,' she assured him.

He sat with that for a moment, stroking her hair and seeming to absorb the reassurance in a way that strengthened the bond between them. 'So what I've been thinking,' he said in the end, 'is that maybe we could make a fresh start – in Ireland.'

Stiffening at the unexpectedness of it, she tried to think what to say. She'd never considered leaving Kesterly; this was her home, she'd grown up here, met

Kian here, the Mermaid was here, so was her mother, and Daisy, in her ethereal way. They couldn't just up and leave everything, everyone, behind. It was making her feel panicked even to think of it.

'I've got it all worked out,' he continued, sounding both anxious and eager. 'My mother and I have been visiting care homes near us and there are a couple I think you'd approve of. Of course, I realise you'd need to see them before making a decision, but if you do give one of them the thumbs up, our Danny's talked to a customer of his who has a private plane – not one of those little two-seater jobs, it's a proper executive jet – and he's agreed to let his pilot fly us all over there so your mum doesn't have to go through the ordeal of a public flight. Danny's even spoken to a nursing agency about hiring a qualified nurse to come with us to take proper care of Marsha on the journey.'

'Wow,' she murmured, 'you have been busy.'

'Of course, if you'd rather your mother stayed here and we came to see her regularly, that would work too.'

'But what would we do in Ireland?' she asked. 'Everyone we know, everything we own, our businesses, this house, is here.'

'We know people there too,' he reminded her, 'and there are plenty of things we could do. I've been working with our Cullum lately. He's got a really good business going now the recession's over. He mainly buys up old properties, restores them the way we did with the Mermaid, then he sells them on. And I got to thinking that with your flair for interior design . . .'

With a choke of surprise, she said, 'And what flair would that be?'

'The one you used on the Mermaid.'

'I had help from a professional.'

'And you could have help again, until you felt ready to take it all on yourself, and even hire someone in to assist you. It's all just a suggestion,' he went on hurriedly. 'If you want us to stay here and maybe even move back into the Mermaid . . .'

'No, we can't do that. It's Misty's and Marco's home now, it would be wrong to make them move out. Not that I can bear to think of giving it up . . .'

'I've had an idea about that. Why don't we ask Misty and Marco if they'd like to buy into the place, you know, become joint owners with us? That way we'd still keep a stake in it, but they'd have one too. It seems fairer than the arrangement we've had with them up to now where they're basically on a salary, with no security if we did decide to sell. And let's face it, they run the place brilliantly, so they deserve to have a proper footing in it.'

Since that was undeniably true, Jules could only say, 'I'm not sure they'd be able to afford it.'

'They could if we set a price that works for them. We don't need to make money out of them, we just want to keep our connection with the place, and do right by two people who've always done right by us.'

Loving him for his crazy and wonderful generosity, she smiled as she said, 'You're a good man, Kian Bright.'

Affecting a full Irish brogue, he replied, 'Now that I won't be arguing with.' Then after a pause, 'So what do you say? About Ireland.'

Still not sure how she felt, she lay quietly assimilating it all, trying to imagine resettling her mother in a different care home, creating a new life with Kian and Aileen and the family and friends they had over there, many of whom she already knew . . .

'You don't have to give me an answer now,' he said softly. 'I just wanted to put it to you as an option, but it's not our only one, and I'm ready to do whatever makes you happy, because that's really all that matters to me.'

The following morning they were off early to Bristol airport with the youngsters, all of them experiencing a dizzying mix of emotions as excitement, nerves and nostalgia got caught up in grief and hope and the bonds that tied them all together.

'We'll keep in touch,' Stephie assured Jules tearfully as they hugged goodbye. 'We'll send emails and texts and . . . Did you sign up for Instagram? Ethan, did you put Instagram on Jules's phone?'

'It's there,' Ethan assured her.

''We'll send photos of everything we're doing,' Stephie ran on, 'well, nearly everything, and you've got to text and email back.'

'Of course we will,' Jules promised, so pleased that Stephie was travelling with Joe and Ethan rather than on her own that she could just about cope with the wrench of letting them go.

There were tears in Kian's eyes as he held Joe tight. 'Take care of yourself, son,' he said huskily, 'and you know how to get hold of us if you ever need us.'

Joe's eyes were wet too as he choked back a sob.

'I've got to say it,' he responded, 'I love you, man, you're the best, you and Jules. I never want to lose touch with you.'

'It's not going to happen,' Kian reassured him. 'We'll always be here for you, you just have to pick up the phone, or email, whatever works best, and wherever our home is, there's always going to be one for you.'

'That goes for you too,' Jules said to Stephie. 'And you,' she smiled at Ethan. 'You feel like family, all of you, so that's how we think of you.'

'Can I tell Dean you said that?' Stephie asked anxiously.

'Yes, of course,' Jules replied. 'I intend to write to him soon. Have you heard from him lately?'

'Not since he rang to ask if I knew about his dad. He knows I'm going to Europe now, but I've promised that no matter what happens, or where I am when he finally comes out, I'll make sure I'm there for him.'

'We all will be,' Jules assured her.

As they rode the escalator to the first floor, Joe said, 'You'll still come to the States for visits? Em's there, so I guess you will.'

'Of course,' Kian replied, with a glance at Jules, 'and we'll hope to see you over this side of the pond from time to time.'

Jules almost added 'with a new girlfriend', but decided it wouldn't be right to mention anything like that today.

Eventually the travellers were going through passport control, turning round every step of the way to wave and blow kisses while laughing through their tears. Jules wondered if they knew how heart-breaking it was for her to watch them go without Daisy being amongst them. She guessed they did, and no doubt felt it just as deeply.

As Kian's arm went round her she leaned into him and gave one last wave as they disappeared. They were ghosts now, like Daisy, but unlike Daisy they'd come back one day soon, please God.

An hour and a half later Jules and Kian were at the Seafront Café where Fliss had reserved them a window booth and Andee was already waiting with the lawyer, Helen Hall. Helen was a petite, pale-skinned woman with a shock of dark red hair, shrewd green eyes and a smile that Jules found herself instantly warming to.

'It's good to meet you,' she told Jules and Kian as they slid into the booth. 'You probably don't recognise me, but my family and I have long been regulars at the Mermaid.'

'Your face is certainly familiar,' Jules responded truthfully.

Kian said, 'I hope the service was always up to scratch.'

'You never failed us,' she assured him.

With a smile he said, 'You're going to be a legend around here now you've managed to get the charges against our Danny dropped; I hope you realise that.'

Helen's laugh was surprisingly girlish. 'I'm afraid that wasn't my doing,' she confessed, 'although I'm having a problem convincing your cousin of that.'

Drily, Andee said, 'From what I know of Danny I think he'd far rather give credit to a lawyer than anyone in the police force, so like it or not, Helen, you're his new best friend.'

With a droll arch of an eyebrow, Kian added, 'Good luck with that.'

'We haven't seen Danny yet,' Jules told her, 'so how come the charges were dropped?'

Andee and Helen exchanged glances. 'It's a good question,' Andee replied, 'and it turns out that things have been going on behind the scenes for quite some time that we're only just becoming aware of.'

Puzzled, Jules said, 'What sort of things?'

Helen said, 'Apparently the Chief Prosecutor for Dean Valley has never been happy with the way Dean's and Amelia's trial was handled. As a result he ordered a confidential investigation, and I'm told that he passed the findings to the Director of Public Prosecutions at the end of last year.'

Jules and Kian could only look at her.

'I've now discovered,' Helen continued, 'that the Crown Prosecution Service is intending to return the case to the courts.'

Jules went very still as her insides turned rigid with shock.

Gruffly, Kian said, 'Can they do that? Isn't there something called double jeopardy?'

'Indeed there is, but last time Amelia was tried for voluntary manslaughter. The new charge, I'm told, will be murder.'

Jules's eyes closed as a dizzying relief was swamped by the horror of having to go through a trial again.

Helen said, 'I'm not sure if you're aware, but since Amelia's trial a new Director of Public Prosecutions has been appointed and she's made it abundantly clear from the start that she will not tolerate cronyism.'

Continuing, Andee said, 'It almost goes without saying that Anton Quentin will know what's going on. It'll be why he hasn't insisted on pressing charges against Danny and Gavin; he doesn't want Amelia's name in the press any more than it has to be, particularly when her actions are very likely to be viewed as the cause of Gavin Foggarty's breakdown.'

Jules was still trying to take it in. If she and Kian had known the CPS was reviewing the case, that someone out there who mattered had seen the travesty of justice and reacted to it, would it have made a difference during the past two years? She thought it would have, but no one had told them, and maybe, on reflection, that was a good thing, because if it had ended up being buried it could have destroyed them.

'What about Dean?' Kian was asking. 'Does this mean he could face a new trial too?'

Appalled by the thought, Jules looked at Helen as she said, 'I'm afraid I don't know the answer to that, but I'll be trying to find out, unless the CPS makes its announcement first, and that could happen at any time.'

'He's innocent,' Jules told her. 'He should never have been tried in the first place . . .'

'It'll break his father completely,' Kian cut in, 'if this ends up with his boy on a murder charge. It'll break Dean too, and what good would that do anyone?'

Andee said, 'If things go the way we hope it could end up clearing Dean's name, but that's all a long way down the road; a lot has to happen yet, and what you two have to think about is what it's going to mean for you.'

Jules took a breath as she looked at Kian. 'It's not about us,' she said shakily, 'it's about Daisy and the justice she deserves.'

Squeezing her hand, he turned back to the others as he said, 'How long before we hear officially about a new trial?'

Helen said, 'In the light of recent events I'd say it could be sooner rather than later. Obviously, if I hear anything before you do I'll be sure to let you know.'

It was just over a week later, as Jules and Kian were driving over to see Misty and Marco at the Mermaid, that Helen Hall rang to let them know that they should be hearing from the CPS sometime in the next couple of days.

Jules's heart twisted horribly. Life was moving beyond their control again, the ugliness of the past three years was on its way back and they had no way of stopping it. Yet did they really want to? That girl should pay for what she'd done to Daisy, and to Dean.

'There won't be an official announcement,' Helen was telling them over the hands-free speaker phone, 'until after the CPS have contacted you, which means you shouldn't, for the moment, be bothered by any press attention, unless it leaks out, of course.'

Kian's hands were gripping the steering wheel. 'I take it she's being charged with murder?' he said.

'Yes, she is.'

The relief that assailed Jules was unexpectedly over-whelming, but apprehension was quick to eclipse it.

'What about Dean?' Kian asked shortly.

Helen said, 'I ought to speak to his parents first, but

if you promise not to call them before I have a chance to, I can tell you that he won't be facing charges.'

Jules felt tears stinging her eyes. Though this was the news they wanted for Dean, considering everything he'd been through it hardly felt like a victory. 'I guess you don't know where Amelia Quentin is?' she asked, picturing the girl's shock, fear, fury – heaven only knew how she was reacting.

'I don't,' Helen answered, 'but I imagine she'll be brought back to Kesterly any day now to be charged.'

'And remanded in custody?' Kian put in.

'I should hope so, considering the seriousness of the offence and how badly things were handled before. Listen, I'm afraid I have to ring off now, I'm due in court, but I'll be back at my desk after four if you have any more questions. Oh, and do let me know once the CPS has been in touch.'

Assuring her they would, Jules disconnected the call and stared at the glittering expanse of sea as they continued down the hill towards it. Though they'd discussed the possibility of a new trial endlessly since learning there might be one, now they knew it was going to happen they'd fallen completely silent. Dealing with the hypothetical was nothing like facing reality. She knew that only too well, for there had been a time when she and Kian would have vowed to kill anyone who harmed Daisy, and they'd have meant it, but what had they done when it had actually happened? Kian had tried to kill himself, and she had lost all sense of who she was or what her life meant. They'd hardly even protested when the murder charge had been reduced to Voluntary Manslaughter – *With*

Provocation, as if to add insult to injury – nor had they fought for a retrial when they'd known proper justice hadn't been done.

And yet here was fate, circumstance, God Almighty for all she knew, about to right the wrongs they'd suffered and see their daughter's killer face the judgement she deserved.

'It seems odd,' she said as they turned into Hope Cove, 'that we should be coming here now after finding this out.'

Kian didn't disagree. 'I feel a bit shell-shocked by it,' he confessed.

'Do you mean being here, or hearing the news?'

'Both, I guess.'

As they pulled up in their old space at the side of the pub's garden, Jules's mind was starting to spin. Too many memories were coming at her at once, as though every day of their time here, every happy occasion and special moment was trying to be remembered and cherished in one go. She was finding it hard to take a full breath as she registered the bed of vibrant daisies that Misty had created at the front of the pub, where friends and family still left candles or mermaid figures as they came and went. Her daughter's face seemed a ghostly reflection at the windows; her laughter was music on the breeze. There were no strange or familiar faces at the picnic tables or down on the beach, just Daisy and her friends playing, planning or putting on a show. She could see her blonde curls as she and Joe strolled hand in hand towards the moor, throwing each other into the surf, or picnicking in the moonlight. Kian was no longer beside her; he was building scenery, cooking up a new deal, striding over the weir to the sailing school.

'This is even harder than I expected it to be,' he murmured.

Turning to him, she took his hand. 'We have to make this about Misty and Marco,' she reminded him, and felt surprisingly bolstered by her own words.

'Of course,' he agreed, and pushing open the driver's door he waited for her to join him and held her hand as they walked across the garden to the open front door. It took a while with so many wanting to greet them, but eventually they were stepping from the dazzling brilliance of the outside sunshine into the comparative gloom of the bar.

The familiarity of the place, the sounds, the smell, the sheer feel of it, almost took Jules's breath away. She hadn't really expected anything to be different, but the fact that nothing had changed was making her heart tighten with longing and painful joy.

Forced to let go of each other's hands as old friends and regulars surrounded them, they rose gamely to the warmth of their welcome, sharing laughter, cries of surprise and plenty of hugs. Everyone wanted to buy them a drink, know how they were and hear all about what they were up to now. As the spirit of the moment carried them to the bar where Misty, grinning from ear to ear, was already sorting the drinks, Jules could only feel thankful that no one knew about the new trial yet. It would be the talk of Kesterly once the news was out, and they definitely weren't ready to discuss it with anyone else at this stage.

The next half-hour passed in a chaos of fun, more

drinks and lots of promises to get together soon, until finally they were in the library with Misty and Marco, the door closed to offer some privacy, and a tray of coffee with home-made biscotti between them.

As Kian outlined the offer they were there to make Jules watched Misty's expression moving from wary interest, to surprise, to outright amazement as tears filled her beautiful eyes.

'It feels as much your place as ours,' Kian told her, as she threw her arms around them, 'so we thought you should have some ownership of it.'

'Are you sure?' Marco gasped, eagerly shaking their hands. 'I mean, everyone thinks of it as yours, and what you're asking for it, it's worth so much more.'

'It doesn't matter what people think,' Jules smiled, 'it's what's right that matters to us, and because the Mermaid wouldn't be the success it is without you two, and means as much to you as it does to us, we couldn't feel happier about including you in the ownership.'

As Misty clasped her hands to her face and danced up and down, Marco and Kian grinned and Jules said, 'Obviously we'll have to talk to lawyers and the business people, we just wanted to make sure you were up for it before we did that.'

'I feel so proud and emotional and overwhelmed,' Misty wept and laughed. 'I can hardly believe it's happening. I thought you were coming to tell us you wanted to sell up, or move back in . . .'

'We'd have been all right with that, I promise,' Marco assured them, 'we've even started packing . . .'

'Then stop,' Jules said gently. 'We won't be selling

or living here again. It's your home now.' As she spoke she was looking at Ruby's shoe on the mantelpiece, and feeling her heart swelling with unbearable loss.

Following her eyes, Misty said, 'It's always there, where you left it.'

'Do you ever get a sense of her now?' Jules wondered.

Misty shook her head. 'Not the way we used to, but sometimes I feel like she might have been around: doors or windows are open that shouldn't be, a light goes on and off for no reason. I always think she's come back to look for you and when you're not here she just goes again.'

Realising how sad that was making her, Jules took a tissue from her bag as Kian said, 'We should go now, but we'll be in touch tomorrow or the next day to sort out when to see the lawyers.'

As they shook hands on their deal and hugged again, Misty said, 'So what's next for you two? Will you stay in Kesterly?' Her eyes were merry as she looked at Kian. 'Knowing you as I do, I expect you've got some amazing scheme waiting to burst out of that sleeve.'

Kian smiled and winked, and taking Jules's hand he led her out through a side door to avoid any protracted goodbyes, and left Misty and Marco to go and celebrate their good news in any way they chose.

'Well, that seemed to go well,' he commented as he and Jules wandered across the weir to settle, side by side, on the rocks at the far side. The cliffs were like old friends rising up steeply, protectively, behind them, while the cerulean sky seemed to be putting on its best display of dazzling brightness.

'I knew they'd be happy,' Jules smiled, gazing

absently at the waves as they swelled gently towards her and she struggled to overcome a deepening sense of nostalgia. Leaving this place had been a terrible wrench the first time they'd done it; it clearly wasn't going to be any easier now.

'Do you remember how we used to sit on the beach when we were kids, planning what we'd do with the pub if we could ever own it?' Kian said dreamily.

Letting her head fall against his shoulder, she said, 'How could I forget? We used to come practically every weekend, although we never really believed it would happen, until one day it did.'

'It took us a while to believe it even then.'

Jules sighed. 'Do you think we should have been more careful of what we wished for? I mean, considering where we are now.'

After a moment he said, 'I was just asking myself the same question, but even the way it's turned out can't take away from how happy we were. And we'd never have wanted to be without her.'

'No, we could never wish for that.'

They sat quietly, their hands entwined, their memories rising and falling with the tide as over on the beach children shouted and laughed and threw themselves wildly into the surf.

In the end Jules was the first to break the silence. 'I think we should go to Ireland,' she said softly.

Kian became very still, as though not sure he'd heard her correctly.

'I think we should go soon,' she continued, 'before the new trial gets under way. We don't want it to hold us back, or become what our lives are about for the next however many months. Of course we'll be here if we have to be when it happens, but we ought to make plans so we have something to move on to when it's over. Something good.'

When he didn't answer she turned to look at him, and seeing tears on his cheeks she slid her arms around him. 'What matters is that we're together,' she whispered, weeping herself, 'and there are just too many memories here for us to be able to cope with.'

Pulling back so he could look into her eyes, he sobbed as he said, 'Do you have any idea how much it means to me to hear you say that? I was afraid for so long . . . I thought you'd fallen out of love with me, or wanted something more than I could give you . . .'

With a horrible rush of guilt, she lifted a hand to his face as she said, 'I've always loved you, more than anything, or anyone, apart from Daisy, but that kind of love is different.'

'Yes, it is,' he agreed, gazing searchingly into her eyes, 'but I felt a rift opening up between us, or not really a rift, we just didn't seem as close . . .'

Knowing exactly what he was talking about, she let her eyes drift away, hating herself for the pain and confusion she'd caused him, for the betrayal that had seeped like a poison into the closeness they'd always shared.

He was speaking again. '. . . so I guess I should have told you that I knew about Nicholas, but I was too afraid that if I did you'd tell me you wanted to be with him.'

'Oh God, Kian,' she sobbed, turning to him. 'I had

no idea you knew . . . I swear it didn't mean anything . . .'

He seemed not to be listening. 'I used to think you only stayed with me because you couldn't bring yourself to break my heart by taking Daisy away. Then I dreaded her going to uni in the States. I thought you'd go with her . . .'

'It never even crossed my mind.'

His eyes fell away. 'Then after, when we didn't have her any more and there was nothing to keep you here . . .'

Sobbing wretchedly, she gasped, '*You* are what kept me here. It's always been you, Kian. I've never loved anyone else and I never will. Oh my darling, to think of what you've been through over something that meant nothing. It was a moment of madness, a compulsion . . . I can hardly put into words what it was, but I've *never* wanted to do it again, and I've *never* regretted anything so much, especially now I know what it did to you.'

His smile was wry, his eyes still wet with tears as he gazed deeply into hers.

'How did you find out?' she asked, brokenly. 'You weren't even there . . .'

Putting a finger over her lips, he said, 'Remember how well I know you. I could tell something was up as soon as I arrived in Chicago, and after that, when we were at the lake, you just weren't yourself. Then one day, while we were setting up a picnic on the shore, I saw you flinch when someone shouted to Joe that his dad was on the line.'

Frowning, she said, 'You knew from that?'

He shrugged. 'I *guessed* from that, and then, when we were back here, I heard you on the phone to Em one night. You didn't say his name, but it was obvious who you were talking about, and so . . . That was how I knew you were afraid the baby was his.'

Jules's heart fractured right through, overwhelmed by the sheer awfulness of it all. How lonely and fearful he must have felt then, how desperate to find the right way while having no idea how he'd gone wrong. She simply couldn't bear to think of him suffering like that; it was almost as bad as losing Daisy.

'If it had been his,' he said, 'I'd decided that I'd accept it as mine, if it was what you wanted. If it wasn't . . . Well, I guess it's not an issue any more, so there's no point going there.'

Clasping her hands to her face, she wondered how she was ever going to cope with the guilt. 'You should have told me,' she choked. 'You shouldn't have gone through all that on your own. We'd have worked it out together.'

'I can see that now,' he said gently, 'but at the time I was waiting for you to tell me. I thought, when you didn't, that you needed to keep the secret until the time was right for you to go . . .'

'I'd never leave you,' she vowed passionately. 'Nothing, no one, means as much to me as you do. We belong together. We always have and always will.'

Tightening his arms around her, he said, 'It's how I've always felt, and hearing you say it . . . Knowing you want to start again with me, in Ireland . . .' He sobbed on a laugh. 'This is the happiest I've felt in a very long time. It's like life might start making sense again now. It'll have meaning and purpose, and I'll always be there for you. I'll never leave you again the way I did, after Daisy . . .'

'Ssh,' she whispered, putting a finger to his lips. 'You did what you had to then, but we must make sure that we always talk about things in the future, no matter how hard they might be. No more secrets, no more pretence, just us and honesty and whatever we make of our lives from now on.'

'It's a deal,' he smiled through his tears.

She smiled too, and pulling him to his feet, she said, 'Don't let's hang around. Let's go to Dublin as soon as we can get a flight so I can see the care homes you've shortlisted for Mum, and when we've made a decision we'll start putting everything in motion.'

It was three days later that they finally heard from the CPS, and soon after Amelia Quentin was returned to Kesterly to be charged with murder. There was no bail granted this time, nor were there any statements from her father, although Helen Hall had heard that when it came time for the plea hearing she would plead not guilty by reason of temporary insanity.

'So that means another trial?' Jules had asked nervously.

'Not necessarily,' Helen replied. 'If the experts on both sides agree that she *was* suffering from temporary insanity then she'll be detained under the Mental Health Act and sent to a secure psychiatric facility.'

'For how long?' Kian wanted to know.

'The term will be indefinite, until she can convince the authorities that she is no longer a threat to society.'

Now, as they prepared to leave the house on the Risings, with Andee and Helen there to help handle the press who'd set up camp in the street, Jules remarked, 'Maybe if Amelia does plead temporary insanity it would be the best way to go, because she isn't right in the head, or not in the sense that most of the rest of us are.'

Not arguing with that, Andee glanced at her phone as it rang. 'Nothing that can't wait,' she told them, putting it away again. 'So, are you about ready to go?'

Jules and Kian nodded. 'Thanks for doing this,' Kian said, shaking her hand.

'It's no bother,' she assured him. 'Would you like to go over the statement again before you leave?'

'No, it's fine,' he replied. 'Short and sweet, just like you said. Justice for Daisy, that's all we want. And for Dean. No news on his release date yet?'

'No, but it shouldn't be long in coming now.'

Jules nodded. 'His parents will be so relieved. Stephie too, of course.'

As they started for the door Helen said, 'Do you have any idea yet when you'll be back?'

'In about a week,' Jules answered. 'Hopefully everything'll be in place by then for my mother to make the next trip with us.'

Andee was looking around, taking in the charming little house that Jules, in spite of everything, had managed to turn into a home. 'So what are you doing about this place?' she wondered. 'I only ask because I could be looking for somewhere to rent.'

Jules and Helen regarded her curiously.

'It's a long story,' Andee smiled ruefully.

'We'll be happy to let it to you,' Kian told her kindly, 'if you're serious . . .'

'I'm not,' she broke in quickly, 'or not very. Anyway, you'll need it when you're here for visits.'

Deciding to broach the subject again when they came back, Jules watched Helen open the front door to check outside.

'Andee and I will go out first,' she said, turning back, 'and make them aware that we'll be giving a statement just as soon as you've been allowed to pass. That way, hopefully, they won't bombard you as you leave, or attempt to follow you. Is Danny in place to keep a check on that?'

Kian nodded and held up his phone. 'He texted about ten minutes ago. He's at the end of the street.'

Turning to Helen, Jules took both of her hands and pulled her into a hug. 'Thank you,' she said softly, 'not just for this, but for everything.'

'Don't mention it,' Helen replied, and stood aside for Andee to hug Jules next.

'You know where I am if you need anything,' Andee said warmly. 'You only have to pick up the phone.'

'I don't know how I'd have got through any of this without you,' Jules confessed. 'You've been the best friend anyone could ever wish for.'

'I've enjoyed getting to know you,' Andee smiled. 'I just wish the circumstances could have been different.'

After they'd embraced again, Andee turned to Kian and gazed fondly into his eyes. 'You're a special man,' she told him, 'and I'm truly sorry for everything you've been through.'

Pulling her to him, Kian said, 'Thank you for being

there for Jules. If there's ever anything we can do for you, nothing will ever be too much trouble.'

With twinkling eyes she said, 'Careful, I might hold you to that.'

'Do,' he insisted.

A few minutes later, having made it to the car and out of the street with the press recording every inch of their progress, they were heading down the hill towards Hope Cove, leaving Andee to act as their spokesperson. Behind them Danny was keeping close to their tail, just in case anyone tried to follow, and Aileen was already calling to find out if they were on their way yet.

'What do you really think of her pleading temporary insanity?' Jules asked, as they pulled up at a set of lights halfway down the hill.

Kian barely hesitated. 'That there's nothing temporary about it, but right now I'm trying to do what we promised each other, and not think about the girl or the trial at all.'

Happy with the answer, Jules reached into the depths of her bag, searching for her phone as it bleeped with a text. 'I expect it's your mother,' she said, as her hand closed around something that clearly wasn't the phone. Unable to make out what it was, she drew it out and felt her heart turn over with surprise.

'Look,' she whispered, holding it up for Kian to see.

He blinked, curiously. 'So you decided to take it?' he said.

'No,' she replied. 'It was still on the library mantelpiece the last time I saw it.'

Frowning, he said, 'So how did it get in your bag?'

'Maybe Misty put it there.' Except she knew Misty hadn't. She'd have seen her do it, and the shoe had still been in place when they'd left the library.

Looking down at it, she turned it over in her hand, remembering all the times she'd found it in odd places around the pub, and the flat, as though Ruby was trying to have fun with her, or even to communicate something. She recalled how attached Ruby had been to Daisy, settling in Daisy's room with the mermaids as if it were where she'd always belonged. She'd even sensed Ruby's overwhelming sadness after Daisy died.

Somewhere deep inside her she felt Ruby was trying to reach her now. Why else would the shoe be in her bag?

Lifting it to her cheek, as though to embrace it, she smiled sadly to herself, and whispered, 'I should have thought to take you with us. Thank you for coming.'

As Kian pulled away from the lights she heard something rattle inside the shoe, and tipped it upside down to find out what it was. When she saw a tiny mermaid drop into her lap her heart filled with tears. 'Oh, Kian,' she murmured, picking it up and showing him, 'look what was inside the shoe.'

Glancing over, Kian started to smile. 'There are probably better ways of putting this,' he said, 'but it looks to me as though our girls have found their own way of coming with us.'

Acknowledgements

An enormous thank you to Andrea Bright at the White Hart in Littleton-on-Severn for guiding me so patiently through the running of a pub. Also to Sabrina, Mark & Nikki at the Royal Oak in Cromhall.

Once again my thanks go to Ian Kelcey for so much invaluable advice regarding the trial. Any errors, or journeys off into dramatic licence, are entirely mine!

Susan Lewis

The Girl Who Came Back

Bonus Material

Susan Lewis

on
The Girl Who Came Back

Dear Reader,

I hope you have enjoyed this book, dark though the subject is.

The idea came to me, as many ideas do, from a story in the papers about a girl who was being released from prison after serving only a few years for the violent murder of a friend. Uppermost in my mind while reading this report was the family of the deceased girl whose lives would never be the same again, while the killer, still under thirty, was being allowed to restart her life. I could hardly begin to imagine how the girl's parents must feel about this apparent travesty of justice.

Naturally, I didn't approach them, it would have been quite wrong to try and exploit their grief, but I couldn't stop thinking about them, and it wasn't long before characters and a story began to form in my head of how a family might handle this kind of horror.

The writing of the book, surprisingly, turned out to be far easier than I had anticipated. Perhaps it was moving back and forth between past and present, something I don't often do, that helped to move it along; or, more likely, it was because of how strongly I connected with Jules and Kian. I also very much enjoyed reintroducing Andee Lawrence, the detective from *Behind Closed Doors* who will be featuring in future books.

Thank you so much for the time you have given this book. I hope you have felt it to be worthwhile, and that you will go on to enjoy many more of my books.

With my warmest wishes

Susan

$\mathcal{S}$usan's travel diary

A trip to New Zealand

Dear diary,

I've just returned from one of the most inspiring and wonderful research trips I've made in a long time. Of course all that fabulous New Zealand wine made it doubly enjoyable! It was all go most of the time, and I developed a love for Hawke's Bay that would see me living there if it were only possible. Since returning I've been fully immersed in the new book (one way of staying in NZ), which is a follow up to *No Child of Mine* and *Don't Let Me Go*.

I've had so many requests for this book that I can only hope that everyone ends up enjoying revisiting these characters as much as I have. Though, as you might expect, it's not all plain sailing for Charlotte and Chloe, nor for Anthony who now has a vineyard, and is so desirable... Well, you'll find out for yourselves soon enough. So, a little recap on my travels with James...

Keri Keri

Keri Keri, in the Bay of Islands, is one of my favourite places. I did a few signings while we were there; it was such a delight to meet so many readers who had enjoyed my books! We also took a trip to Rainbow Falls, a stunning waterfall just outside of Keri Keri, and of course we had to revisit Chloe's beach, which is in the bay you might remember from *Don't Let Me Go*.

From Auckland to Hawke's Bay

On our 6 hour drive through the stunning heart of the North Island to Hawke's Bay, we made a small diversion to Rotorua in order to view the geysers where we caught a great explosion, but by the time I got my iPhone in action it had turned to puff.

The geyser!

We also managed to stumble upon a Maori haka at the same time. Great show with war dances and love ballads. We then moved on to Black Barn vineyard where we would be staying. This fabulous barn – (home from home, but not very like Bagstone!!) – has inspired the setting for Charlotte, Anthony and Chloe's home in the next book (characters from *No Child of Mine* and *Don't Let Me Go*). That evening we took a trip to Alessandro's pizzeria in Havelock North; a great venue for Charlotte and Anthony to bring their kids. Yes, that's more than one child! Time has moved on and there are now two additions to the family – and Chloe is 8.

Writing notes at Alessandro's pizzeria

The time was packed with all sorts of research including fancy dinners at the world famous Wineries of Craggy Range, Mission Hills and of course Black Barn. I've found out so much about wine-making that I've offered to take over for Dave McKee at Black Barn should he ever want to go on holiday! A visit that resonated deeply with me was to Te Mata Primary School where I met Mike Bain, the head teacher, who is so popular with the children that they practically fall over themselves to speak to him when he walks into a room. I had no idea head teachers could be so accessible.

The stunning Craggy Range vineyard!

The trip was rounded off with a stay in Wellington with friends whose gorgeous home overlooks the bay and then on to Lake Taupo which provided even more inspiration so it too will appear in the new story.

All in all it was a really fabulous trip, do keep an eye out for more on the new book...

Read the brand new novel
by Susan Lewis

The Moment
She Left

Kesterly-on-Sea is full of secrets.

Some are darker than others; many are shameful. One is even deadly.

Andee is an ex-detective whose marriage is breaking up. So when a young female student disappears without trace, she throws herself into the search.

Meanwhile, the town's beloved Rowzee Cayne has just discovered that she is terminally ill, and doesn't want to burden her family and friends with the news.

Andee and Rowzee don't know it yet, but their journeys are going to help them uncover a secret. One that is going to affect them more than they could ever imagine.

The Moment She Left

Available now in hardback

About
Susan

I was born in 1956 to a happy, normal family living in a brand new council house on the outskirts of Bristol. My mother, at the age of twenty, and one of thirteen children, persuaded my father to spend his bonus on a ring rather than a motorbike and they never looked back. She was an ambitious woman determined to see her children on the right path: I was signed up for ballet, elocution and piano lessons and my little brother was to succeed in all he set his mind to.

Tragically, at the age of thirty-three, my mother lost the battle against cancer and died. I was nine, my brother was five.

My father was left with two children to bring up on his own. Sending me to boarding school was thought to be 'for the best' but I disagreed. No one listened to my pleas for freedom, so after a while I took it upon myself to get expelled. By the time I was thirteen, I was back in our little council house with my father and brother. The teenage years passed and before I knew it I was eighteen … an adult.

I got a job at HTV in Bristol for a few years before moving to London at the age of twenty-two to work for Thames. I moved up the ranks, from secretary in news and current affairs, to a production assistant in light entertainment and drama. My mother's ambition and a love of drama gave me the courage to knock on the Controller's door to ask what it takes to be a success. I received the reply of 'Oh, go away and write something'. So I did!

Three years into my writing career I left TV and moved to France. At first it was bliss. I was living the dream and even found myself involved in a love affair with one of the FBI's most wanted! Reality soon dawned, however, and I realised that a full-time life in France was very different to a two-week holiday frolicking around on the sunny Riviera.

So I made the move to California with my beloved dogs Casanova and Floozie. With the rich and famous as my neighbours I was enthralled and inspired by Tinsel Town. The reality, however, was an obstacle course of cowboy agents, big-talking producers and wannabe directors. Hollywood was not waiting for me, but it was a great place to have fun! Romances flourished and faded, dreams were crushed but others came true.

After seven happy years of taking the best of Hollywood and avoiding the rest, I decided it was time for a change. My dogs and I spent a short while in Wiltshire before then settling once again in France, perched high above the Riviera with glorious views of the sea. It was wonderful to be back amongst old friends, and to make so many new ones. Casanova and Floozie both passed away during our first few years there, but Coco and Lulabelle are doing a valiant job of taking over their places – and my life!

Everything changed again three months after my fiftieth birthday when I met James, my partner, who lived and works in Bristol. For a couple of years we had a very romantic and enjoyable time of flying back and forth to see one another at the weekends, but at the end of 2010 I finally sold my house on the Riviera and am now living in Gloucestershire in a delightful old barn with Coco and

Lulabelle. My writing is flourishing and over thirty books down the line I couldn't be happier. James continued to live in Bristol, with his boys, Michael and Luke – a great musician and a champion footballer! – for a while until we decided to get married in 2013!

It's been exhilarating and educational having two teenage boys in my life! Needless to say they know everything, which is very useful (saves me looking things up) and they're incredibly inspiring in ways they probably have no idea about.

Should you be interested to know a little more about my early life, why not try *Just One More Day*, a memoir about me and my mother and then the story continues in *One Day at a Time*, a memoir about me and my father and how we coped with my mother's loss.

5 minutes with

Susan

Where does the inspiration for your books come from?

I often write about difficult issues, as you well know.
I don't necessarily write from experience in these cases but
I rely on listening and seeking the experience of others
who might have witnessed or been through challenging
situations. It's important as a writer to imagine how you'd
feel if it happened to you. I enjoy doing it but sometimes it
can be quite distressing – sometimes I cry, which tells me it's
working. This is how I really bring my characters to life.

Do you have any peculiar writing rituals or habits?

Nothing too peculiar! I'm very strict about the hours I write,
starting at 10 in the morning and going through until 5pm
or 6pm, usually six days a week. Then, I love to have a glass
of wine at the end of the day as I read back over what has
happened in 'my fictional world' over the last seven or eight
hours, socialising with the characters and often wanting
to gossip about them with someone else.

What advice would you offer to aspiring writers?

Remember to listen: listen to the way people speak,
to the rhythm of the words you are writing (you're most
likely to do this in your head), and always give your characters
room to be themselves. They'll have plenty to say if you
just let them chatter on to one another, often giving
you ideas you hadn't even thought of!

What is the last book you bought someone as a gift?

A variety of children's books for the recipients of the Special Recognition Award that I'm sponsoring for the local secondary school. They've chosen the titles themselves and what a fascinating selection they've made – from *The Diary of a Wimpy Kid* to *The Curious Incident of the Dog in the Night Time* (one of my own favourites).

What's the best piece of advice you've ever been given?

If you want to be a producer you'd better write. I was working in TV drama and this was what I was told to get me out of the Controller's office! I took him at his word and the rest, as they say, is history.

If you had a superpower, what would it be?

If I had a superpower I'd rescue all the children and animals being subjected to cruelty.

What literary character is most like you?

Definitely Emma from Jane Austen's wonderful novel.

If you were stranded on a desert island what song would you choose to listen to, which book would you take and what luxury item would you pack?

That's a hard one. Song choice would have to be Just My Imagination by the Temptations. Book choice . . . *How to Survive on a Desert Island* by anyone who's been thoughtful enough to write such a useful guide. Luxury item: A double-ended stick with a toothbrush at one end and a knife at the other . . . I could give Bear Grylls a sure run for his money!

Have you read them all?

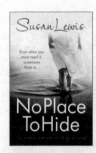

Connect with

Susan Lewis

online

Sign up to Susan's newsletter for
exclusive content, competitions and
all the latest news from Susan.

Want to know more? Visit

www.susanlewis.com

Connect with other fans and join in the
conversation at

f/SusanLewisBooks

Follow Susan on

@susandlewis